Within the Realm of Night and Shadow

A Novel
By
K.B. McKay

NORQUIN
PUBLISHING LLC

Paperback ISBN: 979-8-9996341-0-8

Cover Design by: Marina Veit

Norquin Publishing, United States of America

First edition printing 2025

For the ones who run from the dark when the light flicks off. The ones that keep their arms and legs safely tucked under the covers. Welcome to the other side.

Within the Realm of Night and Shadow

Prologue

The chanting was beginning to give her a headache. Bad enough she had to sit on this stool above the toxic fumes of sulfur and ash, she had to listen to this infernal racket as well? The leaves of the laurel tree were beginning to take effect. If they didn't hurry this along, she was going to be sick right into their sacred chasm.

Finally, when the sweat from her brow began to bead and drip down her smooth, tanned face. When the edges of her vision became blurred and darkened. There was silence.

Pythia took a deep breath, head lolling back. She felt like she could lift up into the air and fly along its currents, it was so thick that air. And though there was little light, her vision seemed to spark and crackle. Shifting, fractured beams of white light, interspersed with blues and purples, fizzled at the edges of her sight. She lifted her arm, reaching for them, only to stop as her hand multiplied from one, to two, to five. She waved it, her vision trailing. The many arms chasing one another until she stilled and they merged. Whole once again, united.

That is so strange.

The priests' chanting continued, and Pythia jumped.

Right, focus.

Her thick, dark brown hair tumbled in dampened curls down her back. It felt so good to sway it side to side against the thin cloth of her tunic. It was so damn hot. Sticky. She wanted nothing more than to strip down, and throw this sweat soaked tunic into the burning lava at her feet. Let the damn thing go up in flames while she danced around it. Give these priests a real show to interpret. The oracle, dancing naked in Apollo's sacred temple. Ugh, she needed some *air*.

Wait, what was she doing? Right, the prophecy. She nearly rolled her eyes, but controlled herself. She was high on the fumes. The last thing she needed was for the priests of Apollo to believe she didn't take her divine appointment seriously. So, she went along with it, spreading her arms wide at her sides, her breaths coming and going in heavy pants. Difficult enough to do in this stagnant, foul air.

Gods girl, don't vomit.

Incoherent babbling began to fall from her mouth, a sing-song that sounded nice in her ears. The syllables made her want to giggle as her mouth shaped their creation. She was *sooo* high. Too high. They really overdid it this time.

Focus, Pythia, she scolded herself.

And then it happened, the vision shot through her so quickly she didn't have time to brace herself. A real vision this time. The priests were going to be pissed that she'd been holding out on them.

There was white, only white, and then...a rain of ash. Blackened roads filled with blood, and creatures of all manner fighting a battle, a war. Among the fallen a dark Queen rose, her footsteps crushing the bodies of her victims beneath her. And at her side, or against her, it wasn't clear, a woman. A key. The realms flashed before her, one by one falling, crumbling, turning to dust. The entirety of the cosmos screamed in pain and fury.

Pythia choked, gagging on the fear brought on by her vision. Or was that the fumes?

The woman with hair of blood will doom or free her people. She alone would break the curse, or...was that another she saw? A shadow at her back? No, two.

She couldn't hold it any longer. With a gasp she shot up straight, her vision clearing. The priests were staring at her, mouths agape, their droning halted as she spasmed on the stool.

"The key to what?" one of them whispered, his eyes wide.

Pythia shot him a scathing glare. "You want me to do your job for you as well?" she snapped. "Don't worry, that one wasn't for you."

"Don't be insolent, girl," the sternest, her least favorite, scolded. "And you were supposed to ask the gods for a vision of this year's harvest, not whatever that was."

Another, one of the true believers in her gift, ignored his fellow priest and asked, "Who is it for, Pythia?"

Pythia's gaze went to the shadows that seemed to beckon and move at her back, deeper in the recesses of her cave. They were thicker now, tension vibrating within the darkness.

"The one it is for knows. They have heard."

That was all she could say, because at that moment her stomach decided to empty itself of its contents. She heaved. Bile spewed from her mouth, and splattered into the smoking chasm with a hiss.

ACT I

ESCAPING DESTINY

CHAPTER

I

Halfway around the block from her apartment the sky opened up, dumping rain onto unsuspecting pedestrians. The normally busy sidewalk suddenly emptied as groups of people ducked into buildings, or under awnings attempting to avoid the unexpected deluge.

Enid sighed happily, turning the collar of her jacket up to keep the cold sting of the rain from her neck as she continued in an unhurried pace down the walkway—enjoying the slight, sweet fragrance that slowly washed over everything. Steam curled around her, born from the cool kiss of rain on asphalt.

Living in the city made her feel safe. One insignificant speck in the ant farm of humanity around her. The constant rush of people allowed her to blend into the background, an unnoticed observer to the daily energetic buzz of life that thrummed throughout the streets and colossal buildings.

Admittedly, she missed the rolling hills and wide spaces of her small hometown. Where, instead of skyscrapers, groves of trees towered into the blue sky, and the songs of birds were as numerous as the honking horns she had now grown accustomed to. Thoughts of home, though far and few between, elicited a sharp ache of pain in her chest and the sting of tears in her eyes.

She focused instead on the smell of the rain and the sounds of the city, pushing the thoughts away.

A strange cackle drew her attention. Perched on a garbage bin, unconcerned about the rain that splattered around it, sat a large raven. Beady, black eyes blinked at her. Enid skipped back as the bird flapped its massive wings and took off, its shadow sliding directly over her as it flew into the stormy sky. She shook her head and continued along, chiding herself for how easily she was frightened.

Within a few minutes she reached the diner. The bell at the top of the door pinged as she ducked inside, her sneakers squishing wetly on the linoleum. A few eyes glanced her way, but the majority of the crowd remained blissfully ignorant of her entrance—absorbed in their conversations or food.

Her shift didn't start for another thirty minutes, but she liked to come early to eat and possibly pick up any stray tables someone was willing to pawn off in the hopes of an early escape. The unexpected rainstorm had driven in more people than usual and her manager, Gladys, yelled table numbers at her as she walked through the throng of people. Tucking her bag and jacket into a locker in the back, she hurriedly threw on her apron, jerked her hair back into a wet ponytail, and ran out to grab drink orders.

The stream of people continued nonstop, and by the time Enid had a minute to slow down she realized she was most of the way through her shift. Outside the rain had stopped, the sun had long since set, and the lights of the city reflected off of the dark, wet street. One by one, the crowd thinned until only a couple booths remained occupied.

She stood at one of the windows, watching the people stroll by on the street as she cleaned the floor-to-ceiling pane of glass. One of the figures on the other side slowed as it passed. A handsome face smirked through the reflection of the window. The motion of the towel in her hand paused as their eyes connected. His smile widened. Wickedness peered back at her through glowing green eyes, reflecting the dim light like a cat's, fanged teeth flashing.

Enid flinched, her face dropping from the window to inspect her feet. She forced her breath into a slow, even rhythm despite the desperate pounding of her heart. Fear kept her from looking back up. The now familiar mantra chanted silently through her head.

It's not real Enid, it's all in your head. It's all in your head.

"You need to eat something," said a warm voice behind her. Enid gasped as she twisted around, her hand going to her already frantically pounding chest.

Cindy stood with her hands on her full hips. Her thick, curly brown hair pulled up into a tight bun. Dark, cocoa skin contrasted beautifully with the white diner t-shirt that stretched over her ample breasts. Large, almond shaped brown eyes raked Enid over, a beige high heel tapping on the floor in assessment, shapely legs hugged by skinny, form fitting black pants. Cindy was the only person Enid knew who wore high heels while waiting tables. She swore that one day the love of her life would walk in, and she refused to be caught in anything other than her best. The woman was made of steel.

"I know you came in here without eating a thing. You are going to waste away," Cindy scolded as she took the cleaning rag and spray.

Enid looked back over her shoulder, out the window at the neon lit street. The stranger was gone, lost in the occasional groups of night owls that stalked the city. She shook her head, pushing out the thought of the strange man with glowing eyes that could not be real. Her stomach rumbled hungrily at the mention of food.

"You are right as always," Enid sighed as Cindy swatted at her with the cloth. She hurried into the kitchen, eager to get a few small bites in between tables.

The cooks sat in the back at the small break table. A deck of cards dealt out amongst them. Good natured insults and loud teasing filled the space—more at home in the small grease filled, stainless steel room than in their own places. Enid wished fleetingly, and not for the first time, that she felt as at home anywhere as these men did here.

"Enid!" The head cook, Leo, shouted above the insults. "Come, I saved you some food." He stood from his chair with a wince and a stretch. "Don't look at my cards, you bunch of cheats!" His slight Italian accent added a delicate cadence to his otherwise stark tone. The other cooks replied with shouted denials and japes as he walked her over to the heat lamps, handing her a warm plate and fork.

"Thank you so much Leo," she said as she helped herself to a generous scoop of the employee meal. Spaghetti. Leo's favorite. Cheap, easy, and hardy. She practically inhaled it. Enid moaned in delight as the warm spices danced across her taste buds, wiggling happily as she chewed.

Leo shook his gray head with a chuckle as he went back to the card table. The people in the diner had become a surrogate family to her. Watching out for her, reminding her to do things like eat when she forgot. And Leo was like a father—stern but caring.

"Enid, did you fall from heaven? Cause you must be an angel!" Jason, one of the grill guys yelled from across the room. Enid rolled her eyes at the corny pickup line. One of many he loved to tell any girl that walked within earshot.

"Shut your mouth! You leave that girl alone, she's too good for a punk like you," Leo scolded, slapping the back of his head. Laughter echoed around the room.

"What are you talking about? I'm a delight," Jason insisted, placing his hand over his heart in mock pain. Enid shook her head.

Taking another big bite, she glanced out the large window into the dining room as the most piercing gaze she'd ever seen landed on her. She froze, a noodle of spaghetti still dangling between her puckered lips. Smokey gray eyes traveled over her before drifting away. A black t-shirt, dark blue jeans, and black, hooded jacket did little to hide the muscular physique. Thick, jet-black hair fell into his eyes. He shoved a hand into it, brushing it back as he slid into a booth near the window, his large frame dwarfing the table before him.

Another glance drifted toward her, curious and amused. She sucked the noodle up, sputtering as she almost choked on it. There was the barest glimpse of a dimple as she ducked away from the window. Great. He saw that. Awesome. Heat flooded her cheeks as she scraped her plate off, thrusting it into a tub before turning to wash her hands.

Cindy swept through the swinging kitchen door.

"Girl, I know it's your turn but if you need me to take this table I will happily fall on that sword," she said as she openly ogled the guy through the window.

Enid giggled as her friend nearly swooned over him.

"It's ok. I can take it."

Cindy groaned, biting her lip, her almond eyes rolling back before cutting over to Enid.

"Are you finally going to at least make a move?"

Enid only gave a shake of her head in response as she walked out of the kitchen with a grin. His eyes seemed to follow her as she went behind the counter. It always felt that way when he came in, even when she didn't wait on him. All awkward awareness. His stare like the stroke of fingers against her skin.

It was a trick of her imagination. Had to be. Someone like him didn't go for someone like her. Though, more times than she could count, she would look up from her work to find those gray, steel eyes locked on her. Fighting the flush that attempted to darken her cheeks, she pulled the freshest pot off the heater, filled a cup, and brought it over to him.

"Coffee, black?" She placed the cup in front of him.

Not that she had to ask. He got the same thing every time he came in. Every night for the past year that she had worked there. All the other girls called him the hot, quiet guy. Several of them had used all of their best flirting tricks to get him to ask them out. Sliding him their numbers, and shamelessly making suggestions. The numbers were always left sitting on the table along with a generous tip.

He smiled as he lifted the cup to his mouth.

"Thank you." he replied, in his smooth, deep voice before taking a sip of the steaming, black liquid. Her attention hovered a little longer on his lips than they should have. She blushed as he raised his eyebrows questioningly.

"Anything else?" she asked to cover the awkward moment.

"Just the coffee, thanks," he said politely. She nodded, turning on her heel.

"Enid," he called out before she could take a step. She stopped, inhaling deeply.

"You know my name?"

He chuckled. "Name tag."

11

Her hand slapped over the plastic tag on her chest.

"Right, of course."

Why doesn't the floor open up and swallow me now, she thought as she forced herself to stand there instead of running in mortification. "What can I do for you?"

"You have something on your face, here," He pointed to the corner of his mouth. "I thought you might want to know."

Oh god no. Covering her mouth with her hand, she mumbled a quick thank you, and took off to the bathroom. Her face flamed scarlet the whole way.

The bathroom mirror confirmed it. The orange spot contrasted horribly with the pale pink of her heart shaped mouth and the deep flush on her cheeks. Snatching a paper towel from the dispenser, she wiped at it furiously. With calming breaths, she smoothed down the stray hairs in her ponytail. Her face was still red. Nearly matching the thick, flame colored locks that fell in waves to the middle of her back. Which, to her surprise, was not as frizzy as she expected from the rain. She rubbed a bit of mascara from underneath her wide, green eyes.

I just need to get through this, she thought as she threw the paper towel in the trash.

Pressing her cool, damp hands along the back of her neck, she mentally prepared herself before looking over her face one last time. The only spots that remained were the small freckles scattered across her nose and high cheekbones. With a satisfied nod, she ducked back out into the diner to face her Achilles' heel. Handsome men.

***

The last few hours of the night went by pretty quick. One of the quirks about working late night was that few people came in, but those that did were strange company. Most were harmless, such as the servers that came in occasionally from places that closed down early, or the couples out for an after-date coffee, not yet ready to give up the solace of a few hours from children. The older gentleman who lives upstairs that could never sleep. Harmless.

Then there was the other type that roamed the night-soaked streets. The ones who exuded the promise of violence. The ones you did not want to find yourself alone with on a vacant road. It's their eyes. Empty and soulless—void of any emotion. Those were the people that chose to walk in the very moment Enid was cleaning up behind the counter for the night.

Discreetly, she checked on the handsome man. The flash of money indicated an imminent departure, to her relief. Her feet were aching. It took everything in her not to groan when the bell above the door pinged, and in walked a small group. The sound died in her throat before she had to suppress it.

They were all strikingly beautiful. Beautiful, but terrifying. Something within her recoiled. The broken part of her brain she tried desperately to hide. They looked around, assessing. Enid felt herself freeze, turning away from those roving gazes. Some instinct within her screamed to stay away.

Run. Hide.

She pressed the feeling away, her mantra running through her mind. One of them glanced over at the large man in the booth who glared back. He elbowed his companion with a sly smile, head jerking in that direction.

"Vidar," the other said with a smirk, blue eyes flashing. His pale skin shone like alabaster in the stark, fluorescent light. If he wasn't so frightening Enid would have thought him a model straight from a photo shoot. Vidar gritted his teeth, jaw muscle jumping as he gave a small nod of his head in response.

The group chuckled taking a booth on the other side of the diner, openly looking around at everyone as if sizing them up, like wolves on a hunt. A shiver ran up her spine.

Cindy caught her eye, giving her a wink and fanning her face before she strolled up to the table to take care of them. Enid grabbed the last pot of coffee to top off cups. She pried her eyes away from her friend, trying to convince herself there was no need to go over and drag her away from those predatory people.

It's all in your head.

Once again, she wondered if she was feeling something others did not. Unreliable senses giving her brain false information. Broken.

Her hand tightened on the handle of the pot, an attempt to ground herself. Her body suddenly felt too small, too contained. Breath locked in her chest, unable to escape, as though it knew it needed to get out, needed to be free of her, but couldn't recall the way. Enid placed her other hand on the counter as she began to sway on her feet. *Not now*, she thought as the anxiety attack came out of nowhere.

Something within her thrummed, a call, a need she couldn't answer, wild and raging. If she released it the world outside would shatter over her—consume her. It was all too much, and too little at the same time. The sound of her heart boomed within her ears, the rush of her blood a gentle woosh between beats. Forcing slow, even breaths she gripped the edge of the counter, keeping her head down.

Briefly, she remembered a long ago, muted argument through a closed door in the middle of the night. Her small, child hands clutching tight to her blanket as tears streamed down her rounded cheeks.

"Howard, she insisted that…" her mother stopped suddenly before speaking again in a whisper Enid had to strain to hear. *"…that the man who worked at the butcher had horns and walked around on hooves. HOOVES, Howard!"* The word was enunciated, somehow making it sound more ridiculous. *"Like some sort of great prancing goat!"* She practically spat the last few words in disgusted fury. *"I had to drag her from the shop while she pointed and screamed at the poor man about horns sticking out of his head. I paid double to apologize."*

Enid shook the memory away, and released her breath in a soft, slow stream. The feeling passed, her head cleared. She calmly examined the flecked laminate top she still gripped. Drops of coffee blended with the pattern. Absently, she wiped at them, attempting to cover up the fact she had been standing there for so long. Finally, she was able to step from behind the counter.

Vidar continued to glare at the group across the room as she approached him.

"Do you need anything else?" she asked quietly, fighting the urge to step back as he turned to her with a scowl. A storm of fury swirled within his gray eyes, softening as he acknowledged her.

"Just a refill please," he said.

"Oh! It looked like you were getting ready to leave," she responded. Enid refilled his cup, trying not to notice the white knuckles of his clenched fists on the table.

"I changed my mind," he said tightly. A loud laugh drew his attention back to the other table and his eyes once more clouded over angrily. Cindy was leaning down flirting openly with one of the gorgeous men, who smiled at her with a row of perfect straight teeth in his handsome, ebony face.

"Do you know them?" Enid asked softly. "It seems like they know you."

He took a sip of his coffee, visibly pulling himself together as he sat the cup back down with exaggerated care.

"We are not friends, I am acquainted with them, yes." Saying no more than that, he put his elbows on the table, steepling his hands in front of him, and continued to glower at the group.

Strange, Enid thought as she walked away.

He sat there with an unwavering glare as the small group ordered food—his coffee untouched and growing cold. There seemed to be a silent war of wills being carried on in front of her as the diner slowly emptied out of everyone but the two booths. Even the cooks had ducked out for the night.

Finally, the group got up and began moving toward the door. Enid sighed happily, grabbing a bus tub. Everything was clean with the exception of those two tables and she was ready to go home.

As they neared the exit, the woman broke away, sauntering over to the other booth. Enid couldn't help but notice the graceful confidence with which she carried herself. She leaned over the table, her long black hair cascading in glossy waves over the pale skin of her arms.

"Vidar, as always it is a pleasure to see you," she purred with a thick, Russian accent.

"Lania," he grumbled. His shoulders were full of tension, his scowl shifting among the four individuals equally.

"Where have you been? We have not seen you around lately."

Vidar looked at her blankly for a few moments. "I've been busy," he finally replied.

"Do you come to this place often? I think I might like it here. It is homey."

Vidar's jaw ticked. The only reply he offered.

Slowly cleaning up the untouched plates of food from the recently vacant booth, Enid kept her head down while covertly keeping an eye on the exchange.

"Lani," one of the other men called, gesturing to the door. They could have been siblings. He shared the same pouty mouth, cool blue eyes, and dark black hair as the woman. As he waited, his attention wandered over to Enid, looking her up and down. Her skin turned to ice wherever his eyes lingered. She forced herself not to balk when he winked at her. Him the calm, cool predator, and her the shaking, terrified prey.

It's all in your head.

The feeling of confinement overwhelmed her again, of her body being too small. Her heart throbbed, the pulse within her pushing outward, needing to escape. She pulled back on the feeling, reigning it in, forcing her breath to stay slow as she turned her face from the stranger to avoid those haunting blue eyes.

The woman smiled, and stepped away from the table.

"I hope to see you around, Vidar," she said.

Enid stopped midway through cleaning while the woman gave her a long look, and the group filtered out the door. She remained there, watching as they walked off, vibrant blue eyes following her through the glass until they faded from view. Only then did she move, sagging in relief.

Vidar slid out of his booth, placing money on the table. There was a hint of a smile, and then he was gone. The bell above the door singing his departure. Enid watched him walk away in the same direction as the others, broad back disappearing into the shadows down the street. She stared after him long enough to twist the lock into place.

A worried frown pulled at the corners of her mouth. The darkness outside whispered to her a promise of violence. With a shiver, Enid pushed away from the door.

CHAPTER

2

The air was thick, but cool with autumn chill. She walked briskly, looking forward to relaxing on her couch and a few hours of mindless television. Enid didn't sleep at night. Hadn't for years now, so the thought of her bed was still distant. Wine and tv though. That she was desperately looking forward to. She hummed to herself as she reached her building and, with aching feet, slowly climbed the narrow, dingy stairwell to her sixth-floor apartment.

Sliding her key into the lock, she jumped at the sound of a throat clearing behind her. Before she could turn, she was slammed up against the door. The side of her face bounced painfully against the solid wood. Her throat locked up as she tried to process what was happening, dread freezing her limbs.

"Oh, how I have missed you darlin'."

No.

Enid's entire body went rigid at the sound of the familiar, southern drawl. The effect was immediate. Years of muscle memory clicking into place. Her stomach knotted. A whimper escaped before she could stop it. And the body at her back pressed her harder into the wooden surface. It was a dance she was uncomfortably accustomed to.

A hand slid down her arm and settled over her own, guiding her to twist the key. Before her brain could catch up, before she could fight the instinct that kept her frozen, she was ushered into the dark apartment. The door softly clicking shut.

The hold on her arm was vise-like as she was shoved against the wall. The paralysis that held her faded as she came face to face with her attacker. She felt the sharp tang of rage and terror on her tongue, a dangerous combination. Dangerous because her fury made her mouthy, and her fear made her slow. Things he would use against her if she defied him. Him being her ex, Charles Wallace. A towering mass of uncontrolled wrath fueled by a lifetime of bitter disappointment.

"What are you doing here Charlie?" She asked before she lost the nerve to speak. Her voice remained steady despite the jackhammering of her heart.

Without responding, he tossed her keys across the room, and one by one pushed the locks into place. His blood shot, brown eyes never left hers. As the last bolt slid home, he leaned in against her, pinning her to the wall. The bruising grip on her arm loosened only for his fingers to find her chin, forcing her to stare up into his hate filled face. He looked like hell.

"I could say the same thing to you, Enid," he replied, his face close to hers, their gazes locked eye to eye.

She tried not to wince at the painful press of his fingers. Showing pain only made it worse. His blonde hair was longer, sticking up in several directions as though he'd been pulling at it. It had been a while since he shaved, the scruff covering his strong jaw line. It scratched against her cheek as his mouth moved to her ear.

"Why are you here, Enid?"

His voice was low and calm. The kind of calm that sent a chill down her spine. The reek of alcohol assaulted her nose. She drew in a shaky breath and held it as his fingers slowly caressed the side of her face, down to her throat, where he gripped her firmly. His other hand braced against the wall, caging her in as he leaned back to give her a long, hard look.

She had to say something. It would get so much worse if she didn't, but she was still drawing a blank. What could she possibly say? Hesitantly, she opened her mouth to speak, and the grip around her neck tightened. He pulled her head away from the wall only to slam her into it again. Her head bounced, spots clouded her vision, and she hissed. Tears stung the corners of her eyes. She tried again to speak. The sound barely made it past her lips before he strangled it from her. His large hand squeezing her delicate wind pipe closed.

Frantically, she scratched at him, attempting to gain another breath. Those hard eyes watched her casually, noting the panic in her face as though calculating exactly how much she was suffering—estimating when it would be enough. The pressure increased and spots began to dance in her vision as tears now leaked freely down her cheeks.

"Why did you leave home?" His voice was eerily calm.

Her mouth moved wordlessly. Still, he didn't bother alleviating the pressure for any sort of response. That's not what he wanted right now, anyway. Years of his abuse had taught her that. Now would be the time that he reprimanded her for her transgressions, made her see the error of her ways. Made her regret the actions with a little bit of pain and violence. Enid tried to keep the panic down as her lungs began to burn. He leaned in, his lips hovering, her own still moving silently as she tried to plead with him. Faintly, he brushed them with his, a feather soft kiss.

"I took care of you," he whispered. Spots of light joined the dark flashes behind her eyes. She struggled to breathe, to understand. It was all happening too fast.

"I watched out for you." He pulled back, his eyes angry slits. It was getting harder to focus. Her hands felt so weak where they struggled against his hold.

"I loved you," he fumed, slinging her to the floor. She gasped loudly, inhaling the sweet air in gulps, before violently coughing and choking.

Before she had a chance to recover, he was there, snatching a fistful of her hair. Enid held fast to his wrist, attempting to keep the strands from being ripped out by the roots. Her scalp ached, forcing a cry of pain. He only wound tighter around her scarlet locks, yanked her flush against him, and crushed his lips to hers.

She struggled to get away, but his arm was around her waist, anchoring her in place. The coarse hairs on his chin scraped like sandpaper. A sob bubbled at the back of her throat as his mouth brutalized hers, all teeth and rough edges.

He was too strong. Too angry. Too determined.

"I would have done anything for you," he rumbled. He gave her hair a harsh jerk. His whiskey laced breath hot against her cheek. "And how did you repay me?" He put his forehead against hers. "You left me at the altar and disappeared without a word."

Fright slipped down her spine at the hardness in his tone. He stood up straight, holding her waist tight, her head pulled back so he could fully take in the discomfort he saw there.

"What do you have to say for yourself?"

Enid whimpered, her body tense, back bowed painfully in his embrace.

"Charlie," she gasped, tears thickening her voice, "I'm sorry, please—"

He let her go. Before she could get another word out, he pulled his fist back and slammed it into her face. Agony lanced through her. Her head whipped back and she thudded to the ground solidly. The last thing she was conscious of, before the blackness took over, was the feeling of him on top of her. His thick fingers fumbling with her pants.

***

Bright light stung her eyes. Her hand automatically shifted to block it. The movement had her hissing. Her body felt as though it was tearing apart. Carefully, she tried to move her limbs one by one, assessing the ache within them. The events of last night washed over her and she stilled.

Looking around, she found herself on her bed, naked and alone, with the blankets pulled up to her chin. The usually drawn curtains were open. The morning light shining through the open slats of the blinds. Throwing the blanket off, she forced herself up only to stop as her head spun. Taking in slow, deep breaths, she pushed through the dizziness and gasped. Dark bruises covered her legs and arms. Marks peppered her torso and breasts. She suppressed a sob at a deep ache between her legs.

Hearing footsteps, she pulled the blanket up to cover herself. The door from the bathroom opened and Charlie walked out, a smile on his freshly shaved face. He had showered, his damp hair was combed back, and he looked more like his normal self. Enid sat back farther on the bed, attempting to keep some of the distance between them.

"Hey, darlin'," he said happily as if he hadn't beat her nearly to death and then raped her unconscious body the night before. He ignored her attempt at space and sat beside her, fingers gently grazing her cheek. She flinched. He frowned. Some of the pain and anger from the night before flashed through his eyes. His jaw clenched before he spoke.

"Now, I know what you are going to say, and I am sorry. I got carried away, and I shouldn't have, but you have no idea what you put me through this last year." He stood up, and ran his hands through his hair before turning to face her.

"I mean, what were you thinkin', runnin' off? Making me think you had been kidnapped or murdered! I had everyone looking for you. Do you have any idea how many sleepless nights I had? We were supposed to be getting married, Enid! My whole family was calling nonstop for months wantin' to know what was going on. The police weren't any help. I had to hire a private investigator! I spent the entire time tellin' everyone you were having another one of your episodes. I didn't know if you were dead in a ditch, chasin' after a leprechaun or some shit. It's the only explanation I had. Do you have any idea what people have been whispering?" He began gesturing wildly around as he spoke.

Enid emotionally imploded as he continued his rant, shriveling into the numb husk of her mind. Her fear swallowed everything she felt until all she had was a gaping hole where her feelings should be. At some point she stopped listening as he droned on about canceled venues and wasted money. Paying attention only to the frenzied movement of his hands. Aware of those hands at all times.

Vaguely, she wondered what her life would be now. Would she be running all the time? Always looking over her shoulder? Or would he finally snap and end up killing her. That thought brought the ache in her head back to the forefront and she winced putting her hand to it. Her long hair fell in waves in front of her face. A small moment of respite from the ranting lunatic in front of her. Charlie sat back on the bed.

"You ok?" he asked in concern, pulling her hand into his and touching her hair softly. She instinctively tried to avoid his fingers. It didn't deter him. Instead, he pushed her hair back and gently put both hands on either side of her face, forcing her to look him in the eye.

"Hey," he said softly. "You know I don't like to hit you. I was drinking, and hurt, and I went too far. It won't happen again. Just—let's go back home. I forgive you." His fingers stroked the strands of her hair. "We'll get you cleaned up, pack your things, and drive home tonight. We will get you better doctors and round the clock care. You won't have to worry about your hallucinations ever again. I will take care of you." He ran his fingers across her cheeks wiping at the tears that she hadn't realized started to fall.

She didn't want to go back. She didn't want him. She wanted to be left alone. She wanted her freedom, and here he was promising her everything she loathed. She hated him. But there was no doubt in her mind that if she told him those things now, he might snap.

Mutely, she nodded. The tears continued to fall, but she didn't feel them. She felt nothing. She didn't feel it when he smiled, leaned forward, and kissed her unresponsive lips. She didn't feel it when his mouth moved down to her neck. She didn't feel it when he pushed her back onto her bed and began to run his hands along her body. She didn't feel it when he dipped down and pulled her abused nipples into his greedy mouth. She didn't feel him pulling her legs apart. And she didn't respond when he pulled his clothes off, and lay on top of her, pushing himself into her aching cavity over and over again.

Her body was numb to the pain, numb to the emotions she knew should be coursing through her, numb to her anguish. She was an empty vessel that he tried to fill with his love, but she was cracked. He didn't seem to mind that she was unmoving, unblinking, unfeeling as he moaned and grunted on top of her before giving one final, hard thrust, his body shuddering.

When he finished, he rolled off, hugging her tight to his side. She lay as still in his arms as she had been underneath him. Her stomach was a heavy, aching stone in her body. She wanted to throw up. She wanted to rip his hands off of her and scream at

23

him. She wanted to make it so that he never touched her or anyone else again. But she could only lay there, trapped in her own body—trapped in his unwanted embrace.

"Why don't you go get cleaned up," he urged, rubbing her arm.

Robotically, she stood and walked around the bed to the bathroom, feeling him watch her until she shut the door. She took her time in the bathroom. The mirror began to fog up as she stood and stared at herself. Her right eye was edged in purple and puffy. A cut high up on her cheekbone had opened up and was oozing slightly. Her lips were swollen and red. Fingerprints stood out darkly on the white skin of her neck.

After he had his way with her last night, he must have cleaned her up a bit. Her torn, bloody work clothes were on the floor of the bathroom—a blood-soaked washcloth among them. She gently dabbed the cut with a fresh cloth from the nearby shelf, flinching at the sting.

Slowly, in the safety of solitude, her emotions began to bubble to life—threatening to overwhelm her. Tears of frustration leaked down her cheeks. Balling her hand, she pressed it into the edge of the sink to keep herself from lashing out. She was supposed to be free from this. Even hiding among millions of people hadn't been enough.

The scalding water did little to soothe her sore, beaten body. Methodically, she attempted to rid herself of the feel of his touch, scrubbing her already sensitive skin until it was red and raw. Still, she didn't feel clean.

She stood under the water, her head pounding, her chest tight from the rush of emotions she attempted to suppress. They raged within her, kicking and stomping to be free. Urging her to lash out, to fight.

Only when the water began to run cold and she began to shiver did she finally feel calm enough to step out into the foggy bathroom. Wiping the haze from the mirror, her jade eyes reflected determination back at her. She was going to get away from Charlie Wallace. Once and for all.

CHAPTER

3

Later that evening they sat at the tiny table in her apartment eating dinner. Half packed boxes and paper were scattered about. Charlie had come prepared with packing materials, and made no delay in throwing the last year of her life into the cardboard receptacles that would most likely be their permanent home.

Enid only grazed at her food, lost in thought. She needed a plan. There had to be a way out of this, away from *him*. In the past she had tried going to the police, and filed restraining orders. They took pictures of her bruises and broken bones, clicking their tongues and giving her empty, whispered apologies. None of it mattered. Family money would buy his way out of it every time. Those that did try to help were quickly transferred or dismissed. It was a miracle the police left well enough alone when she took off.

Maybe she could run again. Farther this time. Change her name. Her appearance. She internally lamented the thought of cutting her long auburn hair and dying it, but she would do it. It was only hair. This was her life. Thoughts, plans, and ideas buzzed around in her head as she slowly chewed on a piece of garlic bread without really tasting it.

Charlie happily talked away beside her, his voice a garbled droning in the background of her mind. Trying to give herself time to think, and hopefully come up with a plan before they went back to their hometown, Enid had been deliberately slow doing everything. The packing sat around half done. She took her time eating. Maybe if she could get him to take her to the diner, she could give him the slip from there. The thought had promise.

"What do you think Enid?" she heard Charlie say suddenly.

"I'm sorry, what?" she responded. The piece of bread she had been nibbling on froze halfway to her mouth and she forced herself to pay attention to his words.

"Well, don't sound too thrilled," he chuckled. "I mean a baby would be hard work, but I think it'll be good for us. A son, to carry on the family name," he said with a grin, wiggling his eyebrows.

Enid sat there staring at him. She thought she might be sick. Panic swirled in her gut. The already tasteless toast turned to dust in her mouth and she dropped it down onto the plate. Giving him a shaky smile, she stood, and dumped the rest of her food into the trash.

Think Enid, think, she thought as she scrubbed at the dish.

Charlie's arms wrapped around her from behind and she jumped. The plate slipped from her grasp, breaking in two at the bottom of the sink.

"Whoa, Enid." Charlie soothed. His arms locked around her as he kissed the back of her head. She stood frozen, her heart pounding like a frightened rabbit's. "You're so jumpy. What's wrong?" His eyes narrowed suspiciously as she stepped away from him and put her back to the counter.

"Nothing," she said, trying to sound calm and collected. "You surprised me. I was deep in thought. You know, so much to do. I actually just remembered that I left some things in my locker at the diner that I really need. I should let them know I'm not coming back in person anyway. It would only be polite. They may have some paperwork to send me, tax forms and what not. I really should leave a forwarding address."

She realized she was beginning to babble and zipped her mouth shut, eyes wide as she gauged his reaction.

Please, please, please, she thought over and over as he seemed to process her words.

"Alright," he said slowly. "But I'm coming with you, and no funny business. I just got you back, I am not letting you go again." Her back bit painfully into the edge of the counter as he gripped her chin, forcing her to look up into his face.

"I mean it, Enid. You are mine, and you aren't goin' anywhere." The words were forced through gritted teeth. Sincerity shone in the depths of his dark eyes—what he was willing to do to keep those words true.

Enid gulped.

"I-I won't," she stuttered. He held her still like that for a few strained seconds, watching her intently, nostrils flared.

"Who do you belong to Enid?" he asked quietly, his fingers threading into her hair, twisting as he yanked her face closer to his, their lips centimeters apart. A whimper rushed out of her. She lifted onto her toes in an attempt to relieve the pain.

"Y-you," she breathed, tears stinging the edges of her eyes. He laid a soft, gentle kiss on her lips before pulling back to look at her.

"It's for your own good, you know. With your family history…"

"What?" she whispered.

"Nothin' darlin'. Something between your mother and I. You keep in mind to do what you are told, and everything will be just fine. I'll take care of you." His mouth claimed hers again, rougher, demanding, until she relented and returned the kiss.

Finally, he let her go. She nearly sank to the ground in relief. Only her grip on the counter kept her upright.

An hour later she was ready to go. Pulling a jacket on, she stood in front of a mirror, and gave herself a once over as she slid her hair back into a low ponytail. The redness had faded and the swelling had gone down. The cut below her eye, and the purple that ringed it, she couldn't do anything about. She would have to say she fell into something if anyone asked. The collar of her jacket did well to hide the marks around her neck, but some still peeked out on the edges. Shaking her hair out of the ponytail, she pulled it around her face to offer more cover for the bruising.

An old backpack sat on a nearby chair packed with a few changes of clothes, her wallet, and a few toiletries. She grabbed it as she walked out of the room. Charlie stood by the door on his phone, glancing up at her as she came out.

"What's with the bag?" he asked as he tucked his phone into the pocket of his khaki pants.

"I need it for the stuff from my locker." Enid shrugged as she grabbed her house keys and walked past. It was difficult acting nonchalant as she pulled the door shut behind them and locked up before they made their way down to the street.

"Let's take my car," he said, leading her toward where he had parked his shiny BMW. Enid pulled back.

"It's only a few blocks. It would be easier to walk than to find parking," she explained as she moved in the direction of the diner.

They strode along the sidewalk, Charlie taking in the city, Enid trying to act casual. Even at night there was a bustle to the place, though fewer people walked the street. The lights flickered off the windows, making everything seem to sparkle in neon. Enid stiffened as he put his arm around her shoulders, jerking her closer to him. To anyone else they looked like a pair of lovers on a date, but she knew he was only keeping her close so she couldn't run. She had learned the difference between his possessiveness and true affection.

The diner wasn't very crowded when they made their way in. Cindy was behind the counter talking to one of the customers seated there. She perked up when Enid walked through the door, her eyes flashing over to Charlie questioningly and their joined hands as they made their way over to her.

"Hey, Cindy, this is Charlie," Enid said as he took a seat on one of the stools.

Charlie reached over, taking Cindy's extended hand.

"Ms. Cindy, it is a pleasure to meet you," he said smoothly, his southern accent thickening the way it always did when he talked to pretty women.

Cindy cocked her head to the side with a flirty smile.

"Oh, we have us a country boy!" she exclaimed, squeezing his hand before letting it go.

"Yes, ma'am," he said smoothly, giving her a smile and a wink as he leaned against the counter. Enid nearly rolled her eyes at the charm he was exuding. It fooled everyone.

"Cindy, is Gladys here?" Enid interrupted. She was getting jittery.

"She's in the back." Cindy gave her a worried look, her gaze lingering over Enid's black eye, flicking to Charlie and back again.

Enid gave a slight shake of her head as she turned to Charlie.

"Charlie, why don't you have a cup of coffee while I go take care of everything."

"Sounds good, darlin'. Don't take too long," he said, reaching out and squeezing her hand. He gave her a meaningful look. She got the warning.

"I won't be long at all," she replied, plastering a fake smile on her face as she pulled her hand away from his too tight grip. Cindy grabbed a cup of coffee, placing it in front of Charlie before following Enid back into the employee lounge where the lockers were.

"What is going on?" Cindy questioned sternly, following as Enid threw open the locker, thrusting an extra set of clothes into her bag. It was all her locker contained. "What happened to your eye?"

Enid shut the metal door, letting out a deep sigh before turning to the only friend she had.

"Cindy, I don't have a lot of time to explain. I'm sorry. All I can tell you is that man out there is a horrible person. I've spent the last year of my life hiding from him, and he found me. Now I've got to go. Please keep him preoccupied. Give me time to get as far away as possible."

Cindy looked at Enid for a moment, her arms crossed over her chest.

"He do that to you?" she asked with a nod of her head toward Enid's eye.

Enid nodded, looking away in shame as she zipped up her bag.

"Can't we call the police on him? He assaulted you."

Enid shook her head.

"I've tried. I've filed a restraining order and everything. His family has money and powerful connections. He gets out and comes back every time."

"Motherf–" Cindy hissed as she glared over toward the door. "Fine. I'm stalling him, and you get away. You better call me and let me know you're safe."

Enid sighed in relief and threw her arms around her friend, giving her a big hug.

"Thank you so much," she whispered.

Cindy pulled back, anger and determination shifting across her face.

"Alright, go out the back. I'll keep that asshole distracted."

She pulled her shirt down and pushed her bra up, causing her cleavage to strain out of her already tight shirt. Enid would have laughed if she wasn't so terrified. She watched as Cindy sashayed out the door and into the main dining room, hopefully giving her enough time to escape unnoticed.

Making her way to the back door that led to the only other exit in the building, she was suddenly stopped by Gladys. She looked longingly toward the door as Jason walked out of it, a bag of trash in hand.

"Enid, can you pick up a couple extra shifts for me next week," the older woman wheezed in her harsh smoker's voice.

Enid cursed her luck. She really didn't want to have this conversation right now. There wasn't time. Not to mention she felt terrible just springing this on her.

"Gladys, I really can't. I'm sorry. In fact, I hate to say it, but I've got to quit."

The older woman's eyes went wide as she pressed her lips together in a thin line. "Why is that? What happened to you?" A frown turned her lips down as she shot a sharp look at the cut and purple bruise on Enid's cheekbone.

Enid's hand went up to her face. "Oh this. I'm so clumsy. I ran into the corner of a door," she said, waving her hand as if to blow it off.

"A door?" Gladys's face hardened. "That must have been some big door." The older woman gave her a disapproving look, but didn't remark any more on it. "Now why are you leaving? Where are you going?" Gladys fired the questions at her rapidly as Enid struggled to think quickly, still eyeing the exit.

She ran a hand through her hair in frustration. She hated doing this, but she needed to get going and didn't have the time to explain everything. Charlie would expect her back in a few minutes and she needed that time to get space between them.

"Gladys, I can't really go into the details, but I have to move. I'm going home. I decided to go back." She drew in a ragged breath as the older woman inhaled sharply, obviously not pleased. "I'll call you later and explain better, I promise. I really need to go now."

Gladys shook her head disapprovingly. "I thought you would have been one of the few to make it. You couldn't have given us some sort of notice?"

Enid bit her lip in frustration. "I'm sorry Gladys. I'll explain later."

She glanced over her shoulder to see Cindy still keeping Charlie distracted. He smiled as she laughed and leaned forward on the bar, her ample bosom drawing his attention like a magnet. Enid rushed past the frazzled older woman, her shoulder shoving against the cool metal, and stumbled out into the night.

CHAPTER

4

The door slammed shut behind her, the sound jarring as it echoed off the brick walls of the alley. Enid rushed toward the street, her feet skipping along the broken up concrete and shallow puddles. As she rounded the corner, she barreled to a stop. Charlie pushed through the door of the diner; a phone pressed to his ear.

Of all the luck.

She ducked back into the alley, her heart thundering.

Now what? Maybe he would go back inside once he finished his conversation. Still, it wouldn't do for him to walk this way and see her. Her steps were quiet, careful, as she moved further into the shadows—willing him to go in. Keeping an eye on the sidewalk, she prayed he didn't come this way. Her hands moved along the brick wall, steadying her frayed nerves as she slid into the darkness, letting it conceal her.

A solid form at her back startled her, a sharp intake of breath the only sound she allowed herself to make.

"Hello, there," stated a thickly accented voice.

Looking over her shoulder, she glimpsed a black t-shirt over a solid chest before scanning up, into a set of amused, ice blue eyes. The man from the diner last night. Her eyes widened in recognition.

"What are we hiding from?" he whispered.

Enid turned to face him, the anxiety within her, that inner voice of self-preservation, urging her to pay attention, to not turn her back. She stepped away, still not willing to move further toward the street. Uncertain, for the moment, which direction held more danger.

The stranger leaned casually against the wall. No threat in the way he held himself, no indication he would do her harm. The warning bells in her head dimmed. He continued to assess her as she shifted uncomfortably—feeling completely exposed.

"I'm fine, thanks," she murmured.

"You do not appear fine," that thick, Slavic voice replied. Muscular arms crossed over a broad chest as he raised a brow, full lips pulling into a frown. "You are running from a lover? A boyfriend?"

Enid didn't bother to respond.

He rubbed his jaw as he studied her. "An abusive lover, it would appear."

His fingers traced a line across his throat, his gaze lingering where the bruises marred her skin.

She shifted her weight between her feet before finally giving a slight nod, her head lowering in shame.

"Perhaps," he mused, "we can help each other." He kicked away from the wall and took a step forward. When she stiffened and moved away, keeping that space between them, he stopped. "You see," he continued, "I am in need of something, and you need to get away from this person, correct?"

"And?" Enid replied, watching him warily.

He lifted a shoulder. "So, we kill two birds with one stone, as they say."

"What is it that you need?" Enid asked.

A smirk shifted across his face, the action transforming him from relaxed to savage in an instant. Fear crept up her spine. There was a moment, a trick of the dim lighting perhaps, or a passing car from the street, where his eyes reflected in the shadows. An eerie green flash in the dark. Demonic.

Please God, let it be the light, she thought.

It wasn't. The only light came from the single, naked bulb by the door of the diner. Some primal part of her sensed the truth, felt it with certain clarity, knew without a fraction of doubt who she was looking at. What, not who. A predator in the dark— vicious, and hungry. At that moment, Enid realized she had made the wrong decision. She should have run for the street.

She didn't stop to consider her actions. Didn't stop to think how it made her look. Survival and instinct drove her as she slammed into the wall at her back, backpack crunching. There was no refusing what she saw this time, no playing it off as a trick of her brain. That part of her that she tried to deny, that she hid away thrummed solidly through her body.

Run. Hide.

It was too late. There was no running now. The look in the hunter's eyes told her as much.

"What are you?" she hissed.

He faltered, head cocking to the side.

"What do you mean?" he purred, the picture of innocence.

She glared at him. He chuckled as he took another small step in her direction.

"I am merely a concerned stranger, in the right place at the right time." His voice was soft, soothing, and persuasive. "It is fortunate I happened upon you."

She didn't trust this act. Continuing to level that hard glare, she took a step to the side—closer to the street. He frowned, mirroring her movement. A warning shot through her, the alarm in her head rang out.

Run!

Even as she began to move toward the street, weight shifting forward, she felt the tug of a strong arm around her waist.

"CHARLIE!" she screamed as her feet left the pavement. Her body was swung around, the arm a steel band caging her against the stranger.

"Now why would you do that, I wonder?" His voice was low in her ear.

At the other end of the alley, a pale face peeked around a dumpster. A woman, small and petite, with raven hair and eyes that matched the man at her back. Lania.

"Have you lost your charm, brother?" the woman called as she stood and walked toward them. Curiously, she picked Enid over as she came closer, the back of her hand wiping at a full, red mouth. She moved like a cat, all stealth and grace. Enid's heart was thrumming desperately, a frightened rabbit in the maw of the wolf.

"I think I may have caught a prize, Lania. Something to tell our Queen about, for sure."

The woman hummed in response, stopping before them. Delicate fingers grazed the skin at Enid's neck, skimming over the bruises with a frown.

"What the hell is going on here?!"

Charlie. Enid nearly gasped in relief.

"Oh good," the man murmured, whispering only for her to hear. "A snack."

The pressure around her waist disappeared and she was pushed, her body stumbling, into the arms of the woman. Despite being smaller than Enid, she was surprisingly strong. Enid yelped as she easily shoved her into the wall, the brick biting into her back even through the material of the bag. One hand against her chest was all that kept her in place.

"Is this the one? The one who did this thing to you?" Lania tilted her chin toward Enid's bruised face and neck; words inflected with the same heavy accent as her brother.

Instead of responding, Enid tried to push her away, to slip out of her grip. It was useless. Lania stood there with an amused expression before she quickly lost interest, and looked, instead, toward the angry man barreling at them.

"Who the fuck are you, and what the hell are you doing with my girl?!" Charlie shouted. His hands were already balled into fists as he stalked toward the trio, eyes narrowing at Enid suspiciously. "What the fuck are you doing, Enid?" he demanded.

The woman, Lania, laughed. "Oh yes," she confided to Enid as though they were just two girls gossiping over a boy. "He is the one." Her lips curled, eyes glittering dangerously. "How delightful."

"Dimitri," Lania called. "Can I play with him, please?"

The dark man glanced over his shoulder, the corner of his mouth tipping upward. "Dah, sister. Let me make our introductions first." He winked at Enid, running a hand through his thick, black hair before turning to Charlie as he rubbed the back of his neck. A sheepish gesture.

"My friend–"

Dimitri didn't get another word out before Charlie's fist connected with his jaw.

The scream of pain that followed did not, however, come from the strange man. But from Charlie as he cradled the mangled appendage protectively against his chest.

Dimitri's face was hard as he stood in place, his arms folding in front of him. "That was unnecessary." Not a mark scarred his pale skin. Enid's jaw dropped.

"What are you?" she whispered once more. Lania chuckled.

"You do not want to know, but you will find out soon enough."

She let go of Enid, stepping between her and the street as she circled around behind Charlie, inspecting him like one would a prized animal. She watched him intently, the pain in his face, the way he cradled his hand. Her eyes brightened when fury replaced agony. Enid wasn't going to bother staying anymore to witness what happened next.

Twisting the other way, she ran further into the alley. She didn't get far past the door to the diner before a chain-link fence blocked her. The diner. If she banged on the door loud enough, someone might come to check. It was so close, but something on the ground stopped her. A body by the dumpster. Enid dropped to her knees next to Jason. Blood colored the neck of his white shirt. A whimper broke from her as she lay a shaking hand on his chest. He was breathing.

Thank God.

She needed to get help. No sooner had she stood, than she was slamming against a hard body. Dimitri's arms folded over her.

"There you are," he laughed. Her backpack was pulled from her shoulders and slung to the ground as he moved them closer to where Lania stood with Charlie, away from the small circle of light and the door.

Lania was teasing the furious man, her finger trailing along his muscular arm.

"Do you want to punish me, as you have punished this woman?" She smiled. "Perhaps my brother will leave her alone to save me," she suggested, sidling closer.

Enid gasped as she was lifted, Dimitri's hands on her thighs tucking them around his waist before he pinned her to the wall. Her hands pelted his chest and shoulders. It did nothing. She was no more than a gnat batting at him. He grinned, placing a hand on the wall at either side of her head.

"Keep fighting me, little flower. I like it," he growled.

Behind them, Charlie's good hand found Lania's neck and he roughly pushed her against the opposite wall.

"Let her go!"

Dimitri ignored him. His head dipped, soft lips grazing hers. She jerked back. He hummed, the sound filled with amusement, vibrating through his chest where her hands rested. Leaning into her once more, his mouth traced a line along her jaw, to the nape of her neck, the pressure increasing as though he was taking his time tasting her, teasing, his tongue flicking out to lap at the salt on her skin.

"Let me go!" Her shout was in vain. He paid her no mind.

Enid's head pounded, the weight of him not nearly as crushing as the one that settled over her chest, suffocating her. She pushed against him again and again, desperate—needing to get away, to breath. Something fractured within her that scared her more than the thought of violence. It started in her temples, moving behind her eyes, building as the panic rose and she felt herself begin to unravel, to lose control.

Her hands were lifted above her head, one of his holding them in place when the feeling overwhelmed her and broke free. It felt as though her entire being spilled out into the night. White light flooded her vision and her back went rigid.

The images came then. Slow at first, and then faster, so fast she couldn't decipher them—only the meaning within them. Tunnels, and strange lights. Creatures of all shapes and sizes. Glasses filled with ruby liquid and a woman. A woman of incomparable beauty as dark as the night with eyes that pierced her soul. Danger, lust, greed, fear. And a different, conflicting emotion that flickered in the background. Hope.

Enid blinked as the vision faded. Dimitri watched her, eyes wide.

"What are you?" It was his turn to ask the question now. Enid only stared, her confusion as evident as his.

37

Behind them, Charlie had Lania off the ground. Her mouth open in a soundless scream.

"You better stop, unless you want me to snap this bitch's pretty, little neck!" he shouted.

Still, Dimitri's attention remained on Enid. He wrapped a strand of her scarlet hair around a finger as he considered her.

"I wonder," he breathed, letting her hair drop as his hand gripped the back of her head. And then his mouth was once again at her neck, with more force this time. The sharp pain of teeth in her flesh tore a scream from her. A scream that was soon muffled by his hand.

Charlie looked over his shoulder, his nostrils flared, face red. Lania's fluttering eyes closed and her body hung limp. Charlie let her drop to the ground without a thought, turning toward Dimitri. Enid could only distantly register that the woman was dead. Charlie had killed her.

"You son of a bitch!" he shouted. Scooping up a nearby brick, he swung it toward Dimitri's back. Still Dimitri kept his focus on her, his mouth at her neck, the pain fading. The sensation both pleasurable and frightening.

Enid watched as Charlie's arm stopped mid-swing. Puzzled, he peered over his shoulder. There Lania stood, her small hand holding his wrist. She plucked the brick from his grasp and tossed it. Her fingers went to the marks on her neck, the prints that lingered there slowly fading away. A purple collar on her creamy skin.

"Your technique leaves much to be desired. Still…was it good for you?"

She gave him a wicked grin before jumping on him, legs and arms clinging tightly. Placing one hand on his shoulder, and the other on his head, she pushed it to the side to fully expose his neck. The petite woman threw her dark head of hair back, her mouth opening wide to reveal long canines. With a growl she lunged at Charlie's neck, shaking at it like a dog with a bone.

Charlie's shouts echoed in Enid's ears. Dark spots began dancing at the edges of her vision. Dimitri pulled at her neck with deep, greedy gulps. She whimpered weakly.

"Please, stop." Her eyelids fluttered as she fought for the energy to keep herself alert. "I don't want to die."

She felt him tense before he pulled away. His pale skin was flushed, his blue eyes glassy and dilated. Lazily, he licked at the drops of red at the corner of his mouth. Her blood. Tears blurred her vision. She was going to die. The press of his body was all that held her in place, her legs still wrapped around his waist. An intimate embrace, almost too intimate for death.

"How would you like to be remade," he said softly, a hand lifting her chin, keeping her bobbing head still. "You know," he mused, "in my world, there were once mates. Souls fated to cleave together—becoming one for all the rest of their days. They had a way of knowing when they found one another, a connection that clicked into place. Our magic is strained now, broken. But perhaps, that is what has drawn me to you?" He hummed, his lips grazing hers once more fleetingly. "Or perhaps, it is the color of your hair. The shade of burnished wheat soaked in blood. It awakens something here." His fingers thumped against his chest, strangely blue eyes contemplative. "I could make you strong, fast, unbreakable."

She was so dizzy. Still his words broke through the haze, echoing in her head, a promise, a seduction. "No one could harm you ever again. You would be immortal. Part of a large, infinite family. Untouchable." He whispered the last word in her ear, the breath caressing the delicate hairs. She shivered.

He cupped her cheek. There was the flash of teeth against the flesh of his lip, blood welling to the surface. Gently, he brushed them against hers. The coppery tang lingered on her tongue as he deepened the kiss, forcing her lips apart. She pushed against him, sputtering as he pulled back and pressed his hand over her mouth and nose until she swallowed.

Her body began to relax, warmth overtaking her limbs as the blood rolled down her throat. No longer fighting, she dazedly looked up into Dimitri's eyes. The deep pools of blue swimming before her like the sky, endless and mysteriously beautiful. She found herself slipping into them effortlessly as the feel of his soft lips returned to hers, and the metallic, sweet taste of his blood entered her willing mouth.

She didn't understand why she had fought the increasingly sweet, nectar-like taste of him. How had she lived without this bliss? Never wanting it to end, she gave herself over to him, wrapping her arms around his neck.

Their tongues danced and twisted against one another. She couldn't get close enough. Needed him closer. Within her. Part of her. Her heart beat strangely as the euphoria became overwhelming, dizzying. He groaned into her mouth, crushing her tighter, hands sliding along her curves. The kiss became heated, frenzied as Dimitri ground himself against her. A yank on her hair had her head tilting to the side, his hot mouth drifting lower.

A loud roar echoed from the end of the alley.

Dimitri jerked back with an inhuman growl, stepping from her toward the looming threat. Enid slipped to the ground in a daze, her arms blindly groping the now empty air.

The earth began to tilt, the shadows shifted and swayed. Lania jumped from Charlie, who fell flat on his face on the concrete and remained unmoving, blood pooling around him.

Enid felt her strength failing. She slumped over onto the dirty concrete as the duo confronted whatever creature dared interrupt their meal. A pair of heavy boots stepped into the fading light as the darkness took her completely.

CHAPTER

5

Her head ached when she finally managed to pry her eyes open. A large figure crouched over her, and for a brief moment the feel of Dimitri's lips flashed through her mind. Trembling with longing, she reached toward the figure. A firm grip clasped her outstretched hand.

"How do you feel?" a deep, familiar voice asked. The bubble of fantasy burst, flooding her senses with harsh reality as she realized it was not Dimitri above her, but rather the rugged voice of Vidar that spoke.

With a gasp she drew back. The shock and embarrassment of what she was about to do, and who she had been thinking of splashed over her mind like ice water, bringing her back to her senses. Confusion crept over her as she fought her inner demons, things she could never imagine herself doing flitting through her mind. The subtle taste of blood in her mouth caused her to lick her lips as her heart pounded deliriously in her chest. The memory of the ecstasy she had so briefly discovered returned to her at the taste of him lingering there.

Vidar only stared, his mouth moving without words, as she blinked up at him, heat filling her core, bringing a flush to her cheeks as the thoughts of Dimitri overtook her. Concern flooded Vidar's face as his eyebrows drew together. His large hand wrapped around her bare arm, the feel of his skin on hers pulling her back to herself like an anchor, snapping her floating mind back to reality.

The ground was cold and hard beneath her. Her forgotten backpack lay under her head. Groggily she pulled herself up. The pounding in her head beat in time to her pulse.

"What is happening?" she asked, looking around. Distantly she realized part of her felt bitter that Dimitri was no longer there. Vidar helped her up, his touch a solid reassurance in the wild storm of her internal crisis.

He looked her over, his gaze seeming to peer into her very soul as though looking for any indication of deception from her. The spot where Charlie had fallen in the alley was nothing more than a smear of red soaked into the concrete. No sign of him lingered with the exception of that stain on the earth. Vidar seemed to anticipate her question as his gaze followed hers.

"They took him," he said simply. "I could only protect one of you." He shrugged his shoulders as he gave the flimsy apology.

His words, as few and simplistic as they were, seemed to bring clarity to her shattered mind. The fear and the pain were real, along with the blood and pleasure that accompanied them. This event had not been the figment of her imagination. Not only that, but she had relished the sensations Dimitri brought out in her. Barely even hesitated to question the turn of events that led her to lust after a demented, blood crazed demon. She shuddered in horror and Vidar gently rubbed her arms, as though trying to help fight away the chill that tumbled down her spine.

Part of Enid wanted to scream in terror at what she had experienced and felt, while part of her wanted to laugh at the audacity of it all. That she who had spent so long running and hiding from a life of panic, of being broken and bloodied; had for a brief moment embraced it with ecstatic abandon. Instead, she stood there staring at the red stain on the ground, wondering if she would ever feel joy that she had been rescued from that demon.

A demon. That was what he had been. They had been. The two of them. Dark siblings, robbing humanity of life and happiness. She shook her head. No, that couldn't be right. It couldn't have been real. Vidar had saved her from a vicious attack. A mugging about to become a rape. Nothing more.

It's all in your head, Enid. It isn't real. Her mantra. Grounding her. Pulling her back from the brink with consistent, comforting words. How much of the assault had been real, and how much of it was an invention of her fragile psyche? A groan drew her attention to the trash bin where Jason had begun to stir. Vidar glanced back at him, discomfort lining his face as he looked around.

"He needs a hospital," Enid said, her voice flat and strangely calm. He was pale, but alive. She was happy about that, but that happiness was only a flicker against the utter emptiness she felt at Dimitri's departure.

"He will be fine. He won't feel good, but he will live. A hospital will not be necessary, and there will be too many questions that cannot be answered cleanly." Once again, his no-nonsense style of speaking broke into Enid's splintered mind. She felt herself shrugging along in agreement, realizing internally that before this happened to her, she would have immediately called the police with little hesitation. Now, she could barely make herself feel anything other than the empty sorrow of abandonment.

"We must go. Before he wakes up and anyone else comes around." He grabbed her bag from the ground, handing it to her as he took her by the arm and steered her toward the street. She threw a final glance back at Jason before she followed along beside Vidar.

She was only vaguely aware as she gave brief responses to his inquiries of where she lived. A few times they missed their turn and had to backtrack as her scattered mind refused to focus on Vidar's task of getting her safely home.

By the time they reached her apartment building the sky was beginning to grow lighter in the east. Vidar grumbled under his breath as he kept glancing toward the ever-lighting line of blue, then down at his watch. His movements were restless and uneasy, every ounce of his patience used to direct her up the steps to her door and help her find her keys. She was distracted, distant. Her responses vague and noncommittal. Anger boiled through him at the Revenant. He should have torn them limb from limb.

Unlocking the door, he pushed it open, and turned to guide her into the apartment. Her eyelids fluttered and she began to fall.

43

Vidar rushed to grab her, stumbling across the threshold in his effort to keep her upright. Surprise and worry flooded him, but he had no time to reflect. Setting her on the couch, he immediately set about drawing all of the shades and curtains after closing and locking the door firmly. Only after the apartment was blanketed in complete darkness did he calm down enough to turn to Enid.

She sat staring off into space. The numbness of shock fully set in as her brain attempted to rationalize the feelings swirling unbidden through her. Vidar sat beside her and placed his hand against her cheek gently. Her skin was clammy beneath his palm.

He felt for her pulse, wincing at the fading bite marks. Her heart beat steady and strong beneath his fingertips. He sighed with relief. Enid looked up then with tear filled eyes. Despair, regret, and grief radiated in the trembling drops that refused to fall from her lashes. He froze at the sight, swallowing thickly as the pure, unspoken emotion awoke a similar feeling from the recesses of his memory.

With a sob she leaned into him, her tears spilling over onto the soft, gray material of his t-shirt, soaking through to his skin. Without thinking he wrapped his arms around her, holding her as she shook against him until the tears were finally spent. Her weeping quieted to gentle, gasping breaths, and slowly she fell asleep—limp and yielding against his solid form.

He sat with her like that, not moving; despite the fact that her breathing deepened and her hands no longer clasped at his shirt in desperation. Those distant memories of the touch of another, and the warmth of a loving embrace tugged at him as he watched her sleep. As the memories and emotions flooded through him, he held her gently and securely, relishing the uncommon feeling of another being, even if only to comfort, even if just for one day.

CHAPTER

6

Enid awoke in a rush. Her hair was plastered to her sweaty forehead. Cotton filled her mouth. She willed her bleary eyes to look around, gritting her teeth at the stiffness in her neck. Still dressed in her clothes from last night, rumpled and dirty, she lay on the couch alone in her apartment. She moved slowly, her limbs protesting as she stood and stretched. Hollowness filled her chest. A bitter ache of loneliness that she didn't want to dwell on. That she didn't want to bring herself to understand, not yet.

The rest of her apartment stood empty and quiet. The packed boxes still piled against the wall—silent sentinels to the pain of the previous day. The shades and curtains were pulled over every window. A peak behind them revealed a darkened sky.

Despite the unusual quiet, Enid was certain there had been another person there with her. The feeling of strong arms around her lingered in her memory, and she wrapped her own arms around herself in a pitiful attempt at replicating that touch. A quick look around revealed that she was indeed alone.

Hastily, she locked the deadbolt and chain on her door, realizing that the only lock in place was on the knob. That was unlike her. Her fingers brushed over the latch, uncertainty filling her as she realized she couldn't remember coming home. She leaned her forehead against the solid wood of the door, attempting to sort the jumble of thoughts.

Images whirled in her mind, each one fighting for recognition. She remembered Charlie, and the strange, beautiful woman from the diner. A voice echoed in her head as she sifted through her memories until the vision of a face popped into her mind. Deep, ice blue, hypnotic eyes.

'How would you like to be remade.'

She gasped, her legs trembling as she remembered being held against his firm body, his breath on her neck, her heart racing in her throat. Pushing away from the door, she stumbled back, fighting the urge to rush out into the night and search for him.

Instead, she staggered into her bathroom, flicking on the light and rushing to splash cold water on her face. Anything to cool the sudden heat that sprang up through her at the thought of him. The liquid splashed along her hands and face as she rubbed them over her skin, the frigid water already helping to clear her muddled senses.

Grabbing a towel, she dried off, finally ready to face herself in the mirror. She froze, the towel slipping from her fingers. The bruises, the swelling and cuts that had graced her face and neck had disappeared leaving her skin clear and unblemished— glowing.

Her green irises were vibrant against her flushed cheeks and red, full lips. Gently she ran her fingers along her cheek. The cut had vanished. It was as though it was never there. Enid shook her head in disbelief. She hadn't imagined the beating and the rape. The half-packed boxes scattered through the apartment were proof of that; yet, somehow, she had healed overnight.

The memory of Charlie laying in a pool of blood cut through her. She remembered the rage on the face of the blue-eyed man whose lips tasted like ecstasy. She remembered Vidar looking down at her in worry, helping her from the ground and walking her home.

She needed answers. And the only way she could think to do that was to go to the diner. Enid grabbed her keys. As she rushed down the stairs and onto the darkened sidewalk, she sent a fervent prayer out to the universe that Gladys would forgive her, that Cindy was working, and that Vidar would choose tonight to make another appearance.

***

The jingle of the bell was a welcome familiarity as Enid entered the diner. To her surprise, only a few of the tables were occupied. A glance at the clock revealed it was past eight. She rubbed a hand over her face and through her hair in frustration. She had slept a whole day away. The kitchen door swung open and out walked Cindy with plates in hand. As soon as she saw Enid, she set them on the bar, and rushed over to pull her into a hug. Enid embraced her tightly, tears stinging her eyes as she struggled to keep her composure.

"Excuse me, but can we get our food over here!"

Enid winced as Cindy pulled back and cut her eyes over to the scruffy faced man who sat scowling at her across the room. With a quick pat to Enid's arm, Cindy grabbed the plates she had abandoned from the bar and stomped over to the two men at the table, throwing them down with a loud clatter.

"You're welcome!" she huffed before spinning around and dragging Enid over to a nearby booth.

Cindy sat there for a moment, her eyes widening as she took in Enid's face.

"You look way better than you did yesterday. Are you wearing makeup? You don't look like you're wearing makeup."

Enid bit her bottom lip nervously as her observant friend looked her over.

"It must not have been that bad," Enid muttered as she looked down at her hands.

Cindy gave her a sharp look of disbelief. "Girl, you looked like you fell down several flights of stairs. Now I can't see even a single bruise."

Enid only shrugged, tucking a strand of hair behind her ear.

"Well, what happened? Why are you here and not halfway to some remote hideaway? Is that abusive, good for nothing, jackass gone? That bastard disappeared when I had my back turned for one second. I was so worried you didn't have enough time. Then Jason came stumbling in from the alley covered in blood; only he didn't know what happened. Said someone must have hit him from behind." Cindy shook her head, her eyes flashing around as though looking for some invisible perpetrator. Her protective nature hungry to lash out at anyone deemed worthy of such an assault.

Heaving a deep sigh as she grabbed her hair in her hands and pulled, Enid looked on as Cindy rambled worriedly. She should have realized this would be harder than she thought with her friend's naturally curious and questioning personality. Suddenly she regretted her rash decision to rush over. There would be no answers for her here.

"Honestly," she shook her head, shoulders sagging in defeat, "I'm not sure. I can't remember a lot of last night. I woke up in my apartment alone only about an hour ago."

Cindy's eyes widened further as concern flooded her features. "Shut up. You don't remember anything?"

"I remember going outside. I remember seeing Jason out there, and then there were a couple people that I can't seem to remember, and Charlie showed up. The rest....is a blur."

There was no way she was going any further in detail. Not even with Cindy. The more Enid thought about that night, the crazier it seemed, and the more certain she was that she suffered from one of her constant hallucinations brought on most likely by head trauma and emotional stress. At least she hoped so, there were no other logical explanations. Tears flooded her eyes and she wiped at her nose, blinking them back.

"You need to go see a doctor!" Cindy exclaimed, worry evident in her large almond shaped eyes. "What if you have a concussion?"

Enid shook her head, tears leaking out at the sudden movement. Wiping them away, she once again emotionally steeled herself and looked her worried friend in the eye.

"Cindy, I'm fine. I feel fine. I was under a lot of stress yesterday, and now it's over. I'm safe and I'm still here, which is a lot better position than I thought I would be in. Please, don't say anything to anyone, and don't worry. Okay?"

Cindy sat back in the booth, giving her a hard look as she seemed to think over everything. Finally, she nodded.

"Thank you," Enid choked out in a near whisper before clearing her throat and glancing around. No one seemed to be paying any attention to them at the moment, thankfully.

"How's Jason?"

Cindy sighed heavily, the concern in her eyes thickening as she glanced toward the kitchen where the boisterous man usually could be heard throughout the diner. It was unusually quiet that night.

"He's ok. Weak, tired, and beat up. Whoever attacked him did a number. There was blood all over his shirt but no cuts, and no superficial wounds that anyone could find. He thinks he may have been knocked out but they didn't take anything. He still had his wallet on him. I don't know what happened last night, Enid, but the whole thing is nuts. He's as stubborn as you. He wouldn't go to the hospital either." Cindy sucked at her teeth and waved her hand in the air as if dismissing the whole mess. "You all are crazy as hell," she mumbled, crossing her arms over her chest and pursing her lips.

Enid chewed at her bottom lip, guilt weighing on her as she stared down at the laminate under her fingers.

"I'm sorry Cind," she said, her voice soft as she spoke. "I want to put the whole thing behind me. It was a rough twenty-four hours and I'm lucky to even be here. I just want to get back to work." Enid lifted her gaze at the thought. "That is going to be a rough conversation with Gladys."

Cindy smiled, her face lighting up. "I can help you out with that."

CHAPTER

7

Voices echoed around the cavernous room—raised in merriment and excitement. Most were flushed from the bounties of their hunt. Some relayed the stories of their conquests in grim detail, weaving a tale of seduction and drama, while others were more modest in their detail— finding no glory in their actions beyond the necessary will to survive.

Dimitri prowled at the fringe of the chatter, lost in his thoughts of a red-haired seductress with a touch that burned him to his core. He spent the time since he last held her in constant torture, yearning for her. Aching. It was the only goal he had any focus for. To have her in his arms again. To claim her completely. His Queen would be most interested as well. She spoke often over the centuries of a curse placed upon her, and a red-haired woman who would be able to break it, who would be the key to unlocking their future.

Dimitri rolled his shoulders, his neck moving left to right as he stretched those muscles in anticipation. The Queen would be pleased, and Dimitri would finally have a true companion after all this time. She was the one, she had to be, with the way her blood sang to him. He couldn't wait to hunt her. To show her the life she could have with them, how much better everything could be.

Most of the others still clung to their fragile humanity. It leached at them, diluting their strength, gifting their emotions control over their actions, and muting their natural Revenant impulses. Dimitri had no such qualms. His humanity had its time, and it had left him broken, unwanted, outcast. Becoming Revenant had changed all that. Now he was going to gift that feeling to another lucky human.

The easiest ones to convert were the unfortunate souls that had been horribly and savagely wronged. Their rage and desire for revenge fueled their transition. Dimitri already had an idea of what tactic he could use. His sister's new companion had been most helpful in divulging information.

As Dimitri paced, lost to the thoughts of temptation and deception, there was a sudden burst of chatter behind him. It wasn't until arms grabbed him about the neck, and a happy, flushed face pulled him closer that he realized his sister had arrived. Pale blue eyes rimmed with thick black lashes, the same as his, peered up at him from a pale, heart shaped face. Her raven hair cascaded in thick waves down her back.

"Brother!" she squealed. "Did you see how clever my new pet is? He is adapting quickly. Already he has had a successful hunt. On his first night, too." Her eyes danced with joy as she kissed his cheeks. Dimitri chuckled, removing her arms from his neck and gently pushing her away.

"Dah, sister. I thought you might enjoy it."

Lania clapped her hands together gleefully. "My last one was so bad. It kept running away."

"Lania, what do I tell you? If you are going to keep a pet, you must train it correctly."

"This time will be different," Lania promised. "I like this one." She spun away, her dark hair swirling around her as she wandered over to eagerly chat with some friends.

The dull roar of voices in the crowd began to slowly fade to a buzz as the Queen entered the room. She was the epitome of feline grace, her movements smooth and precise—head held high. Her dark skin glistened with blue highlights in the orb light. Intricately braided hair hung to her swaying hips. Gold beads and crystals woven into the braids caught the light and glimmered brightly against the velvet darkness of her skin.

As always, she was dressed as a goddess should be. A golden skirt hugged the curves of her body where it sat low on her hips, her long, muscular legs peeking from slits on either side of the thin material. The same shimmering fabric hung in a small triangle over her chest, held in place around her neck and back by two delicate gold chains. One large ruby pendant hung heavily between her breasts, tapping against the slight curve of her exposed midriff as she moved. Gold bands ornamented her arms, and gold sandals adorned her feet, the laces curving around her slender ankles.

The Revenant Queen stopped in front of the large, throne-like chair that dominated the head of the room. A red velvet pillow was placed upon it, and she sat, large onyx eyes taking in her loving subjects—her children.

The murmurs and whispers of adoration came to a stop as every eye in the room was reverently drawn to the dark beauty before them. Her full, lush lips pulled into a slight smile as she approvingly looked on at her captivated audience.

Before them sat the center of their universe. Her beauty matched that of no other. She was the model of grace, the archetype for sexuality. Artists and historians alike clamored for her affection. She was the muse to Aphrodite, the inspiration of Venus. Their beginning and their end.

The Revenant stood transfixed. One by one, their hearts began beating in time to hers, until eventually they were as one. Finally satisfied she had their full attention, she motioned for them to sit. The group moved to sit where they stood, their eyes glued to their queen.

"My children," her honeyed voice carried easily around the cavern—delicately melodic. Dimitri shivered as the sound sent a pleasant tingle through him. He drank her in. His untouchable goddess. His savior.

"I am so very proud of all that you have accomplished for me. We thrive as a species. I am only saddened that I cannot do more for you," her soothing voice cracked with emotion, and a solitary tear fell from her eye, leaving a wet trail. Her full lips trembled.

Gasps and murmurs of dissent sprung out through the crowd. Dimitri was awash with sadness and fury. His Queen was upset. Heaven and hell would be moved to ensure her happiness.

"As you know, since my marriage to King Fenri, we have grown in numbers, but we still face the prejudices and mistrust of the other clans. They are jealous of our ability to adapt to the world above, and seek to keep us confined to their rules and limitations. They have poisoned my dear husband's ear. Our numbers will not be allowed to grow beyond what they are currently. We may only replace those that are lost to us. A stipulation, no doubt, to keep us in check."

Dimitri inhaled sharply, his chest tightening in dread. Would this new decree keep him from his woman? Fury began to fester within him at the thought. No, his Queen wouldn't allow it. There was something special about her. She might very well be the one they've hunted for these many centuries.

A buzz began to grow in the crowd, worry spreading over what this would mean for their kind. Many voiced concern that this was the beginning of the end. The Queen gracefully lifted one of her hands and the talking ceased suddenly.

"I have asked my husband for a concession for those of you who do not have a bonded partner. No creature should be forced to live their lives in loneliness. I only want happiness for my people."

Her eyes traveled the room, seeming to land upon each face individually.

Dimitri felt a thrill as they settled on him. He wanted to dive into their black depths, to pause the moment and bask in its glory. He lived for these small moments. Even if only for a split second, he was rewarded with the intimacy of her glance. Once again, he was reminded of how he must obey her, serve her, worship her. She was a benevolent mistress.

"He has graciously agreed to my request," she continued, her soothing voice lulling them to calm. "Those of you with no mate please come forward to speak with one of my attendants after the meeting. Each request must be approved. If this law is not upheld, both the newly made and the maker will be destroyed." Her voice echoed through the chamber as she spoke the last word.

Dimitri shivered at the power behind the statement. The order binding itself into each of the Revenant in the room, locking into place with finality.

One of the Queen's attendants stepped up and whispered in her ear. Her lovely mouth turned down in the slightest of frowns. Dimitri's eyes narrowed, watching the movements of her features with rapt attention. The frown melted from her face within seconds, and a bright smile dazzled her waiting audience.

"I will be in my personal chambers for the next hour for those of you who need to make requests. The rest of you, I will see at the next new moon. Remember, my loves, only do what is best for our collective. Do not let me down." With those parting words the Queen stood and left the room, her attendants following behind. A sigh broke through the group as everyone watched her until she was out of sight. Then one by one, they shook themselves out of their haze.

As Dimitri came back to himself, he noticed his sister had already vanished. Probably off to play with her new toy. He stood from where he had been kneeling and followed the small group of people who were making their way toward their Queen's chamber. Thankfully there were only a handful of others who were waiting before him to make requests. Patience was not a virtue he possessed.

They were funneled in groups into the interior waiting room of their Queen's private quarters. Large, hand carved wooden doors stood at both the entrance to the waiting area and the main rooms themselves. Each with a set of guards standing sentinel. A small wooden desk with a single chair stood in a corner, at which one of the Queen's private attendants sat scratching down the names of those that came to wait.

Dimitri left his name with the brown-haired woman in the customary red attendant garb before going to sit at one of the wooden benches lining the edges of the room. He leaned back against the solid stone wall, looking up to where rectangles had been cut high along the top. There, wooden paneling had been inserted. Candle light and the smell of incense filtered through the hand carved designs. Dimitri watched the flicker of that light, allowing the perfumed incense to lull him into a sense of calm. He would not give up hope that the object of his desire would soon be his.

More patiently than usual, he waited. One by one the others were called in and escorted out. Finally, he was the last one left.

He glared at the attendant in the corner. Others who had arrived after him had come and gone and still he sat, unnoticed. Anger bubbled within his chest. Unfortunately, he knew arguing would get him nowhere. The Queen regulated every facet of the Revenant collective, and her attendants were extensions of herself. So, he bit his tongue as the woman in the corner gave him cursory glances, obviously not impressed with his furious stare. His knuckles cracked in his lap as he tightened his hand into a fist and released it, over and over.

At last, the inner doors creaked open and another attendant stepped through.

"Dimitri," she beckoned.

The main chamber was warm. A small fire crackled in a large stone fireplace. Obviously there for show as temperature did not affect their kind. Dimitri recognized it as the status symbol it was. Their Queen was important enough to have multiple rooms and a fireplace to heat them with, in case a visitor from one of the warm-blooded clans were to stop in.

The Queen herself sat in one of the large, cushioned chairs that perched in front of the fire. The soft light casting a golden glow against her smooth, dark skin. She had changed during the time she had been in her rooms, an elegant red dress now draped her voluptuous body, the color bright like a jewel.

She leaned forward in the chair as she turned to see him. Dimitri's breath caught. Focusing around his Queen was always so hard, but he must remember why he was here. He closed his eyes and brought forward the memory of green, cat shaped eyes. Eyes belonging to a woman he would soon possess.

With his intention firmly set in mind, he sat in the chair opposite his Queen. On the table between them were two large wine glasses filled with a deep burgundy liquid. The enticing scent of blood hit his nose causing his mouth to water hungrily. With delicate, long fingers the goddess before him picked the glass up and handed it to him.

"I have saved my favorites for last," his Queen said with a smile. He nearly choked on the thick blood as it ran down his throat. It was warm and good, but not as satisfying as the beauty he feasted on the night before.

"Your favorites, your highness?" he questioned.

"Of course," the Queen purred as she placed her glass down and leaned toward him, her captivating eyes holding him in place.

"My Dimitri. I remember when you and your sister first joined us centuries ago. Your anger and pain called to me, like a song in the night. The intensity of it…" She stopped speaking as a hand went to her neck, her gaze far away as she lost herself in the memory. "I haven't felt rage of that severity in longer than I can remember," as she finished her statement, her eyes, now filled with heady desire, once again locked on his.

Dimitri swallowed thickly.

A nervous energy pulsed through him. For a second his mind drifted back through the years to the pain and misery of his human existence. Memories he never wanted to recall. Memories of suffering so consuming that the survival of it smelted a flame of fury so intense, it burned the very soul from his body. His non-beating heart fluttered erratically.

The Queen's full lips tipped up in a smirk as though the sound amused her.

"My attendants tell me you are putting in a request to claim a mate," she stated, taking another long sip from her glass, her eyes never leaving his.

Dimitri nodded as he sat his glass back on the table, his appetite long since satiated. "Yes, my Queen," he said, resting his arms on his knees.

"If I remember correctly, this would not be the first mate you have requested over the years. I do believe I have a couple attendants who were some of your discarded lovers." She chuckled. "I have heard many tales of your prowess."

Dimitri gave a low laugh. He was both pleased and embarrassed that his Queen knew of his inability to remain satisfied long term with any of his past conquests.

"In fact, I do believe dear Rebecca, the attendant who escorted you in, was one of them."

Dimitri sat upright, unable to recall anything of the woman. All he remembered of her was the red robes, and a blonde bob.

"She must have done something to her hair," he said with a shrug.

"Tell me what is so special about this human, that you are tempted to try again for a mate."

She leaned back, her fingers playing absently with one of the crystals in her thick, dark braid.

"Her name is Enid," he began. He spent the next ten minutes describing everything he could think of about Enid, from the color of her hair, to the smell of her skin, to the taste of her on his tongue. The longer he spoke, the more lost in the idea he became of his fire haired temptress. Not even his Queen was able to pull his attention away from his descriptive fantasy. He stopped short of telling her about how he seemed to burn for her—how he seemed to feel a flood of emotions he hadn't felt in centuries after he had taken her blood, and how he couldn't tell if the emotions came from her, or him, or some mix of the two.

She sat patiently, waiting for his explanation to end, her eyes following the movement of his hands as he spoke. Finally, he stopped and slumped back in his chair. His hand raked through the inky black strands; pushing the longer locks at the top away from his eyes, smoothing nervously around the shaved sides. There was only one thing left to say.

"I think she may be the one we've been searching for, my Queen."

Her black eyes sparkled with delight.

"And she appeared to go into a trance, her eyes turning white?"

He nodded. "Yes, my Queen," he whispered.

She seemed thoughtful.

"You will go find her and bring this girl into our family, but you must be discreet. Dimitri, I am going to tell you something now that is to remain between the two of us, do you understand?"

Her eyes held his, the warning in them clear. He nodded his head solemnly.

"My marriage to King Fenri is one mostly of convenience, rather than intimacy. It is no secret that there is no love lost between us. Our marriage stopped a war, but it also allowed me to navigate the politics of the clans more readily, which has allowed us to have the freedoms we have benefited from for the last few decades. He turns a blind eye to our hunts, as long as we stay within certain parameters, and our clan is allowed to grow and flourish. Until recently." Worry was evident on her beautiful face.

"I believe the other clans are planning something, trying to do or say things that will turn Fenri against me. There is a very strong possibility that they are going to try to assassinate me." Dimitri growled low in his chest, his need to protect his Queen overwhelming.

"We must tread carefully in how we handle ourselves, and in how we interact with the other clans. We do not want to call any attention to ourselves that will send the King's Enforcer after us."

Swallowing thickly, Dimitri rubbed a hand along the back of his neck. "I may have already had an…altercation with the Enforcer," he mumbled guiltily.

The Queen's eyes narrowed darkly. "Tell me everything."

***

Dimitri hurtled through the air. Splinters and dust shattered around him as his back slammed into the great, heavy wooden doors of the Queen's chamber. Pain lanced through his ribs. He hit the ground and rolled before coming to a hard stop against the outer doors of the waiting room. Groaning, he lifted his head slowly. Lania was perched on the bench by the now demolished doors, her bright blue eyes wide as she took in the state of him.

"You made her so angry, Dimitri."

She shook her head, clicking her tongue. Raven hair swayed in her face before she sat up with a sudden gasp, lighting up with excitement as a thought popped into her head. Her smile was bright as she hopped up. "Don't worry brother. I will fix this."

Lania skipped in glee as she pushed through the splintered fragments. Dimitri groaned and let his head fall back to the ground with a thud.

A small giggle drew his attention.

At the desk in the corner sat the two attendants from earlier. The blonde, Rebecca he remembered briefly, was perched on the desk. The brunette was resting her head on the other's leg; arms wrapped around her tiny waist. They both seemed pleased to witness his discomfort, wide smiles adorning their pretty faces.

"Rebecca," he said with a nod, lifting himself to sit.

"You remembered. I am shocked. I don't think you've acknowledged me in a little over fifty years, Dimitri. You recall Genevieve?"

Dimitri glanced down at the brunette as Rebecca rubbed her hand along the chocolate strands of the girl's head lovingly. A tiny hint of a memory came back to him. Those wide hazel eyes looking up at him in the middle of a hay field, the moon reflected brightly in them. She really did have some of the largest eyes he had ever seen. That's what had drawn him to her. Those innocent doe-like eyes.

"Ah Genevieve," he said as he used the nearby bench to help him stand. "Your father was a cattle farmer?" he questioned as he brushed the splinters from his hair and clothes.

Genevieve jerked upright, anger flashing in her eyes.

"He was a goatherd," she snapped. "You nearly got me stoned by my village. My whole family disowned me before you turned me and had me kill them."

"Huh," Dimitri said in surprise. "Well, that certainly sounds like something I would do."

Rebecca murmured soothingly to Genevieve as the brunette hissed, her fangs flashing ferociously.

"He's not worth it, dear one. Our Queen has plans for him," she whispered, peppering soft kisses at the corner of Genevieve's mouth. With a frustrated groan, Genevieve captured Rebecca's lips in a deep kiss that soon turned heated. Dimitri looked on in pleasant surprise until Genevieve pulled away to glare at him.

"Leave now," she spat.

Dimitri held his hands up in surrender as he turned to walk out the door.

"You two make a beautiful couple," he called over his shoulder before slipping through the outer doors.

"Fuck you," came the response from the two women on the other side.

Dimitri chuckled darkly as he continued down the dimly lit corridors of the Revenant compound until he reached his rooms.

By now the sun would be high in the sky in the world above. He would take this time to go over his options. He wandered over to his bed where he kept his black t-shirt from the other night. Holding it to his nose, he inhaled deeply. Her delicate, flowery scent still lingered on the material—her blood dried within the fabric. He snarled with need as he pulled it tight against his chest and dropped heavily onto the mattress, lost within his thoughts. Before long he drifted to sleep with the smell of her pressed against him.

In his dreams he stalked her.

CHAPTER
8

After a brisk conversation with Gladys, and a fervent argument given by Cindy, Enid was once again behind the counter pouring steaming coffee for patrons who vibrated with the exhilaration found only in those who relish late nights, darkened corners, and the hum of artificial light. Cindy whisked behind her, perfume wafting in her wake as she hurried to her tables. For a moment she stopped, backing up as she looked Enid up and down.

"Seriously though, you have got to give me your makeup secrets." She shook her head, continuing in her haste. Enid smiled weakly.

Her friend had no idea of the events that had taken place on the other side of the brick wall in the alley next door. No one knew. Only Jason's haunted expression as he met her eyes briefly before looking away, was any indication anything happened at all. Enid kept her mouth shut. Throwing herself into work. The assurance that Charlie was gone was all her friend needed as an explanation for why she was back. Guilt bit at her. She was grateful for Charlie's disappearance, but the omission of the events leading up to his departure weighed heavily on her. He was most likely dead.

Despite her trepidation and confusion, Cindy's good mood was contagious. Her friend flitted around anxiously, eager to prepare for an upcoming date. She was so excited that Enid agreed to cover the rest of the night so she could go early.

The trickle of customers had died down to nearly nothing by ten. Lightning flashed through the sky, reflected from the windows of the towering buildings around the diner. Cindy threw her a quick wave as she ducked out the door, the bell chiming her departure. The rest of the kitchen staff was gone. Jason sat alone on a stool in the corner of the kitchen—dark shadows around his glazed eyes.

Enid had attempted to speak to him about last night's events only to have him stare at her with that hollow look before turning back to the grill. His movements were nearly mechanical as he flipped burgers on the sizzling flat top. Gladys had resigned herself to the office, paperwork keeping her late into the night.

It was unusually quiet. The steady sound of rain on the pavement outside lulled Enid into a state of peaceful contentment as she refilled salt and pepper shakers. The storm was far enough away that she didn't have to worry about the cracking booms of thunder that would reverberate in her bones, causing her to jump with every clap. So, she happily sat cleaning and filling the shakers for each table in the deserted, fluorescent lit diner. Enjoying the stillness of the moment.

The jingle of the bell at the door, and a gentle breeze carrying in the scent of fresh ozone had her turning with a welcoming smile that immediately froze, and then melted from her face.

In the doorway stood a tall, dark figure. A neat black suit hung on his too thin frame. Gloved hands lay crossed atop the shiny, silver knob of a cane. Despite the late hour, and the cloud filled sky, he wore dark sunglasses that hid his eyes. Even still, she could feel his gaze crawling over her. His long gray hair was twisted into dreads that were pulled into a low, thick ponytail at the nape of his neck. His skin was dark as ebony, but ashen in a way that made her think he'd never seen the sun. It seemed too tight, like taut leather over the sharp bones of his skull.

A slow smile stretched over that face, seeming too wide, like it may cause his delicate looking skin to crack. When it seemed to stretch nearly ear to ear, he tilted his head toward her slightly. His eyes slowly came into view over the top of his glasses, flashing a bright red. The rag slipped unnoticed from her hands to fall on the floor at her feet.

"Enid," he said. His voice was the deepest tone she had ever heard, like gravel in her ears. It crept over her, spiking horror into her brain as she processed the gritty, raw timbre. That tone, along with the fact that he knew her name, sent a wash of terror invoked adrenaline through her system. Feet locked in place, body frozen, Enid watched in silence as he slowly stalked over to her. She felt like prey in an open prairie, alone with nowhere to hide.

As he moved, he seemed to test the smoothness of the floor beneath his shiny black shoes. He took in every feature of her posture, as though he anticipated she might sprint away like a gazelle from a lion. The cane clicked along the floor. All the while the creepy smile stayed plastered to his face.

"I've been watching for you everywhere," he said, coming to a stop on the opposite side of the counter. Setting his cane before him, both hands resting atop its smooth, round head, he stood, and waited. Enid swallowed past the beating of her heart.

"What do you want?" she whispered. Her voice was barely audible—even to her own ears.

He chuckled darkly. One of his gloved hands lifted to straighten his already impeccable tie before flicking an invisible piece of lint from the sleeve of his suit jacket. As that wide smile turned fully back to Enid, she couldn't help but think that those teeth would be perfect for ripping and tearing at her delicate flesh. Everything about the man before her screamed hunter. Monster.

Run. Hide. That primal part of her pushed within her, urging. She gripped it tight, crushing it down.

"Want is a trivial sentiment. Wants ebb and flow like the tide. I am not here for anything as petty as want." He waved his hand in the air, dismissing the very idea with distaste.

Another moment passed where the two merely looked at each other over the counter. Enid forced herself to remain still, taking calm, measured breaths in an attempt to control the frenzied rush of blood in her ears. The man tilted his head to the side, the grin on his face impossibly wide. He remained there, dark lenses fixed on her unwaveringly as he waited with an unnatural patience. Looking at her as though he could sense the struggle within.

"What do you need?" Enid asked finally, her voice a little stronger, her hands a little less shaky as she fisted them at her sides.

"Ah!" he hissed in apparent glee. "That," he said lifting a gloved finger to the sky, "is the right question."

Standing taller, the smile faded from his face as he rolled his shoulders back, an air of authority and dominance radiating from him. The lights in the diner flickered and grew dim. Shadows seemed to pulse around him like an inky aura. The red glow of eyes shone through the lenses of his sunglasses like two burning coals.

"What we need, Enid Washbourne, is for you to accept what you are. You have a destiny that must be fulfilled. You have been hiding too long, and now much is at stake. You are the intermediator, and the arbiter. The conflict has already begun, and you have been too blind to see."

Confusion laced with dread settled in the pit of Enid's stomach. Instinctively, she took a step back from the terrifying figure. As she felt the muscles of her legs flex to take another, the lights of the diner went out. She inhaled sharply. Before she could even think of releasing the breath the lights flickered on and her back hit something behind her. The air whooshed out of her in a strangled gasp.

The dark stranger was no longer before her. Only his cane remained, standing in place in the middle of the floor as though held up by invisible strings. From the corners of her eyes, she could see dancing shadows. Slowly, she lifted her head to find twin burning coals peering down at her. The wide grin on the skeletal face. Her breath caught within her throat.

"I see," he hissed.

His eyes blazed brighter through the glasses. Strong, bony fingers latched onto the sides of her face, and her body locked up, each muscle paralyzed. She whimpered, her temples pulsing in time with her heart as full-fledged terror spread like liquid nitrogen through her body. Her wide jade eyes fastened onto those floating red dots, unable to look away.

"You've blocked it," he murmured, the nearly maniacal grin turning down into a frown of concentration. "You are stronger than we thought. That is good, you will need it." He tilted his head to the side, examining her like some strange insect.

"What you won't need is this block. That will have to go now." With that he yanked a glove from his hand with his teeth, the other firmly holding her head still. The hand beneath the glove was nothing more than skin over bone. Pointed talon-like fingernails wickedly curved from the end of each bony finger. Enid could only watch in mute horror as he lifted a hooked nail to the space between her eyes.

"Not even the sons and daughters of fate can escape their destiny."

Enid couldn't cry out. Even as a needle-like pain cut into her skin, the nail slicing from between her eyes to the middle of her forehead in a searing line.

"They will find you, the ones you need to guide you on your path. Beware, not all who come looking mean you well."

The words barely registered. All she could see was the blaze of his eyes. All she could feel was the burning pain lacing through her skull. When she thought she would break apart, there was a flash of lightning that seemed to wash her vision in complete white light. Her head snapped up and she pulled air into her lungs with a shocked gasp.

He was gone.

There was only her—alone in the empty diner, with the flash of lightning brightening the sky, and the steady sound of rain.

Enid dropped to her knees. The peace she had only moments ago gone. Voices rushed at her in a muffled, garbled jumble. Pain continued to throb in her skull, pulsing from the middle of her forehead. With shaky fingers she reached up and gingerly touched the spot.

In a flash she was surrounded by haphazardly strewn bodies and rubble. Creatures of every shape and size crawled or flew through the chaos. Some were tearing into bodies hungrily. Others had fresh victims to play with. Many of the beings were fighting each other. Locked in a deadly, fierce battle. Above her the sky was dark. Ash rained down from the thick, boiling clouds. Everywhere there was a blanket of gray covering cars and buildings, like a black winter landscape of death.

A loud, deafening shriek filled the air to her right. Enid turned toward the sound as a skeletal hag flew at her. Thin, gray strands of ash-littered hair streamed behind her as she reached with claw-like hands. Screaming, Enid flung herself away.

She slammed painfully into a cabinet—arm raised to deflect the oncoming blow. Looking around in shock, she realized she was once again in the diner. The bell above the door rang. Nervously, Enid crawled on her knees to the counter before slowly raising herself up to peer over the edge. Over and over, she pleaded in her head for it not to be that skeletal man again.

Vidar stood inside, looking around curiously. She pulled herself up, relief flooding her system. Sagging against the counter, she pressed her hand to her chest as though to physically stop her heart from pounding so violently.

"Enid? Are you okay?" Vidar briskly strode to the counter, reaching over to grasp her shoulder.

Suddenly, she was standing in a bright, sunlit meadow. Before her stood Vidar, eyes black as coal, roaring in agony, every muscle wrought with tension. His skin began to flake and harden before her, the flesh and blood man turning to stone. Then he was still. Nothing more than a frightening and horrified statue in a field of wildflowers, mouth opened in a silent scream.

CHAPTER

9

"Enid?" She shuddered as Vidar shook her shoulder. With a startled gasp, she jerked back.

"Don't touch me," she warned, her hand lifting like a shield before her.

"Enid, you're bleeding." Concern filled his features, but he didn't try to reach for her again. Though the way he scanned her for further injuries gave the impression he wanted to.

The tips of her fingers shook in the air between them. The same ones she had used to touch her forehead. And they were covered in blood. A small drop slid between her eyes, creating a warm line along her nose. Hastily, she grabbed some nearby napkins, dabbing at it.

"What happened?" Vidar pressed.

Enid shrugged, lowering her gaze to the counter. She could barely process it all, how was she going to explain it to someone else? If it weren't for the cut, she wasn't sure if she even believed it herself. Taking a deep breath, she pulled the napkins away to see the bleeding had thankfully stopped.

"I'm not sure what happened to be honest," she finally confessed. "There was a man, he was strange, with red eyes and these shadows…" Her voice trailed off as she finally looked up, bracing herself for the judgement she was sure to see.

Vidar's eyes were completely black. Not just dark, but solid black, the white of his eyeballs, and the gray of his irises disappeared beneath the inky darkness. Anger radiated from him.

She looked on in shocked disbelief. It almost seemed that smoky snippets of shadow were slithering around him. Not as thick and full as the red eyed man, but a hint of the same dark aura.

"Your eyes," she breathed.

Surprise overtook the anger on his face and he stepped back, glancing around before focusing on Enid.

"What?" he asked softly, his voice lowering significantly as if afraid of someone overhearing.

She shook her head, squeezing her eyes shut. "I'm not crazy," she whispered to herself. "It's happening again. Why do I keep seeing these things?"

"Again?"

Enid nodded, her eyes large as she looked up to the solid black pools staring down at her, her own reflection within them so small.

"That's impossible. Not unless you are fae," he whispered.

"What?" Enid instantly latched onto the unfamiliar word. "Unless I'm what?"

"Nothing," he said. "I wanted to make sure you were ok. I need to get going."

"Wait!" Enid exclaimed.

She walked out from behind the counter, only stopping when she was close enough to touch him. Hesitantly, she reached out, waiting to see if he would stop her. When he didn't, she became bolder, stepping closer. His dark eyes flicked along her face as she stared into them. Enid tried to keep her cheeks from burning. She was close enough to feel the heat from him. The broad expanse of his chest so near she could see how the fabric of his shirt strained across the hard planes of muscle. It was strange how drawn she was to him. Even now the urge to close the distance, to press against the firmness of him, was staggering.

There are more important things to focus on at the moment, Enid, she chastised.

Rocking to her toes, she brought her hand up slowly to the side of his face, hovering for a heartbeat, seeking assurance. Still, he did not move to stop her. The tips of her fingers slid along the skin of his cheek, slightly cool to the touch but very real, resting in her palm. The muscles of his jaw tensed. She allowed her hand to drop to her side, her heels setting solidly back to the floor. A breath she didn't realize she was holding, rushed out in a shaky exhale.

"This is real, isn't it? I'm not hallucinating. This whole time, the things I've been seeing—I'm not crazy."

He studied her for a moment with those depthless black eyes.

"What if you weren't? What if I told you, it was all true? That there was another world within this one, made up of all of humanity's worst nightmares?" His voice was low, the barest hint of danger thrumming in the gritty timbre.

"All of my life, I've seen things. Things that shouldn't be there," she murmured, looking up into his face in awe. "Things that were dark and terrifying. Things that couldn't be real. And now I'm here, looking at something impossible, but very real. ...I'd be relieved. Relieved I'm not crazy. Relieved to have control of my own life. I have no idea what is going on, or what you are, but I'm not scared. Not of you."

"You should be," he whispered.

"Why? Are you going to kill me because I know what you are? Is it because I'm—whatever that word you said?"

Vidar's troubled look only got deeper, contemplative. When he did speak, it was carefully, as though weighing each word before he uttered it.

"I would tell you everything you want to hear. I would spend all night, into the next day answering your questions. However, the less you know in this situation, the better. While you remain distanced from this world, I can still protect you. The more you know about it, the less of a blind eye the creatures of that realm will turn toward you. You *do not* want the attention of these beings. They will destroy you in every way imaginable."

Enid blinked at him with wide eyes. "Creatures like you?" Her voice came out low, merely a breath in the air between them. Outside, thunder rumbled.

Vidar stared at her, a war raging across his features. Restrained and uncertain. It was unnerving how easily she could read him in this moment, like he was showing her his true self— all of him.

His hands clenched into fists at his sides, and he leaned toward her. He took a breath, mouth opening as though to say something that would shed some light on the secret he protected. She wanted so bad for him to close that distance, to confide in her, trust her. But whatever held him back won the battle. The emotions washed from him, face turning to stone, his black eyes hardening. She tried to hide the way her stomach dropped when he took a step away from her.

"Far worse than me, Enid. Far worse."

She recalled the red, coal-like eyes of the man encased in shadows as he grinned down at her with that unnaturally wide, sinister smile. The glow of Dimitri's eyes in the dark alley as he pressed her against the wall. An involuntary shiver went through her.

"So, what happened last night, those people...Dimitri."

Vidar's mouth drew into a thin line.

"Stay away from them. They are more dangerous than you know."

She nodded her consent. Even now the thought of the dark-haired hunter had her trembling with desire. *No, dread. It was dread*, she hurriedly corrected.

"What should I do?" she asked.

"Lay low while I figure out what is going on. I will give you a number to call, should you need it. It may not work right away, but you can leave a voicemail or text if it is urgent. It will alert me."

"Why would you help me?"

He looked away for a moment, taking a deep breath, his shoulders sagging as though under a great weight. When he looked back at her, it was with gray, storm filled eyes. The sadness in them made her heart ache.

"I think, you..." he stopped, his eyes shifting away from her. "You remind me of someone that was very dear to me. Someone I lost." He turned toward the windows, looking as though he was searching the streets for something.

"I will walk you home when you are ready. If you go out, then do it in the daylight. There are fewer horrors in the daylight."

Enid looked at him for a moment. "Fewer? Can any of these creatures you mentioned still find me during the day?"

His eyes clouded over once again. A single nod was his only response.

*****

Securing a few days off was easier than Enid thought. Gladys took one look at the blood on her forehead and Jason's quivering form on the kitchen floor before she declared them both in need of some time to recover from their attacks.

Nothing in her demeanor made Enid believe she had seen anything from the comfort of her little office. However, the look in Jason's eyes as he avoided her gaze before running off made her think he had most certainly seen something. She fervently hoped he would be okay.

She wasn't even sure *she* was alright. The last few days would have been enough to test anyone's mental stability. Though, it had the opposite effect for Enid. The events of the recent nights only ensured she was more mentally sound than she had been willing to give herself credit for over the years. Except now she had different questions. Why was she this way? How could she see creatures she shouldn't? There was only one place she could think of to get the answers she so desperately craved, and she was not looking forward to it.

When he walked her home, Vidar was incredibly quiet. They both remained lost in thought, the silence strangely comforting. He walked her all the way to her door. And when she shut it between them, peering from the peep hole, she noted how he remained standing in the hall until all the locks clicked into place. Only then, did she see him turn and leave.

CHAPTER

10

Enid slept fitfully, tossing and turning.

It was cold and dark. So very, very dark. Wind whistled past her, swaying the oversized cotton t-shirt around her bare thighs. She rubbed her hands along her arms, attempting to soothe the chill.

The sound reminded her of a long-ago trip to the Grand Canyon. Standing at the edge of that great chasm had both terrified and inspired her. Standing here listening to the wind wail in gusts as though traveling over a great distance, was very different.

If she could see anything in the suffocating darkness, then perhaps she wouldn't be so scared. Perhaps the view would inspire awe like that long ago childhood trip. But she couldn't see, and the thought of falling through dark, endless nothing kept her in place. She reached out a tentative hand. Her heart almost as loud as the whistling in her ear.

A deep chuckle echoed from the void.

Enid gasped, snatching her hand back.

"I can smell you, little one," purred a familiar, accented voice.

Dimitri.

Against her better judgment, she leaned toward the sound. Equal parts longing and terror entwined within her. She had to remember, the rational part of her brain argued. Remember the predatory gleam in his eyes as they followed her. The sharp bite of pain at her neck. His strong hands holding her hostage against the rough brick.

"I smell your fear." His voice was closer this time. Behind her. Whirling, she strained to see into the thick shadows. There was nothing. Only the endless dark.

The drum of her heart continued, faster and faster, unheeding of her need to calm it.

"Do not fear me," he whispered into her ear, lips grazing the delicate shell. Tingles erupted along her skin. The sensation brought to mind the feel of his lips on hers, the taste of him on her tongue. How he felt pressed against her. Trembling, she reached out, only to find empty space.

"Hmmm." It came from all around her this time, humming along her skin—vibrating along the small hairs of her body. "I also smell your desire."

Enid bit her lip, shame filling her. Step by miniscule step, careful not to make any noise, Enid crept back. If she could just find a way out of this place.

A shrill scream tore from her, echoing into the void as strong hands found her, gripping her arms tightly and crushing her against a firm body.

"While your fear is delightful, I would rather taste the desire in you, my flower," he murmured.

Dimitri's arms encircled her, and she melted into his embrace, all doubts vanishing. Her hands were trapped against his chest. A small barrier between the crush of bodies, anchoring her as his lips found hers—the featherlight caress destroying her already crumbling defenses.

A hand slid into the mass of her hair, gripping firmly as his lips blazed a heated trail down her neck.

"I like how it makes your blood rush," he breathed against her skin. The cotton fabric molded along her body suddenly felt stifling. The chill from earlier forgotten as his fingers kindled a flush of warmth with each stroke.

"You taste of honey," he whispered, mouth claiming hers once more. "Of vanilla and sunshine." The kiss was deep and slow, savoring the flavor of her lips.

She shuddered, her moan mingling with the howling of the wind. His hand drifted lower. Fingers reaching for the edges of her shirt. Lips following the erratic beat of her pulse.

Without provocation his name fell from her lips like a whispered prayer.

"Dimitri."

A possessive growl erupted from him, vibrating into her hands still pressed to his chest.

"I will have you, my flower. You will scream my name," he rumbled, voice low with need.

Gasping, Enid shot up in bed. Her skin cold, her heart slamming in her chest. Although she was enveloped in darkness, it was not all-encompassing. Recognizing her room, she relaxed and breathed a sigh of relief. It was only a dream.

"Enid, you are seriously messed up," she scolded.

Once again, she slept the day away and was still exhausted. She was used to being a night owl, but normally woke up sometime in the late afternoon. Tomorrow will be hard. She would have to catch the train soon if she was going to make it at a decent hour.

Enid ran a hand over her face, and down her neck, her fingers lingering as the images in the dream flashed through her mind. With a groan of disgust, she pushed it away, and began to prepare herself for the journey ahead.

**

Dimitri awoke with a roar. His skin slick with sweat. Muscles tense with want. She was not here with him. The thrill he had through the blood link was short lived. He was sick with need— knowing it was only a shadow of what he would experience with her when they were together on the physical plane.

The link was soon to dissipate. He could already sense how weak it was, fragile. The thrall would last only as long as his blood was in her system. Her blood still flushed him with life, fanning the flames of his passion, his need for her. But that yearning she felt, there was no telling if it would remain once the blood was gone. He couldn't risk it. Steps would need to be made, and soon. He had his orders, the permission of his Queen, all that remained was to set the plan in motion. The thought set his blood soaring with anticipation. It was a fine line he was about to walk. Between fear and seduction.

He rose from the bed, the candles around him flickering weakly as they began to die out. Pacing around the room, his head spun as he thought out ways to get to her, to have her there with him—to own her body, mind, and soul.

A knock at the door interrupted his thoughts and he roared, throwing a nearby chair against it. The brittle wood burst into pieces, dust and splinters littering the floor. There was silence. Silence that was soon punctured.

"Dimitri?" came the soft voice of his sister.

"Go away, Lania!" he shouted as he resumed pacing. He laced his hands behind his head. His whole body was tense with bitter disappointment and fury.

"Dimitri, you need to eat. You are getting frustratingly difficult." Lania called out stubbornly.

Stomping to the door, he flung it open to find his twin sister leaning against the frame. Her new play toy at her back—fear widening his eyes. He was shirtless, his neck and chest peppered with red bite marks. Black and blue bruises covered him. They must have stopped mid game if he was still not properly healed.

Dimitri glared at the blond-haired man who lowered his gaze and took a quick step back. Terror radiated from him, filling the hall with the sharp, tangy scent. Lania glanced back with a smirk before facing her brother again.

"Dimitri, will you please put on some pants? Unless you want to use my new pet."

She grinned widely, a wicked gleam lighting up her face. The male went pale. Charlie, Dimitri remembered, was his name.

Dimitri shook his head, grumbling as he grabbed some sweats and stepped into them, sliding them over the boxer briefs he usually slept in.

"I want the woman. My Enid." He said her name softly, almost reverently, as though the sound of it was pure joy on his lips.

"Dimitri, we can get you any woman right now."

"NO!!" He ground his teeth together, eyes wide with rage. "I want her! She is perfect. She smells of the sun and lilies after a fresh rain, and tastes like rich honey, vanilla and wine. I can still smell her desire thick on my skin. I can feel her wanton and writhing against me. She is the only one I will have. No other." He fisted his hands through his hair again as the thoughts of Enid caused an unbridled need to rush through him.

When he glanced back toward his sister, he was amused to see the dark look that clouded her pet's face. Instead of fear, rage reddened his skin as he glared toward Dimitri and mumbled under his breath.

"Is there a problem, dog?" Dimitri took a step forward, forcing the man to look him in the eye. Panic once again wiped away the anger, and the male shook his head.

"I-It was nothin'," he stuttered.

Dimitri recalled their brief interaction in the alley, how this man so fervently fought. How he seemed to think he could best him. Before Dimitri had lost himself in his Enid, his flower, and lost any interest in the annoying swats of the human.

Grabbing him by the throat, he slammed the male against the stone wall. His head bounced with a wince, hands pulling futilely at the one held firm around his throat.

"Do not forget, you are only recently turned. You are no match for me. Not to mention, as long as my sister's leash is around your neck, you will remain subservient. Do not dream you can challenge me, you pathetic, weak, useless plaything."

Lania sighed dramatically.

"Dimitri, that one is mine. You can play with him, but don't kill him."

She pouted as she crossed her arms and stamped a foot against the hard floor.

"Repeat what you said about Enid," Dimitri continued.

His canines lengthened as his fury overtook him. With his keen hearing, he already heard the mumblings of the insipid male, but he wanted him to repeat it. He wanted the weak, vapid creature to understand that Enid was his to claim. His to possess.

The coward gulped.

"She was mine first," he wheezed, dread causing his voice to squeak.

"Do you have a death wish?" Dimitri spat. "Tell me please, I would love to make it come true." He took one of his hands, and crushed it in his grip. Screams echoed off the walls and down the hallway as the bones crumbled. Lania leaned forward, a wide smile on her face, a gleam of excitement in her eyes.

"Dimitri, don't break him. I'm not done playing," the sound of her voice was whiny and insistent, but the smile on her face betrayed the joy she felt at the infliction of pain.

"He is too loud," Dimitri said, tightening his hold around his neck.

He grinned, watching Lania's pet rasp as the air to his lungs was cut off, eyes bulging from his head. Not used to immortality, he still had all the instincts of humanity. It was highly entertaining to use those instincts against the recently turned. No doubt his sister had been doing just that for hours now.

"Wait," came the quivering gasp between thin breaths.

Dimitri merely watched with a detached expression as the male's face gradually took on several shades of red.

"I can.... take... you.........to.........her." He finally got out through agonizingly small puffs of air.

With that statement, Dimitri's eyes sparked with interest and he let go. The thud of his body hitting the ground was musical, as was the desperate coughing and wheezing.

Dimitri sat back on his heels. Arms perched on his knees as he looked down at the sputtering male. A small, sly smile graced his lips. Lania tapped her hands together, bouncing lightly on the balls of her feet as she watched her pet cradle his hand while fighting to breathe.

"Charlie, was it? I am listening, my friend."

CHAPTER

II

The next afternoon, Enid stood in front of her family home. The pediment molding along the top of the double wood doors appeared like a curious eyebrow waiting with infinite patience as she stood at the wide porch steps. '*Have you decided to come back,*' it seemed to say to her in the quiet, reproachful whisper of her mother.

Her desire to turn and flee from the formal, colonial style house was so strong that, for a moment, she nearly pivoted on her heel. Instead, she reached out and pressed her hand flat against one of the nearby columns, its solid length stretching to the balcony above. Calm flooded through her as though the strength of that column helped to support and ground her as well as the structure of the massive house.

With a deep breath she stepped forward, setting her small suitcase down, and lifted the perfectly polished brass knocker. The weight of it was solid and reassuring as she rapped it against the striking plate. The sound reverberated through the door, faintly echoing in the large foyer she knew lay beyond.

She threw a cursory glance at the doorbell that sat nearly inches from her right hand. The musical tone would travel louder and farther through the reaches of the house, but this was her father's knocker. The last project he performed in the care of their home before he became too weak and frail to move far from his bed.

She remembered how excited he had been with the find at a local antique store, and the hours he spent polishing and shining it to perfection before affixing it to the grand front door. Those memories came back to her in a comforting rush before scattering as the knob turned, and the large door cracked open. Before her stood the perfectly poised and manicured figure of Isadora Washbourne.

"Enid?" She blinked in confusion, bright green eyes wide with surprise.

"Hello, Mother," Enid replied.

Isadora Marie Washbourne was not the delicate, meek southern bell she so profusely attempted to portray. Behind the soft, lilting words and elegant demeanor, was a sharp tongued, demanding, overbearing, vicious woman with an iron will and need to control all those around her. She rose to the top as queen bee of every social club she became part of. Those who spoke against her were quick to be outcast, the unlucky souls rejected from clubs and ostracized by the community while Isadora calmly batted her lashes and uttered a heartfelt, 'Bless your heart.' The whole of Enid's life had been spent under her well-manicured thumb.

"So, you finally have the decency to show up."

Isadora didn't even try to conceal the anger in her clipped tone. The coldness of her mother's voice sent an icy shiver through her. The older woman's glare hit her like twin shards of jade, puncturing the last vestiges of Enid's calm. She found herself standing taller, back straightening like an iron rod as she fought to maintain her composure against that hardened bitterness.

"I would have called, Mother, but you wouldn't want to hear what I have to say." Enid sighed heavily. "You never listened to anything I had to say," she muttered, more to herself.

Isadora replied with a loud sigh of her own. "Enid, don't mumble. It is unbecoming of a woman of your social standing." Enid could hear the disappointment that seemed to be the theme of her childhood. Once again, she was reminded of one of the reasons why she chose to leave it all behind.

Her mother opened the door wider, ushering Enid in with a furtive glance. As though her neighbors would be able to see through the high fence surrounding the ten-foot-tall privacy hedge, into the yards of pristine lawn, to the large, covered porch.

She could see the gears turning in her mother's head now. The whispering as they gossiped about her runaway bride daughter, and the shameful excuse of a mother who raised her. She was barely through the door before Isadora restarted her tirade, away from the imaginary prying eyes and ears.

"Now, please tell me you have come to your senses, and are coming home."

Enid gritted her teeth as Isadora continued without waiting for a response. Instead, she turned to take in the comforting familiarity of her childhood home while her mother continued her rant.

"Of course, it was absolutely mortifying how you ran out of your wedding. Poor Charlie was beside himself. Not to mention all of the work I spent over a year organizing and planning, flushed right down the drain. All of my friends were talking for months. I know I raised you better than that. I don't understand. How could you? Do you have any idea how badly your actions have impacted me, and our standing in this community? You are a disgrace to the Washbourne name. If your father was still alive—"

"Mother!" Enid shouted in frustration, slamming her suitcase down on the polished marble floor.

Isadora always knew the best place to attack any opponent. She hit her mark now as Enid was filled with remorse. The memory of her father was a sensitive subject. Thoughts of him evoked the smell of leather, aftershave, and old books as they sat and read together. The only time in her life when she felt comfort and safety. Her heart ached with loss, and anger filled her at her mother's careless words. This would not be a win for Isadora. The two women glared at each other, their eyes mirrored images.

"It is unfortunate that you feel you have been so callously betrayed, Mother," Enid began. "However, I will always do what is in the best interest of my health and, despite what you think, the memory of my father, which includes preserving the integrity of our family name. None of those things would have remained intact and vital if I married Charlie Wallace."

Isadora inhaled sharply, no doubt building up to an epic rampage. "I never—" she breathed before Enid cut her off.

"You know very well that Charlie was not a good match for me. He has always been incredibly controlling, violent, and quite honestly, emotionally unstable. I understand that I could have gone about the matter in a better way, but at the time I felt like I was in an unsafe situation. I couldn't tell anyone where I was going. I couldn't risk him finding me." Enid paused to breathe, her heart racing and her head spinning a little as she pushed to get all of her words out without interruption.

"I don't understand," Isadora said, her voice softer and higher as though portraying the epitome of innocence. Enid braced herself for whatever tactic her mother was going to attempt now.

"He comes from an upstanding family. They are very well off. You would never have to want for anything. I've never seen Charlie be anything but a caring, devoted partner. Enid, you really should have seen him when you left, the poor boy was broken." Isadora's voice cracked and she let out a shaky sigh as though the memory of Charlie's despair had her in tears.

Enid gritted her teeth and rolled her eyes, anger ratcheting at her mother's overly dramatic display.

"He obviously loves you," Isadora continued without missing a beat.

She almost laughed out loud. It was like reading a script with the notation, *pause for effect*, and Isadora was a master actress at work.

"Now I know there have been times when he may have gotten a little rough in how he went about protecting you, but can you hardly blame the man? He is an elite athlete and you are so very petite. I could see how he could accidentally cause some bruising when trying to detain you during one of your episodes."

Enid did laugh then. Not a lighthearted laugh, but a deep, full, painful laugh that burst from her very soul. She couldn't believe what she was hearing. Enid wanted to scream, to cry, to throw something and hear it shatter. The way she felt like she was shattering right now as she listened to the woman who brought her into this world defend her abuser. She choked it back.

"Charlie played football in high school and for one semester in college before he got kicked off the team for drinking. He's hardly an elite athlete."

"He dislocated his kneecap!" Isadora hissed.

"Doing a keg stand! The man is a horrible drunk with anger issues. It's what got him kicked out of his boxing gym. Not to mention, I don't have episodes and I really wish you wouldn't have told him that I did. It was his favorite excuse to use whenever he felt like putting his hands on me." Enid unconsciously lifted her fingers to her neck as she spoke.

"Enid, you know you are prone to bouts of delusion, and your future husband should be privy to that information. It is for your own good. Like the time right before your poor father and I had to have you committed. You insisted that—" Isadora stopped suddenly before speaking again in a whisper. "—that you had a little friend with wings living in the rosebush. Who told you if we hired the cook I wanted, he would try to eat us in our sleep."

Enid rubbed the skin between her eyes in exasperation. Flinching when she touched the still healing mark.

"Mother, are we in public?" she asked as her eyes went to the ceiling as though praying for patience from some higher being.

"No," Isadora replied, perplexity stopping her cold.

"Then why are you whispering?!" she snapped, restraining herself from outright yelling.

"Because some things should not be spoken of!" Isadora uttered in annoyance.

Enid began to question her logic in coming here. No matter what she said the woman would not believe in her. There would be no getting her to understand, no reasoning with the way Isadora had the world mapped out in her head. Enid held her hands over her face, attempting to contain the overwhelming anger and bitterness. This arguing was pointless. If she was going to get the information she needed, she would need her mother in a better mood.

"I-I'm tired," Enid murmured. "I think I need to lay down for a bit."

Isadora's eyes still flashed with anger, but whatever scrap of motherly instinct she had was still in there. "Of course. I'll take you to your room and you rest for a bit. I have a dinner this evening that I need to prepare for and would like you to attend. Afterwards, we can sit down and talk about everything, and plan for what's next. Ok?"

Enid nodded, gathering her bag as she followed Isadora up the stairs. Nothing had changed in the house as far as she could tell, with the exception of a few new pieces of art. She was led up the grand staircase and down a wood paneled hallway, their footsteps muffled by the designer carpeting.

Her room remained as she left it. Pictures and numerous books still where she had placed them on the floor to ceiling bookshelves at either side of her door. Her desk still contained the same various pens, notebooks, and knickknacks along with the desktop computer she was gifted at sixteen—a relic now. The four-poster bed sat on the long wall with a matching set of nightstands perched on either side.

She stepped around the bed to the French doors leading to the upper balcony. The small wrought iron cafe table remained with a single matching chair, nestled within a grouping of pots filled with brightly colored flowers. Many mornings and evenings were spent there in an oasis of quiet and bliss—away from the ever-watchful eyes of her mother and the staff. Part of her, surprisingly, was happy things had been left this way for her. As if despite the years of seeming disappointment she brought her family, and her swift departure the night before her wedding, there was always a place there for her—a home.

"I've got a lot of work to do before I need to get ready. You should have plenty of time for a nice, long nap," Isadora said going to the walk-in closet and reemerging a short moment later with a dress that she laid upon the bench at the foot of the bed. "Here, this will be perfect for this evening. Go ahead and rest. I'll help you unpack later."

Enid turned away from the view of the balcony and gave her mother a tight-lipped smile as Isadora stepped from the room. As soon as the door clicked shut, Enid hurried over and quietly cracked it open. Her mother walked down the stairs, cell phone already in hand as she rattled off precise orders. When her faded red hair disappeared from view, Enid crept out into the hall.

Only a door down and across from hers, was her mother's pristine office. If there was anything to be found, it would be there. Thankfully, Isadora kept the door unlocked. Enid quietly closed it behind her before turning to look around. Nothing had changed.

A fireplace sat to the left. White plaster molding and antique tile surrounded it. Above, a large painting of a landscape hung in a gilded frame. The matte blue paint offset the mahogany wainscotting and floor to ceiling bookshelf behind a solid mahogany desk to the right of the room. In the center, before the fireplace, sat a buttery yellow loveseat with small, pink, chintz floral print, and a pair of brown leather wingback chairs.

Enid hurried to the desk, already sure of where she needed to look first. There was one drawer that always remained locked. Enid had wondered why for years, but never felt the need to snoop. The only time she saw it open was when her mother locked away her medical records. Those she didn't need to see, she knew what they contained. But there were other things she glimpsed inside. Today would be the day she found out what they were.

It was an easy matter to get the key from the back of a picture frame on the bookshelf. Sure enough, it slipped into place easily, turning without effort. Inside, there was a simple brown box. Enid lifted it out and set it on the desk before removing the lid.

She frowned when she saw two photo albums inside. Curiously, she picked the first one up. Yellowed newspaper clippings and antique photos filled it—pressed neatly onto the heavy scrapbook cardstock, newspaper carefully laminated to preserve the brittle paper.

The first headline she saw read: 'Local Girl dies from Drug Overdose, Prestigious Family in Shambles.' A sepia toned photo beside the article showed the image of a young woman in her mid-twenties with a large smile and vibrant, light eyes. Her face was framed by straight, pale hair. Beneath the photo in elegant cursive was the name, May Sanderson. The article itself outlined the discovery of the woman's body, and some quotes from the bereaved family. One quote stood out in particular–

'My sister was a troubled spirit, prone to delusion and flights of fantasy. I begged her to stay away from the drugs, but they were the only thing that seemed to separate her from some false reality only she was privy to. I can only pray she is at peace now.' When pressed for further explanation Ms. Adilynn Sanderson refused any additional comments.

Enid's head shot up. Adilynn was her grandmother.

The rigid plastic of the scrapbook creaked as she turned it. The next page contained an old letter, with tearstained, smudged ink—words scrawled in a shaky hand. The penmanship otherwise would have been exemplary.

My Dearest Millie,

My time here at Northspire Institution has shown me many things about my fragile state of mind. I understand the things I see cannot possibly be real; however, this understanding does little to help me recover my sanity. If anything, these beings that appear to me have come all too frequently, and with more violence than ever before.

They say the shock treatment should be helping. God help me, my sister, I lie and say it does for fear that if I am truthful the quantity of these horrible treatments will increase. Despite my most fervent of prayers, I fear that will never be the case. I beg for alternatives, but the doctors tell me it is the only way.

I think I will die from this daily torture. I cannot take the jolt of electricity through my already fractured brain much longer. What little sanity I have left dissolves with each session.

Please, my dearest sister, talk with our parents. Have them remove me from this place, which I know will be the death of me. If you have any love for me at all, get me away from this constant nightmare. I will shut my eyes to the world and the monsters I see in it. I will close my lips, leaving their renditions unspoken. If only I can come home to the warmth and comfort of my family. If only I could lie in my own bed, safe and free from the terror and agony that has become my constant companion. Rescue me.

Your loving sister,

Elspeth

Tears ran freely down Enid's face. Her hands shook against the page. She sat back with a strangled sob, falling into the desk chair. Heart breaking as she felt the emotions of the woman who wrote her pain so freely. This was a horror Enid could understand only too well. How many times had she questioned her own sanity, her life, her free will with the things she had seen? It was only due to her parent's refusal to permanently admit her to a similar institution that Enid was able to avoid the same fate. Even her short incarcerations had been a struggle.

On the opposite page of the tear-streaked letter was an old black and white photo of a beautiful young woman. Her wide, sad eyes gazed toward the camera over her shoulder. Her dark hair curled to perfection and pinned in a low bob. She seemed to be haunted. Enid allowed her fingers to graze the picture. The same flowing handwriting beneath the photo read, *Elspeth Ardmore*. Millie had been her great-grandmother's name. This woman must have been her great aunt.

The following pages of the book contained newspaper clippings of a car accident, and an obituary for Mr. William Ardmore dated August 1945. Next to this was another obituary for Mrs. Evelyn Ardmore dated February 1946. She was barely forty-six years old. The grainy black and white picture showed a woman who bore a striking resemblance to the photo of Elspeth, with the same dark hair and haunted eyes. Enid's great-great grandmother. Nothing else spoke of delusions or bouts of insanity, but it was there—reflected in their eyes. Something in her family line, some sort of gene.

She turned her attention to the next album.

Enid took a deep breath, an attempt to steady her nerves, and then she opened it. Inside were pictures of a happy family. Enid had never seen these photos before, but she recognized the people in them. Her mother as a child, her grandmother and grandfather. All, except one.

Another young girl, a year or so younger than her mother. Her full, cheerful smile was bright in the older photos, then slowly dimmed as the years progressed. She had large brown eyes, and thick chestnut hair that curled in full waves around her pale face. In the last photo, she wasn't smiling at all. The family was in front of a large waterfall, everyone but her looking happily into the camera. Her eyes were wide, almost frightened, with the same wary expression as young Elspeth.

Did her mother have a younger sister?

There was a large, manilla envelope tucked into the box, underneath the albums. With shaking hands, she opened it. A birth certificate, social security card, and a thick folder were all the envelope contained. The name on the card and birth certificate read Aislinn Worth. Enid's grandparents were listed as the parents on her birth certificate. Enid dropped them on the desk, running a hand through her hair. She had an aunt. How did she not know this?

The folder itself held documents with a heading 'Northspire Institute for the Mentally Impaired'. Her grandmother's signatures were on the older documents in the back. Her mother's familiar signature on the new. Papers listed details of Aislinn's mental instability, a chronicle of her attempts to self-harm, and doctor's notes stating her inability to function in the day-to-day world.

Enid slumped back in the chair. An aunt. An aunt with some sort of affliction similar to her own. One that had been locked up because of it. Northspire Institute. That would be her next stop. She had to see for herself. Had to meet the woman who could understand her fears, who lived her daily nightmare. Had to—

The door to the office opened and Jane, her mother's assistant, walked in. Her hand went to her chest with a gasp when she saw Enid.

"Oh! You scared me," she said with a light laugh.

Enid replied with a chuckle. "You scared me too."

She waved her hand around at the items on the desk, packing them away. "I was looking through a few things, trying to find something to surprise my mother with. Please don't tell her."

Jane looked uncomfortable, but finally gave a hesitant nod. Enid locked the box back away as the assistant came over and grabbed a notebook from the desk.

"Jane?"

Pushing her glasses up on the bridge of her nose, Jane turned to her with a shy smile.

"Do you know where Northspire Institute is?"

"Well, yes. It's about twenty minutes away. Mrs. Washbourne does volunteer work there and sometimes has flowers delivered. Why?"

"Well, I was wondering if you could give me a ride there for a quick visit. I know you have to be busy organizing the dinner tonight, but I could really use the help."

Jane bit her bottom lip, glancing at her tablet. "I do need to run an errand that isn't far from there. I could drop you on the way and pick you back up after? I'm afraid it would have to be a quick trip. I can only spare an hour, tops."

Enid smiled widely. "That will be perfect! Thank you so much."

Finally, something was going her way.

CHAPTER

12

Jane dropped her off with brief instructions, her words clear and precise despite her timid demeanor. With a quick thank you, Enid stepped out of the car and gazed up at the gray stone walls of the clinic. The brass plate fastened into the stone next to the door read:

Northspire Institution for the Mentally Impaired
Est. 1864.

Enid frowned up at the facade of the building. Dread and fear seemed to lace the exterior like mist on a mountain. The kind place you would find in a horror movie. She shivered.

The front doors opened into a large room. It felt sterile, despite the warm wooden beams and cheery, yellow painted walls. Most likely due to the aroma of disinfectant and medicine that seemed to permeate the air, like most hospitals. A row of stiff, wooden chairs faced a large semi-circular desk, granting a place to sit without being comfortable enough for anyone to linger.

The receptionist greeted Enid with a bright smile.

"Good afternoon, how can I help you?"

She did her best to hide the trembling in her hands as she stepped up to the desk. Thankfully, she was able to keep her breathing calm. No sign of a panic attack yet.

"Yes, I'm here to see Aislinn Worth."

Enid tried, and failed, to keep the uncertainty out of her voice. The receptionist turned to her screen, fingers flying over the keys with a rhythmic tap.

"Are you family?" she questioned, her large brown eyes turning to Enid. "She's only allowed to have visitation from family, I'm afraid."

"I'm her niece," she replied with a nervous smile.

"Oh yes!" the pretty receptionist exclaimed, her face lighting up. "I'm so sorry. I see the note here now. Your mother's assistant already called ahead to say you would be coming. Right this way."

She stood from the desk, leaving it unattended as though sure no one would be calling or walking in while she was away. Enid made a mental note to thank her mother's assistant for her foresight as she followed the woman past the elevator to a small door on the other side of the room.

The tiny window inlaid with a grid of thin metal wire showed a plain white hall beyond. The receptionist unlocked the door, ushered her through, and walked briskly down the corridor, all the while chatting about the history of the hospital. Unfortunately, Enid could not bring herself to pay attention to the bubbly words.

Trepidation filled her, fed by the uncertainty of what she would encounter. Was her aunt really as bad off as her mother claimed? Enid couldn't shake the feeling that she was walking in on a glimpse of her future, or what her future could have been. Perhaps a broken woman, silent and staring into empty space. Or panicked and pleading, wrestling with the demons in her minds, jacketed and shoved into seclusion.

"You actually came at the right time," the receptionist was saying. "She is in the back garden for her outside time." She continued talking about the benefits of fresh air and sunshine in her cheerful tone. "It's so nice that you came to see her," she continued in nearly the same breath. Enid was almost dizzy with how little air the woman seemed to take in between sentences.

"She barely gets visitors anymore since your grandmother died, and Mrs. Washbourne comes less and less." Her pert, brunette ponytail waved as she gave a sad shake of her head, before bouncing up again as she came to a sudden stop. "She will be so pleased to see you, I'm sure of it. She is well loved around here. Practically one of our most popular guests. After all, she has been here longer than most of the staff."

Enid's eyes widened at that comment. The receptionist pointed through the open doors of a bright, airy sunroom to a small, grassy field. There, under the shade of a tree, sat a thin, older woman. The dappled light through the tree branches fell upon a brassy, light brown head of hair streaked with gray.

Two orderlies in white uniforms sat at a nearby table, watching over the few patients who fidgeted in chairs, blinking around them at the sun-drenched little garden. The drab, gray attire they wore was at odds with the bright green landscape and fragrant, flowering bushes. The cheerful receptionist flitted over to the white clad men while Enid made her way toward her aunt, pulled as though by an invisible string.

The grass sunk softly beneath her shoes. Compared to the miasma of fear entrenching the building, this little garden was a sanctuary of peace and serenity. Not daring to disturb that peace, Enid walked quietly over to the older woman and sat beside her, allowing the silence to hover as she collected the words she wanted to say. She took a moment to enjoy the feel of the breeze on her face and the flash of sunlight through the filter of leaves in the weaving branches above them.

There was a tinkling sound, like a windchime on the breeze. Enid glanced around for its source, but only saw the movement of shadows in the branches above. The flutter of a wing.

Her aunt tilted forward, wisps of hair falling from a messy braid. She gave a low whisper, soft but insistent, beneath her breath. Enid tilted her head, trying to make out the buzz of words. She couldn't. She pasted a smile on her face, hoping it veiled her nerves.

Where to begin?

"Hi, Aunt Aislinn, you don't know me, but my name is Enid. I'm Isadora's daughter."

Aislinn rocked herself gently side to side, glazed eyes staring straight ahead, unhearing.

Enid was about to try again when the woman stilled, head turning. Large brown eyes met hers hesitantly, wide with wonder, and a hint of fear. Enid kept her smile, praying it was reassuring. She couldn't help the spike of sadness and pity that shot through her at the lost, broken look.

"Isa," she whispered. Her voice was scratchy from misuse. A pink tongue darted out to moisten her chapped lips before she continued, words cracking, slightly louder, but still barely more than a whisper. "Isa, you haven't aged a day. How long have I been here now? It seems so long." Her eyes drifted forward once more, the rocking continued.

"I'm Enid, Aunt Aislinn. Isadora's daughter." Enid kept her voice soft—a balm to soothe the woman's brittle nerves.

"Enid? Poor Enid," Aislinn muttered. "So young, the sweet little thing. Too young to see such monsters." She turned to Enid then, eyes wide and insistent, thin hands grasping hers tightly. "You must tell her, Isa, don't let them know she can see. If they know, they will take her. They will hurt her. I know you don't believe me, but please. She'll understand, she'll know."

Her head turned to the side, away from Enid. That soft, frantic whisper again, only this time Enid could make out the words. "I know, but she doesn't believe me. I tried to help the girl. I tried."

"Aunt Aislinn, I believe you, I do. I know," Enid spoke softly, trying to break into the chaos of her mind. "I see them too."

Her Aunt stilled, her grip tightened painfully. Enid forced herself not to jerk away, to remain calm

"What game are you playing now, Isa? It isn't like you to be so cruel. Cold yes, but not this. I told you I tried to help her. I took hold of that bright, blazing aura and I pressed it back into her. I tried to hide it, to conceal her ability. I pressed it into a shell, a barrier of protection against the creatures."

Aislinn's voice cracked. Tears pooled in her eyes. She released her hold on Enid's hands and wrapped her arms around herself.

"I wasn't strong enough. Fissures, cracks broke out before you even took her from here. I told you last time. I'm sorry."

The tears fell from her eyes. She continued her rocking—seeking comfort. Strands of hair that had fallen from her braid danced in the breeze. Above them the tree swayed gently and the musical notes of the hidden windchime drifted in the air.

Enid stilled.

The block was her aunt's doing. Which meant, at some point, they had met. Her mother had brought her here. She stared at the woman, swaying back and forth on the bench, face streaked with tears. This could have been her life, her fate. Her mother had gone to great lengths to hide this from her. Could she have been trying to protect her this entire time? To shield her from this trauma? Maybe to keep her from ending up the same way? Enid wanted so badly for that to be true.

"Aunt Aislinn, do you think you can show me, or tell me what you did to...my aura?" It felt strange even saying those words.

"She's wrong, she's wrong," her aunt mumbled, her head moving to the side as though talking to someone opposite her. "She can't see, she doesn't know."

Enid reached for Aislinn's hand, holding it gently as she spoke, trying to break through to her. Trying to get the older woman to hear her, to see her.

"But I can see, Aunt Aislinn. Please, teach me how it works. Help me to control it."

The rocking stopped and once more those crazed eyes fastened onto her. Enid jerked as Aislinn grabbed her wrist with her other hand, and leaned in close.

"You think you see? That you know?" She hissed angrily. "Then look." That thin hand grabbed her chin, turning her head toward the table with the two orderlies.

As Enid's face turned toward the white uniformed men guarding their dazed patients, she noticed for the first time the strange glimmer around them. The two men appeared to be clean cut orderlies, one bald and broad shouldered, the other wiry and lean with short, crew cut brown hair, but beneath that image were beings Enid had never seen before. Her hand tightened in her aunt's, her heart beat spiking. The air was getting harder to breathe.

"You can't see, you don't know what really lies beneath the glamor these things project. You don't know how they torment us. How they feed on our fear."

Enid shuddered.

The bald orderly was a great, hulking beast with horns erupting from either side of a massive head, similar to a bull. Minotaur, she thought—Greek mythology coming to mind at the sight of the creature. His thickly muscled legs stretched the fabric of his white uniform, ending in large hooves instead of the white tennis shoes that glimmering image portrayed.

The other orderly was thinner, smaller, and a ghastly green color. Greasy, black hair hung in knotted fringes around sharply pointed ears. A large hooked nose nearly covered over his thin-lipped mouth. Red eyes flashed toward her. With a soft gasp she turned her head away. Not wanting to alert them.

She grasped her aunt's hand, pulling it from her face, holding it tightly. Looking back toward the orderlies, she flashed a smile.

Everything is fine. I can't see what you are.

Inside, she trembled in terror.

Aislinn continued, her voice a hushed whisper—bordering on hysteria.

"The minotaur feeds on fright, terrorizing and menacing all who come to this place. And the ghoul? The ghoul comes with pain and torture when the fear grows dull, punishing us, especially when he's hungry. When the dead bodies have all run out and he is greedy for more, he comes and whispers to us tales of how he will devour us when we die."

Enid shivered at the horror of it, but Aislinn wasn't finished.

"When they are bored with you, they send other creatures to haunt your dreams, to etch their promises into your flesh."

She winced. Aislinn's fingernails had dug themselves into her hands—red moons marking the pale skin.

"Pray, Isadora, that you never see. Because once you do, they will find you, they will hunt you, and they will destroy you. Don't look at them. Don't see them. Keep Enid away. Don't let them know. Tell her. Tell her."

Her hands dropped Enid's, instead gripping her arms roughly, pulling her closer, the whites of her eyes clear around the brown irises. Insistent, knowing. Enid resisted the urge to wrest away from the bruising grip.

"Enid can glimpse the future, I've seen it. She told me when she was here." Aislinn let go, pulling back to herself with a soft laugh, rocking once more. Whispering, her gaze distant. "She told me, 'Aunt Aislinn, I'm so sorry about your dinner tonight. They are giving you brussels sprouts. Yuck.'"

She snickered, swaying as she continued to speak. "It was true. It was true. She told me to run, to hide. Hide from the bad man with the red eyes. He's coming."

"We had brussels sprouts that night. The bad man came." Her face went pale, haunted. "I couldn't run. Couldn't hide."

She went quiet, her legs drawing up, her arms wrapping around them as she continued to gently sway. A child-like tune humming from between her lips—a lullaby meant to comfort.

The tune itself licked a streak of fear down Enid's spine.

She left her aunt to her thoughts. Her own mind now in jumbles. Absently she rubbed at the marks on her wrists. The beastly orderlies remained playing their card game, unbothered or indifferent to the conversation taking place under the arching boughs of the great oak tree. From the corner of her eye, she watched them. Discreetly observing that false image hovering over their grotesque forms.

Glamor, she thought.

That is what her aunt called it. Her own head spun with the information that she was still trying to understand. Enid's heart thumped in her chest, not in the fast-paced beat of fear, but with the deep, slow thud that comes from a shocking revelation.

She was incredibly overwhelmed.

Sifting through her earliest memories, she tried to place the ones Aislinn spoke of. She couldn't.

A rustle of the leaves above drew her attention. The light through the boughs fell upon her face, blinding her as she searched for the source of the sound. Had she sat in this garden before, as a small child, looking into these very trees for the birds—the windchimes clinking their musical notes.

Next to her, her aunt gave a low, keening moan, startling her from the reverie. The sound was full of dread and horror. The hairs on the back of Enid's neck stood on end.

"Visiting hours are over," came a rough, deep voice next to them.

Enid jumped.

The bald orderly stood over them, mimicking the movements of the hulking minotaur. Before she realized what she was doing, her eyes drifted up past the head of that normal, human mirage to the massive, horned head of the beast behind it. His frame towered feet above the average six-foot height of the projection meant to represent him. Breath blew from his snout in a huff. A large brass ring in his nose vibrated as he did so.

Enid's mouth dropped open.

Her aunt's hands clamped down against hers, the older woman's nails digging into her soft flesh. Briefly, her eyes met the large brown ones of the minotaur. Alarm flooded her as she was met with suspicion. Jerking her head down, she forced herself to meet the squinting eyes of the bald apparition instead.

"Of course!" Enid replied, a little too loud, bobbing her head blandly to the false face, urging herself not to look up at the terrifying true face lurking above.

The minotaur and human puppet reached their hand out expectantly. Aislinn extended her trembling hand to take that of the orderly illusion as it blended with the true hand of the minotaur. It looked so fragile and delicate in the gigantic, hairy palm of the great beast. Her aunt gave her a wide-eyed look of agony as she was gently pulled away from the little bench, her legs wobbling beneath her as she stood.

Patiently the minotaur helped stabilize her before he led them along the flagstone pavers of the walkway to the patio. Enid was surprised at how unexpectedly gentle he was as he walked alongside her aunt, keeping her from tripping on the uneven ground. She trailed behind, trying her best to remain stoic as the phantom face of the orderly and the beast kept turning back to look at her quizzically. All the while her aunt's voice played in her head.

Don't let them know.

At the bank of glass doors, the Minotaur motioned her aunt to go in before him. Enid gasped, sucking in her breath as he lowered his head, deadly horns aimed at Aislinn's back. She was rooted in place, her feet unable to move, her voice trapped within her while she watched in mute horror.

The image of the orderly walked in time to the beast, its horns slicing through the projection harmlessly. Then he was through the doorway and stretching his impressive bulk as though ducking through the human sized opening had been rough on his back. Enid's breath blew out in a rush, the icy fear melting away as Aislinn, completely unharmed, turned to look at her with those haunted eyes.

"It has been so nice to visit, Aunt Aislinn," Enid said, unable to contain the slight tremor in her voice. Her aunt said nothing, merely stood there, eyes darting around. The shadows beneath them deep, her body quaking.

Unable to resist, Enid enveloped her in a hug.

"I won't let them know," Enid breathed into her ear. "I'll be careful."

As she pulled away, Aislinn grabbed her arms once more, eyes searching her face. As though, for the first time, she was actually seeing Enid for who she truly was. As soon as it was there, it was gone. The detached, glazed expression once more washed over her features, as though she was too broken to feel anything for too long.

Enid watched silently as the frail woman was escorted through a set of doors. The goliath once more ducking behind her as he ushered her along. Guilt tore at her, leaving an ache in her chest, as the doors shut behind them. She had an overwhelming feeling of loss—a foreboding, that as those doors swung shut, so did the book on Aislinn Worth's life. Enid's shoulders drooped, grief and despair flooding her.

She turned to leave.

And ran right into the narrow chest of the ghoulish, green orderly. His red eyes seemed to brighten as he took in her shocked appearance.

"What do we have here?" His raspy voice sent shivers of terror tumbling through her, numbing her fingertips.

"H-hi," Enid sputtered. "I was just leaving."

She did her best to keep her face neutral, but she knew she was failing horribly. Already her hands had begun to tremble and she clutched them tightly in an attempt to hide it. With a tight smile she stepped to the side to walk past, only to have him mirror her movements—blocking her exit. She stared into those red eyes, transfixed as he leaned toward her, his greasy black hair hanging between them. His face level with hers.

"I saw how you were looking at Artemis. I know you can see."

"S-see what?" Her voice was barely audible, even to her own ears. Vidar's words rang in her ear.

'You do not want the attention of these beings.'

He leaned closer so that his beaked nose was in her hair, inhaling the scent of her shampoo, his lipless mouth at her ear. Enid's feet turned to lead. She was suddenly hyper aware. Aware of the prominent hump on the creature's back. Aware of the fiend's foul, hot breath. Her knees felt as though they may give out, her legs as strong as cooked pasta.

"You can see what I am." That voice nearly sang with menacing delight. He pulled back to gauge her reaction, hands behind his back, body arched so they were eye to eye. Enid's head began moving back and forth, shaking in disagreement. She didn't trust her voice to speak.

"My, my, you are entertaining," the creature mocked. "You haven't even realized my glamor is gone."

Enid's eyes widened as she realized her mistake, scanning for that clean-cut, human image from earlier. As the creature stated, it wasn't there. Only this ghastly *thing* confronted her.

She had given herself away so easily. So quickly. She staggered backward, wanting to be away from the devil. Its eyes gleamed with elation.

"Oh yes, run. Run, run. Go now." A laugh rippled out of it as it drew itself to its full height.

Enid couldn't help it. She ran. Back away from the creature. Away from those maniacal red eyes. Further into the unfamiliar, sterile hallways of the sanatorium.

CHAPTER

13

Metal doors slammed against the tiled wall with a crack that echoed down the hall ahead of her. Fear hammered against her heart, the beat keeping time to the pace of her footfalls. The laughter of the ghoul followed, pushing her to go faster, look harder for a way to escape.

Inwardly she cursed her stupidity. Why didn't she pay attention to the glamor? Why did she run further into this accursed building? How could she be so careless?

Each door in the hall was locked, probably harboring some poor soul wrestling the demons in their own heads. They wouldn't be able to comprehend the very real devil that trailed Enid down the stark hallway, his taunts following her as she tested door after door. Finally, she set eyes on a way out. The stairwell.

She hit it hard, dodging to the side as it bounced off the cement wall before slamming shut behind her. The stairs wound up, one flight after another. She didn't bother counting the levels as she sped up them, pulling herself along with the aid of the hand rail. Only when she heard the door below swing open with a bang did she lunge toward the nearest one. The shoes of the ghoul tapped hurriedly against the cement stairs, his laughter mocking.

Hoping he wouldn't suspect her location, she caught the door, letting it click shut silently behind her. This level seemed quieter, empty, the buzz of the fluorescent lighting the only sound besides the rasp of her breathing. She rushed from room to room and found, to her relief, another unlocked door.

A sob nearly broke from her as she rushed in, keeping the door open a crack as she crouched behind it, unable to control her breathing, and the frenzied pounding in her chest. It was so loud. Focusing, she counted the beats, forcing herself to take slow, even breaths until the shaking began to dissipate, her heart rate slowed.

It wasn't the stairwell door opening that had her creeping away from the door. But the ding of the elevator. Heavy footsteps made their way down the hall. A glance around offered no escape should she need it. She had found refuge within some sort of operating room. A table sat in the heart of it, a row of cabinets at the back, a metal cart on wheels off to the side. Not one suitable place to hide.

She ducked behind the padded table, the best she could do, when she heard the soft hum of voices. They whispered to her from the depths of a shadowy corner. Her name reached her ears, the sound a balm to her frightened nerves. They spoke to her of safety, of comfort. In a daze, she walked toward them, stepping away from the table. She reached out—the cloud of shadow nearly at her fingertips.

The door to the room flung open, jarring her from her trance. A line of light scattered the shadows as the massive form of the minotaur hunched through the opening. He seemed somehow larger as he stood to his full height. The light from the hall spilled into the room behind him, casting his shadow across the tile floor. She backed away from the dark image of the creature as it skimmed the tips of her shoes. As though even his shadow might cause her harm.

She was so screwed.

There was nowhere to go. She didn't have the capacity to think on it for long as the creature reached for her. He moved quicker than she would think for such a large beast. Hands grabbed her shoulders, lifting her and slamming her down on the table. The air flew from her lungs. Stunned, Enid lay there, gasping for a breath she couldn't reach. The large, brown eyes of the minotaur peered down at her.

"Human with the sight," his deep voice rumbled. "It is rare I get to see one of you, so fresh and unbroken." His large nostrils dipped toward her as he inhaled loudly. "Ah!" he grumbled, his breath a warm fan across her face. "The fear of one who knows, who can really see us. So much more fulfilling than that of these fracture-minded mortals."

He reached above them with one of his massive hands, turning the light on overhead, yanking it closer to her face—examining her. Her mouth opened and closed soundlessly as she desperately worked to pull air in. Vidar had warned her. Her aunt had warned her. *How could I be so stupid?* A trickle of air reached her hungry lungs. It wasn't enough. Water pooled in her eyes.

Releasing the light, he grabbed ahold of her jaw, turning her head first one way, and then the other. Inspecting her stricken expression from all angles. His enormous, horned head lowered further, and he gave a great huff, taking in as much of her scent as he could. While his eyes roved over her hungrily, she continued to wheeze beneath the hand holding her. Struggling to breath, to move, to get away from the creature that toyed with her. Her own eyes were wide with fear as the wickedly sharp tips of those horns moved ever closer.

The beast wasn't going to lose this opportunity. His large hand around her chin, fingers digging into her cheeks, amused by her struggle. Once he had her secure, he loomed directly above her, locking her in his stare. Then, with intent, he took a deep, long breath. Holding it before taking another and another. White light seemed to pull away from her. Strands of it funneling into the minotaur's mouth with each inhale. Every time Enid felt weakness wash over her. A single tear crept down the side of her face. She wasn't ready to die.

A soundless scream erupted from her when she felt his course, sandpaper tongue run along her cheek. Scraping from jaw to temple in one swipe, tasting the salty drop of water. It left behind a wet and sticky trail that had her throat constricting in a gag. His nose nuzzled into the hair behind her ear, snuffling.

"Such terror," it rumbled in delight.

"There you are!"

Enid's breath finally came back to her in a whoosh. Tears streamed down her face. Between that and the blinding light above her, she couldn't make out the figure at the door. But she recognized that grating, chill voice. The ghoul had found her.

"Let me play with her, Artemis," he groused, moving toward them.

"I'm not done," snapped the minotaur. The hand not holding her down pushed the other creature away.

"I saw her first!" The ghoul hissed.

As she looked on helplessly, it rushed at the minotaur. Green arms wrapped around that great, furry neck. Blackened, rotting teeth bared in fury. The minotaur reared back in response, hands slipping away from Enid as he reached for the creature astride its bulky back.

She took the opening, sliding from the table. Oblivious to her, the two fumbled, growling and spitting—each vying for dominance. She rushed across the room and out the door. Running as fast as she could.

The sounds of fighting continued uninterrupted as she made it to the elevator doors. The button clicked frantically beneath her fingers. Tears streamed down her cheeks—painting the world in a watery canvas. There was a ping and the doors slid open as a bellow erupted down the hall. Panicked, she threw herself into the metal box, her fingers hitting the close button over and over. Torturously slow, they began to shut.

Just when she thought she was free, a green hand jerked between the small opening, reaching for her, and the doors stopped their movement. Enid reared back, her horror-stricken face reflected in red eyes, when suddenly, the creature was thrust to the side. The mass of the minotaur rammed the ghoul. Its momentum too great for a sudden stop. His size worked to Enid's advantage as he took out his competitor and himself—both laying in a furious tangle on the floor.

Her fingers ached from how hard she smashed them into the button. When the doors shut, cutting off the shouted curses of the creatures, she slammed her palm against the lobby button. The metal room around her shimmied, and began shifting downward.

It will be ok now, she told herself over and over.

102

The reflection staring back at her from the metallic wall was a mess. Mocking her soothing thoughts. She still needed to get out of here without drawing anymore unwanted attention. Smoothing her hair down, she wiped her tear-streaked cheeks. *Acceptable, well...better.* The elevator shook to a stop, the bell pinging just before the doors opened. The lobby sat before her. Thankfully monster free. The cheerful, perfectly ordinary human receptionist greeted her.

"There you are! Your mother's assistant is here. She is in the parking lot waiting for you."

Enid nodded, gave her a shaky thank you, and walked as quickly as she could for the doors.

Jane sat out front in her little Volvo. The engine was running, probably for the heat against the brisk chill, but Enid was never happier to see such a sight in all her life. She opened the door, falling into the seat and ducking low as they drove off.

Through the side mirror she watched as the two beasts hurried out the front door, searching. Their glamor was back in place. Those false human images scanning the parking lot in confusion. She didn't relax until they finally slipped from view.

Even then, she couldn't bring herself to speak, or listen to the gentle murmurings of her mother's assistant as she put up some pretense of small talk. Once it became clear Enid would remain unresponsive, she stopped. Instead turning the volume of the radio up a bit and humming along to the music. Enid wished she could be that carefree and unassuming, blind to the horrors of the world. Her life would never be that way again.

CHAPTER

14

Esmelial sighed contentedly, fingers tracing patterns along the chest of the naked male next to her. A chorus of moans on the other side of the room drew her focus. Sharp cries of ecstasy rising in harmony. The sound waves of desire curled around her, resonating along her skin—a sensual buzz of anticipation. The other male they enticed for the night drove himself hard into a petite blonde-haired siren.

Esmelial stretched, relishing the tingle of energy in her limbs as she turned to watch the blonde's eyes begin to glow. Mouth open in a gasp, she drank deep from the life force of the man above her. Her back arched high off the bed as she pulled him closer. Breasts bouncing with the force of his thrusts. His life force shimmered around them, face shining with euphoria as he neared completion, grunts growing deeper.

The Siren's full lips drank it down greedily, her eyes an electric, blue topaz. Their glow brightening with every drop she devoured. It was a sight to behold, watching the young siren work. But if she wasn't careful, she would kill the male. They couldn't have that. It would make things very difficult.

"Thea," she purred. A soft, careful warning.

The human jerked and spasmed with pleasure, caught in her snare. Thea held the release, savoring her meal. He cried out, hands fisting the sheets beneath him. Crumpling the fabric between curled fingers. Shouts swallowed by the skilled fae as she held him in place. Thea sat up further, stabilizing herself on one arm as she rocked her hips. Her ankles locked behind his taut ass, forcing him harder into her. And all the while she drank deep of his essence. He groaned—a deep, guttural noise.

When Esmelial was certain she would have to tear the seductress away, Thea's head fell back. Cutting off contact as she screamed out, allowing orgasm to crash over the both of them. The human's face and neck were so red, Esmelial was afraid it would be his heart that killed him instead of the Siren.

She tensed, watching with collected calm. She did not want to explain another burst heart either. As soon as his body stopped shuddering, the man fell atop the small blonde. His heavy breaths punctuated by frantic laughs against her supple breasts as he nuzzled them.

Esmelial relaxed.

"Oh. Holy. Fuck." He managed to get out between gasps. "How?" His arms tightened around her narrow waist, pulling her on top of him as she giggled.

Esmelial chuckled, checking on the one at her side. He was still breathing. Good. It had been such a long time, almost a month, since she last ate. She shouldn't keep such large gaps between meals. It made her careless. As it was, she could only get the two of them out of Dokkalfar undetected. Their sisters could handle a few more days, but they would need something soon as well.

Thankfully, frequent visitors to one of the Revenant owned nightclubs were plentiful, and this Revenant owed her a favor for helping to quietly settle a dispute in front of dozens of humans. So, when the need arose, the Revenant let them in and gave them access to a private room. Usually, it was reserved for the Revenant's hunts. Giving human blood bags a place to rest between meals. But it was equally satisfactory for the Sirens needs. She needed to keep it a secret until she could get their hunting rights reinstated. The time tables were strictly enforced for this reason.

Fucking Revenant and their backstabbing bullshit. They were the reason the Sirens had to go to such lengths. Too bad she needed them to survive, or her sisters did. If Esmelial had only herself to worry about, she would drain the whole lot of them. If they had any life force worth taking that is. She hated them. Well, she hated their queen. Some of them weren't that bad. A couple of them could be really fun. When allowed away from that bitch Isis.

Esmelial climbed from the bed, slowly moving about the room as she gathered their things. The one holding Thea watched her appreciatively with sleepy eyes. She swayed her hips for him. Letting her fingers trail along the curvy planes of her body, savoring the praise she saw reflected back at her before his eyes fluttered shut.

"Such a tease, Essie," Thea murmured as she slid away from the sleeping human, his arms thumping solidly against the mattress.

"I couldn't very well take any more from the poor creature. You very nearly drained him dry," Esmelial replied.

Thea laughed, squirming into the tight skirt and low-cut shirt she wore to get here. "Ugh, these clothes. I can't wait to get back home and take them all off again."

"Me too, dear one. Let's hurry."

They slipped from the room, smiling to the Revenant standing guard. He replied with a distracted nod of his head. Focused on a young brunette in the middle of the dance floor giving him eyes.

Males, even fae males, so easily distracted, Esmelial thought with a huff.

"It's too bad we can't dance, Essie," Thea mumbled with a longing look toward the sea of bodies. "I haven't felt this good in so long."

Esmelial stopped, her gaze moving to the dark glass window of the office that looked down over the club. She gave Thea a small smile. "We can take another few minutes. Go. Dance." She bumped her shoulder and gave her a wink. "I will come find you."

Thea gave a delighted squeal that had Esmelial's heart lifting in happiness. The blonde rushed down the stairs, her body already falling into the rhythm of the music. Much to the delight of several lustful faces in the crowd. Esmelial leaned over the railing long enough to see the happy fae throw her head back.

Hair piled high on her head as she danced. It took seconds before she was surrounded by eager men and women.

The door to the office was closed, but no noise reached Esmelial's ears from within. So, without bothering to knock, she turned the knob and waltzed in. William Monroe sat at the large desk, a drink in hand. Black dress shoes propped casually on the shiny wood as he watched the mass of bodies writhe below. His tie hung loose around his neck. The top buttons of his white shirt undone. Suit jacket thrown casually on the nearby leather couch.

It was unusual to see the Revenant so relaxed. In clothes not sanctioned by his queen to wear. He looked so very…human. That could be due to the fact he had recently eaten. She could smell the scent on him. See the glow in his naturally bronze skin. Her hunger peaked despite the recent meal.

He cast a glance over to the siren. Not surprised to see her, but not particularly thrilled either. His brown eyes were nearly as dark as his expertly styled hair—almost black. He was beautiful, but he was Revenant. She tried to contain her disgust.

"I see your girl has been satisfied," he said, a nod of his head toward where Thea swayed within the crowd.

Esmelial smiled.

"Very," she replied, closing the door. She drifted over to the large window behind him. Her gaze flicking briefly to the stunning siren below.

"You seem rather pleased, yourself," she crooned, letting a slither of her magic hum through her words as she stepped closer. Her hands slid down his broad, muscular shoulders. The Revenant relaxed a little. The human whiskey in his hand clicking onto the desk as he leaned back into the chair with a sigh.

"I need to take advantage of the freedom while I can," he said.

Esmelial hummed in question, a little more of her magic threading into the sound. It was delicate work, seducing a Revenant without them knowing. As creatures of seduction themselves, they were quite adept to the sensation.

"It's nothing," he murmured as she walked around him. Her fingers trailed along the length of his calf to the tip of his shiny, black shoe. Dark, hooded eyes met hers as he lowered his feet to the floor, giving the siren room to perch herself at the edge of his desk.

He swallowed, eyes trailing along her curves. She had worn this annoying piece of material for that reason. The thin fabric hid nothing of what lay beneath, while showing enough to leave the mind wanting more.

Watching carefully, she crossed her legs. Angling toward the Revenant, her heeled foot slightly grazed the side of his thigh. Subtle, careful. Not too much. The Revenant licked his lips.

"Have things been *hard* for you?" she asked, a slight emphasis on the right word. A tiny sound from the back of her throat. Not a full song, only enough of a tone to entice. "Can I do anything for you. Something to help you relax? Since you have done so much for me." She leaned forward, her hand going to his knee. Some of her long, black hair fell forward. As though he couldn't help himself, William reached up and pushed it back. His fingers lingered along the spill of her cleavage. Eyes darkening as a finger found the edge of a nipple so near the fabric's edge.

She uncrossed her legs, arching into the touch with a shiver. Only a woman, unexpectedly pleased by the attention of a man. *Don't gag*, she told herself. Playing the part to perfection, she slightly wet her lips as she parted them. The hungry look he gave her had nothing to do with blood.

She could see the moment his control slipped in the tightening of his jaw, the flare of his nostrils. Suddenly, the Revenant had her straddling his lap. Strong hands gripping her hips. The Siren gasped in mock surprise. Another opportunity to unleash a bit more of her song. A thrum of desire meeting her as she felt him harden through the fabric of his pants.

"There is something you can do for me," he murmured against her mouth.

Her fingers made quick work of the zipper and button of his pants. Freeing him from the confining material. The Revenant groaned as she slid down atop him, his eyes flaring at her lack of underwear. Moving her hips in a rhythm that seemed to please him, she uttered the necessary moans in response. The required amount of attention to stroke his ego, while allowing her magic to further entrap him.

It wasn't all bad, actually. Though she was loath to admit this part of the seduction required little acting on her part. The Revenant was well endowed, and knew how to give pleasure much more readily than the human she had earlier. The only thing he couldn't provide was a meal. Siphoning whatever stolen essence he contained would be merely a snack. Still, it was better than nothing, and using her magic was so very tiring.

"William," Esmelial moaned. "Do you enjoy helping us?"

The Revenant held her waist, directing her up and down his shaft. Attention focused on the place where they came apart and together again. "Not particularly," he gasped. "But you're a great fuck, and *that* I like," he replied.

Esmelial hummed appreciatively. Delightfully honest. He was almost ready.

She pushed her song into each cry and gasp. Blending a crescendo of magic and seduction. His eyes began to glaze over. She lowered her dress, baring her breasts. Letting her song slip out a bit louder now that she felt her magic firmly entangle him. He fondled them reverently. Devoutly kissing and suckling each nipple to pert attention. Her power thrummed excitedly within her, invoking a spasm through his body.

She brought her lips to his ear.

"What worries you, William?" she whispered.

The Revenant groaned, his head falling back as she picked up the pace. "The Queen. She's got us looking for a girl."

"A girl?"

The Revenant blinked, eyebrows furrowing. Esmelial hummed, her song working into him as he worked deeper into her. His fingers biting into her flesh.

"A girl with scarlet hair, from a prophecy," he gasped, hips bucking beneath her. He was so close. If she extended this too long, he would suspect. Already she could feel him picking at the edges of her seduction as his talented tongue danced around her nipple. Damn Revenant, so fucking tricky.

"Why is this prophecy so important?"

She panted, clutching the back of his neck and arching into him. Obviously enjoying his ministrations despite herself. His arms tightened, her nipple popping out of his mouth as he answered.

"The girl will destroy humanity."

Esmelial's rhythm wavered. William guided her. Hands firmly gripping her rounded bottom as he helped her find the cadence once more.

"Then the Queen wants to kill her?"

"No." A moan, deep and guttural. His thrusts harder. "She wants to find her, control her. The Queen wants to rule this realm, and others. The girl can help. The girl will be the key."

Esmelial let out a soft sigh. Feeling the rush within her that meant her silver eyes were beginning to glow. "The key to what?" she murmured against his mouth. She curled her magic around him, beckoning to the human essence locked within his blood.

"Oh, fuck!" William cried out. "The key to another realm!" His hips snapped upward, muscles tense. Rubbing against that place inside her that was her undoing.

Esmelial nearly lost her control then. It took her full concentration to keep from unraveling.

"I will give you your release, Revenant, and in return you will forget we had this conversation."

William growled low in his throat. "Yes," he hissed.

She opened her mouth over his as she pulled that sliver of life force from him. And then she let go. Let the pleasure rush over the both of them in a wave that had them both shuddering. William roared, his fangs snapping into sight. Before he could use them, Esmelial shoved the entirety of the orgasm into him. Letting it consume him.

"Fuck," he gasped.

His eyes rolled back into his head, and he passed out against the back of the chair.

Climbing off him, she fixed herself, and straightened his pants the best she could. She was happy with tonight's progress. It had been a satisfying venture. In more ways than one. Taking her time, she walked over to the door, opened it, and then slammed it shut. William jerked awake.

"You look like shit, William," she said, her hands on her hips. "Have you eaten?"

The Revenant looked around, running a hand over his clean-shaven face. "I-I don't know."

"Well, you should," Esmelial scoffed as she walked over to the desk. "We finished with those humans and left them sleeping. We will need another couple for the rest of my sisters as soon as possible. Can you make that happen?" She leaned her hands on the desk. Watching the rumpled fae as he stretched, and rubbed his hands along the back of his neck.

Such talented hands, she thought briefly before immediately dismissing it.

"Um- yeah, sure, whatever. Yes." He was utterly perplexed.

Esmelial straightened. "Thank you," she called over her shoulder as she sashayed from the room. Behind her, she could hear William pick up his phone. Calling down for a fresh girl— a walking blood bag. She smirked.

Downstairs the sweaty bodies still swayed to the beat. Thea, face pink and glowing, danced in the center of the mass. All jostling to watch her, touch her. Flashes of topaz light danced in her eyes.

"It's time," Esmelial yelled as she walked through the throng, not needing to push aside the people who naturally moved aside for her. Their expressions of longing called to the song in her blood. It was tempting. To stay there in the middle of that mob of lust. Siphoning little sips of life-giving nectar from each eager mouth. But she couldn't. They would be caught if they didn't leave soon.

The humans around them groaned in dissent as the two sirens left. Thea leaned into Esmelial, her arms threading into hers as though she were drunk.

"Did you get anything interesting, sister?" Her mouth was at Esmelial's ear, her voice low so any other fae wouldn't hear. Esmelial glanced over at the flushed, honey haired beauty, and smirked her response. A smile lit up Thea's face.

The atmosphere outside was the complete opposite of the claustrophobic heat they left. Esmelial breathed deeply as they walked past the line of humans. The women shivering in their tiny dresses. Flush with energy from the recent meal, Esmelial felt amazing. The cool air didn't faze her. She wanted to run. To strip naked and dive into the ocean. To scream her happiness into the sky as she danced along roof tops. Thea gave her a knowing look as they walked the dark street.

"Good thing we have a long walk home, right Essie? It's rare to feel this exhilarated anymore. It makes me want to do foolish things."

Her giggle died as a large shadow stepped into their path.

"You mean like sneaking out to do unsanctioned hunting?" A deep, male voice rumbled through the shadows before coming into view.

The Enforcer.

Dread snaked through Esmelial even as Thea gasped, her beautiful face draining of color. Esmelial stepped forward, angling herself in front of the younger fae.

"Champion of the High King Fenri, Lord of the Between," she purred, directing his attention to her. "What a pleasant surprise."

"You know I don't answer to that title, seductress. That title died along with my father," Vidar sneered, impatience evident in his voice.

"Oh, but you should Lord Vidar, for there are those amongst the Fae who believe you hold more claim to our throne than the King. Many who, despite your tainted blood, would bleed to see you sit upon it."

"You speak of treason," Vidar hissed, his eyes flashing to the solid black of his father's people. A thing which only happened when he was angry. She needed to tread lightly. The Enforcer's ire was legendary.

"Treason? Me? Never," came an overly mocking protest. *Shit*. She couldn't help herself.

Swallowing back her fear, she put on her most charming smile and walked invitingly toward him. She had to tilt her head up quite a bit to get a good look at those black eyes. He was taller than most humans. Over six and a half feet, closer to seven if she had to guess. Trying hard to hide her apprehension, she stepped close enough that her chest grazed the front of him. Her eyes filled with desire, full lips slightly parted. Those ink black eyes looked down at her. Eerie, even for one of their kind. But she needed to keep him preoccupied, needed to find a way out of this for her sisters.

Her cleavage had to be on full display for him at this angle. Using the knowledge to her advantage she bit her bottom lip suggestively. He gripped her biceps and hauled her roughly against him, leaning down so his face was close to hers. She gasped, threading her song into the sound. The taste of triumph on her tongue. Men were so easy.

"You forget yourself, Esmelial," he growled. "You know your tricks don't work on me."

He let her go suddenly and she stumbled back into Thea's arms. Undeterred, she straightened, regaining her composure.

"Can you blame me, Enforcer? Seduction is my nature, and you are such an appetizing specimen. Too bad you hold the human aversion to nudity." She slid closer to him, her gaze drifting down his body.

"I am not your prey," he gritted out, his voice harsh.

"Ah, but you would be such a fulfilling victim, if you were only susceptible to our song," she purred, stepping so close that her chest was nearly touching his, but not quite. She was a little more cautious this time. Her normal devices weren't working. Time to change tactics.

"It is so fascinating, even with that taint of human blood, you still possess so many of the strengths of your father. I wonder which of the fae will be so critical of that flaw of yours when they have withered away to nothing in this rapidly changing world."

She circled around him, a finger running down the side of his large bicep. Noting how still he was—unflinching. His jaw clenched as she traced a line along his shoulder, letting her nail scrape against him lightly.

"Certainly not the Revenant," she continued, relishing the way his muscles tensed. Good, she got to him. This could work for her. She flashed a smile as she moved around him. The tip of her nail trailing along the broad width of his back. Her eyebrow arched at the well-defined muscles beneath the fabric of his shirt.

A specimen indeed.

"Many of them still remember their frail humanity."

Vidar stepped away, whirling to face her. Obviously no longer able to tolerate the feel of her touch.

"Do not speak to me of the Revenant," he hissed.

"Oh?" she questioned, regarding him sternly—deathly calm.

Behind the Enforcer's back, Thea faded into the darkness. Esmelial suppressed her grin. *Good girl.*

"Such disdain you hold for the blood suckers, not that I blame you. Though, you seem to hold such disregard for the majority of fae."

Vidar took a single step toward the siren, just one. His head tilted to the side. Those eyes seeming to peer straight into her soul. Esmelial couldn't help the icy shock of alarm that pressed at her chest, or the way her eyes widened slightly. But she quickly recovered.

"You are awfully concerned about my prejudices, seeing as you were the one to bring up my mixed heritage."

She shrugged.

"I did say I don't blame you for hating the Revenant. You and I have that in common. What I am worried about is if those feelings extend beyond that clan. Say…to half-starved fae trying to survive in any way they can."

Vidar's frightful gaze turned toward the nearby alley. A set of blue eyes reflected in the shadows before disappearing. Thea. Esmelial nearly hissed her frustration. If she knew what was good for her, she would be halfway home by now.

"Do not worry, Siren. I am not without compassion."

The unexpected words startled her.

"I did not come seeking you and your sisters. I come looking for answers to questions of my own."

Interesting.

"Perhaps I could be of service, Enforcer. For a price, of course."

He grunted. "Obviously. Our kind does nothing for free."

It was true. Esmelial grinned. "Get the King to grant my sisters and I our hunting rights, and I will be your spy. I will find what you need."

He appeared to consider her words. "No killing humans."

"Of course. We deal in pleasures of the flesh, not the consuming of them. Why would I destroy my food source?"

Vidar crossed his arms over his wide chest, frowning.

114

"We don't *intentionally* kill our food source," Esmelial corrected with a roll of her eyes. "Our control slips when we are starved."

He rubbed his jaw as he looked down at her. Finally, he extended his hand.

"Deal."

With a smile she reached out and took it in her own small one. The Enforcer jerked her forward, his tight grip causing her to stumble.

"If at any point you give me reason to doubt your loyalty, I will hunt you and your sisters down. One by one."

Esmelial held her breath, the smile wiped from her face. She nodded.

"I give you my oath, Enforcer. I will not betray you," she said, trying to hide the way her voice wanted to quiver. As she spoke the words, she felt the promise lock into place within her. Unbreakable. He must have felt it too, because he instantly dropped her hand.

"This is what I need," he spoke low so his voice didn't carry down the empty, dark street. "There was an incident with a human woman. The shadow man paid her a visit."

Esmelial's mouth dropped open. The shadow man hadn't been seen in centuries. Not since...she shook her head. Memories were a fuzzy thing when you lived for so long. She focused on Vidar's words.

"The night before that, she was attacked by Revenant. It seems like too much of a coincidence, and..." He hesitated, seeming to consider his words as he looked her over darkly.

"I am oath bound," she reminded him.

"There is something unusual about this woman."

Esmelial frowned.

"Does she have red hair?"

The narrowing of his eyes answered her question before his words did.

Fuck, she thought.

"How did you know that?"

This could be dangerous, but it could also give her an opportunity to kill two birds with one stone. She would get the hunting rights, of that she had no doubt. The Enforcer had the

King's ear more than anyone. And she would get her revenge on the bitch Queen.

"Because, the Revenant are looking for her. There is a prophecy."

She explained what she learned from William. Vidar listened, thoughtful, but inexpressive—as usual.

He hummed when she was finished. "A key," he whispered.

Esmelial swallowed. "Could she be *the key?* Could the myths be true?"

Vidar shrugged. "There is no way to tell right now. But if the Revenant get their hands on her, we may never find out. This Revenant, he seems to know a lot for one who takes such risks. Keep working. See what you can find out. I will get your rights to hunt reinstated, but keep the ruse with the other fae. They must continue to think you are desperate."

She nodded.

The Enforcer turned to leave. Before he had taken two steps he stopped, looking back over his shoulder.

"Oh, and Esmelial," he called. She met his gaze. The black no longer hid the gray of his eyes that seemed to swirl like a storm. "Try not to let *your* prejudices interfere with this job."

He didn't wait for a response before he disappeared. Swallowed by the shadows.

CHAPTER

15

The house was already prepared when Enid arrived. Lighting set just right. The smell of dinner wafting through the air. Probably from a hired chef and crew, knowing her mother. Enid's mouth watered at the delectable smell. She hadn't eaten in a while. The events of the past few days had messed with her appetite.

Her mother came around the corner. Already dressed in a tasteful burgundy pant suit that brought out the green of her eyes and the brassy remnants of the vibrant red hair she once possessed. She faltered when she took in Enid's disheveled appearance.

"Where have you be—"

The words were cut off as Enid threw her arms around her. The smell of her mother's Chanel perfume was a welcome balm to the turmoil inside her. Tears sprang to her eyes, and she blinked them back, not wanting to succumb to her emotions and have to make up an excuse for them.

Her mother patted her back before pulling away gently. Concern filled her eyes. Enid merely smiled reassuringly. Despite the anger they had toward each other most times, and despite the secrets, she still needed her.

"I'll go get ready now," she said softly. Isadora nodded with her own small smile before turning to go. Most likely checking details for a third or possibly fourth time.

Enid eyed the dress laid out on the bench. It was one her mother bought for the honeymoon that never was. She frowned down at it. Split between finding a new one or wearing what her mother wanted. It was only a dress. With a sigh she pulled it on and stepped into the bathroom to do something with her hair. Before long there was a tap at the door.

"Enid, it's me, may I come in," her mother's voice called from the other side.

"Yes!" She dropped her hands from the mass of scarlet waves. Already realizing it was a futile attempt.

Isadora walked into the marble clad bathroom, her eyes running over Enid. No doubt checking off some mental list as she took stock of her appearance.

"I do love how that dress looks on you," she exclaimed before stepping up to help tame Enid's unruly locks.

It was stunning, Enid had to admit. A deep, navy-blue cocktail dress with a cinched waist. The skirt hugged her hips and thighs, flaring slightly above her knees. She still couldn't think about the fact it was meant for her ex. Pretty wrapping paper for his new gift. Enid thrust the thoughts away, a bitter taste at the back of her tongue.

In no time her mother had her hair twisted into a perfect chignon, a faraway look on her face as she gazed at Enid through the mirror.

"I do wish your father was here. Things were so much easier when he was around."

Enid patted her hand. Isadora's eyes came back into focus.

"Come," her mother said, heading for the door. "Our guests will be here shortly."

***

Dinner was, as always, an elegant affair. Each guest tucked into their seat with a sparkling glass of liquid, either amber or ruby—depending on the taste of the drinker. Isadora's best matching silver candelabras stood tall at either end, surrounded by large blooms of fragrant magnolias in low crystal vases. Polished silver shone in the dim light. The crystal glasses were spotless. Their faceted flutes reflecting prisms of rainbowed light around them. A name card on the silver rimmed china plate in front of each chair directed the diner to their assigned position.

Enid was never comfortable at these gatherings. Even less so with the tight bodice forcing her to sit upright in her chair. And her mother's best friend, Meredyth Wallace, eyeing her coldly across the table.

Earlier that evening, as the last arrivals were trickling in, the tall, blonde woman had breezed into the room as if she owned it. A fur shawl wrapped around her shoulders. A prop for the show of revealing a shimmery, golden wrap dress. Her large brown eyes narrowed at the sight of Enid. Mouth pursing as though a bitter taste had entered it.

Isadora had taken her hands, their heads lowering in a private conversation. Meredyth's long, graceful neck arched toward Enid, a hard warning in her eyes. Then she twisted away, fingers grabbing the jacket of a passing friend. Once more the light hearted social butterfly as she chatted animatedly.

The meal was delicious, and gratefully, uneventful. Not a soul brought up the events of her ruined wedding. Her dining neighbor instead filled the conversation with small talk about the community and weather updates for the year. Enid was doing her best to suppress a yawn as the plates were cleared. Guests were already saying their goodbyes.

The ringing of the doorbell caught her alone with the busy staff rushing to clear the table. So, Enid took it upon herself to answer. The click of her heels echoed in the grand marble foyer. She swung the door open with a friendly smile, and froze.

On the front porch, backlit by the flickering glow of the lamplight, was the striking figure of her ex-fiancé. A perfectly tailored, black suit accentuated his broad shoulders. Hair gelled back from his chiseled face. He seemed paler than the last time she had seen him, and somehow more dangerous, deadly. An eerie beauty marking his features. He took her in hungrily, making her fidget with unease. Behind her, the voice of his mother called out.

"Charles, my dear, come in sweetheart!" Meredyth's voice was sweet as honey. Her sophisticated southern accent making her sound warmer than Enid knew her to be.

Charlie looked down at the threshold, the corner of his mouth ticking up in a way that sent a shiver down Enid's spine. His eyes locked onto hers as he took an exaggerated, intentional step onto the marble tile. She backed up, the click of her heels quick. Her spine a rod of steel. Charlie stepped in front of her, close enough she had to look up to make eye contact. She felt her hand being lifted, his eyes dark as they held hers.

"Enid," he murmured, his skin cold as he pressed his lips to the back of her hand. Her heart pounded. Ice flooded her veins.

"You look lovely, as always," he said softly before moving away. Enid remained where she was, her body a statue holding the door.

Meredyth took his arm with a wide smile.

"There's my handsome boy," his mother said, looking at him adoringly. "You've kept us all waitin' so long. Dinner is already over." She was pouting.

The fact that a grown woman acted like a petulant child to get her way always sat wrong with Enid. She didn't try to hide her frown.

"I'm sorry, Momma," Charlie stated, his gaze still on Enid. "I was unavoidably detained."

Something within his face flashed with the promise of violence. Enid's eyes widened, unable to look away. Isadora took that moment to break the tension, gently guiding Enid away from the door and closing it.

"Why don't we go into the drawing room for a night cap," she said, her warm smile directed at Charlie.

"Of course, Mrs. Washbourne," he said, his manner the epitome of poised grace. "And how lovely you look this evenin'."

He stepped forward, drawing her into a brief hug. The position set him close enough to Enid that he was able to run a hand along her waist. His eyes locked onto hers with deadly intent. She flinched. Then he was pulling away, that friendly look on his face as her mother ushered them into the comfort of the drawing room.

Enid had always hated this room. A room so eloquent that children were banned from entering. She spent her childhood outside the door. Small toes reaching out to tap at the lush cream carpet in defiance.

Ornate plaster molding decorated the square façade of the fireplace. Reclaimed cobblestone, the worn edges of the stone perfectly butted together, protected the carpet from the pop of embers. Should any make it past the antique grating perched before the soot-stained opening. Designer, silk wallpaper lined the walls, catching the light of the flickering flames within the hearth. The finest works of art Isadora could find were proudly displayed. The envy of any museum. Enid glanced around, noting the details, taking in the art. Anything to keep from looking at Charlie.

Her mother pulled her down onto one of the antique loveseats sitting opposite each other before the fireplace. Charlie and his mother claimed the other. The silky, white brocade material beneath her, normally a luxurious comfort, only felt strangely cold against her palms.

A maid entered bearing a decanter of wine and four glasses on a tray, which she left on the gleaming coffee table before taking her leave.

Charlie's stare never faltered from Enid. She couldn't bear to meet that intense scrutiny. Her eyes flicked everywhere, avoiding. But no matter where she looked, she was uncomfortably aware of him. The heat in those deep brown orbs pressed into her—filled her with trepidation.

"I believe," Isadora began, her voice firm, "it is time we address the elephant in the room, so to speak."

Enid's already tense body stilled further at the statement. Her jaw clenching with anticipation and dread.

"Of course, Isa dear, you are quite right. I have been hoping we could talk about the unfortunate circumstances involving the wedding for some time." Meredyth's sugary sweet voice was grating to her ears. The other woman once again piggybacking off her mother—as usual. Enid wasn't sure she had an original bone in her body.

"Before we do that, I have something for Enid," Charlie said, the deep baritone of his voice making her shiver with something other than fear. The thought instantly disgusted her. What was that?

He motioned toward an attendant who beckoned to others outside the room. Two people walked in, carrying between them a large, gold frame housing a painting. Enid's breath caught as she took in the masterful work.

Depicted within the gilded frame was a woman dressed in black. The elegant curve of her neck revealed through a veil of golden hair as she leaned toward a black winged figure. An angel reached toward her from the other end of the canvas, his beautiful face twisted with sadness. However, the woman didn't acknowledge his earnest gaze and outstretched hand. So enthralled was she with the shadowy individual who wrapped her in his tumultuous embrace. Instead, she stared up at her dark angel with longing—seemingly unaware of the hand hovering perilously close to her throat. A savage look held her in thrall. While behind her the angel of light reached for her in vain.

Without realizing it, she left the loveseat. Her feet moving of their own accord, drawing her closer to the painting. The attendants set it against a wall and left. The room was quiet. There was only the crackle of the fire as Enid took in the scene before her, riveted.

"What do you think?" Charlie's voice whispered in her ear, close enough his chest grazed against her back. She jerked away, and looked around. They were alone.

Enid glared at him.

"I think the subject is quite telling." Anger fueled her words, but fear subdued her voice.

Charlie chuckled. The sound sinister and forbidding as he moved to stand beside the gilded frame, watching her with dark amusement.

"Dimitri sends his love. The painting is from him." His eyes flashed ominously, a wolf in the dark.

"Dimitri," Enid breathed. Sudden heat thawed the chill she felt earlier. She was nearly dizzy with it.

Charlie's jaw ticked, his hands curling as his eyes furiously moved across her face, not liking what he found. Powerless to keep his volatile temper at bay, he crossed the space between them, arm capturing her waist and yanking her against him—his grip a steel vice. She twisted her face away, unable to meet his fierce scowl.

"I always knew you were a whore."

His voice was low and harsh. Words pressed between gritted teeth, his mouth brushing against the delicate skin of her outer ear.

"And now you've gone and damned me, as well as yourself."

He snapped each word with barely controlled rage. A whimper slipped past her lips. Her heart a hammer in her diaphragm.

"Dimitri will have you. He has set his claim. He will ruin you, and when he has used you up and tossed you aside," Charlie leaned back enough to grab her chin, forcing her to look into his fiery brown eyes, "I will finish the job."

He released her roughly. The thick carpet absorbed the sound of her stumbling.

"Neither you, nor Dimitri can have me," Enid retorted as she righted herself, her voice quivering.

Charlie shook his head, a smirk crossing his lips.

"You don't get it. You can't fight him. He's not human. He is a god. No, he's a devil. And he's had a taste of you. What's more, my precious, beautiful, harlot," Charlie grabbed her face again, his thumb running across her lips, "you've had a taste of him. He's in you now."

She jerked away, his touch repulsive on her heated skin.

"No matter where you go, no matter what you do, he will hunt you. He will find you. And he will own you. And you, sweetheart, you will crave him. You will yearn for him with the heat of a thousand suns. When you come together, you will beg him to devour you, and he will burn you up from the inside out." He glared at her wickedly. "You will be left a ruined, exquisite shell, and I will be there to fill you up again and make you scream."

Enid stared in shock as his smile widened. Two deadly, pointed teeth drew down—fangs, eager for blood. His eyes blazed with hunger. To her surprise, he took a step away, his hands sliding into his pockets moments before the click of heels on the tile right outside the door reached Enid's ears. His neck cracked to the side and a composed mask slipped over that evil expression. Those terrifying teeth tucking behind grim lips.

Isadora ducked her head into the room, a look of hopeful anticipation on her face. Charlie turned toward her mother with an expression full of pain and flashed that straight, white smile that used to make Enid weak in the knees.

"May I use your bathroom, Mrs. Washbourne?"

He sounded defeated, heartbroken.

Isadora drew a hand to her chest with a concerned gasp.

"Of course, Charles dear. You know where it is."

Shoulders slumped in sadness, head bowed in defeat, he left the room. Isadora's sympathetic expression followed as he disappeared around the corner. Then with a heavy sigh, she turned back to Enid.

"He really only wants what is best for you. You should hear how he talks about you. He loves you so much. Can't you give him another chance? I will happily pay for counseling if it will help."

"Mom," Enid choked out, still reeling from what Charlie said, from what she saw. He had changed into something…other. He was like Dimitri, and that woman from the alley.

And he was here. He knew where she was.

Dimitri knew where she was.

She needed to leave immediately, needed to see Vidar.

"Please, Enid? No one is perfect, and he already knows about your… issues. He can help you when I'm no longer here to do it."

Enid had to sit down. So that was the reason her mother pushed Charlie on her so much. He was the backup plan. The one who would hide Enid's mental instability from the world when she no longer could. Enid hid the nausea that rolled through her. Charlie was a monster before, what had he become now.

"Mother, did-did you tell him I was here? Did you invite him here to see me?"

Isadora froze, blinking a few times as she wrung her hands together. "I called him shortly after you got here. I had to tell him. He's been so desperate, and this was a perfect opportunity. Meredyth was already coming tonight as it was."

"I can't stay here," Enid said, fear filling her voice as tears stung at her eyes. "I have to go." She stood on shaky legs.

"Enid, wait," Isadora rushed forward, taking Enid's trembling hands in hers. "Stay tonight. I'll send everyone home. Don't go yet. You just got here." Her eyes shimmered with unshed tears. Enid winced.

"O-okay," she said softly.

"Let me go talk to them, I'll be right back."

Enid watched her walk away, nervous at the thought of her anywhere near Charlie. Who knew what he was capable of? The only reassurance she had was that he would never harm his own mother, and hurting Isadora risked putting his mother in the crosshairs.

Meredyth's loud, outraged voice came from the foyer a few moments later.

"I can't believe this. The nerve! What does she have to say for herself?"

"Merry, please," Isadora crooned, obviously trying to appease her oldest friend.

"NO!" Meredyth shouted, her heels clicking furiously over the marble floors. "No one embarrasses my family the way she did and gets away with it. She made a mockery of my son, of me, of my husband."

Isadora groaned wearily.

"Let me talk with her. She's obviously confused. I can smooth this over."

Meredyth huffed. "I don't know why my Charlie is wasting time on her. He could have anyone, but for some reason I can't fathom, he is set on marrying that disgrace of a girl."

Enid peaked around the door, watching the scene before her as Meredyth waved her manicured talon furiously. She snatched her fur wrap from the nearby attendant, eyes blazing. Charlie strolled down the stairs at that moment, his face a calm mask as he approached his mother. Enid ducked from view, not wanting to draw his attention.

"Have you heard, Charlie? My *best friend is* kicking us out—like rabble!"

"Meredyth," Isadora sighed, "it's not like that."

"Oh, isn't it?! After everything your daughter has put us through!"

Enid slowly peered around again, just enough to see what was happening. Charlie put a hand on his mother's shoulder, turning her to face him.

"Mother, I was just going to suggest we leave. Enid is havin' a hard time with everything, and I think she needs some time to think. I'm afraid I pushed her too far with my sentiments. You know how fragile she is. We must be strong for her."

Her face relaxed. A maternal glow lighting it as she put a hand to his cheek. "You are so thoughtful," she said gently. "You are too good for her."

Enid ground her teeth as she watched Charlie shake his head. He was putting on quite the performance.

"I love her so much," his voice cracked with the threat of tears.

Meredyth pulled him into a motherly hug. Catching her eye over his mother's shoulder, he paused sniffling long enough to give her a wink. With a flash of fangs, he slashed a finger across his neck. The warning was clear. He was going to fucking kill her.

"There, there, my sweet boy. Let's go."

She didn't relax until the door clicked shut behind them. Only then did she wander over to the painting. Drawn to that intense longing between the woman and the dark angel holding her hostage. Somehow, she couldn't help but notice how similarly those features mirrored Dimitri's. She felt like that woman—dread and desire pulling her with equal fervor toward certain doom.

CHAPTER

16

Isadora stood in the doorway of Enid's room, watching her sleep fitfully. Legs thrashing beneath the sheets. She sighed. Recalling so many similar nights when her only child lay in the safety of her bed, fighting her invisible demons. How many times had she stood here like this? How many nights had she prayed to ease her child's pain? Quietly, she stepped back into the hallway, pulling the door shut behind her as soundlessly as possible.

In the darkness of the room, the red eyes of a Mare gleamed. He smiled savagely, two large, tusk-like teeth pointing up from his bottom lip, as the watchful mother stepped out of the room—blanketing him in blissful gloom once again.

Beneath his hairy, squatted body the human girl twisted in vain. He rolled his large head back on his neck, his hands finding purchase on the girl's temples as he sat firmly upon her—holding her in paralysis. She stilled. Such deliciously terrible dreams this woman contained. He could spend hours watching and feasting. But this one was claimed by another much stronger than him.

The foul creature leaned closer, relishing the tension in the girl's face, the way her lips parted sensuously in a silent scream. A thrill rushed through the Mare. He wanted to taste those screams. The temptation was almost too much.

He bent low, hovering over the curve of her lips. His breath escaped in ragged gasps, blowing over her, sending scarlet tendrils of silky hair wafting from her forehead. She whimpered. The Mare groaned, eyes rolling back into his head. The horror, the dread was so strong, so powerful that it vibrated from every pore—ripe fruit to pluck from such a tender tree.

No, he scolded himself.

The Revenant bastard would be after him for taking even a sample. Dimitri was territorial and fierce. Not to mention, his sister would be sure to punish him if her brother was disappointed.

The Mare grumbled in dismay, reaching through her dreams, pulling at the fading link she had to the Revenant. He pushed against it, leading it to the forefront, strengthening the connection—tying it to her dreams, her sleep. It was as simple as knotting a single strand of hair. Tiny and unnoticeable. When the knot was secure, the connection vibrated like a live wire under his touch, firmly seated in her mind. Fed by the nightmare that haunted her, it blossomed and grew.

He regretted letting Lania know he could help the Revenant dream walk. At first it had seemed like a fun way to gorge himself on the terrors they would induce in the fragile human psyche. Especially Lania. She was an artist with blood and terror.

The thought of the Revenant woman made him ache with longing. Her nightmares were pure poetry. A feast of delights. He should have known better. His appetite came at a cost. Here he sat, acting at their command with not even a taste for himself.

In her sleep, the woman ran.

***

Within the shroud of her nightmare, Enid rushed down an ever-lengthening hall. The ground beneath her feet shuddered with the heavy footsteps of cloven hooves close behind.

When she looked over her shoulder, the massive shape of the minotaur bore down on her. Taking a quick turn down another hall, she ran right into the narrow chest of a green creature. Red eyes sparkled with wicked glee.

She screamed.

Rank breath blew along her face as the ghoul laughed maniacally. Spinning away, she ran again until she found an elevator. The button lit up beneath her fingers. A glance back had her shrieking in terror. The monsters were so close. Prowling nearer and nearer as she impatiently banged against the cold metal.

Just as she thought she was going to be overwhelmed, the doors pinged and she fell forward into emptiness. Red eyes glimmered in the dark shaft. Watching as she fell endlessly.

She stopped with a bounce.

Hesitantly, she shifted to her feet. She couldn't see a thing. The only sound was the rustling of the thin, silken fabric around her body, and the light swish of her hair in the howling wind. The cold, hard ground was rough under her bare feet. She strained to hear anything that may tell her if she was truly alone here in the void. Apprehension twisted her stomach. There was a shuffle of movement ahead. A footstep that reached her waiting ears, causing her to draw in a breath.

She'd been here before. He had been here with her. Whispering to her, touching her. Unsure of whether or not to move, trying to deny the eagerness she felt at the thought of him, Enid stood still—waiting, listening.

She was soon rewarded when a deep, throaty chuckle vibrated through the air. Her heart beat wildly. Before she could take a shaky, hesitant step, there was a solid presence in front of her.

Even unable to see, she knew it was him before he reached out and touched her. His hand slowly grazed the skin of her arm leaving a trail of goosebumps, causing her to shiver as he stepped closer. Then there was the solid muscle of his body against the soft, thin fabric of her slip. She felt him lean over her, the gentle whisper of his breath against her ear.

"There you are, my flower."

His breathy, Slavic voice pulled at the cord of desire within her. Full lips grazed the edge of her cheek. She tilted toward him, desperate and aching as she felt the tip of his nose trace a line along her jaw, down her neck, to the crook of her shoulder. Powerful arms held her tight while firm, lingering kisses heated a flame of desire within her core. Tingles of pleasure erupted in their wake. A moan escaped her. Fingers snaked into the soft tresses of her hair, a solid grip holding her steady against the tide of passion.

"Come to me, little one. I need you," he purred. His hand tightened in her hair, the other rubbing small circles against the silk at the curve of her hip.

Enid pressed herself against him. She couldn't fight it anymore, this pull, this need to be near him. Her arms curled around his broad shoulders, and she found herself running her fingers up his neck. Encouraging him to continue as she gave in to the raging desire. A groan rumbled through him, and he was lifting her, his hands guiding her legs around him.

Then, they were falling, her body held flush against his. Her back bounced into the billowy softness of a mattress, forcing a gasp from her. Dimitri lay above her, a muscular arm on either side of her head, illuminated by the soft glow of candlelight. He gazed at her. Desire in his ice blue eyes.

She blushed, realizing he was shirtless, the planes of his body on full display. Heat erupted within her anew as she drank in the sight of him. Openly appraising his body down to where his hips were nestled in the cleft between her legs. He gave her a satisfied smirk.

Strong fingers ran down the side of her neck and over her shoulder, pushing aside the flimsy strap of her silk, purple nightgown. The fabric gave way with little effort, and he dipped forward. Lips tracing the line of her collar bone to the hollow of her neck. His tongue flicked across the beat of her pulse, the pressure thrillingly sweet. She sighed.

Dimitri groaned at the sound, his mouth moving to the peak of her nipple, rolling the hardened bead around his tongue. She arched against him, moaning loudly.

This dream felt so real.

Ecstasy clouded her mind. His heavy body creating delicious friction in all the right places. He gripped her hip, anchoring her in place with a hiss when she bucked against him. Releasing her nipple with a pop, he gazed down at her. She wanted to drown in the blue of his eyes. Need and hunger reflected back at her, but it was the barely contained yearning that was her undoing. Dimitri captured her lips, his tongue dominating hers. Desire fueled urgency that she returned with equal fervor. He reeled back, teeth lengthening as he fixated on the steady beat of the vein at her neck.

Enid froze, her breath catching. Fear doused the flame of passion that had nearly consumed her. His pupils were dilated so that the blue of the iris was barely a ring around them. He stopped short of sinking those teeth into her neck. A hand cupped her face. His thumb brushing over the center of her lips.

"Do not fear me, little one," he breathed.

"You keep saying that," she whispered, her throat suddenly dry, "and yet you chase me in the dark, you trap me against my will, and look at me as though you will drain every drop of blood from my body."

Dimitri's arms flexed as he lowered himself further against her. He rocked his hips, causing her to gasp at the sudden friction.

"You do not enjoy being trapped against me?" he teased.

She shuddered, unable to respond, her body betraying her. He drew back, brows furrowing as he examined her face, fanged teeth vanishing.

"Your beautiful mouth says one thing, my flower, and yet your body tells me another. I do not intend to take you against your will." He sat up on his knees, arms crossing over his muscular chest. Black sweat pants stretched over thick legs.

Enid's dry mouth filled with saliva. She ran the back of her hand over her lips. Praying he didn't notice her almost drooling as she pulled herself up so that she could sit, legs folding to the side. His eyes followed the movement. The muscles in his arm tensed as though he itched to trace his fingers along their length.

"I would have you give yourself to me freely," he grumbled.

"Why?" She found herself questioning, stunned at her own bravado. "So, you can enslave or kill me?"

A menacing growl rumbled at the back of his throat.

"NO," he barked.

"Then why?"

She winced at how desperate and needy she sounded.

"BECAUSE!" he roared. Enid jerked.

"Because," he said softer, his hands raising as if to calm her. "Because I can't stop thinking about you. Because my body begs to be near yours."

His fingertips found the edge of her knee and began to slide slowly up her thigh. Goosebumps erupted in their wake.

"Because I yearn to hear the sound of your voice."

He found the lacy edge of her nightgown, pushing the silk up to her hip as he rocked forward. His other hand finding purchase on the headboard.

"Because nothing can satisfy me until I have you by my side, in my bed, underneath me, around me."

Inching nearer, his tongue darted out to wet his full lips.

"I hunger not for your blood, but to know you, your desires, your dreams, your wishes."

His words fell upon her lips. Each breath mingling with hers as the tip of his nose slid along her cheek. She melted at the sensation, following the movement, wanting to close the distance between them.

"I would grant you whatever you wished, satisfy your every desire, and deliver to you your every dream."

A strong hand pressed at her waist. The air cool against her exposed hip. Her breath caught, body buzzing with the electricity that tingled between them.

"Give yourself to me, and you will know only ecstasy. You will want for nothing. You will be a goddess, and I will spend every waking moment of my being on my knees in servitude to you."

That sensuous mouth drifted above hers, a hair's breadth away. Letting her decide whether or not to close those few millimeters between them. With a moan, she acquiesced, her lips crushing his. His hand moved from her waist to her lower back, drawing her against him. Her thighs wrapped around him tightly. He released the headboard, fingers threading through her hair.

***

Enid shot up with a gasp, heart racing. Relief flooded her when she realized she was alone in her room. She flopped back on her bed, attempting to calm her erratic breathing.

The dreams were getting more intense. Almost real. Her lips felt bruised and swollen like Dimitri had actually been kissing them. She stood, fixing the purple slip that had ridden up her hips in her sleep. It was soaked in sweat. The moon was high, the crescent of it waxing in the night sky through the glass doors.

A notification alert lit up her phone. Vidar had responded to the text she sent earlier in the evening.

Go somewhere safe. Meet me at the diner. Night after next.

Perfect. She was working that night. She sent back a quick confirmation.

The air cooled her heated skin when she stepped out onto her private balcony. The silk of her nightgown absorbed the crisp breeze, helping to further relieve her. A sigh fell from her lips, and she leaned into the slight sting, savoring the smell of decaying leaves and mowed grass. The smell of fall. A raven took flight, its body dark against the star flecked sky.

She should try to get some rest.

Turning to go back inside, she shrieked when she noticed the still figure reclined on the cast iron chair by the small table. Charlie scanned her body, not disguising the fact that he appreciated what he saw.

"Hey darlin'," he drawled. "Havin' any interestin' dreams lately?"

Enid pressed a hand to her chest, attempting to calm the erratic racing of her heart.

"What are you doing here? How did you get on my balcony?"

She took a step toward the door.

Charlie sighed, his elbow resting on the table next to him, his head leaning on a steepled finger.

"I'm not goin' to hurt you," he said. "You, my dear, are. *Off. Limits.*" He twirled his other hand in the air to punctuate the last two words. "I couldn't wring that pretty neck of yours, even if you asked me nicely."

That twirling hand dropped to the leg he had propped on his other knee, giving it a slight squeeze as he eyed her throat thoughtfully.

"You sure do like to talk about it though," Enid replied.

"Well, honey, it's good to have goals," he said, a bitter smile twisting his lips. "A man can dream."

Enid didn't like the crazed look in his eyes.

"And why is it that you suddenly can't hurt me again? I'm *claimed*?"

133

Charlie only stared at her a moment before he spoke again, his patience strained.

"That's what I said. Claimed, taken, appropriated. To be seized."

He stood then, his hands going into his pockets. He was still wearing his suit pants and shirt from earlier, minus the jacket. The buttons were undone part way on his shirt, a bit of chiseled chest peeking between the white fabric. Sleeves rolled up along his forearms.

"Not under any circumstances, even if you begged me, could I touch you. No matter how badly I wanted."

The dark look he gave her had Enid taking another step toward the door. Like he was tempted to test the theory.

"And why would that be?" she asked, still not sure she trusted his declaration.

"Because, Darlin', you had to go off and run away so that I had to go find you, and then we stumbled upon a couple of fucked up, inhuman, sons of bitches. Now, you've been claimed, I'm possessed, and I can't do a damn thing about it. Not unless my new psycho ass girlfriend releases me from her hold, or gives me permission."

"Her hold?"

"Yes, dammit," Charlie said, frustration evident in his voice. He slammed back down in his chair.

"She's in my head. I can't get her out. I hear her, I see her, I smell her. Wherever I am, I itch to get back to her. It's like my whole being craves her. And this woman!" Charlie rolled his eyes. "You thought I was bad, she is a sadist and a masochist all rolled into one hot little body. It's very confusing."

"Okay, then why are you here, Charlie?"

He bit his bottom lip, standing to walk over to her. Enid started to back away again, only to have him snatch her toward him. Hands gripping her biceps roughly.

"I'm here to give you a message. To let you know Dimitri will have you. It will be easier for you if you go willingly to him. He doesn't wish to see you harmed, but he won't ever give up."

Enid whimpered, her arms bruising under his grip. The sound seemed to excite him. His face inched closer.

"There isn't anywhere you can run from Dimitri now," Charlie's voice was a hushed whisper. One hand released her arm, fingers walking along the side of her temple. "All you have to do is fall asleep and he will be there." His pointer finger pressed into the center of her forehead before he let her go, thrusting her away.

She allowed herself to fall back against the rough brick, stunned. Was what she just experienced not a dream? He had been there. Dimitri. He had called her into that void, asked her to come to him willingly. It all felt so real because it was real, and she had given in like a harlot. She closed her eyes, her head against the cool brick. Cursing her stupidity and inexperience with this new, strange world and its creatures.

"Look at you," Charlie said, his eyes greedily raking down her body and back again. "Finally starting to realize how fucked you are."

Enid swallowed thickly, turning her face away from him. He stalked forward, placing a hand on the wall next to her and leaned in close.

"I've never seen you dressed like this before."

His breath tickled her ear. His fingers slid down the strap of her dress, the tips grazing the tops of her breast, hovering along the skin above the fabric. She slapped his hand away.

"I thought you couldn't touch me," she hissed.

He gave her a slow, contemptuous smile.

"I said I couldn't hurt you. And I can't touch you, not really," he said, biting his bottom lip as he looked down at her thin nightgown. "Not like I want to."

He lifted his hand, placing it on the wall on the other side of her, caging her in.

"Now, Darlin', what will it be? Will you come with me so I can deliver you to Dimitri and ease both of our sufferin' or, are you going to continue to be an insolent little bitch and keep makin' us work for it?"

She glared up into his cold, dark eyes.

"Well Charlie, I would hate to disappoint you. I know how much you love when I make you work for it."

Her voice was hard. The thought that he couldn't cause her any actual harm bolstering her.

The look on his face was murderous.

He punched the wall next to her head. The brick crumbled to dust, leaving a crater in the shape of his fist. She let out a squeal. Shrinking away as the broken pieces rained down on her. Not a scratch marred his knuckles.

"I'll be seeing you around, Darlin'," he growled before pushing away. He backed slowly to the railing of the balcony, eyes never leaving hers. In one fluid movement he was over the railing, flinging himself into the air.

Enid rushed forward, looking below for his ruined, crumpled body. Charlie stood on the gravel drive below, pristine as before, staring up at her. He put his hands in his pockets and, whistling a tune, turned and strolled off into the night.

CHAPTER

17

A short flight and a taxi ride the following day had Enid standing in Cindy's apartment. Her dynamic friend pushed her onto the couch, thrust a glass of wine in her hand, and immediately ordered her to open up.

Unable to say much about anything inhuman, Enid told her what she could, glazing over certain things. She told her about her estranged aunt, and her family's history of mental disorder. Though, slightly played down so her friend wouldn't think her to be a lunatic. She told her about the dinner party, and how Charlie was invited. She also mentioned him showing up that night to threaten her. Minus the fact that he was now a freak of nature who could jump from a second story balcony with the ease of descending a step.

"Girl!" Cindy declared after she was finished. Her second glass of wine sloshing perilously close to the rim as she waved her arm around. "I thought you said Charlie was a done deal."

Enid groaned, her head falling against the back of the couch, arm dropping over her face.

"I thought he was," came her muffled reply. She lifted her head, pushing her hair from her face. "I don't know what to do at this point," she mumbled, taking another gulp of wine. The ruby liquid was tart on her tongue. "I need to get that man out of my life once and for all."

Cindy nodded thoughtfully as she looked into her glass. Suddenly, she jerked her head up, her face shining with excitement.

"I don't know why I didn't think about this before! The fine ass man I've been seeing is a cop! I can give him a call and see if he can give us any ideas!" Cindy picked up her phone and began to scroll through her numbers. "Plus, it'll give me an excuse to see him again without looking desperate," she mumbled as she gave Enid a wink.

Enid shook her head, laughing at the thought of her confident, vivacious friend coming off as desperate, and pushed the phone down so she would stop scrolling.

"Don't. I'll think of something. Cops haven't helped so far."

Not to mention, she couldn't involve human authorities. What would she say? Officer, the bogeyman is after me and wants to claim me as his mortal slave? Enid chewed her lip as she considered what else to tell her friend without pulling her into the chaos that was becoming her life. If she knew too much, she could become a target of the fiends that seemed intent on hunting her.

"I think I have someone who can help."

Cindy arched a perfectly tweezed eyebrow at her. "Oh?" she asked, sounding way too intrigued.

Enid nodded. "His name is Vidar. The really attractive guy that comes in and sits at booth three. With the leather jacket and killer gray eyes."

Cindy fanned her face. "Ooh! Mr. Hot and quiet, coffee black, no sugar? Girl, yes! Please tell me you have that man's number and have given him the tour of your secret garden." She batted her eyelashes at Enid.

Face aflame, Enid gasped in feigned shock.

"No! I haven't slept with him. But he's supposed to meet me at the diner tomorrow night. I'm hoping we can talk after my shift."

Cindy wiggled excitedly, bouncing in her seat, wine swirling out of the glass and onto her hands.

"Oh shit," she exclaimed, rushing off to grab a towel.

"Marcus is coming tomorrow too. I can't wait for you to see him," she squealed as she dried the liquid. "I'm going to get my date outfit ready. Make sure you get your beauty sleep tonight. We need to show these men what they are missing in their lives!"

"Vidar is helping me with a stalker, not taking me out," Enid scolded, the blush still flushing her cheeks.

"Maybe it can be both," Cindy said, shaking her hips suggestively.

Her friend's enthusiasm was contagious, and Enid found herself laughing despite the frantic thoughts in her head. If only she were able to enjoy simple pleasures like dating. As attractive as she found Vidar, tomorrow would not be a social meeting.

ACT II

INTO THE UNDERWORLD

CHAPTER

18

Vidar sat in his usual place drinking black coffee. The diner was quieter than usual. Though, from what he heard, people had been avoiding the area lately due to the rising number of attacks. He had been busy elsewhere. The Enforcer was not omnipresent. Normally the threat of his presence was enough to keep the creatures of his realm at bay. That it no longer worked was disturbing. He swallowed down the anger that rose within him and took a sip of his coffee, allowing stillness to settle over him. Once more he made a mental note to speak to the King about a task force.

Despite his relaxed exterior demeanor, he was vigilant. Senses in overdrive as he surveyed the night outside the pane of glass. The traffic was minimal for the normally bustling city. The people all tucked away in the safety of their dwellings, wary of the danger that lurked in the night air like a heavy fog.

Laughter and loud voices came from the direction of the kitchen. A defiant jab at the fear shrouding the neighborhood. Enid was currently finishing up her work for the night. The hint of a smile etched the corner of Vidar's lips as her soft, tinkling laugh drifted through the swinging door. He marveled at her strength, that she still had the ability to find joy despite the horrors she's been subjected to so recently. The thought of taking that happiness from her weighed heavy on him.

Very soon he would be changing her life for good. There was no other way—not one that he could find. He had wrestled with other thoughts, plans, and strategies. He and the King had spent the majority of the night before discussing it at great length. Now he only searched for the words with which to tell her. To ease her into it.

The bell jingled, and someone he never expected to see in this place entered. Thoughts left him, the expression draining from his face as he felt the mask of indifference he normally wore settle over his features. The door swung shut behind the unwelcome patron. Vidar's hand tightened around the mug—the only indication of his irritation. The heat reminding him to keep control of his volatile strength.

The intruder found Vidar quickly, mouth tightening in a line as he shook his head. Amber clashed glares with stormy gray until something in the newcomer's eyes softened as he took the opposite seat in the booth.

"I suppose you know why I am here." His words were clear and concise. His manner polite and businesslike. Straight to the point.

Vidar gritted his teeth, feeling the muscles in his jaw pop tensely as he scowled over the tabletop. The space between the two was thick with tension. Slowly, calmly, Vidar leaned back, lifting his cup as he regarded the other man, searching for any hint of hostility. Despite the tenseness in his shoulders and arms, there seemed to be no indication he meant harm. He wore only a plain black shirt and jeans. Hands in plain view on the table to show that he carried no weapons. Most likely an intentional choice to lower Vidar's guard.

"How about we pretend I don't, and you can inform me of the situation, Marcus."

Vidar brought the cup to his lips and welcomed the steaming liquid down his throat. Never losing sight of the Revenant before him. Marcus frowned. Vidar could tell he did not want to be there. He considered Marcus to be a fair and honorable person, despite being Revenant. His presence could only mean that he was trying to avoid a conflict. One that Vidar would feel obligated to get in the middle of.

Marcus had always been loyal to the King as well as his Queen, but the marriage between the Revenant Queen and the King had changed things. The new High Queen, as she was calling herself amongst the clans, was pushing boundaries. Boundaries which had long been established. Those changes included new laws. Laws that were altering the regulation of the clans. As a Revenant under the Queen's thrall, Marcus was bound to honor them, whether he wanted to or not.

Vidar knew this. He respected it. What he didn't know, was how far the Revenant would have to go, how badly this order needed to be carried out, and to what extent.

Marcus ran a hand over his face, his worry apparent, shoulders slumped with the mental weight they bore.

"I've been commanded as an ambassador of the Revenant clan, to clean up the mess a few of our clansmen have created."

Vidar gave Marcus a cold stare. His guard up.

"A few of your clansmen have been greedy and sloppy. They require enforcement."

Vidar was trying to be careful in his wording. He didn't want to outright defy whatever the Queen's order may be, but he had a job to do, and only certain concessions he was willing to allow.

Marcus remained calm and reasonable as he surveyed the room. "So, you are involving yourself in the matter?" He asked quietly.

Vidar regarded Marcus coolly for a moment before he leaned forward. "Three humans were attacked in the alley right outside. You don't have to be a mind reader to know that. There are eyes everywhere in this city. Then one of those humans was confronted by another fae. The Revenant are not exactly being covert."

Marcus stared unblinkingly back at Vidar. "We had nothing to do with the other fae. But you are correct. There are eyes everywhere, and some of those eyes know that you got in the middle of that attack. I don't think I need to remind you that we have blood rites to this place. We are allowed to hunt freely here." His fingers poked at the table as if driving his point home.

As he spoke, the door swung open. The bell pinged. A tall, willowy figure walked into the diner, looked around the place, and then chose an empty booth on the other side of the restaurant. Vidar registered the arrival with a cursory glance. He didn't want a human sitting too near for this conversation. Too much delicate information was being relayed.

"You are correct, my friend," he began, his tone even, "but, you are over hunting the area. I do think you can see that. The humans are starting to become wary. Look at the street outside. The fear that sharpens the scent of the air. My job is to keep us hidden. To keep the factions in check."

The door opened again, the ringing of the bell a distracting nuisance. Another straggler moving past their booth. Both fae quit talking while the man passed. Bloodshot eyes caught Vidar's and jerked away nervously. Vidar narrowed his eyes, watching until the person was seated a good distance away.

Marcus shifted in his seat, drawing Vidar's attention. "I will not deny that my people have been a little…zealous lately. I will speak with our Queen about it. The new laws have caused some…confusion."

A couple entered. The bell noting their arrival. A man and woman, pale and unkempt. Vidar couldn't help but watch as they whispered to each other. The woman's eyes met his and widened before she looked away, pulling the man over to an empty booth. He glanced around, his intuition thrumming to attention. It was rather late for it to get busy. Cindy and Enid rushed from the kitchen. Each going to opposite sides of the diner to take care of the last-minute customers.

"There tend to be growing pains during such times," Marcus was saying. Cindy walked up then, her face aglow with delight.

"Hey sugar!" She said to Marcus as she refilled Vidar's cup. "I didn't expect you until later."

A bright smile flashed across Marcus's face as he gazed up at her. Vidar could read the adoration there. That smile dimmed as Marcus glanced at Vidar.

"My shift ended earlier than expected," he explained. "You think I can get a cup of coffee while I wait?"

The bell jingled, another person slouching into a seat. Vidar registered the sound with irritation. Cindy nodded toward Enid who rushed over to the newcomer, notepad at the ready, before turning back to Marcus, her smile never wavering.

"Be right back with that!" She patted his arm affectionately before giving him a wink and sashaying away. Marcus's stare followed her for a moment before he glared around the room and turned back to Vidar.

Vidar looked at the Revenant questioningly. "Are you here on behalf of your clan, or to clarify why you appear to be hunting here. In the very place that has already drawn so much scrutiny."

Marcus's face grew hard. "I'm not hunting," he grumbled. "I have petitioned for a mate."

He said the words so softly that Vidar was almost certain he had misheard.

"A mate?"

If a Revenant could blush, Vidar was certain that Marcus's face would have reddened, even with his ebony complexion.

"As you know, I have been alone for centuries now. With our...longevity, it's no easy thing to find someone worthy of spending a near eternity with." His eyes drifted toward Cindy, her curls bobbing around her face as she rushed around dropping off drinks. "Not that it's any of your business."

Vidar lifted his hands in surrender. "I wouldn't dream of coming between you. My regard is for those who break the laws."

"Our laws, or your laws?"

Vidar tensed. "What do you mean by that, Marcus?"

The bell clanged. Another patron drifted in. Vidar glared at the swinging brass above the door. Cindy dropped off a steaming mug of coffee before rushing off. Vidar's gaze shifted around the room as it continued to fill up despite the late hour. He shifted. Something felt off.

"I mean that you halted a legal hunt. I mean that you interfered with a human who has knowledge of our existence. An existence that could be in peril if humans were actually aware and believed in it. But I'm not here to tell you how to do your job." Marcus picked up the mug, leaning back into his seat. "What I am here to tell you is to let us handle it. Dimitri won't drop it, and neither will the Queen." He took a sip of the steaming liquid before placing the mug on the table. His long fingers fiddling with the handle as he continued. "The truth of the matter is, he got into her head, but somehow, this girl got into his too."

The door rang again, another late-night diner. Vidar winced. He was going to rip that damn bell off the wall. He couldn't concentrate. The newcomer made direct eye contact with Vidar. A smirk upon his thin mouth. A fang glistening in the fluorescent light. Vidar growled, a short, deep rumble from the base of his diaphragm.

"Explain." His patience was running out. Even as he spoke to Marcus, his glower was locked on the newly arrived Revenant.

"You can't keep her from this. It's already gone too far. The Queen won't have...turbulence among her people. She will do what it takes to make sure this girl bows down to her. To keep her grasp upon us all."

Marcus glanced about before lowering his voice so that Vidar had to strain to hear. "Something is off, things are not as they seem with her."

Marcus slid his mug away, resting it at the end of the table. Vidar followed the movement.

"From what I understand, there are two humans in this establishment who are now considered loose ends. Loose ends that you, the Enforcer, knew about. Yet it is us that you hunt," Marcus continued, his voice slightly louder now.

Loud enough for fae hearing at least.

Vidar raised a brow at the strange display. As if the Revenant across from him was putting on a show. Marcus lay an arm along the back of the booth. Staring at him with cool indifference.

"So, whose interpretation of the laws are you following, Vidar? Are you enforcing for the good of the fae, or do your loyalties lie with these humans?"

Enid was rushing away from one of the tables, her green eyes on the notepad before her. Small pieces of her scarlet hair fell from her braid as she hastened along. No one else was looking at her. The diner was strangely quiet despite the crowd.

Vidar noticed with a start that every eye in the place was on him.

Marcus continued to regard him, a hint of a warning in his eyes. Vidar's attention drifted back to Enid. She lifted her head. Her eyes met his as the door opened, the bell chiming once more. Her head turned in greeting.

Suddenly, she halted, hands dropping to her sides. The notepad fell to the floor. Vidar felt like everything slowed as he followed the direction of her stare.

Dimitri stood there. Eyes only for Enid.

Vidar could see the intensity in his profile, as though nothing but the petite redhead before him existed. Behind him, Lania grinned widely. Her eyes moved around the room, hand looped in the arm of a bulky, blond man Vidar didn't recognize.

He realized everyone in the diner except the staff, was a Revenant. As he sat, distracted by Marcus, they had been stacking the deck in their favor. Vidar leaned back in his seat, his hands moving away from his coffee to the edge of the table. Marcus gave him an apologetic look.

"I am sorry for this, my friend."

At the slightest tensing of Marcus's muscles, Vidar sprang to action. His grip on the table tightened and he slammed it forward. Pushing it firmly against the Revenant across from him, caging him in the seat.

All of the Revenant moved at once, as though given some sort of signal. Several of them darted into the kitchen through the swinging door. Yelling and growling erupted from within. Through the kitchen window a splash of blood paint the wall red. Most of the Revenant converged on Vidar, the bloodthirsty creatures slashing and kicking. He swung at the nearest, sending the Revenant flying into a wall.

Cindy screamed as one hopped over the counter, grabbing her. Marcus roared, rushing to her side in a blur to shove the Revenant away. Dimitri was in front of Enid now, her hand in his, the other stroking her hair affectionately. Her green eyes were glazed and unfocused, her cheeks bright pink. Fury twisted his gut at the sight of her, so vulnerable to the leech's influence.

The Revenant all jumped him at the same time. One wrapping around his neck. Others gripped his arms to keep him from swinging. He felt the sting of fangs in his neck and biceps. Two more rushed over as he struggled against their hold. Through the tangle of bodies, he watched Marcus leave with Cindy. Her body held close against him as she lay unconscious in his arms. Lania whispered something in her brother's ear and he glanced toward Vidar. Amusement glinted in his eye.

Dimitri bit his lip, drawing his own blood.

Feeling utterly helpless, Vidar thrashed against the Revenant holding him as he witnessed Dimitri lean into Enid, pressing his lips to hers. Forcing that trance inducing liquid into her mouth. He roared, his control balancing on a knife's edge. The Revenant on his right arm was tossed away like a ragdoll as the white-hot rage fed his strength. His hand reached back to tear another away. Focus solely on the woman he had come to protect.

Eyes rolling back into her head, Enid's legs gave way. Dimitri scooped her up, cradling her against him. With one last smug look toward Vidar, he ducked out the door.

Vidar snapped the neck of the Revenant trying to keep his left arm immobile, using his thin, limp body to send a female flying across the room. He started for the door, only for two more Revenant to fling themselves in his way before he could take three steps. Lania blew him a kiss as she followed her brother out. The blond-haired one didn't bother to look in his direction. His expression impassive.

The fury he felt multiplied by magnitudes, becoming a devil on his shoulder. Vidar gritted his teeth. He felt it boiling over with dangerous ferocity, and for the first time in centuries he let it. Without a thought, he reacted. His hands snapping out to grip whatever part of a Revenant body was in his way. Arms were pulled from sockets. Heads twisted from shoulders. Bones snapped like dry twigs.

When he came back to himself, he stood in the middle of the diner. Blood blanketing the walls. A window was busted open with a Revenant body hanging impaled on the glass. A severed arm was in his hands. The mass of body parts lay at his feet like a puzzle of gore. Sirens blared in the distance.

"Fuck," he rumbled, letting the arm fall from his hands into the pile.

Calmly, he moved into the back of the diner. The kitchen was covered in blood. The bodies of the cooks lay across the tiled floor and stainless-steel counters. A door to a small room with a desk and computer hung open. An older woman slouched in a chair, her throat ripped out. The security system merely bits of wire and metal scattered across the desk, monitors smashed.

With nothing to do for anyone here, Vidar stepped out the back door, into the adjoining alley. Red and blue flashing lights reflected in the distance. As quickly and silently as possible, he jumped onto a dumpster and pulled himself up a fire escape, climbing effortlessly to the top of the building. From there, he made his way along the rooftops as far from the diner as possible.

The Revenant would pay for this. He would make sure of it.

CHAPTER

19

When Enid came to, she found herself walking in the middle of a dark forest. The sounds of night chirped and sang. Bugs and birds, and the high croaking chorus of frogs. The rustle of unknown creatures within the brush somehow felt welcoming instead of frightening. Or could it be that she walked with a far more dangerous predator? One that kept even the mountain lions and bears at bay.

Despite the fact that she should be scared, she wasn't.

Where was she? No idea.

How did she get there? Not a clue.

What she was sure of, the only thing that mattered, was that she followed someone who needed her. Someone she, herself, needed in return. Dimitri.

He had come for her. Whispered his desires as he pulled her to him. Strong arms encasing her in comfort and safety. His lips had been firm and sweet. The depth of his demand clear as he kissed her. His tongue tangling with hers in a warm, sensual dance. They would finally be together. No one would tear them apart.

Yes, she had whispered.

Forever, she moaned as he ran his fingers through her hair.

They had driven for so long. She couldn't remember where from. The name of that place evaded her. For a moment her thoughts went back there. Someone waited for her.

Weren't they? She couldn't recall.

What was she doing?

Her brain felt foggy. She stumbled over a root, and nearly lost her footing. Strong arms caught her. Someone's hand held hers. Confused, she looked up into the face of the man keeping her upright. Dimitri.

"Careful, my flower," he purred, his hand caressing her cheek.

The blue of his vibrant eyes reflected in the hues of his raven hair in the moonlight. He was a beautiful god, dark and cold. Where did he come from? She looked around, fear and uncertainty worming their way into the back of her head.

"She is shaking off the thrall, my brother," a woman chuckled. Lania, that had been her name. There were others with them. A group. Her head felt so fuzzy.

Dimitri continued to stroke her cheek.

"My flower," he hummed to Enid. Her heart quickened as she lifted her face toward him. "Kiss me again. Show me how much your heart yearns for me, as mine yearns for you." He bit his lip.

Enid marveled at how red they were, as though stained with the juices of cherries. She reached for him, her hands curling around his neck, her lips parting as she eagerly answered his request.

His strong arms lifted her to him, pressing her firmly against his solid chest. He did taste of cherries, of honey, of the sweetest nectar that ever passed her lips. Whatever he asked she would grant. Whatever he desired she would become. His large hand on the back of her head, holding her firmly in place felt so right.

With a moan she deepened the kiss, savoring the feel of his lips, soft and demanding. The way his tongue swirled along hers, teasing and tasting. She returned the fervor, exploring him, tasting him with more passion than she'd ever felt.

She whimpered as he pulled away, setting her back onto the ground. Did she do something wrong? Was he displeased with her? She would do better. Frantically she reached for him again, her breath quick with need.

"Not yet, my love," he whispered, his forehead against hers. He peppered kisses along her cheek to her neck in a trail that felt like a low flame against her skin. He groaned deeply as his mouth lingered on the throbbing pulse that beat there in time to her racing heart. "Soon."

The trees around them stretched up into darkness, nearly blotting out the moon and stars, as he lured her further into the forest. A raven landed on a branch above her, its cry loud and mocking when her face turned its way. Dimitri pressed her on. She followed him, eager and needy.

Before long they began to climb. Up and up, high into the sky. Above the towering trees. The small path undefined beneath their feet. She knew only that she needed to follow. It was what he wanted, and she happily complied. She was a kite, pulled along by the string of his wants and desires. Only by fulfilling his every wish could she be happy. Lifted into bliss by the glory of his approval.

They walked for hours. Steadily, it became colder. She began to shiver uncontrollably, feet and legs burning with fatigue. Why had she come up here, to this strange wood in the middle of nowhere? She peeked over the edge of the mountain. The wind whistled around her. She was afraid. Someone called out from up ahead, and Dimitri turned her to look at him.

"Whatever happens, my flower, you must remain by my side. Do not wander, do not even look at another being. There are many in this place who would try to take you from me."

Enid was bewildered. What place?

He leaned into her, the smell of him pleasant. She took a deep breath. He smelled of frankincense, of some exotic spice she couldn't place. It was heavy and seductive. He rewarded her with a slow smile.

"You are about to see a world shown only to a chosen few. It is a world of magic and wonder. A world where you and I will live forever young and strong for all of eternity. We will be part of a wondrous family, free to love each other, to pleasure each other, for all of time. It is my gift to you."

She swayed.

It was so cold. She was on a mountain. Why was she on a mountain in this thin, cotton shirt, without a coat? When did she leave the diner? Vidar would be worried.

She was pressed onward, Dimitri urging her to follow. Hesitance slowed her steps, but he was persistent. Soon a cliff loomed before them. Vines laced the craggy rock surface. Shivering, Enid was led to where they converged into a thick sheet of leaves and stem.

Dimitri disappeared beneath the mass of greenery. His hand still gripped hers. With a tug, she was pulled through. The vines were lighter than they seemed, sliding along her arms easily.

Heat touched her chilled skin. She was standing in a tunnel carved into the earth and rock. Bare roots broke through the dirt, hanging about their heads. The only sound was the whisper of the wind outside the green curtain at her back.

Dimitri guided her on, deeper into the tunnel where she could no longer see. Her breath hitched. The others chuckled as they led the way, obviously unconcerned. Dimitri soothed her with soft whispers, his arm around her shoulders, his scent comforting her.

Further in, the ground began to tilt beneath her feet. She felt as though she might faint. She shouldn't be here, couldn't be here. This was wrong. Wrong. She fought. Struggling against the grip that pulled her onward into the place she couldn't go. The earth rolled and tumbled.

"I know," Dimitri whispered, "it will pass."

The suffocating feeling of panic nearly made her numb with fright. The horror of her situation sent dizzying waves of anxiety through her. Her muscles seized. She couldn't go on. Planting her feet, she refused to take another step. Air burned in her lungs as she hyperventilated. Sucking in deep, gasping breaths that did nothing to soothe her.

Vaguely, she felt Dimitri scoop her into his arms. Carrying her into the dank earth while she struggled against him. Then, like a bubble popping, she felt herself break through the thick aura of hysteria. Her body relaxed. Relief flooded her. Dimitri pressed a kiss to her head before he placed her on her feet. The ground nothing more than rock beneath her once more.

"Stay close," he said. She nodded, fear and apprehension keeping her obedient.

The quiet of the outside was a misleading introduction to the melodious mayhem that soon reached Enid's ears as they moved further into the corridor. The musical sounds of pipes, strings, and drums reverberated amongst the clamor of voices.

Stepping out of the tunnel she audibly gasped. The cavernous area before her was larger than she could have imagined. Larger, even, than the mountain seemed it could safely hold. Dimitri's eyes crinkled at the corners as he smiled. Joy lighting up his face at her reaction.

They stood upon a ledge of stone that corkscrewed its way around the walls of the enormous complex, winding downward. The ground far below, several turns of the walkway down, was crowded. Filled with covered booths and tables. Creatures walked dim paths. The shadows broken only by the soft, sporadic twinkle of light.

Though subdued, the light was surprisingly plentiful. Lanterns hung from vines and trees that magically grew and thrived without the aid of sunlight. The luminescence within the hanging orbs and pendants was magical, flickering brightly. But, not from flame. Instead, tiny lights sparkled and danced like fireflies fluttering in the glass membranes.

Many more doorways littered the walkway as it spiraled down. Dark mouths hinting at a vast network of tunnels. Between them, large niches were set into the stone walls, in which shops were housed with creatures haggling and bartering over goods and food.

Wooden platforms thrust off the edge of the walkway over the open air. Some had rope pulleys connecting them on which baskets and buckets were hung and pulled up and down or, back and forth across the chasm. Many were lined with tables and chairs for eating, drinking, and conversing. Some held more creatures distributing wares, or playing odd sounding instruments. A few platforms moved up and down the vast abyss on ropes. Primitive elevators for those without wings.

But it was the creatures with wings that had her stopping to stare. Big, beautiful butterfly wings, wings like birds, dragonfly wings. Wings of so many colors and shapes. The creatures fluttered along, slowing only long enough to give her curious looks before flitting away. Large and small, creatures of all shapes and sizes.

Above it all a large clock hung, ornately carved with flowers and vines. And on its face, where the hands of the clock punctuated the time, a large smiling moon danced across, moving in time to the rhythmic ticking. On the opposite side a blazing sun perpetually chased it. Dimitri's hand found her lower back, pressing her forward.

The thick, floral fragrance of jasmine, wisteria, and gardenia filled the space. Laced with the heavy scent of spices and roasting meat. She inhaled deeply as the smells of cinnamon, bergamot, curry, and garlic wafted from a nearby oven built in the back wall of a niche. Flames sparked as a large creature with horns tended a turning spit of meat that dripped juices onto the sizzling coals. Her mouth watered.

From other stands more heavy, musky scents like frankincense and sandalwood lingered, as thick as the music that drifted in the air. Enid was in sensory overload. Never in her wildest dreams did she imagine a place like this existed.

As they walked along, creatures gave them open, curious looks. Many looked human at first glance, but a second look proved otherwise. Their eyes shimmered, reflecting in the low light like a cat's, like Dimitri's and Lania's. Sharp fangs, or pointed ears peeked out here and there. Then there were the creatures that were very much not human. Some had small, bent shapes with large eyes, and ears. Some with horns or tusks. There were some that were terrifying, and some that were terrifyingly beautiful.

This was the other world Vidar had warned her about. A great, vast, mysterious underworld. The thought of him sent a flash of guilt through her. She remembered. They were to meet after her shift at the diner to talk about the Revenant and Charlie, and the Shadow man. Only, the Revenant had gotten to her first. Enid edged away from Dimitri a bit as she continued to look around at the strangeness of this place.

They passed under the branches of a tree perched on the edge of the walkway, growing right through the large blocks of stone. Delicate limbs shivered above her head. No lights hung from this tree. Instead, strange pink flowers bloomed in clusters among the silvery leaves. As she hesitated, gazing in wonder at the unusual blossoms, the smooth, papery trunk shifted. A beautiful face peered out at her with a smile before melting back into the tree. Enid's mouth dropped open as Dimitri pulled her along. The astonishing sights continued and she took it all in—wide eyed with wonder.

She watched in awe as two stunning women strolled by. Both had cloaks of soft fur draped over their curvaceous bodies. They were eerily the same. Same face. Same body. But one had pale, luminous skin with long, shimmering hair as white as the moon. The other velvet, ebony skin with silky, black hair cascading to her lower back. Their eyes were the same. Large, dark, and beautiful.

Enid felt herself drawn to them like a fish on a hook when they glanced in her direction, reeling her in. She shifted toward them. Her body answering a call beyond her will.

Dimitri grabbed her arm, jerking her to a stop. Enid stumbled, the spell broken. The women gave twin smirks and a slight tilt of their heads toward her captor as they continued. Not even the slightest hesitation in their movements. Hips swinging alluringly.

Holding her closer to him, Dimitri leaned over her protectively. "Do not look anyone in the eye," he breathed in warning, his lips close to her ear so only she could hear. She was trembling. All the possibilities of what could have happened flashing through her mind. Unable to form words, she merely nodded her head.

They continued down the spiral pathway. This time she stayed much closer to Dimitri, her eyes lowered. Behind them, Lania laughed darkly. She murmured something incoherent. The other Revenant burst into laughter. Enid couldn't help the flush of embarrassment.

The crowd thickened. Creatures who had begun to take much closer notice of them were now whispering amongst themselves. Pointing as they went by. Dimitri did not seem to notice the glances, gestures, or the whispers. He moved confidently, with purpose. Until, suddenly alert, he stopped. His focus drawn forward along the wide, winding path.

Enid glanced around, avoiding eye contact with the creatures who leered at her. The crowd parted around them, continuing on their way like a stream around a boulder. On a hanging platform to their left fae stared openly, enjoying mugs of a yellow-colored drink. Their attention no longer on their own conversations, but on the entertainment the small group was about to provide.

Emerging from the throng of people, five heavily armed individuals materialized. There was a commanding presence about them. Each in the same black tactical pants and long-sleeved shirts with heavily padded vests. Here and there, weapons of different types were strapped to legs, waists, and backs. Everything from knives, to guns, a few swords and an axe. One man even had a bow with a quiver strapped across his back.

They could have easily been a human special ops group. With the exception of the otherworldly glimmer in their eyes, the variation of weaponry and, not to mention, the sharpened teeth and claws a few seemed to possess.

Enid held still as the men surrounded the Revenant in a loose half circle. Dimitri pressed her behind him. Her heart felt like it was going to spring from her chest. She squeezed her hands into fists and licked her lips nervously as a few of them eyed her openly.

The leader of the group stood in front of Dimitri, a slight frown on his face. His dark hair was short and slicked back. Shaved on the sides where intricate tattoos trailed down his neck and beneath his shirt. His piercing, honey-yellow eyes never wavered from Dimitri's face as they stood assessing one another.

"Dimitri," the man finally spoke in a deep, guttural voice. "We have been sent to detain you, and your…friend. The King demands to see you both immediately."

Dimitri shrugged his shoulders nonchalantly, and glanced back at Enid.

"You should be speaking to my Queen. I applied for, and gained consent before I confiscated the woman. My claim is valid."

The leader's eyes shifted to Enid, giving her a once over. Enid stepped closer to Dimitri, and gasped when she bumped into his solid frame, bouncing off of his hard body. A few of the King's guards and some of the Revenant in their own group gave small chuckles before effectively dismissing her. Their attention on the more dangerous creatures.

159

"King Fenri is aware of your situation and has asked to see you. We will escort you." The guardsman looked around at the others before giving a nod of his head. They scattered, clearing the crowd away as they surrounded the group of Revenant.

Enid glanced at Dimitri who clenched his jaw. Looking around at each of them in turn as though assessing his odds. They stepped in closer, herding the Revenant in tight. Dimitri must have decided to relent, because when their leader gave a brief nod, they followed. The guards ushered the Revenant between them through one of the doors.

The tunnel took many turns, and branched off in several directions. Enid was hopelessly lost in the maze of them. The only thing she could tell was that they were moving deeper into the heart of the hive-like complex.

Before long, they came upon a large rectangular room with a vaulted ceiling. Shimmering orb lanterns hung at different heights all over like scattered stars. A row of sconces lined the walls, flickering with smokeless flames that gave off a warm, comfortable heat. At the far end of the room a dais contained a large, white, marble throne. It looked strangely out of place among the natural gray, brown, and blue granite that seemed to make up the caverns and tunnels around them.

They were herded into the middle of the space. A couple of the guards peeled from formation to take up position on either side of the entrance. The rest stayed in a loose circle around Enid and the Revenant. The leader stepped up on the dais and disappeared behind the throne. There was a loud knock against wood, followed by a clicking sound, and the slight squeak of a door opening.

Vidar stepped out. His gray eyes narrowed angrily at Dimitri. Enid drew in a sharp breath. She barely had time to take him in completely before another figure emerged.

He was a small man. Not small by normal means, but small in comparison to Vidar. More guards filtered out behind him as he stepped into the room forming a protective barrier of bristling teeth, cold weaponry, and black tactical apparel.

Even without the security, there was something dangerous about this man. Enid assumed he was the King when he sat upon the cushioned marble throne. Hard, steel eyes cold against his tan skin and thick brown hair. His whole persona radiated aloofness, and arrogance. He was still as he observed them, his body tense. It made the smile on his face appear unnatural and harsh within the bushy confines of his scruffy beard. Like a wolf baring its teeth. A predator, through and through.

Vidar stood at his left. His expression briefly softened as his eyes turned to Enid, roving along her as though attempting to account for any harm done. Dimitri shifted in front of her, blocking their sight of one another. His cold stare a challenge. Enid leaned around him, the sight of Vidar helping to sooth her scattered nerves. He was obviously angry. The muscle in his jaw ticked, his eyes bled to black as he returned Dimitri's hard look. Openly accepting the challenge within.

The King glanced at the large, brooding man, observing the tension, before turning back toward Enid. He stood from his throne, forgoing the stairs on either side, and hopped straight off the dais with surprising agility.

As he moved, his guards gathered alongside him, collecting themselves at his flanks as he stalked forward. Vidar followed suit, his large hands clenched into fists at his sides. The King stopped in front of Dimitri, jerking his head to the side. After a moment of hesitation, and a dark glare from the King, lip lifted in a warning sneer, he stepped aside.

Enid felt so small standing there alone.

"Is this the one all the trouble has been about?" The King asked, scrutinizing her like an insect as he spoke.

She looked up at him cautiously through her lashes. Careful not to make eye contact. He didn't appear to have the same worry. His countenance hard, eyes cold. She glanced away, her skin itching unnervingly under his consideration.

He chuckled as he circled her. She felt him lift a lock of hair before dropping it. Nervously, she shrunk away from the touch as he moved, taking inventory as he went. She gasped when he leaned in close, inhaling deeply, as though purposefully taking in her scent.

Dimitri growled.

Instantly, one of the guards had a knife at his neck. A firm grip on his shoulder. Dimitri swallowed thickly, relaxing back from the knife. His gaze still intent upon Enid as she remained under the King's scrutiny. King Fenri stopped beside her. She had to keep herself from flinching away when his arm grazed hers.

"You are certain she is as important as you say?" came the low rumble of the King's voice. Despite her fear, she risked a look. What on earth could he be talking about? His attention remained locked on Vidar.

"I swear it on my father's name, my King," came Vidar's reply.

Now it was her turn to stare at him skeptically. His expression was full of some emotion she couldn't quite read. It pulled at her heart, creating an ache within her. When he met her confused look, he only offered a small smile. The black blanketing his eyes faded to show the beautiful gray beneath.

Dimitri looked scared. Gone was the arrogance he carried himself with earlier. Pain lanced his expression and he winced away from the biting edge of the knife, having leaned too far in an attempt to reach for Enid. He resigned himself to remaining still.

"And you wish to claim this human as part of your clan?"

A snarl erupted from Dimitri's mouth at that statement, the knife edge drawing a bead of blood at his throat. The King glared at him in reproach.

"I do, your Highness," came Vidar's reply. Those gray eyes held Enid captive as he spoke over Dimitri's outburst. Seeking permission and asking for forgiveness. Enid was breathless with the weight that settled over her. It was as though this moment was a turning point in her life. A path she did not foresee stretching forward into an unknown future. Significant.

"I do believe a claim has already been issued for this woman," came a soft, feminine voice.

The guards in front of the doorway melted away from the opening with a bow as a woman strode into the room radiating power and confidence. A pure white cloak of fur over her shoulders and silky white dress. Radiant ebony skin glistened in the soft light, a beautifully stark contrast to her clothing. Deep onyx eyes held a warmth that comforted Enid. She found herself returning the smile that adorned the woman's full lips. Her

162

attention turned from Enid, her head lifting regally as she faced the King.

"Husband," she said with a slight dip of her head.

"Hello, *dear wife*," the King replied. A hard, slightly sarcastic tone accompanying the sentiment.

The Queen's eyes narrowed incrementally before she turned to Dimitri. A line of blood made its way slowly down his neck. The knife pressed so tightly that a sniffle would embed it deep within his bleeding throat.

"Now that's not necessary," she said. Her voice was soft, her expression unconcerned as she looked to her husband.

He flashed her a razor-edged smile.

"It would appear that my guard believes it is."

He stepped closer to the ebony goddess, his hands behind his back. She didn't give any ground, holding her space as he moved so close that his barrel of a chest grazed against her. Her eyes never wavered from his, never backed down.

"Of course, now that you are here, I am sure my Queen is quite capable of handling her Revenant."

A slow smile played upon the Queen's lips before her face inched closer to his.

"Of course, my King," she breathed, her lips nearly brushing his.

From where she stood, Enid could see the way his hands clenched at the movement. It was the only indication he gave that the woman had any effect on him. She stepped back from her husband and walked over to Dimitri. A hand reaching out to touch his arm.

"Dimitri, you won't cause any problems for our King, will you?"

The knife at his throat released a fraction, enough for him to talk. His thick Slavic accent was a rasp as he spoke.

"I would not dream of it, my Queen."

"There," she said with a radiant smile. The King nodded, and the guard released him, backing away. Dimitri pressed a hand to his bloody neck. Glaring at the blood that came away on his fingers even as the wound sealed shut.

"Now what is all of this about the Enforcer claiming this woman. I expected her with Dimitri for the rebirth ceremony in my quarters."

The King shrugged his shoulders. His smile nearly a snarl on his rugged face.

"It would appear there is another claim that your Revenant was not aware of. As my Enforcer tends to be…prudent about such things, I thought it necessary to hear him out."

"Is that so?" The Queen said, head tilting to the side as she looked over at Vidar. "And what does your attack dog have to say on the matter?"

She sneered before turning the same fierce look on the King. For the first time since the beautiful woman walked into the room Enid felt a flash of disdain for her. Vidar didn't take notice of the jab, remaining unexpressive. The King, however, did not seem pleased by the comment.

The smile on his face widened savagely.

"Now dear," he retorted, "you know I'm capable of being my own attack dog."

His eyes flashed menacingly as he snapped his teeth toward her. Enid shivered, attempting to control the fear that snaked down her spine. The King truly looked like a wolf in sheep's clothing. The human figure merely a cover for the creature beneath.

The Queen didn't falter.

"The Enforcer is not allowed to interfere in a claim. Yet tonight when my children went to retrieve the intended, several of them were slaughtered. I had to have one taken from a morgue before humans discovered what he truly was. He shouldn't be rewarded with this woman. He should be punished." She hissed her fury into her husband's face.

"Vidar has learned that the woman has Fae blood." The King's face morphed into a mask of indifference.

Everything went quiet. Enid's eyebrow shot up. The Queen walked over, her black orbs staring into Enid's green ones as though searching for something.

"A witch? You are sure?"

"She has the scent," the King murmured. "It is faint, but it is there."

The Queen backed away, flapping a hand in dismissal. "It is of no consequence. She is still human. A drop of Fae blood means little."

"It is of consequence, because that little drop of blood gives her the rights and liberties available to all fae. Should the bid for refuge be accepted. Vidar has already asked for the claim to be validated. I can't ignore it now. The woman shall have the choice."

"She has chosen."

"Has she?" The King asked.

The Queen turned to Enid at this point. "Tell them. Tell them you have chosen Dimitri."

Enid started at being addressed directly for the first time since she got here. "Um," she seemed to have a hard time finding her voice. "I wasn't given much of an option."

The Queen lifted her chin as she turned hardened eyes to Dimitri. He swallowed thickly.

"I just needed more time, my Queen." He seemed to physically shrink under her withering gaze. "I maintain the claim. We have shared blood. I followed all the correct requirements. She followed willingly."

"Under thrall," Vidar muttered.

Dimitri hissed. The Enforcer took a step in the Revenant's direction. Only the King's hand on his shoulder stopped him.

"The woman is here now. She is part of this world, whether it was forced or not," the King stated.

"As such," the Queen interrupted, "she will need a protector. This world is not safe for one as frail as her. Which is why she should be allowed to be claimed by Dimitri as intended."

"And we should reward the Revenant for bringing the human here under thrall? With no warning or choice in what she would be losing?"

"What, exactly, do you mean by that?" Enid cut in.

The Queen's dark gaze turned to her. "It means that you will no longer have any part in the human realm. You will live and abide by the rules and laws of the Fae. This city will be your only home for the rest of your life."

"I could never go home again?"

"Never," the Queen whispered darkly.

Vidar cleared his throat, his voice gentle. "It means that while you could visit the human world, it wouldn't be your home anymore. There are certain laws the Fae live by and secrecy is our biggest one. What you should know, Enid, is that the only other option left to you is death." His eyes pleaded as they burned into hers. "The only reason the Fae have survived this long is because we have remained hidden. The Revenant knew that when they kidnapped you."

Vidar turned a hateful glare on the Queen. "Stop playing with her emotions. You took her choices from her when you brought her here."

"You dare speak to me this way. I am your Queen." Venom dripped from her words as she spat them.

"He does speak the truth," the King interjected. "The girl wasn't going to be able to leave the second she stepped foot in this city."

The Queen gave a graceful shrug of her shoulders. "I am only letting the child know what is in store for her."

"What will happen to me now? What will my life be like?" A tear slipped down Enid's face. She rubbed it away.

The King stepped closer, surprisingly gentle as he tilted her face up. "This is no consolation for what you have lost, but I can promise that you will be treated with the same respect and freedom as any of my people. You will have the support of myself and my dignitaries in your quest to find your place in this realm."

He let go of her, his hands clasped behind his back again, his voice stern as though speaking to a child. "What I can't promise you, is safety from some of the other creatures who call this place home. It is a dangerous place for someone unprepared and so frequently used as a food source. Which is why a claiming is necessary for humans. You will need a protector, someone who is capable of keeping those predators at bay."

"All the more reason for her to become Revenant, dear husband. She wouldn't need that protection. She would be one of us and she would have a great family to aid her." The Queen gestured to the group of Revenant around them.

She stepped up to the King, her hand resting on his chest, a look of compassion gentling her features. "It is the best way, my love." She reached for his cheek. His hand snapped forward and grabbed hers, holding it away from him.

"It would seem, *my love*," he taunted, "that we are at an impasse. Vidar asserts he is protecting his claim, while Dimitri maintains the claim is his. We will have to come up with some way to rectify this situation." He dropped her hand.

"What do you choose, girl?" The King looked to Enid curiously.

Enid turned instantly toward Vidar.

"I will not give up, my flower," Dimitri blurted, stepping toward her. "I know you feel the pull toward me as well. I have tasted it in your blood."

Heat flooded Enid's cheeks, her gaze moving to study the floor. She knew it was true. There was something in her that ached for him. Something she couldn't explain or describe.

"Tell me you cannot choose me," he persisted.

Quiet tension hugged the room. When she finally spoke, her voice was so soft it barely seemed to rise above the rush in her ears. "I can't choose."

"He's had her under thrall," Vidar spat. "Of course she is conflicted."

The Queen appeared deep in thought, her eyes shifting from Dimitri, to Enid, to Vidar. Enid could only numbly follow what was going on. Vidar's earlier statement echoed over and over through her head.

The only other option is death...

"I believe I may have a suggestion, husband. If you approve, of course."

"I'm all ears, wife."

The Queen moved in between Vidar and Dimitri, commanding their attention. "What I am about to suggest is quite dangerous. Someone may very well lose their lives. So, I will ask one more time. Is this human worth that to you? Will you be willing to lay your life on the line to claim her?"

Vidar remained stoic, his face giving away nothing of what he may be feeling inside.

"I would lay my life on the line, yes."

Dimitri glared at Vidar, his hate palpable. The Queen cleared her throat and he looked toward her instead, adoration softening his expression. "Dah, my Queen. I would."

The Queen looked over at Enid, curiosity gleaming in her eye.

"Then I propose the Elemental challenge. One of you faces the trial. If you win, you win the girl. If you lose, she belongs to the other."

The King's poised, teasing demeanor was forgotten. His arms crossed over his chest. "That challenge hasn't been done in centuries."

"A worthy test then. If they are both adamant for the claim, they will have to earn it."

"But only one of them can run it. The other faces no risk. What would be the purpose of that?"

The Queen shrugged. "If one is dead, there will be only one left to do the claiming. We can't very well have both of them dead."

"And who will face the challenges?" The King seemed distrustful. The Queen smiled up at him beatifically.

"Whomever wants her the most, husband."

"I will do it," Vidar's deep voice broke into the conversation. Dimitri snarled angrily until the Queen touched his arm, silencing him with a look.

"Very well, Enforcer," the Queen said simply. "We will gather what is needed for the challenges. It should take us a few nights to set up the first one. In the meantime, the girl may be comfortable staying in the chambers of our last human resident."

That look of distrust on the King's face only deepened. "Those rooms are next to Vidar's. For someone who was so intent on making the claim for her own people, you are being rather lenient on this."

The Queen shrugged. "If he is to make a claim on her, he should introduce her to our world, and allow her to get to know it. After all, he is the one risking his life. Perhaps during the course of the competition, she could learn a bit from both of her would-be champions."

Dimitri perked up at that statement. The light in his eyes that had started to dim while Enid was pulled farther from him suddenly flared as hope filled him again.

"Vidar, Dimitri, and I will escort her to her new room. Husband, should we meet after to discuss the details of the challenge?"

King Fenri looked her up and down as though attempting to see the flaw in this arrangement.

"We will meet in one hour in my chambers."

The Queen nodded. "Very well. Vidar will have until the first trial to teach Enid about our world and prepare her. After the first challenge, Dimitri will spend time with her. You will alternate until a choice is made."

The two men glared at each other over the Queen's head.

"Is this satisfactory?" asked the Queen, authority rippling through her. Her words like a knife slicing through their anger.

"It is, my Queen," Dimitri murmured.

"Fine," Vidar said, his jaw muscle ticking furiously as all his quiet resolve finally started to dissipate.

"Very well. This way dear," the Queen said, stepping next to Enid, and threading her arm in hers.

"Enid," King Fenri called before she was pulled from the room. They stopped, and Enid looked back to the rugged figure of the King.

"Welcome to Dokkalfar."

CHAPTER

20

Enid was led back into the labyrinth of hallways. Vidar and Dimitri followed, avoiding each other's glares. The Queen's guard took position at the front and rear of the group. Each Revenant guardian a stone wall of walking muscle in scarlet garb. It was an opulent procession of awkward tension.

No one spoke as they took a tunnel that wound lower. The corkscrew-like passage wrapping upon itself several times. It looked as though it had been carved by some great worm weaving a den. The sides were completely smooth and round, the floor ridged with steps.

Enid was grateful for the silence. It gave her more time to really examine her surroundings. And the presence of the Queen and her guard kept the other fae at bay. Soon they stepped out into a larger hall a level below.

The square tunnel had sconce-like lanterns along the flat rock walls that, paired with the hanging fairy lights on the ceiling, helped light the entire width of the cavernous space. It was easily wide enough for four or five creatures to walk side by side comfortably. Every doorway they passed along the way was larger than what Enid was accustomed to. It brought to mind the Minotaur ducking through those comparatively tiny openings. Even that creature would have no problem walking upright through these doors.

Her thoughts were like a leaf on the wind. She kept finding herself swept from one to the next without any organized construct. Only days ago, she was leading a quiet life. Hidden and afraid, but quiet. To presently being escorted through an underground city overrun with creatures that should only exist in fairytales. Not to mention that two very scary, but alluring men were competing to claim her.

Also, she had a drop of blood from one of these creatures from some distant ancestor. At least that helped to explain a bit about her family history. What about her friends and fami—don't think about that. She shook her head, the thought of her loved ones flying away from her.

She cast a wary eye toward the human looking Queen, who was actually the monarch of these strange beings. Something in her gut told her she couldn't be trusted. It could be the sly smile she directed at her, or the icy glare she shot at any fae who didn't bow as she glided by.

Before long she looked up from her reverie, only to stare in astonishment at the sight before her. They were in a large, circular room. A beam of moonlight shone down into the center through a hole in the ceiling. Directly in its path, as if on display, stood a large statue of a man. The bright, silver light made the pale stone shimmer with a soft glow.

Enid gazed in amazement at the level of detail, stepping closer immediately to better scrutinize it. The man was large and muscular. Every curve and tendon meticulously carved from the hard rock. Shoulder length, wavy hair was realistically rendered as though the artist meticulously coaxed every strand lovingly from the stone. The eyes were sad, the face full of longing. The way he stood, slightly tilted forward with one hand out before him, appeared like he was reaching for someone.

It was a tall statue. A foot taller than even Vidar who stood over everyone in the room by an easy six inches. At the statue's feet vines twisted out of the ground, wrapping themselves around the muscular legs and waist. Large, sweet smelling white blossoms hung from the vines.

Enid resisted the urge to reach out and take its hand.

"What do you think?" The soft voice of the Queen spoke right next to her ear. Enid jumped. She was so entranced, she didn't even notice the Revenant step up beside her.

"I think it's beautiful," she breathed, her eyes drawn back to the haunted face.

"Hmmm," the Queen hummed. "You should have Vidar tell you all about him."

Vidar stood a few feet behind her, eyes glued to the statue. He seemed lost in thought, his normally unreadable face full of sadness. He blinked, and once again that expressionless mask covered his features.

"You should know, even if he wins, keeping you safe will be a nearly impossible task. Not even the Lord of the Between can be everywhere at once. He knows that better than anyone."

She gave Enid a small smile. "I look forward to speaking with you in the future," she declared before turning and grabbing Dimitri's arm. "Let's go, Dimitri. There is much to be done."

The intensity of those stark blue eyes tingled. He stumbled alongside the Queen, gaze transfixed until he was pulled through the door and into the tunnels. Only then did she feel like she could breathe, away from the magnetic pull he manifested within her.

Quiet settled over the room at their departure. Enid turned to Vidar to find his attention on her. That stone mask firmly in place.

"Come, Enid, I will show you where you will be staying."

***

The room was much cozier than Enid expected. Even with the stone walls, there was a warmth to the place. Rugs were layered one atop the other along the floor. A wood stove sat in the corner, a fire already burning in its cast iron belly. Opposite the door, tucked into its own little niche, was a fluffy bed stacked with blankets and pillows. A small dresser stood to one side, over which hung an oval mirror. Soft looking chairs with a small table were perched closer to the warmth of the fire. A bookshelf carved into the rock wall loomed at their back, books already tucked into the various niches along with shiny rocks and nicknacks. She felt safe here, secure.

Enid took a moment to examine a tiny statue of a horse on the shelf before exploring the rest of the room. Paintings hung along the walls. Various landscapes and gardens in bright, golden light. They seemed a bit out of place in the dim, cave-like room, but did help add color and cheer.

There were also those enchanting orbs that seemed to be everywhere, small and medium sized ones set at different heights. She lifted a finger to tap the side of one. It was cool, the glass thick. The lights stayed in the center of the orb as it swayed beneath her touch.

A small door beside the bookshelves drew her attention. Curiously she pushed it open, peeking her head in to find a bathroom. A tub was carved into the rock wall and floor, a shower head directly over the top to rain water down. Opposite was a small sink of the same carved design in a ledge of rock jutting from the wall. A mirror hung over it, reflecting the light of the fairy orbs that blinked to life as the door was opened. The most surprising thing to see was the oddly modern human toilet next to the sink. She eyed it for a moment, before turning to Vidar with questioning eyes.

He stood in the hall, leaning against the frame. "We have many proficient plumbers among the water fae," he explained with a shrug of his shoulders. "They have devised a system of plumbing within the rock. It is extremely proficient. They are very proud of it."

"That is impressive," she said as she closed the door, turning back to the room.

She wandered over to the dresser, her eyes drawn to a blue glass vase filled with beautiful, white, trumpet-like flowers surrounded by heart shaped, deep green leaves.

Vidar cleared his throat. "I thought you might like something to cheer up the place," he explained.

Enid blushed as she fingered one of the petals.

"They are beautiful," she responded. "Are these the same flowers that are growing on the statue in the other chamber?"

Vidar nodded, sadness flashing across his face. "They were my mother's favorite. This used to be her room."

He stood there, looking into the space as though seeing it in another time, with another person as its occupant.

Enid stepped closer to him. "What happened to her?" she asked.

His hand ran along the outside of the door, his shoulders raising and lowering as though shrugging off a weight. "She died, not long ago."

"I'm so sorry," Enid responded.

He shook his head, his eyes staring toward the flickering flames through the grate of the wood stove. "She lived a long life, and she was ready to join my father."

Enid nodded in understanding, not wanting to say anything else that may bring up bad memories. And there were many other things they needed to discuss.

"What is going to happen now, Vidar?" she said simply.

Part of her wanted to go to sleep and pretend none of this was happening. Maybe when she awoke, she would find herself in her own bed. All of this only a terrible dream. The other part needed to know every detail immediately. Since she couldn't deny that everything happening was real, her only other option was to get as many facts as possible.

"Now," his deep voice sighed out in exhaustion, "we prepare."

"How?"

"I'm going to teach you everything I can about this world. You will need to know much if you are going to survive this place." He pointed at the wooden door as he spoke. "Starting with this. This is your domain. Your safe space in this realm. You, and only you, have access to this room now that you have claimed it and made it your sanctuary. No one else may enter unless they are invited."

Enid smirked. "Like in vampire movies?"

Vidar rolled his eyes as he gave a heavy sigh. "The Revenant are narcissistic. There are many who have their hands in the movie business, and they do love to put themselves on the screen. It also helps them with their hunts, that their victims have unrealistically romanticized them."

"So, you can't come in?"

Vidar shook his head.

"Show me?"

His eyes went to the ceiling as if asking for patience. "If that will help you feel better."

Backing a step away, he rushed toward the door only to bounce back against an invisible barrier. He stumbled, catching himself as he was thrown. Once he had his balance, he held his hands up as though to ask if that was sufficient.

"Does that rule apply only to fae? What about above ground, in people's houses?" Her mind went back to the night Charlie came into her mother's house. How he had stepped over that threshold so deliberately. Her head pounded at the thought of her mother, she pushed the thought aside, focusing on what Vidar was saying.

"It applies everywhere, yes. And only to fae. For some reason none of us can remember, we are bound by a different set of rules than humans. Maybe it is because the Earth is the place you were meant to be. Your true realm. My kind came from somewhere else."

Enid was mystified. "Vidar, will you please come in and tell me about it?"

He leaned in, his foot going through the doorway as he stepped into the room. "That could have been a very foolish thing to do, Enid," he said softly. "What if I was only trying to earn your trust so that I could kill you easier?" He crept toward her as he spoke, his hands clasped behind him, head tilted to the side.

Intimidating, fearful, terrible. These were all things he could easily portray to anyone. He could be terrifying. She had seen that. Only something inside of her, maybe her gift, maybe only naive stupidity, told her that he was safe. He was trustworthy. Stopping only inches from her, he scowled down at her menacingly.

"I promise only to invite in those I know I can trust. I would already be dead if it weren't for you."

Vidar gave a low hum in the back of his throat as though contemplating her response. "And what if I was only trying to make sure I would have you all to myself?" He stooped lower. His face only inches away. Something within her tightened, but not with fear. She didn't back away, didn't break eye contact. Instead, she smiled up at him innocently.

"I suppose you'll just have to have your way with me then."

Surprise flew across Vidar's face and he stood, taking a step back.

Enid laughed.

She laughed, when only moments ago she wanted to cry, to scream, to rage. And now, with this man, in this moment, she laughed. It surprised her so much that she instantly stopped, a single tear slipping down her cheek.

"What if I went back to my apartment and didn't invite anyone in, ever. Could I stay away from all of this?" She whispered the question. Her eyes refusing to focus as she fought the tears that threatened to follow the first fugitive drop. Vidar reached a hand out and gently wiped it away.

"That place is no longer your sanctuary. I was able to enter it the night Dimitri and Lania attacked you."

His voice went quiet, his eyes looking at her full of concern, or sympathy, she wasn't sure which. Either way she didn't want it. "Something very bad must have happened to you there."

Enid only nodded, anger flaring before she brushed it off.

"Yes, well it seems many things are happening against my will now."

Vidar gazed at her sadly. "Unfortunately, there will be no escaping. You will be hunted, persecuted, and destroyed in any way possible if you even try. I am very sorry. I did not want this for you."

Enid took in a deep breath and let it out shakily. "You should probably tell me everything you can then."

CHAPTER

21

The next night, Enid awoke in her room, the foggy mist of sleep confusing her mind. At first it seemed she was back in her apartment. The black out curtains drawn. The city outside remarkably quiet. Then, as she shifted, a soft light began to glow. Low at first and then brighter, allowing her eyes to adjust gradually. The orb was joined by another, and another, until the room was entirely lit.

A clock on the bookshelf ticked. A smiling moon on the right. A beaming sun on the other. The hand of the clock pointed at the number nineteen. Night time. Above ground it would be dark.

Dokkalfar. It was real. She was here. She lay there for a moment, allowing her brain to process everything. Ending up in this strange place. The Revenant. The Claiming. Vidar's brief synopsis on fae and Dokkalfar, and his promise to return at sundown to continue her education.

Groggily, she pushed herself out of the soft, warm bed. The fire in the stove burst to life as she stood. She stared for a bit, blinking in wonder. It was all so strange and magical. How would she ever belong here?

The bathroom mirror held no further answers as she splashed water on her face, and managed to push her hair back into some semblance of order. She had no other clothes to wear.

Her work shirt was rumpled from sleep, and slightly dirty from the long walk up the mountain. She was still contemplating the state of it, and how to procure a toothbrush, when there was a knock at the door.

Vidar stood in the hall, dressed in black, a steaming mug in his hand that he passed to her with a smile. The liquid was warm and comforting. Resembling something like coffee and chocolate but with a thickness that wasn't cloying. Enid hummed in delight as the heat warmed her.

"I thought you might want to go to your apartment tonight to gather your things," Vidar was saying as she examined the contents of her mug.

"Yes!" Enid exclaimed, tugging at her wrinkled shirt as she sat in one of the overstuffed chairs to enjoy her drink.

Vidar gave a quick rundown of dos and don'ts for their excursion. Do be quick. Don't try to talk to anyone. Don't take anything unnecessary. Do remember that this will be your only trip to the human world until you are declared a fae citizen of Dokkalfar.

"Why?" Enid interrupted, her curiosity getting the better of her.

Vidar paused. "Because once you are officially a citizen, you will be sworn in and pledge an oath. This oath will bind you to our people, and prohibit you from speaking of our kind, or giving away our secrets."

Enid took another sip of the warm liquid. "So, no one has ever broken this oath?"

"No one can. The pledge and the oath literally prevent the words from being spoken. Until you swear the oath, I am duty bound to make sure you don't say anything. That you are kept here in the city and unable to tell our secrets."

Enid put the mug down on the small table next to her. "But I can go get things from my apartment? And the King is trusting me not to give away the location of the city?"

Vidar chuckled. "The King is allowing me to escort you to your apartment on pain of death if you so much as whisper a word. I am trusting you, with my life, not to do that."

"Oh."

He stooped before her, his hand tilting her face to look into his stormy eyes as he spoke.

"I need you to understand how serious this is."

Enid gave a slight nod. "It is. I- I do," she stuttered softly. Now that she was forced to look at him, she couldn't help but stare.

A few heartbeats passed, him studying her as though attempting to expose any falsehoods. Finally, he gave a nod of his head. For a brief second, the pads of his fingers grazed along the edge of her jawline. His eyes glanced to her lips. She followed the movement, breath catching. Then he stood and moved toward the door.

"Ready?" he called over his shoulder.

***

Dokkalfar was a confusing city. Granted, this was only her second time walking around the earthen tunnels that made up the underground kingdom. Vidar held her hand, pulling her along whenever she stopped to gawk at some strange new sight. The fae seemed just as interested in her. Curious faces watched her pass. Creatures stopping to openly stare until Vidar gave a glare that helped expedite their quick departure.

They passed into a section of the city that hummed with excitement. Fae hurried about with bags and suitcases. Nervously buzzing in anticipation. Vidar slowed, letting her take in the sight as they passed. Human clothing hung in a shop. More modern than some of the old-fashioned things worn by many of the fae.

Now that she took the time to notice, she realized she saw as many creatures wearing furs and leathers as blue jeans and t-shirts. There was even the occasional toga and linen shift among three-piece suits and flowy dresses. An eclectic mix of fashion from over the centuries.

In another store, a large, one eyed fae stood in front of a mirror. An attendant presented him with a cuff that snapped around his thick wrist. Instantly a glamoured image appeared, a plain, normal human male—completely nondescript. Enid's eyes vaguely moved over the brown haired, pale skin, male figure before flicking back to the giant cyclops who was nodding his head in approval.

"So that's how it's done," Enid murmured.

Vidar smirked, obviously enjoying her interest in the day-to-day operations of his home.

They moved on, a line forming along the pathway that Vidar pulled her around. Several glass windows sat in a row at the beginning of that line, a small hole in the middle and an open slit at the bottom for sliding paperwork back and forth. Enid craned her neck to watch as gold coins were exchanged for familiar, and some unfamiliar, stacks of money.

"We use gold in the city," Vidar explained as they continued on, "human currency is too fickle. Not to mention, we have easy access to mines down here."

At the last window they passed, a form was stamped before being slid out to a waiting fae.

"What's that?" Enid asked.

Vidar glanced over briefly as they kept moving.

"It's a pass to the portal. Every fae is granted access to the world above for a certain amount of time, sometimes a year, sometimes a few days or weeks. It depends on what they are going for. If it's just to hunt, it's a night or two. If it is for work, or schooling, or a trade, or even a vacation, then it can be anywhere from a week to a year. If it's longer, then there is a yearly assessment and renewal. Every citizen of Dokkalfar is accounted for. Everyone has to maintain our laws or face punishment."

Enid's brow furrowed. "Why is everyone watched so closely? It seems a bit extreme to monitor everyone so intensely."

Vidar stopped then, turning to her with a frown.

"Because when our kind are left unfettered, humans tend to die very quickly. When too many humans die, they look for something to blame. This could lead to our exposure. What do you think would happen to us if humans discovered this place existed? That creatures of magic and nightmare were real?" Vidar stepped closer, taking her chin in his fingers and tilting it toward him. "We would become the hunted. The most fearful of them would turn everything they had against us. Do you fully understand the horrors that have evolved in weaponry with the advancement of technology? Would you really like to see those things unleashed on the core of this earth? Humanity would wipe themselves from existence because of their fear."

Enid's eyes were wide as they stared into his. He nodded, taking her hand in his again as he turned and continued past the glass windows and the fae receiving their paperwork.

Her mind still swirled with all the legalities involved, the requirements to live and work above ground. They came upon a guarded tunnel. Vidar pulled a set of papers from inside his jacket pocket, handing them over. They were checked over carefully before the guards let them pass. This happened once more before they reached a shimmering pane of liquid light within a doorway. Heavily armed guards stood at either side.

Once more their paperwork was reviewed. The guard took it to a console of some sort. A flat pane of clear glass held aloft in a gold frame. He ran his hand over it, and it thrummed to life, a light humming from within. With a few quick taps, they were waved on.

Vidar offered her a reassuring smile.

"Hold your breath and walk through. I will guide us. Don't worry, you'll be fine."

She must have looked as nervous as she felt. Rubbing her hands on her jeans, she took his hand and a deep breath, squeezing tight as they stepped through.

There was a moment of claustrophobia. The shimmering liquid had no feeling. Almost like walking through air, but then pressure around her tightened. Her body felt compressed and small. Suddenly, they were on the other side, the feeling dissipating as quickly as it came.

The air in the city was crisp, despite the obvious smell that could only be found in places where humans clustered together in large quantities. Garbage and musk mingled with the burnt rubber smell of asphalt and the tang of car exhaust.

Enid stopped to look back at the wall they had come through. It appeared to be only an old bricked up door in the alley. A lost relic from another time. She reached out and met only the rough, hard brick. Vidar took her hand in his, gently guiding her along.

"It's one way only," he murmured. "We will take another way back."

They moved quickly, avoiding the more populated streets. Enid realized, with some relief, they weren't far from the diner. For a heartbeat she thought about asking Vidar if they could stop in, only to swallow the words. She couldn't. That wasn't her life anymore. Only, step by step, they were getting closer. Maybe she could see it after all, if only from a distance. Dizziness flooded her, and she shook the thoughts away.

Rounding a corner, she almost stumbled out into the street. Her feet catching beneath her in shock. Across from them sat the dark, ruined exterior of the diner. Broken glass littered the walk. Dried blood streaked the busted window. Police tape stretched all the way around the scene, leaving only a fraction of the sidewalk for pedestrians.

Even the other stores next to it seemed sad and forlorn. The whole of the block that was usually lit from the diner's neon sign, and the bright fluorescent that would shine through the windows, was dark and cold. For a second, Enid thought she saw the flash of glowing eyes deep within the diner's shadowy hull. A fae perhaps, drawn by the violence and blood that lingered in the air.

Vidar took her elbow, guiding her along past the ruined shell of the building. "My old life really is over, huh? There won't be any going back," Enid whispered.

"Yes," Vidar replied. He took her hand in his, giving it a gentle squeeze. "Are you ok?"

"I don't know," she said softly, her head pounding. Forcefully, she pressed away the thoughts and the concerns for her friends. There was nothing she could do for them. It didn't stop the sting of tears that she battled for the next few blocks.

Within minutes, they were in her apartment. It didn't take long to pack up the things she needed. Sadly, she blinked around at the half-packed boxes. There were surprisingly few things she would need to take to her new life. The life she had hoped to build here in this place was over. Crumbled to dust by forces outside of her control.

Her bags were still packed from the trip to her mother's. It held most of her essentials. Wincing, she put a hand to her head. What was she doing again? Oh right.

Throwing on her jacket, Enid grabbed her backpack, looping it over her shoulders as Vidar took her small overnight bag stuffed with her meager wardrobe. And then they were off. Back to the tunnels and rock of the underground city.

Their path zigzagged unusually through the alleys and streets—backtracking in places. Every shadowy movement and slight noise had Vidar's alert gaze darting suspiciously about. Hyper aware, hyper vigilant. Enid didn't comment, but the oddness of it had her heart racing, her paranoia on edge.

It wasn't until she heard the distant sounds of taunting laughter that she understood the reason for his abnormal behavior. They were walking around a corner, for the third time, when a figure emerged from the shadows and stepped into their path.

"There you are, my flower."

The sound of Dimitri's voice caused a flutter in her stomach. Goosebumps tingled along her skin, and Enid trembled. Whether it was in fear or some other emotion she refused to name, she couldn't tell.

"What are you doing here, Revenant?" Vidar grumbled.

Dimitri smiled, his manner all smooth charm and charisma. He was a magnet attracting her in ways she couldn't resist. A planet luring her into his orbit. Overwhelmed by that pull, Enid planted her feet. Her eyes locked on his despite knowing better. He winked and her whole body flushed. She ached to take a step toward him. Just one.

"I heard you were taking my flower out for a quick trip. I couldn't resist the opportunity to check in."

A full body shudder went through her at the intensity of his gaze. She couldn't stop it. Vidar moved in front of her, a wall of muscle interrupting the magical tug. She leaned her forehead against his back. The warmth of him through the soft t-shirt helping to ground her. The tight feeling in her core loosened. Touching Vidar seemed to stop the pull she felt toward Dimitri. She took full advantage of the opportunity, her hands lying flat against his hard back.

"You will have your time Revenant. The thrall has barely worn off yet and you know it."

"Are you accusing me of something?" Dimitri's voice dropped low, anger coloring his tone.

"It seems suspicious you are pushing yourself on Enid so much. Do you doubt your ability to win her on your own? Do you feel the need to press your thrall to keep her attention?"

Enid heard a low growl from Dimitri. Vidar continued, undeterred.

"Tell me, Revenant, why are you doing all this? Why choose Enid, out of all the women you have taken over the centuries."

There was silence. Enid held her breath, desperate to know the answer. Keeping close to Vidar, his body a barrier to the temptation of the thrall, she peeked around his arm. Needing to see Dimitri's expression as he responded.

"She reminds me of someone I killed once," came the reply. His face wistful. Eyes unfocused as though seeing something far away.

"Hmm, someone you wish you could kill again?" asked Vidar.

Dimitri cast a dark look toward Vidar. His eyes reflected eerily in the dim light of a nearby streetlamp. Enid ducked behind him once more, her pulse racing with fear. She gripped Vidar's shirt in her fists as she felt the blood rush from her head.

"I think the only way you will know for certain, that Enid will know for certain, would be for you to leave her alone until after the first challenge. Then it will be your turn to spend time with her. Allow the thrall to dissipate. Let her see your true self. No tricks. No external influence. Just you. Otherwise, she may as well be another kill."

There was a pause. "Fine. I agree. I will show her that I intend to win her over completely. No tricks."

Peering around Vidar once again, she saw determination on Dimitri's face. He looked to her, his voice calm and clear. "You will desire to be with me, my flower, or I will not have you at all."

With that he blended back into the shadows of the alley. His eyes a green glimmer in the dark. A nocturnal predator in motion. And then he was gone.

Vidar put an arm around her, pulling her against him gently. His large hand rubbing her back. Her arms wound around his waist, and she pressed her head to his chest. The beat of his heart helped to steady her nerves. Setting time to its slow, rhythmic thump she took in deep breaths until her heart slowed to match his. His arms stayed around her, giving her time, letting her take as much as she needed. Once the quaking in her body had eased, she looked up at him.

The light from the nearby street lamp etched the angular planes of his face, enhancing the rugged masculinity of him. His gray eyes were bright in the light, stark against the darkness beyond.

"I will do everything I can to make sure you have as much of a say in all of this as possible, Enid," he said softly.

His hand cupped her face, and she found herself leaning into the touch. Her eyes closing with a soft sigh. When they fluttered open, she was surprised to find a look of unrestrained need staring down at her. The muscles of his chiseled jaw tight. His eyes fixated upon the curve of her lips.

She was so tempted to reach up and smooth away the furrow between his brows that her fingertips flexed as she considered the movement. However, a twinge of doubt settled within her. Ultimately, that is what held her back.

The future for her was so precarious right now. What if she gave in to these desires, only to have him ripped away. What if she was imagining these fleeting glimpses? Exchanging them for another, less desirable, emotion. What if he was doing all of this out of some gallant sense of decency. No, best to keep her heart safe for the moment—guarded.

Her head ached. She stepped back, adjusting the straps on her backpack as though it were uncomfortable.

"We should go," he whispered, his voice strained.

She nodded.

They walked a few more blocks. Now moving in a direct route, before stopping at a large, unassuming brick building. He motioned her before him down a flight of stairs to a basement door which he banged against sharply. A slat within the metal slid open. A face peered out before it slammed shut and there was the sound of locks clicking open. The door swung open and Vidar stepped through. Nervously, Enid followed him inside.

The thump of music vibrated through the air. The small hairs on her body tingling from the sensation.

"There is a club upstairs. A favorite hunting ground for fae. I usually try to avoid this entrance, but it is the closest one," Vidar explained. Even muffled through the thick concrete the bass of the music created a buzz within her. Her chest a cavity pounding in time to the deep beat.

"Why didn't the Revenant take me this way last night?"

Vidar gave her a lopsided smile. "I got the King to ban the Revenant from taking humans through the city portals. It was a security measure. In case the Revenant lost control and the human got away, they couldn't lead anyone back. It's become a rite of passage for the humans now. To enter the city through one of its physical doors." He leaned closer, his breath in her ear as he spoke lower. "Really, I wanted to make the claims more difficult for them."

"You really don't like them, do you?"

The smile dropped from his face.

"No. I don't."

She was ushered along through empty rooms of concrete. Between hallways of brick and rock. Down more flights of stairs, and through pillars of concrete braced between floors. Until, finally, they reached a guarded door.

The air felt thicker here. Ominous. Similar to how she felt when she went in through the mountain entrance, but less. As though whoever made this door knew it would be guarded enough on its own in the concrete jungle of the city. Or the humans who lived here were too self-absorbed to go looking.

Though, if anyone did manage to make it this far, the look of the two heavily armed, black-clad guards would make them turn around and run immediately. They were two of the most intimidating men Enid had ever seen in her life. With their dark uniforms covered in sheathed knives and pistols at their hips. Something about them screamed killer. Professional.

Enid slid closer to Vidar who took her hand in his and greeted the men with a nod of his head. They returned the motion as one of them gripped the handle of the door and pulled it open.

Beyond lay a shimmering haze of light, like a rippling blue lake hanging in midair. Slightly different from the portal they had used earlier. She sucked in a breath and held it as Vidar walked forward, yanking her along with him.

Between one step and the next, they went from the concrete room, to the smooth granite floor of the tunneled kingdom. Enid released her breath in a woosh. Her lips parted in awe as she gazed around them. They were in the hall outside her room. No trace of the portal in sight. She wasn't sure she would ever get used to that. Vidar chuckled.

"I'm going to enjoy putting that look on your face as often as possible."

CHAPTER

22

The next few nights were a flurry of information. It was announced the Elemental Challenges would begin in three nights' time. Consisting of a series of trials based on each element—as its name implied—earth, air, fire, and water.

Since Vidar had no other way of preparing, besides his daily workouts and practices with the guards, he spent the majority of his time teaching Enid. Not that he would have spent the time any other way. He barely let her out of his sight. They spent hours going over the various fae in Dokkalfar. He brought her old books detailing each clan, as the factions referred to themselves. Each tome was beautifully adorned with brightly colored pictures depicting some of their ancient histories.

"Even the fae have myths and legends," he mocked as she carefully leafed through the brittle pages. "Most of them are hearsay at this point. Many of us believe the histories have been twisted into something far from the truth."

Her eyes lingered on a colorful picture of a white-haired woman with pointed ears. The vivid purple of her eyes stood out starkly on the aging paper. Vidar gingerly took the book from her. "We can go over these another time," he said, putting it away and picking up another.

"One such myth, which is actually considered truth instead of hearsay, mostly because we have proof of it, is the concept of witches."

Enid's ears perked at that. The Queen had said that, about her. A witch. She frowned. Somehow the idea of pointed hats and riding on brooms didn't mesh with her idea of herself, or any of the women in her family.

"Witch," Vidar was saying, "is a human word. One that the fae adopted over the millennia. At first, they were called other things. Wise women, seeress, priestess, völva, oracle, druid. Then with the advent of Christianity, witches."

He leafed through a book, showing her the pages. A woman with slightly pointed ears, and glowing eyes, fingers dug into the soil as new plants sprang forth.

"That was also when they began to be hunted and, exterminated. Their affinity with magic or a deformity inherited from a fae ancestor marked them as other. As something to be feared and ostracized." He flipped the page to show the woman tied to a stake. Orange and red flames licking at her feet as tears streamed down her cheeks.

"Shortly after this began, it became frowned upon to mate with a human. It gave us away. Made us vulnerable. Only the ones who stayed within Dokkalfar, cutting all ties to the human realm, were allowed to stay. It is rare to find one with your genetic makeup anymore." Despair settled heavily within her at the image of the burning woman. Vidar gently took the book from her and handed her another.

"This book talks mainly about water fae." He handed her the thick, ancient tome, delving into another lecture.

Enid did her best to focus. It was an incredibly interesting subject, after all. But something about the way his eyes narrowed when he focused, or how he would steeple his finger along the side of his jaw as he listened to her questions, would captivate her. She tried not to pay attention to the way the muscles in his arms would flex as he moved a stack of books, or how he would sweep the dark strands of hair from his eyes when they would lean over a page.

When they weren't studying, he would take her on walks around the tunnels. Allowing her to draw a mental map. It seemed there were many levels to the complex system of subterranean passages. Each with four to six stories. The levels all contained public rooms, shops, restaurants, and gathering halls surrounding the center shaft with its pulley powered wooden decks hovering in the air. The ground floor was where the best shopping could be found. Booths, large shops and restaurants lined the spaces between doors and meandering walkways.

Looking up at the mass of the complex from the lower floor was especially awe inspiring. Enid found herself doing it often as they roamed. Vidar hovering over her protectively as she stared up at the walkway winding up and up. The clock hanging above it all. The rope bound platforms shifting across the open air.

Enid was terrified of using these floating platforms. Fearful she would fall to certain death. Corkscrew shaped tunnels connected each level, like a spiral staircase from one floor to the next. She made a point of using them to travel from floor to floor. Avoiding the platforms altogether. Vidar would give her a knowing smirk, but he never pushed whenever she refused the primitive elevators.

Particularly hardy vines grew everywhere. Anchoring themselves in the rock and growing in a mass of hanging tendrils throughout the open chasm. Some grew along the walls and platforms. A living tapestry of greenery and sweet-smelling flowers. Enid would make a point of admiring them, taking in their heavy perfume at every opportunity. Vidar was more than accommodating, waiting patiently while she explored. Trees sprung from stone and flowers thrived in pots and hanging baskets. The numerous hanging glass orbs of fairy light scattered about giving off enough light to sustain the multitude of plants.

Vidar explained there were still some fae who could talk to the plants. Encouraging them to grow despite the lack of sunlight. And how the wood nymphs loved to root themselves into the earth for days at a time, enjoying the open space to spread their branches. Enid began to notice when some of the trees moved position, or disappear altogether.

Large hallways branched off from the public space, spreading further into the earth, from which smaller tunnels and private residences were located. Enid and Vidar's rooms were in a private tunnel located on the second level from the top. The same level in which the King's court and the shifter fae resided. They found that keeping each clan separate helped to quell, though not stifle, the fighting between the sects. Enid found it telling how each grouped together. Much like how humans segregated themselves based on religion or creed, these creatures banded around those they considered most like them.

The third level contained the Queen's court and her Revenant. And the fourth many of the water fae and the Underlings. The fae who were so terrifying and dark, that only the blackest of places would placate them. While there were other levels below those, Vidar mentioned, no one ventured very far past them. For those were the places even the most wicked of them feared to go.

When they walked around the city, Vidar never let her wander far from his side. His menacing glare, and intimidating figure were enough to keep even the most dangerous fae from approaching. The extremely curious would try to catch her eye, but one look from Vidar was enough to send them scurrying off in the other direction.

Enid found herself beginning to enjoy her time in this strange place. Safe in the company of her champion, the fears of her first night in the strange world soon subsided. Often, she found herself believing she could find some happiness here. Or she could hope.

The food was wonderful. The meats were tender, juicy, and well flavored. Vidar nearly doubled over in laughter when she hesitantly asked him what kind it was. Terrified they would try to feed her human flesh. But he assured her there was plenty of game to be had around the mountain, and many creatures who didn't eat human flesh or drink human blood. Thankfully, there were various vegetables and fruits that she recognized, as well as breads and pastries. There were so many incredible, exotic flavors in their strange world that Enid could spend hours trying to smell and taste them all.

One of her favorites was a pale golden wine made with dandelion and honeysuckle flowers. The drink was surprisingly sweet, but not achingly so. With a deep golden hue. She found it incredible. On her second night in the underground world, she drank enough that she had an alarmingly painful headache upon waking the next day.

They had spent the last few hours of that night exploring the market while Vidar pointed out the different fae, whispering to her their unique attributes. He spoke to her of the magic of the place, and how it had begun to fail them over time. How they feared one day it would be gone completely. That possibly, when it did, it would mean the end of them. They bought the bottle of golden wine and shared it over dinner in his room. It felt good to talk and laugh. Especially after the shock of her visit above ground.

She was delighted to discover his rooms were down the corridor from hers. Knowing he was so close made her feel more at ease. She laughed as she entered with no invitation. Reminding him of how he had bounced off of that invisible barrier. Vidar only chuckled, his large hand tussling her hair affectionately. She batted it away, fixing the scarlet locks that had covered her face. They drank and ate until she was giddy.

Excitement overcame her, and she dragged him out of the room, down the corridor. Breathlessly, she pulled him to a stop in that first cavern. Vidar's smile dropped as she asked him to tell her the story of the statue. Mesmerized by the artistic detail taken to portray the handsome man. He looked up at it, a haunting sadness filling his face.

"This is not a statue," Vidar whispered. "It is the body of Lord Halvar, my father," he explained, his voice full of emotion.

Enid sucked in a sharp breath, gazing up at the statue with new eyes. No longer stone, but flesh and blood transformed into what looked like pure marble.

"The Revenant Queen meant to give me a message by delivering you here herself. That I may meet the same fate as him, should I continue to fight for your claim." His eyes narrowed, growing distant. Anger flushed his face.

Enid did not want anger in that moment, nor sadness, but she had the strongest urge that this was a story she desperately needed to hear. She laced her fingers in his, giving his hand a comforting squeeze as she leaned into him. "Tell me what happened?" she asked.

Vidar looked down at her with a small, pained smile before he looked back up into the frozen face of his father. "My mother was human, you know. Her name was Gerda."

"Really?" Enid whispered.

Vidar nodded.

"How did she survive this place?"

He heaved a breath, and released it before he continued.

"Despite their contempt of her, none would dare openly threaten or wish harm upon her for fear of rousing their Lord's anger. Though, in spite of her kindness and compassion to all the creatures of her new home, she was not openly accepted by the people she came to live beside. Some felt that her being bound to a Lord of such power weakened him, and thereby weakened the whole of the Dokkalfar. They could not accept having a human as part of their court. They felt that mixing with humanity was the cause of the old magic beginning to fade."

Enid looked up at him with wide eyes, her head falling against his arm. "So, you are a witch too?"

He laughed. A deep belly laugh that made the room seem brighter for its creation.

"I am fae," he replied, his finger tapping the tip of her nose playfully. "My blood is not that diluted, but yes, I am part human. My father loved my mother with a passion most never find."

Vidar sighed deeply, pausing as if trying to gather his thoughts.

"They were perfect together. Two hundred years after she came to this world there was a rebellion. My father was called to this room in a message sent by mother's hand. Unbeknownst to him, it was not my mother that sent it. When we discovered the trick, we rushed here, but the trap was sprung. We arrived in time to watch rubble rain down on my father from the hole broken through the ceiling. Sunlight flooded the room, and my mother watched as her true love turned to stone before her eyes. I was forced to stand helpless in the shadows, unable to help for fear I would meet the same fate."

Enid's heart broke for him. She found herself unable to speak. Only stood with him, her hand holding his, squeezing it tightly. Tears ran down her face as they both stared at the statue. Reaching out his other hand, Vidar stroked the delicate petals of one of the white flowers. The glow of moonlight reflecting from it bounced around as the flower trembled beneath his touch.

"She wept here at my father's feet, as he was taken from her before her eyes. These moon flowers were planted where her tears fell. The final symbol of her love for her husband."

His hand fell away from the flower, his eyes drifting back up to his father's face. "My father was one of the last true Jötnar. The Lord Protector of that which Lies Between. At one time, we were the guardians of the bridges between realms. But as the bridges disappeared, and the realms began to drift apart, some of us were trapped here. Only able to shift within the veil of this realm from place to place. I haven't been able to traverse the shroud between places in over a century. But I am half human. It may only be me."

"Wait, your mother was human but, she lived for over two hundred years?"

Vidar nodded, his eyes slipping to her. "My mother began to age when my father died. She passed away, an old woman, fifty years later."

A shiver went down Enid's spine, as though somewhere within her a quiet voice was telling her to witness what would come to pass. A prophecy trapped within the confines of her soul. Scratching to be released, but sealed off from her somehow. She tried to push the feeling away, but she couldn't shake it.

"Does that happen to all humans who come here?"

Vidar shrugged. "A fae-human bond is very rare. There aren't enough instances of it happening to know for sure."

"How old are you?" Enid asked.

He raised a brow, his mouth tilting at the side.

"Three hundred and fifty."

Enid's mouth dropped. Vidar laughed.

"How old are you?"

His eyes glistened with amusement. She knew he only asked because she had, or maybe to help hammer into her addled brain what she was getting into with this place.

"Twenty-six," she replied hoarsely.

She was a bit more sober now. And still that sensation of floating crashed over her. The feeling that she was at a crossroads.

"How long do your kind usually live, half human fae, or...Jötnar?"

Vidar lost his smile, his eyes shining with the ache of loneliness and sorrow.

"I don't know. There are none to ask."

Enid swallowed the ball of emotion that lodged in her throat. The edges of the world felt brittle. As though this small moment was only a fragment of tapestry and beyond it stretched an endless void of unknown possibilities. Were she to only shove aside the fabric, she could snatch one into her hands. Could read it, and know it to be true. A chill came over her.

"Are you alright?" Vidar asked.

She forced a smile to her tear-streaked face, reaching up to cup his cheek.

"I think we both need another glass of wine," she murmured, pulling him back down the tunnel to his room.

She glanced back only once at the face of Halvar. Full of yearning and sorrow as he stood forever reaching for the love he would never again hold.

CHAPTER

23

Nightfall had always been a time of uncertainty and trepidation for Enid. Risk dwelled within the long shadows swallowing the earth as the light faded from existence. The setting of the sun was a cry of warning. A beacon to the frail, and the timid. Run. Hide. Dark was for the strong, the menacing. The shadows were their playground.

All of that still rang true, but there was so much more. Now Enid saw the faces of the creatures lurking in the shadows. Now she lived among them. A lamb taken in by the nocturnal hunters. Night meant activity, life, excitement and wonder.

Fae bustled along the market. Their strangeness familiar thanks to Vidar's instruction, and the nights spent within their domain. Wings, horns, and talons were displayed with pride. No glamour needed to hide them in the safety of their city. They were free to be themselves, to flaunt their true images.

In the world above, the darkness of night once again claimed its post. The predators would be out in full force, taking advantage of their uneasy prey. At one point she would have been one of them. Still could be, given the sharp, hungry glances that were thrown her way. Only Vidar's presence snuffed the temptation from their gazes.

They stood in line for food. Gold coins clinked together as she occasionally shifted them in her palm, and contemplated the feeling of this world to the one she left above. A commotion further down the walkway drew her attention, interrupting her internal rumination. Vidar stiffened, standing to full attention. His height allowing for a better view. Slowly, a smile spread across his face and he took her elbow in his hand, guiding her out of line.

"Come, I have another lesson for you to see." Satisfaction laced his voice.

"But we haven't eaten," Enid protested. The delightful smell of food caused her mouth to water. She leaned longingly toward the heavenly scent.

"I will feed you after, I promise," he assured, pressing her into movement. Enid huffed, reluctantly allowing herself to be swept along.

Before long they stood outside what Enid referred to as the throne room. Vidar called it the receiving hall, the great room where Enid first met the King. Raised voices and angry hissing met them before Vidar even cracked the door open. The single guard at post outside merely nodded him along, obviously expecting him. A curious eye drifted over Enid before returning his focus back to duty.

Once inside, Vidar closed the door behind them. Placing a finger over his lips to signal silence before motioning her against the back wall to watch the proceedings. Enid settled against the rock, Vidar's ever vigilant presence next to her—alert and assessing.

The King's guard stood in a group around two arguing creatures. A small woman Enid had never seen before faced them in the tactical black. Her snow-colored hair in a long braid. Vibrant red eyes darted between the two threats. Body poised for sudden movement. The two fae jabbed fingers toward the King, who stood behind the marble throne. His crossed arms propped on the back of the chair, chin resting atop them. An expression of sheer boredom on his face.

The guards were obviously not pleased with the treatment their King was receiving. Rough snarls and snaps punctuated the air whenever one of the creatures became too animated. Enid's stomach dropped to her knees. Her appetite suddenly gone as she recognized the fae.

One of the creatures stopped shouting long enough to lift its long, beaked nose and sniff the air experimentally. It whirled, a solid red glare narrowing on Enid. Beside the ghoul, the minotaur shifted, turning to look over its shoulder. A puff of air blew past the large ring in its nose.

"You!"

The ghoul's rattling hiss sent a wave of fear through her that nearly turned her legs to jelly. He crouched low to the ground, gaunt body coiling like a spring. Next to her Vidar tensed. The ghoul's blackened teeth lashed the air as he sprung forward. He barely made it a foot before he was jerked back. Red eyes widening in surprise as he slammed face first into the floor. The white-haired woman released his ankle.

"Stay down," she spat.

The minotaur shifted nervously as she squared her shoulders and faced him. "Are you going to give me any problems?"

Shrinking from the woman, the minotaur shook his horned head. His large brown eyes glanced to Enid and back. He remained pinned in her red eyed scowl. Clearly intimidated despite the fact that her head barely reached his chest. Enid's mouth dropped open. Next to her Vidar relaxed, his massive arms crossed. One boot planted on the wall behind him, obviously at ease.

"Good," the woman grumbled before turning to the ghoul who sat on the floor, cradling his nose. Blood, black as ink, oozed down his face. "Now show your King some respect."

The ghoul climbed to his feet, and both fae turned to their King, heads bowed. King Fenri heaved a sigh and lifted his head. Arms still crossed lazily along the back of the throne.

Awe and trepidation thrummed through Enid in equal measure. These beings respected strength and power. Ruthlessness was their way of life. Their mantra. She wasn't built like that. From the corner of her eye, she examined Vidar. Relaxed and at ease with the ferocity that played out before them. Her guardian, her mentor. Her champion. Survival in this world would be impossible without him. The King's deep voice pulled her from her thoughts. Her attention shifting once more to the dais.

"Secrecy, discretion, stealth. These are concepts that have been drilled into the very makeup of all fae from the moment of our births. Our world remains hidden. It's how we survive. It's our primary and most upheld law." The King's jaw clenched, his hands fisting. "So why has it come to my attention that the two of you were spotted chasing a human through a hospital? Without glamour. In the middle of the day." The King moved from behind the throne, his fisted hands at his sides. A hard glare leveled at the cowering fae before him. His words were sharpened daggers, spearing the quivering creatures with every biting syllable.

"Not only that," the King continued. "But the human. Got. Away." His body trembled with suppressed violence.

Enid swallowed thickly, grateful that look wasn't aimed at her. She was that human. A loose string that would have been snipped from the world had she not already found her way to Dokkalfar.

The ghoul lifted his head a fraction, his eyes meeting the King's before averting with a wince. "But the human is here... your majesty." A sneer marred the begrudgingly added title. "Our secret, our world, remains safe."

"NO THANKS TO YOU!"

The King's words echoed around the chamber. His shout causing more than the two sniveling creatures to flinch. A heartbeat was all it took for composure to slide over his features. Indifference and boredom covering the boiling rage. The effect was dizzying. Enid drew in a breath and held it. The racing of her heart counting the moments until he spoke again.

"I would be within my rights to call for the immediate execution of you both." His narrowed eyes moved over to the minotaur. "Or internment could be your punishment."

The minotaur seemed to shrink even more into himself. The King paused to examine this reaction before turning toward the ghoul. "There is a reason I waited until now to handle your punishment, however. Both of your clans have been spoken to, and your cases have been reviewed. As this is a first offense, and given the circumstances involving the human ..." All eyes turned to Enid. Some cursory, some curiously, and two with a deep seeded, volatile fury. "... I have chosen to strip you of any above ground privileges. You will be confined to the city for the foreseeable future. Until I have decided you have learned your lessons and proven your competency."

The ghoul seethed, his breath a sharp rasp through his broken nose. "You would deny us the ability to hunt? What kind of King represses his people?"

A dangerous glint reflected in the King's eyes. A warning of the perilous beast that lay beneath the mask of the man on the surface. The ghoul paid it no heed.

"The thrill of the hunt is a primal part of our nature. It is an urge that must be fulfilled, and you would crush it beneath your boots." His high-pitched voice sounded shrill in Enid's ear. "You are a mockery of what a true fae is meant to be. You are no King. You are barely a shifter. You are no better than a human. A weak, pathetic, *man*." The last word was uttered with disgust before hawking a glob of blood covered phlegm at the King's feet.

A low, rumbling growl vibrated through the room. The hairs on the back of Enid's neck stood on end, and she found herself looking for escape, for a hiding place. Her eyes shifted nervously in reflex to the noise that evoked the strongest sense of fear within her. The sound that would have sent her oldest ancestors scurrying for shelter. It called to the ancient impulses that pushed early humans to seek the safety of numbers, of light, of fire. It was a sound that helped spur the creation of civilization. Primal, threatening—horrifying.

The ghoul had the good sense to blanch as the King slowly brought his gaze up from the black blob of spit at his feet to the trembling, sickly green face of the creature that dared to insult him. The guards answered the volatile rumble with their own. Their growls merging in a chorus of promised savagery.

Enid began to feel faint, adrenaline rushing through her. Vidar leaned in closer. The warmth and hardness of his body assisting to stabilize her. Her fingers grasped the fabric of his shirt, twisting it within her fingers as she clung to him. She didn't miss the way he shifted toward the group even as he comforted her. The gleam of anticipation in his eyes as he observed the events unfolding before them.

Across the room, the white-haired woman watched her. Blood red irises staring into her soul as though she could physically see the panic that latched within. She seemed...disappointed. Enid's breath tore itself free in a gasp, dizziness threatening to take her to the ground. Vidar's arm snaked around her waist, anchoring and lifting her.

Before she could blink, the King was off of the dais, his hand wrapped around the throat of the ghoul who sputtered and choked as his gangly form was lifted into the air. Elongated nails drew blackened blood to the surface of green skin. The King snarled, his eyes flashing a golden amber. Teeth lengthening into sharpened points.

"Tell me, ghoul," the King ground out, his voice warbled with the elongation of his teeth. "...how human do I seem to you?"

Hair began to sprout along his face and arms. His clawed hands pressed deeper into the ghoul's neck. A splintered whimper slipped between the ghoul's thin lips. The King grinned in sadistic delight. Teeth gnashing as he forced the ghoul onto its knees.

"Remember," Fenri bit out, snapping at the empty air as he spoke, "you live and die at my leisure. Defy me to your detriment, mock me at your peril. It will be nothing for me to end you. I will throw you into the deepest, darkest hole we have in this city, and forget you existed at all. You will spend the last of your days attempting to claw your way to freedom in darkness and solitude. Unable to hunt, unable to feed, until the day your body expires. Do. Not. Tempt. Me."

The ghoul sniveled, the sound merely a breath, before the King finally let him go. His body sprawling upon the smooth rock floor.

Enid shivered against Vidar. Her face pressed into his side. Embarrassment filled her as she realized how tightly she had lashed herself against him in her desperation to avoid the conflict unraveling before her.

The King stepped back as the two fae were surrounded. His glowing amber eyes followed as they were escorted from the room.

"Two nights in confinement for each. No access to the human world until I lift the mandate. Death to either should they choose to ignore my command."

The ghoul's narrowed gaze remained fixed on Enid as they passed. His eyes nothing more than red slits in a pale, green face.

His lip lifted in a sneer. The black of his teeth stained darker by the black blood that still flowed from the broken hook of a nose. Feet dragging as he was pulled out by the guards flanking him. The minotaur followed behind, his large eyes briefly settling on Enid before drifting to Vidar and jerking away. His large head hung heavily as he walked in shame between the guards. The white-haired woman followed, red eyes peering into Enid's as she passed.

Once they had gone, the door clicking shut behind them, Enid sagged in relief. Vidar rubbed her back in soothing circles. She leaned into the touch, savoring the sensation, seeking the solace it provided. It would have helped, had she not looked directly into the rage filled eyes of the King. He remained standing in front of the dais. Golden eyes still flashing. Still fighting to control the frenzy that so nearly took him. Those eyes were now locked on her. Her blood turned to ice.

Slowly, quietly, with the anger that fueled him lacing his words, he spoke. "This will be my only lesson to you, *human*. Never endanger the peace and tranquility of our world. The whims of one do not override the good of the whole."

With that he spun on his heel and jumped onto the dais, disappearing through the door behind the throne. Vidar gave her a sympathetic grin.

"I am sorry to expose you to that, but that is the essence of our world. It is important that you see what is expected, the dangers you will be facing. This world is not fairy tales and magic. It's predator and prey, hunter and hunted, and above all, secrecy."

Enid nodded, too shaken to form words. His arm around her waist tightened and he lifted her face to his. Studying her as though attempting to see how broken she truly was. She met his watchful expression, letting her fright seep from her. She didn't want to disappoint him. Not with everything he was doing for her.

His hand cradled her cheek, thumb stroking a line along her skin, soothing. She drank in his warmth, letting it ease her. A war of emotions shifted across Vidar's features. A war of her own was also brewing. Desperately, she yearned to close that distance. To discover the feel of him, the taste of him, but the trial loomed closer. Their fates hung in the balance. He held her for two more heartbeats before, reluctantly, releasing her.

They drifted back out into the market where Vidar, true to his word, bought her a sandwich filled with shredded meat. Her stomach clamped at the thought of food. She picked at it politely, unable to stomach the meal.

Around her the eyes of the fae seemed to watch. Their gazes accusing, hungry, savage.

Inwardly, she trembled, even as she felt herself reinforcing her spine with steel. Forcing the weakness in her to melt away. She would become something stronger, something capable of survival. This world would not be her undoing. Sitting up taller in her seat, Enid glared down at her sandwich before lifting it and sinking her teeth in deep. Tearing into it with ferocity.

Vidar watched, his own meal halfway devoured. The corner of his mouth twitched into a knowing smile.

CHAPTER

24

Their final night together, Vidar took her to the highest levels of the mountain city. Enid couldn't help but feel trepidation. Tomorrow night Vidar would face the first trial. Fear of what could happen to him, and the thought she would never be with him like this again, made her feel hollow. Maybe that was why he chose to bring her there. The beauty was mesmerizing.

Fae most closely linked to nature inhabited these chambers. The fae that could survive the sun if a bit of the mountain were to crumble away and expose them to the surface. They were also the gentlest. The least likely to venture out and harm humans wandering too closely. Which was excellent foresight on the part of those who set up the city, as these levels held the most passages to the human realm. Passages warded with spells meant to keep out wandering humans and animals. Thinking of them now, Enid could feel the pressure on her skin, the panic set to have her claw herself away from this place. They were effective.

The garden fae—gnomes, satyrs, and brownies, along with many of the nymphs—rushed about chatting merrily with seemingly endless energy. Small pixie-like creatures stared out at her from their hanging huts woven of sticks and mud. Others peaked their heads from between screens of vines and flowers covering the doorways of their homes cut into the rock.

Some had wings like large butterflies, their tiny, humanoid bodies light enough for the gentle flapping of the delicately scaled wings. Others were no more than wisps of air with dragonfly wings. They moved so fast, fading and reappearing as though they were the very breeze itself, seeming to find joy in pulling the petals from the flowers and swirling them around her. She couldn't help but laugh in delight watching their aerial acrobatics.

Vidar took her through open gaps in the mountain. Raised beds of various vegetables, herbs, and fruit grew in abundance under the expanse of sky. The stars twinkled in delightful patterns above her as she stood among the rows of greenery.

This area was heavily warded. Spelled so that if any human should wander close, they would immediately be compelled to leave. Glamour hid the openings to the world below, keeping them protected from prying eyes overhead. It was fascinating to hear him talk about it all. The intricacies involved in keeping the city safeguarded while allowing them to thrive. Vidar came alive as he showed her his home.

In case the magic here began to fail as well, there were also hidden greenrooms, currently used to farm mushrooms. Sadness hollowed his eyes as he looked around at the happy fae twirling about in the open air. At the lush gardens, vibrant and prosperous. Enid knew what he was thinking. The fae would survive, but it wouldn't be a life of content. Not for these creatures, should the wards fail. They would not thrive. From the discussions they had, Enid knew that the possibility of the magic fading all together was very real.

Grabbing Vidar's hand, she looked around at the gardens before her. Seeing it with fresh eyes—Vidar's eyes. Who would fight to protect this world with the same ferocity if he were gone? A lump formed in Enid's throat. Guilt had been her constant companion today. She swallowed it down, looking once more up into the starry sky. The first time she had seen the outside world in days. It was much more peaceful here than the towering skyscrapers and neon lights of the city she had left behind. The stars plentiful in the blanket of darkness.

How had she ever taken that sky for granted? Her heart ached at the sight. Her mind reaching back for the memory of the sun on her face. The blue of the sky in the day. Light popping through white puffy clouds. Fingers of gold drifting through a leafy canopy.

She wandered over to a great, majestic oak, nearly weeping beneath its graceful arching branches. The elegant limbs twisted toward the open air. Her hand rested against the roughness of the bark, a tear falling from her eye. The tree beneath her hand shook, the thick trunk vibrating. Enid stepped back in alarm, pulling her hand away. The leaves shivered, and then a sudden gust of wind surrounded her. A group of swift winged pixies gently nudged her away, their high-pitched voices soft yet urgent.

"I'm sorry," Vidar said, coming to rescue her from the cloud of fairies that buzzed about. "I forgot to warn you about Daphne."

Enid glanced back toward the oak. "The tree, is it a nymph?"

Vidar looked at her sideways with a smirk. "Yes, Daphne is a dryad, and she is painfully shy." He gestured toward the tree. "Years ago, she took this form and has remained that way ever since. No one has seen her in her human form in about ten years."

Enid gaped back at the graceful oak, at the elegant branches, the curves in the trunk that hinted at a feminine form. "I'm sorry," she called out to the tree. "I'm so sorry. I didn't know. Please tell her." She told the hovering pixies.

As they walked away, Enid glanced back once. Relieved to see the rustling leaves had calmed. The branches lowered as though at ease.

***

Later in the night, Vidar led her to an open overlook within the top of the mountain. The tunnel they took ended in a pool of water that reflected the light of the moon and stars like a second shimmering sky at their feet. Enid touched the pool, sending ripples through the reflected image. Water dripped from the face of the mountain in a steady stream, keeping the level of the pool even with the edge where it spilled out further down the mountain. A hidden, natural infinity pool. Excited, Enid threw off her shirt.

"What are you doing?" Vidar asked as she was about to unbutton her pants. His face flushed as he suddenly spun around. Gallant as always, and protective—even of her virtue.

"I'm going to get in the water," Enid giggled. "I promise my modesty will remain intact. I still have my bra and panties on. It's the same amount of coverage as a bikini." She paused then, her eyes going to the cool, rippling water. "Unless there is some creature in there I should worry about?" She froze, suddenly unsure.

Vidar laughed, the sound surprising her. It was a joyful sound, one she wanted to keep hearing, loud and deep. Something about it made her heart feel light. A smile crept to her lips.

"No creatures to worry about, no." He turned back toward her. His eyes never left her face. Never wandered lower to the vast amount of skin she displayed. *A true gentleman*, she thought.

"Well then let's go," she said. She pulled her shoes and pants off and delicately stepped into the water. It chilled her instantly. After a couple of wobbling steps, she found herself sliding deep into the star flecked depths. No longer able to touch the bottom. She dunked under, and pushed her hair back from her face, sighing in relief. The cool water felt refreshing.

There was a splash and Vidar surfaced beside her, shaking wet hair from his face. An easy smile lighting up his normally stoic expression. Enid squealed, shielding her eyes from the spray with a light laugh before lowering her hand. Her breath caught.

He was beautiful. His skin glowed in the moonlight, giving a subtle radiance to his pale, gray eyes that made them seem startling. She found herself more entranced by the view of him, than by that of the night sky. Bright as it was against the darkness of the valley below. The water slithered along the angles of his face, the muscular swell of his chest. She followed the meandering rivulets, captivated.

"Is everything ok?" Vidar asked, searching her face. She blushed as she realized she had been caught staring. She dipped a bit so her mouth and nose were below the surface. Hoping to hide her embarrassment as she mentally shook herself. He gave her a questioning look.

"Yes, it's a bit cold," she said as she up, letting out a shaky breath that had nothing to do with the chill water. Vidar stood, chest rising out of the water. Of course he could stand here. He was a giant. She swallowed as he came closer. His arms reached around her and pulled her to him.

"Here," he said, lowering himself so that they were face to face, "I'll try to help keep you warm."

Her heart quickened as her legs instinctively wrapped around his waist. Her arms looping around his massive shoulders. It was warmer this way. That was the excuse she used as she pressed against him. The race of his heart pounding in time to hers.

His arms, circled tightly around her waist, were strong. She had never felt such security before, such safety. What would it be like to allow her hands to run along the ridged muscles of his shoulders? To tease her fingers through that thick, dark hair? She itched to do that. Her eyes following the path her fingers longed to travel. Her head rested on his shoulder, her breath against his neck. She watched the beat of his pulse there. The way his throat bobbed when he swallowed. If she tilted forward a bit, her lips would be able to feel the thrum of it. Would taste the salt of his skin. Her tongue darted out along her lips, tempted to do just that. She shivered. They were walking a fine line.

Reluctantly, she sat back. His arms tensed, fingers splaying wide along her back as though wanting to keep her close. It was only a fraction of a second, but it filled her with hope. Then the hold on her relaxed, allowing her to glide away. She didn't want to break the spell of this moment, but they had very little time.

"The first challenge is tomorrow," she whispered, the reminder slowing the race of her heart.

His face darkened, becoming somber. She winced, internally cursing herself.

Why do I have to ruin everything, she thought.

Because, her inner voice responded, *you know you don't deserve him. Stupid, broken girl.*

That's all she would ever be.

"You shouldn't be risking your life for me, Vidar. I'm not worth it."

His arms reached out, grasping her and pulling her flush against him once more. They were so close, she could feel the warmth of his breath against her cheek. Those gray eyes hardened as he forced her to look into them.

"Yes, you are," he reprimanded. Her body trembled involuntarily. Eyes wide as she stared into the intensity that was all him. The calm certainty and demanding dominance that he exuded focused only on her. The hand on her back flexed, inched upward toward the nape of her neck. Her heart skipped. Her breath caught. Then he stopped.

Frowning, he glanced toward the depths of the mountain before his gaze shifted to her once more. His tongue wetting his bottom lip. His eyes scanned her face, mouth so tantalizingly close. She wanted to beg and plead. Eager to taste. To touch. She nearly did, the words catching in her throat.

With a sigh he inched away, looking out into the star lit sky. The moment shattered like glass, leaving her feeling raw and jagged. Dismay settled like a lead weight in her stomach. He led them to the edge of the pool for a better view as she wrestled away the longing.

Never before had she seen so many stars. The sky was awash with them. The milky way was a strip of shimmering light in the deepness of space. The expanse of a dark valley stretched out before them. Touched by silver moonlight, and the vast array of stars. It was achingly beautiful. Just like him, she thought. How she wanted to stay here, locked in his arms. Looking out onto that gorgeous view forever.

Shame once again filled her at the thought of what he was doing for her. Everything he was risking. *Broken*, her mind taunted. When she turned back to face him, his attention was once more on her. Only now instead of hesitation, determination settled along the angular planes of his features.

"Come, we should get you warmed up."

Gently he guided her to the edge of the pool and helped her out. The air was cold against her chilled skin. She stood there, shivering, feeling achingly empty. Alone.

Vidar whistled down the tunnel, and suddenly there was a flurry of wings as some of the pixies raced around them. She felt a breeze along her body. Her hair lifted up and flew around her, the light wind quick but warm. Enid gasped as a tickling sensation rippled over her skin, and she spun around trying to see the tiny sprites as they whipped around her. Joyful surprise filled her as she marveled over the delicate beings.

She stopped when she noticed Vidar staring, eyes dark as he looked her over. His jaw clenched. He was dry now. Pants held in front of himself as though he got distracted before pulling them on. The muscles in his arms tensed as he surveyed her. Enid felt her cheeks redden, suddenly self-conscious. Her hair fell back around her shoulders. Perfectly dry, soft curls bounced against her skin.

Vidar's throat bobbed as he swallowed and then coughed. "That's enough, you pests," he said lightly, as though speaking to much beloved children. "Go on then."

There was the soft tinkling of tiny laughter as the small fae flew back down the hall. He stepped into his pants, pulling them over his briefs before picking her clothes up and handing them to her. Her fingers grazed his, sending a slight electric tingle through her. The thought of throwing that clothing aside and allowing her hands to explore the bare expanse of his torso was so tempting that for a moment Enid paused. Frozen in indecision. But then Vidar stepped away and grabbed his shirt.

The moment passed. Disappointment and mortification remained as she quickly dressed and followed him back to their rooms.

CHAPTER

25

Enid paced, her eyes drifting to trace the patterns in the carpets strewn along the floor. Guilt and despair pecked a hollow within her chest and curled within the aching cavity. Vidar was, as always, unreadable. He ate his breakfast without haste, and looked through some books on his desk. Acting for all the world as though he wasn't about to risk his life in a few, brief hours. Her breakfast sat on the corner of that same desk, next to a stack of ancient tomes, untouched.

Unsure of what to do, where to divert her nervous energy, she walked up behind him, peering over his shoulder at what he was reading. She itched to reach over and touch the soft, dark waves of his hair as she glanced in her periphery at the profile of his face. He was locked in concentration, his attention on the pages of the book before him. Brow furrowed, lips pursed. Forcing her eyes away, she was drawn to another book that lay open on his desk. A beautifully drawn, circular maze took up a full page. Her eyes followed the varying paths, searching for the most direct route.

She had loved mazes and puzzles when she was a kid. Had practically begged her parents to build her a maze of hedges in the yard, so that she might run through them and find her way like some lost voyager on a daring quest. Her mother had vetoed that idea.

Best not to think about those things, she thought, pushing it away. Her mind went blissfully blank.

A portrait she never noticed before lay halfway beneath some papers. Curiosity getting the better of her, she moved the pages aside and gingerly picked up the old, faded, tintype portrait. A woman gazed back at her. Her cheeks were flushed pink. Hand painted by the photographer, most likely. She was achingly beautiful. Pale hair spun into a delicate knot, with spiraled tendrils hanging around her round face. The photographer had taken great care to hand paint her eyes a delicate shade of blue. A soft smile curved her lips as she gazed into the camera. Her simple dress displayed a somewhat thin, but lovely figure.

Vidar's hand froze, his head lifting to watch as she held the ancient photograph. Appreciating the woman within it. "Who was she?" Enid asked as she moved around to sit in the chair beside his. The chair she had been using these last few days as he taught her about his world.

He reached out, taking the small oval of metal away from her, his fingers lightly touching the image. "Her name was Grace," he said. "We were to be bound."

Enid didn't know how to feel. Vidar was hundreds of years old. Of course he would have had relationships over the years. Why wouldn't he have been bound to someone? He wasn't offering to be bound to her. He was only going to claim her. She would be more of a pet for him to care for, not a partner in life. Still, part of her ached at the thought of him with another woman. Enid reprimanded herself. When did she become so irrational? She had no right to be jealous.

"What happened to her?" she asked instead, pushing away the pang of envy.

His eyes filled with love and sadness as he looked over the portrait of the beautiful young woman. Unable to help herself, Enid set her hand on his arm. The urge to comfort him was overwhelming. He stared at the lovely face for a few more moments before he finally found the words.

"She was someone I thought for a moment would be my salvation. A steady ship in a tumultuous ocean." His thumb grazed her face.

"Will you tell me about her?" Enid asked.

"She was a lot like you," Vidar said, after a long pause.

His gaze lingered upon the portrait for a second longer before placing it in a wooden box, and closing the lid gently. "She was killed by Revenant," he said simply.

Enid cast him a worried look. Was all of this payback for a slight he suffered long before she was even born? Suddenly she felt so very small, unsure of her place in this world once again. She did not want to be one of the Revenant, but was Vidar really in this for her, or was he only interested in revenge for his lost love.

"That must have been very difficult for you," she found herself saying.

"It was," he replied honestly. He glanced at her before running a hand through the thick mane of his hair. Pushing it away from his pale, stormy eyes. "But it was a long time ago."

Enid wasn't sure who he was trying to convince. Her, or himself. Suddenly, he stood up and went to one of the carved niches within the walls. Vidar had more than one room, each connected with an arched doorway, covered over by vibrantly colored fabric. This one was his private study. One of the end rooms without an external door into the outer tunnel. It contained a desk, a few chairs, a loveseat and coffee table, and walls of books, boxes, and trinkets displayed within niches.

From within a wooden box, he pulled out a metal bracelet. It was made up of several different types of metals braided together. At the top there was a circular, smooth green gemstone. It was beautiful, with the braids of silver, gold, and a dark brassy metal all swirled within itself. Vidar tenderly lifted her arm and looped the metal band around her wrist, pressing it until it was secure.

Enid stared at it, her eyes drawn to the stone that seemed to twinkle and shift. Almost like she was looking at some moving picture of green grass and towering evergreens. Her fingers reached toward it, wanting to feel the smoothness of it, to test those shifting patterns. Vidar stopped her, his hand grasping hers before she could touch its surface.

"This is a very ancient relic passed down through my family for generations," he explained. Enid stilled, wonder filling her as she gazed at the delicate braiding. "Every generation, the men of my family passed this along, to give to someone they hold dear. It offers a bit of their magic to the one who holds it."

Her heart thrummed in her chest, her throat constricting with emotion. He was giving this precious family heirloom to her? *Not worth it,* that hateful voice whispered within her. She felt like she was going to be sick.

"This stone has been set to a position of my choosing. One in which I know you will be safe. If for any reason I fail this challenge you must smash this gemstone. The magic within it will bring you through the veil to this place where the Revenant will not be able to reach you for a time. At least while you figure out where to go and what to do until they forget about you. Unfortunately, it has a one-time use."

Enid didn't know how to feel. The part of her that had been hurt and betrayed so many times was concerned this was another way to get back at the Revenant, and not about her. The other part, the part that wished fervently that happy endings were real, was honored that he chose to give this very important family heirloom to her of all people. Either way, she wanted to beg him not to continue this. To save himself. Her vision blurred as tears threatened to fall.

He cupped her cheek in his hands, and tilted her face to meet his. His thumb tracing the curve of her bottom lip. His hooded eyes were on her mouth as he leaned into her. Uncertainty and desire fought in equal measure along his striking features. She felt herself responding, reaching toward him, her eyes fluttering shut. Enid's chest pounded, her lips parting as she ached to close the miniscule space between them. There was the feather light graze of his lips against hers for the slightest second. Then came a knock at his door.

Vidar groaned, head dropping in defeat. Enid sat back, her eyes wide. The pounding of her heart still quick in her chest as Vidar got up. The cloth covering over the opening between rooms swung back to block her view as he went to answer the door.

She put a hand to her chest, trying to calm the erratic flutter. What was she doing? What would come of this? Not only was she uncertain of his intentions, but now she was unsure of what she wanted due to that uncertainty. Would she ever be able to trust him? Would he want more than her company? Could she handle this? Her whole life revolved around the outcome of today's event, and on the man who faced it. Not a man, she recalled. A fae. One who had a solid grip on her heart, and didn't even realize it yet.

The murmur of voices in the other room drew her attention. She stood to peek around the cloth. The guard that had escorted them her first day in the underground city was standing outside the door. Ull, she was told he was called.

"The King is calling everyone for the first challenge. It is in the level below the Underlings, in the great Labyrinth." Worry colored his voice. "Vidar, are you sure about this?"

"Of course," Vidar answered. "I would never have done this if I wasn't."

"Do you understand what is at stake though? She is not Grace. Helping this woman will not bring her back."

There was a rumble of rage that had Enid ducking out of sight behind the curtain.

"I know that," Vidar hissed. She leaned against the side of the arched opening, straining to hear the next words.

"I have my reasons for protecting her, and they are mine alone. I don't need to justify myself to anyone. Do not forget that."

There it was. The only explanation she was probably ever going to get.

"Of course, your—I mean, I'm sorry, sir," Ull replied. "If that is the case, we must leave now. The King wishes to speak to you beforehand. He has many worries."

Vidar gave a heavy sigh. "Yes, let him know I will be right there."

The door clicked close.

Enid pulled herself together before stepping around the curtain. Vidar turned from the door, lines of worry smoothing from his face as he looked at her. She drew her shoulders back, reaching for the new found strength she was striving so hard to cultivate. This may be the last chance she would have to change his mind. The very subject he kept brushing off every time she brought it up.

"Dokkalfar means a lot to you," her voice came out steady, despite her shattered nerves.

He was slow to respond, watching her with vigilant patience. "It does," he agreed.

"You are an integral part of this world, of the people within it. You bring balance and order." She held his gaze without faltering. Determination keeping her steady, her words firm. "Do not sacrifice yourself for me."

His eyes narrowed, hands sliding into his pockets as he slowly walked over to her. Something in the set of his shoulders had her drawing in a quivering breath. Suddenly, she couldn't bring herself to meet the stern look in his eyes. Then he was standing in front of her, her focus locked on the tight fabric of his shirt. He took her chin and lifted it.

"Do you wish to be Revenant, Enid?" His voice was dangerously low and even.

She gasped, her eyes widening in horror. "No!"

His fingers brushed along her jawline. Gray eyes moving along the contours of her face as though memorizing it.

"Then let's not speak of this again. I will protect you. I will defend you, because you are worthy." He stooped, eyes burning into hers. "Do you doubt my ability?"

"No." The word was a breath in the air between them.

"I don't doubt you either," he murmured. The tip of his nose brushed along hers, and her breath caught. "The choice is out of your hands now, and I have made mine." He drew back reluctantly. "It's time," he whispered.

Enid's heart thumped so strongly within her that it felt as though it would break free. She took a shuddering breath.

"I'm ready," she said.

***

The King met them in a small chamber furnished with only a few chairs and a table. It was well guarded, with a thick, soundproof door. Given the amount of care taken by the King and his guards, Enid was sure privacy was their intention.

They sat around the table, a grim look upon the King's face.

"These last few days we have been busy preparing for the challenges. I've also had my clansmen searching for any signs of deception." Fenri looked over to Vidar. "We have found nothing, but I can't get rid of this feeling." He shook his head, leaning back in his seat. For all of his attempts to appear detached and unfazed, there was something about the King that struck Enid as vulnerable. The King and his Enforcer had a special bond. It was clear. "You must remain vigilant," he grumbled.

Vidar nodded. "Always, my King."

He ran a hand over his face. Exhaling loudly before his gaze wandered to Enid. His words only for Vidar.

"And you are certain you are willing to take this risk? You above all people understand what it will mean if you fail."

The muscle along Vidar's jaw ticked as he gritted his teeth. He glanced over to Enid before turning a glare on the King that would make Enid wither.

"It appears that everyone is suddenly doubting my decisions today. I'm only answering this question one last time. Yes, I'm certain." He leaned back in his chair. Arms folding over his chest as he and the King scowled at each other across the table.

"It is time for Vidar to prepare. My men will take you to your seat. The Revenant will be waiting for you. He is quite determined," the King grumbled, his eyes never leaving Vidar's.

Enid shuddered. "I don't understand why. He doesn't even know me."

She jumped as the King barked out a laugh and broke the stare down to give her an exasperated look.

"My dear, you have much to learn about the ways of the fae. We do not think or feel the same way that humans do. He wants you because he feels like he has the right to you. He has tasted your blood, felt your compulsion to him. For him that is enough. The Revenant are fickle creatures. Especially that one from what I hear."

She frowned, frustration and anger filling her at the thought of her life being upended once again due to a possessive male. Vidar shifted in the chair, his emotions mirroring her own. Enid couldn't help but feel anxious for him again. This was all her fault. Here he was, her savior, her champion, risking everything to give her some semblance of a normal life.

They stood to go their separate ways. Vidar and the King to some unknown location to prepare, and Enid to the creature who hunted her. She would sit and bear witness, and await a fate that was out of her hands. Tears filled her eyes and she rushed to Vidar, flinging her arms around his waist.

Breathing deeply, she took in his scent as though she could commit it to memory. Earthy sandalwood and warm musk. She looked up, searching his face, uttering a silent prayer that this wouldn't be the last time she saw him. If this challenge didn't go well, this would be the last moment they had. The thought kept her words balled in her throat, unable to escape. Her eyes burned.

His expression softened as he noticed the shimmer of unshed tears. Gently, he touched her face, his thumb softly grazing the curve of her cheek bone. Then he pulled away, and was gone.

She stood alone in the circular room, holding in a sob. Only the guards flanking the door remained. Silent witnesses to her pain.

***

King Fenri mumbled under his breath. They stood in the hall before the entrance to the great labyrinth, deep in the bowels of the kingdom. Usually, the ancient maze remained abandoned. The purpose for its construction long ago lost to the passage of time. Fenri paced, his hands laced at the back of his head. Vidar ignored him, his focus on the door.

He had only seen the ancient labyrinth two times in his life. Once, when he was a boy, from the balcony overlooking the maze as his father told him stories of heroes and feats that required not only strength but mental acuity. The other time was now, as he stood outside its forbidding entrance. Torches lit either side of the massive rectangular opening. The knotted design of a snake chasing its tail chiseled into the granite surround.

"You shouldn't worry so much, Fenri," Vidar grumbled.

"Easy for you to say," Fenri snapped. "You're sure I can't talk you out of this? You know what you mean to this kingdom."

Vidar huffed. "We have been working for two hundred years on the probability this day would come. I am not immortal, that we know of. Besides, today is not the day I die."

Fenri continued his pacing. "You don't know that."

"Not today."

Vidar's steel gray eyes flashed black. Fenri stopped pacing, his arms dropping to his sides, shoulders sagging.

"I promised your father I would look out for you—protect you. You're my godson. And you are asking me to turn the other way and let you sacrifice yourself for a human. Why?"

Vidar turned his head to his godfather. The black of his eyes seeped away at the agony on Fenri's face.

"I've received a prophecy."

Fenri frowned, his eyes narrowing. "Do you care to share?"

Vidar ran a hand through his hair and shrugged.

"All I know is that she will be powerful, and she doesn't realize it. We will need her and, she will be dangerous in Revenant hands."

Fenri rubbed his eyes, pinching the bridge of his nose before giving a nod and crossing his arms over his chest. "I'll respect your decisions, as usual. Do not go seeking Hel this night."

He held his arm out. Vidar gave him a small smile as he reached out and clasped his own arm against it, gripping firmly. With a final pleading look the King turned and stalked out of the hall, preparing to make his way above to announce the beginning of the trial. Vidar turned back to the doorway. He took a deep breath, readying himself for what lay within. Though, he couldn't stop the drift of his thoughts to Enid.

He still didn't understand the hold she seemed to have on him. How he looked forward to seeing those inquisitive green eyes every morning. How he couldn't seem to keep his hands to himself. Taking any opportunity to touch her soft skin, that vibrant red hair. The way the corners of her full mouth tilted when she was contemplating something, her eyes narrowing at the edges as if she could see the solution.

Running a hand over his face, he groaned aloud. What had he gotten himself into? He shook himself out of it. He had to focus. Too much depended on him making it through this challenge.

The flicker of torchlight sputtered beyond the opening. He took another deep, steadying breath. By some twist of fate, he actually knew the way through the twisted puzzle, having traced the design of this very one in his childhood so often it was etched into his mind. He fingered the slingshot at his hip. A bag of smooth stones beside it on his belt. His weapon of choice, the only one he was allowed. As the breath drifted past his lips, he stepped forward to wait at the mouth of the ancient door. Prepared to face whatever he might find.

***

The halls were filled with fae chattering in excitement as they made their way toward the location of the challenge. Several whispered and pointed in her direction as they passed. The guards on either side of her shoving a few of the bolder ones away. Through a break in the crowd, Enid caught a glimpse of a familiar head of soft, curly hair and wide, almond shaped eyes. She gasped, lurching to a stop, fervently searching the crowd.

"Cindy!" she called out.

There was nothing. Only the snickers and mocking japes of the fae imitating her frantic shout in a whining sing-song. Wincing at her foolishness, she followed the guards who urged her along. Was her imagination tricking her? There could be no way her friend was here, trapped and alone among the dark and horrific beings of this feral realm. Enid shook her head. The pain in her temples bracketed to a mind-numbing pound. She let the thoughts go, and the pain drifted away.

They walked through several sets of the tightly spiraled tunnels. The air becoming increasingly dank. The atmosphere gloomier the farther down they went. The chattering of the fae around her grew soft as though even they sensed there was something oppressive within the bowels of their mountain home.

Here, within these lower levels, something ancient and evil crept. The image of fear made real as it slithered its way into the minds of the beings who dared enter its lair. Or that's what it seemed to Enid as she scrutinized the demeanor of those around her. The fae seemed to distance themselves from one another. Distrustful, even of their friends. The guards stepped closer, wary of the duty to protect their charge. They seemed to walk forever into the depths of that bleakness.

Finally, they came upon their destination. Stepping out from the tunnel onto a stone shelf, she looked out upon the enormous maze stretched out below. Her breath stolen by the sheer size of the structure. Attached to the stone she stood upon, and anchored into the granite wall by giant iron rods, was a wooden ring of benches, five tiers deep. On the upper stone ledge was a separate structure, obviously set up for the King and Queen. Their seats positioned slightly above everything else. The carved wooden seats were regal. Especially compared to the rows of bench seating everyone else occupied.

It all looked freshly built. Made to overlook the intricate labyrinth far, far beneath the wooden structure. No glittering orbs of fairy light shone here. Instead, there were flickering torches aflame in metal sconces set along the walls around them, and in the maze below. The wood creaked beneath the footsteps of the creatures who shifted along it, making Enid pause nervously. There would be no surviving a fall into that maze should the whole structure come loose from its moorings.

"Move it, meat!" A furious, guttural shout came from behind her. An enormous creature pushed past. It towered over her with a bald, bumpy head and a large slit of mouth that did nothing to hide the grotesque teeth erupting from it. Its barrel-like chest loomed feet above her head. Enid gulped, her mind no longer bothered by the possible drop.

Ogre, she recalled. The precise detailed explanation playing through her head in Vidar's soothing, patient voice. Deadly, but slow and stupid, and, most importantly, craves human flesh. Another potential hunter among the deadly fae.

"Watch where you're going."

The guards around her bristled, their hands moving closer to their weapons. Eyes flashing dangerously. The ogre let out a huff, throwing Enid a last lingering look before muttering under its breath and trudging off around the upper platform to be seated.

Dimitri waited next to the seat she was ushered to. A dark red rose in his hand.

"You look beautiful as always, my flower," he murmured, leaning toward her as she sat.

Though the circumstances involving the challenges were never far from her mind the last few days, thoughts of Dimitri were. Whatever she felt for him before, that pull which drew her like a moth to flame, appeared to have lessened significantly. Looking at him next to her now, she realized that while he was indeed very handsome, she did not have that soul searing, intense reaction to him. She found the thought comforting. When she went to meet her fate, she wanted to do it with her own feelings and thoughts.

The rose was pressed into her hand, his eyes peering at her hungrily. Bright in the low light cast by the flickering torches.

"Thank you," she said, turning to admire the labyrinth below.

"I look forward to our time together the next few days, the first of an eternity," he said.

She frowned then, turning to look at him, and met those pale eyes with a look of indifference. A small smile tilted the corner of his mouth expectantly.

"We will see," she said simply, turning back to face the challenge area. She didn't miss the flicker of disappointment as she turned away. The way his smile crumbled. He leaned back, giving her space, though she could still feel that penetrating stare.

They were in the front row. A solid railing of wood kept her from plunging to the rocky terrain below. She could see most of the labyrinth from here. Only the farthest pathways were too far to see into.

Enid's eyes followed the network below, scanning for the way through the intricate pattern. Recognition flared within her. The book from this morning. Vidar had been studying this very maze. She almost laughed aloud, but held back, glancing around with a smile. They all came to see him fail, but they would be sorely disappointed. Only Dimitri was watching her. His blue eyes strained.

The crowd was restless, the various types of fae grouped together. All intent on witnessing the fate of the King's Enforcer. The dull roar of their chatter carried through the large chamber. The sounds echoing strangely against the domed ceiling. Conversations grew faint as the Queen and King entered the chamber, moving to sit in their chairs overlooking the crowd. Eager anticipation filled the atmosphere.

The King leaned over to speak with the Queen, their heads drawing together for a moment. Hers dark and regal, his scruffy and savage. She nodded once, and the King stood, motioning for silence. Within seconds the last of the echoing voices faded, the crowd rapt as they waited for their King's words.

"My people," he began, his deep, rasping voice carrying easily among the crowd, "we gather to witness the first challenge of the Elemental. Earth!" The crowd began to clap and cheer. Whistles erupting from among them. A few of the smaller fae flinched at the noise.

The King beckoned for quiet once more.

"At the gong, our champion will enter the labyrinth of the ancients. He will have one hour to complete the maze. However, it will not be as simple as that." As he spoke, three doors opened within the outer wall of the labyrinth, one directly below Enid. From them stepped three hulking minotaur.

The fae cheered, stomping their feet. The wood beneath them groaned at the animated praise. Enid's smile faltered and withered as she watched the beast below shake his horned head. He was even larger than the minotaur that chased her at Northspire. Beside her, Dimitri shifted forward, wicked glee bright upon his face. The King calmed the crowd again, his jaw ticking in irritation, eyes narrowing.

Silence descended.

"In order to complete the challenge, the champion must get through the labyrinth. The Minotaur have each been promised early release from their imprisonment should they succeed in keeping our champion from completing this test."

Soft murmuring broke out among the crowd and was quickly dispensed. Enid frowned. These creatures were prisoners? What had they done to earn such a fate in a world full of savagery.

The King looked out over the crowd, his eyes pausing on Enid before he lifted his hand. There was a single, clear boom of a gong. The sound vibrated on the air around them, tickling her eardrum until it faded to silence. And then Vidar stepped into the mouth of the Labyrinth.

He moved confidently among the turns, working his way through the beginning with ease. Every so often he would hesitate, his head twisting to the side—listening. The minotaur moved quickly, noses twitching, hooves stomping. Breath and spittle flew from their noses and mouths as they rushed through the maze, searching for their prey. They were determined creatures.

Enid's heart was in her throat. Worry like ice through her veins. She cried out when he reached a bend, one of the minotaur on the other side.

"It is no use, my flower," Dimitri said. "The labyrinth is warded. He cannot see or hear us."

Enid's eyes were wide, her teeth biting into her lower lip as she sat on the edge of her seat, unable to look away but terrified to see. Her fingers moved to the bracelet on her wrist, running along the twisted metal.

"All will be well." Dimitri whispered. "I will be here for you when he is gone."

"Don't," Enid snapped, her eyes cutting to his.

"I only want to be your champion, to keep you safe, to hold and serve you," his voice was full of passion and sincerity. His fingers grazed against hers where they dug hard into her knees.

"Stop," she hissed, focusing on the movements below.

Vidar stepped away from the wall. Silent as a shadow. His arm lifted a simple slingshot, drawing the strip of leather back. It whipped forward, an object flying from it and arching over the top of the labyrinth, clattering some distance away. The Minotaur, so close to stepping around the corner and coming upon Vidar, stopped. Its horned head turned toward that noise, and it rushed in the opposite direction. Away from its intended quarry.

Enid breathed a sigh of relief, slumping in her seat. Vidar hurried on, his feet taking him unerringly along the most direct path she had mapped out among the false turns and dead ends.

He was in the middle of the great maze when the second Minotaur ran at him down one of the long, straight passages. He reacted so fast it had to be instinct, drawing the leather pad and releasing it.

The stone struck the Minotaur between the eyes.

The enormous creature stopped mid run as though in surprise. Its large body swayed back and forth. A thin red line trickled down its wide, furry snout. Its eyes rolled back into its head and it fell backward. The ground shaking as it slammed into it. Enid gasped as she felt the shudder through the wooden structure.

Vidar was nearly through. His footing sure as he hastened along. The final passage was within sight. The etching of the great serpent eating its tail carved deep around the exit. Suddenly, he was thrown into the air. Body slamming into the wall beside him. He roared in pain, the muscles along his large arms rigid. Within his hands, he gripped the horn of the third Minotaur, the tip of which was speared into his side. The other horn scraped against the stone of the wall.

Enid screamed, her hands flying up to cover her mouth.

A grimace of pain was stark across Vidar's face. Blood gushed between his fingers. Those gray eyes turned hard. Blackness covering them completely. He bellowed his rage as he glared with those depthless, black eyes into the wide, brown ones of the Minotaur. With a mighty shove, the Minotaur was sent reeling back. The horn Vidar held within his grasp broken in two.

The beast touched the fractured stump with a shaking hand. Vidar stood tall, having dropped to his feet from the wall. A streak of blood bright along the dusty stone where his falling body smeared it. He yanked the pointed horn from his side, scattering more of the crimson liquid along the floor.

They faced each other, the Minotaur frightened and shaking. Somehow smaller as it cowered before the fearsome, fury filled visage of Vidar.

With a ferocious yell, Vidar rushed the Minotaur, the broken horn clenched tightly in his hand. The Minotaur lowered its head in response, his other horn taking aim between Vidar's ribs, hooves planted firmly. With a leap, Vidar sailed above the

Minotaur and grabbed that lowered horn. As he flew around it, the Minotaur's head was forced back, fully exposing the length of its thick neck. Vidar landed, jerked the beast to the side and then struck.

The fragment of horn dug deep before Vidar twisted and slashed it away, spraying blood in a wide arch across the door of the Labyrinth. The face of the endless snake stared down at the scene below, stained red with the blood of the Minotaur. Covered in that same blood, the vestiges of rage still bright within him, Vidar stepped through the exit and completed the first challenge.

Enid lowered her trembling body down onto the bench. She wasn't aware of when she had shot to her feet, along with the rest of the screaming crowd as they watched Vidar's gruesome battle with the final Minotaur. Its body now still, large eyes open and glazed, staring at the door of the Labyrinth.

Vidar had done it. He was through. But at what cost? His side appeared to be a bloody mess from where she sat. Blood gushed from the wound at an alarming pace. She wanted to see him, to know he was ok. Without thinking, she stood, turning to look for an exit, a way to go to him.

A firm grip on her arm stopped her, and her body was jerked against Dimitri's.

"I wouldn't do that, my beauty," he whispered into her ear, his voice low enough that none of the other creatures nearby would hear. "There are many who would be more than happy to take advantage of a lone human woman wandering about the tunnels." He released her arm, letting her take in the hungry fae that glanced her way.

She frowned. "I just want to know he is ok."

There was a flash of jealousy. He twisted away from her, jaw ticking, blue eyes scanning the crowd.

"He will be fine. I can assure you of this. I do not like him, but he is the Enforcer and I can respect his strength."

His intensity turned on her with the force of a powerful wave. "You will know when all is not well, because I will not hesitate to make you mine."

His fingers twisted a lock of her hair, eyes on her mouth as he stepped into her. She leaned away, her body wanting to take a

226

step to keep that distance between them. Only the creatures hovering around the slowly emptying arena kept her in place.

"You are hesitant. I see that. But I will win your heart." His voice grew deep as he leaned toward her, voice buzzing along her skin. His lips brushed the outer edge of her ear. "You will beg me to take you."

Enid shivered involuntarily.

"I want to go now," she murmured.

Dimitri bowed his head and offered his arm, an imitation of gentlemanly behavior. She swallowed her protest, glancing warily at the lingering fae eyeing her with interest, and took the presented arm. A luminous smile stretched across his face as he placed his other hand over hers. Holding it as though she were a precious jewel. They passed leering creatures, making their way out to the tunnels.

"My family is preparing a dinner in your honor tonight. I have a special gift for you."

Enid's eyes narrowed. How appealing his words were. She had learned how the Revenant were masters of seduction, whispering words of flattery and praise. Promises of power and wealth, of passion. Whatever their susceptible prey needed to be lured into their dark embrace. Enid would follow along for the moment, but she would keep her wits about her. He wouldn't fool her again.

CHAPTER

26

The chair wasn't uncomfortable, but even so Enid couldn't help shifting. Seeking relief that she knew wouldn't come. Revenant laughed and chatted amicably in the large hall meant for dining and entertainment.

Like the other rooms in this underground world, this one was carved into the granite of the surrounding mountain. Large pillars lined either side, roman in style, creating a ring around the outside. An enormous table dominated the interior of those columns. It appeared to be carved from one solid slice of tree. The uneven edges buffed to a finish so smooth that it felt like velvet beneath her fingers.

Fairy orbs of different sizes hung over the center of the table, their luminance reflected in its polished surface. The vines growing along them were vibrantly green, trumpeted flowers opening their faces toward the soft, shimmering glow.

At the back of the room, through the towering columns, a sheet of water rippled from the ceiling, splashing into a rectangular pool of water. Lily pads floated upon the surface, their fragrant flowers a dash of pink amongst the gray and green. Lights hovered freely over the water's surface, flickering and floating along trembling leaves like huge fireflies. Their illumination scattering like falling diamonds amongst the spray of water.

Dimitri sat to her right, the Queen's empty seat to her left at the head of the table. When they first entered, Dimitri took the opportunity to press closer, whispering that she held the seat of honor at the massive table.

His voice caused her to shiver. Lips delicately brushing her skin as he spoke, breath warm and soft. That air of seduction was suffocatingly thick around him as he coaxed her to her seat. The silk of the dress she was made to wear slid like water over her bare skin, drawing Dimitri's icy gaze to the curves that lay beneath. It was a beautiful dress, the soft material a deep, inky black. Her skin gleamed like moonlight in contrast, her hair the color of shining copper, her eyes a vibrant jade. As beautiful as it was, it made her feel very exposed. The filmy fabric left nothing to the imagination.

The Revenant were strangely generous in their treatment of her. Before dinner she had been led to a room to prepare. The Queen having sent one of her own attendants to help. Dimitri waited outside, refusing to have her away from his exceptional hearing. Obviously distrustful of his own people despite their claim of family.

The attendant had drawn a bath in a large copper tub, perfumes and oils hovering heavily in the steaming water, before leaving her to her own devices. A small vanity with a bench sat in a corner, a partition beside it, behind which she had found the dress hanging next to a towel and robe.

She had wandered around in the robe for a bit after her bath, poking curiously at the jars and combs laid out on the vanity, when the door opened again—the attendant returned. Silently she was prepped, the blonde-haired woman with cold blue eyes working a comb through her hair until it tumbled in shiny waves along her shoulders. She dabbed something pink along Enid's cheeks and lips before lining her eyes lightly with a black kohl pencil.

The dress itself fit surprisingly well, hugging her chest, waist, and hips. It made her a bit nervous wondering how they managed to figure out her size. Even the height was correct, the fabric swishing around her ankles. A slit on the right side opened up to her thigh, showing off the length of her leg when she moved. Thin straps circled along the tops of her shoulders and around her sides. Leaving her back completely exposed to the curve of her waist. The black slip-on shoes she was given were soft, and well-padded against the cold of the stone. At least part of the outfit was sensible.

Dimitri stood as she walked out of the room. His jaw clenched while his eyes traveled over her, ravenous when they returned to her face. Enid ignored him, turning away from that heady look. Without a word he moved beside her, motioning down the hallway. That charged silence remained between them until they had reached this place.

The room was obviously decorated for celebration, and Enid found herself wondering how often they used it. Dimitri chivalrously pulled out her chair as the other Revenant looked on with varying looks of approval, mockery, or distaste. Only as he pushed her seat in under her did he risk a touch. Fingers grazing along her shoulder as he moved her hair away to whisper into her ear. Then he took his seat, his chair scraping loudly as he pulled it closer to her own.

Platters of food were scattered along the table. Enid eyed it skeptically, as well as the thick ruby liquid in the delicate stemmed glasses in front of the Revenant. Her own glass contained the golden liquid she recognized as dandelion wine.

The sight of it made her think of Vidar. Once more her mind wandered to him—worry pricking through her. She lifted the glass, sipping at it lightly. The sight seemed to please Dimitri. He grinned, placing a few things on her plate, murmuring to her about the delicious qualities of each.

"Do you eat actual food?" she asked. He chuckled.

"Dah, the flavors are more pronounced now that I am Revenant. We need the human blood to help give us power, to flush us with life, but we enjoy normal food just as much."

Hesitantly, she lifted a flakey looking pastry to her mouth, taking a small, investigative bite. The flavor was amazing. The taste of honey and sweet syrupy dates exploded in her mouth in a symphony. She hummed in delight, tongue flicking out to lick the delicate crumbs from her lips. Dimitri leaned his head against his hand, his eyes following the movement.

"I could watch you eat all day, my flower," he murmured, his voice low.

Enid nearly choked, putting the pastry back onto her plate before taking another tiny sip of her wine to help wash down the bite. Dimitri's smirk faltered. He shook it off, the easy smile slipping back into place.

"Would you like something else to drink? We have many more delicious wines you may enjoy. The Queen has a cavern full of all of the rarest wines."

She shook her head, "This one is good, thank you."

"Brother!" A loud voice called, cutting through the stream of voices around them.

Enid went rigid as Dimitri stood and embraced his sister. Images from their first meeting flashed through her mind. The mirthless humor in her voice would always send a tremor of loathing and fear through her. Even in a dark blue mini dress with matching stilettos she moved with the feline grace of a predator. Behind them Charlie glowered at Enid. Dark eyes blazing murderously.

Dimitri gave a low, dark laugh. "I suggest you do not look at my intended with such hatred in your eyes." He stepped closer to the blond man, hands in his pockets as though completely at ease despite the hostile tone. "Unless you would like me to pluck them from your head."

Gleeful laughter erupted from Lania as Charlie's head jerked to the side. His eyes roaming the room lazily instead.

"Brother, you have such a way with my pet. But look at how well he is behaving. My good little puppy."

She draped herself over Charlie, fingers sliding along the nape of his neck. He turned toward her, a smile curling along the edge of his lips as she whispered to him sweetly before rewarding him with a deep, lingering kiss.

Enid's stomach turned. The small amount of wine and food threatening to come back up.

"After all," came her velvety, thick voice as she pulled away from the kiss, still clinging to Charlie's solid form, "we are to be family soon. We must get along. Is that not correct, dear sister?".

Enid tried not to flinch as the woman's calculating gaze turned to her. Charlie appeared unfocused, his eyes glassy as he stared at Lania as though drugged—his whole world revolving around her. Enid only gave the woman a small smile. Thankfully, Lania and Charlie moved further down the table away from them. Lania excitedly hugging and kissing people along the way.

Enid once again found herself studying the crowd, never allowing her eyes to stray too long or meet any others directed at her. All of the men were dressed the same. Black dress pants with belts and black dress shirts with sleeves rolled up along their forearms. Top two buttons undone to give a peek of skin beneath the fabric. Only the women were dressed differently. Their many different dresses showing off the unique beauty of each, like glittering jewels in a crown.

She was puzzling over the meaning of that differentiation, when the seats across from them were pulled away from the table. Her eyes shifted in their direction.

Stunned silence whisked away every thought. Every careful rumination.

Wide brown eyes met hers with a soft, soulful sadness.

Cindy.

Enid couldn't move, couldn't breathe. Pain fractured her. A tear slipped down the curve of her cheek as she took in the sight of her best friend sitting amongst these bloodthirsty creatures. She seemed somehow more beautiful, but also more fragile than ever. Deep circles hung below her eyes, but other than that, her skin was luminous. Gold, shimmering fabric draped over one shoulder highlighted her rich, cocoa skin. Her hair was undone, combed out into a soft, caramel halo around her oval face, a golden comb pushing the right side back above her ear. She was as elegant and stunning as usual. But Enid could see the sorrow in the curve of her full mouth, in the dimness of her eyes, the delicate arch of her brow.

Next to her sat the man Vidar had been speaking to at the diner the night she was taken. His ebony skin was nearly as dark as his shirt. His warm brown eyes strikingly amber against that darkness. One muscular arm was slung protectively over the back of Cindy's chair, the other beside his plate. His back was turned slightly toward the rest of the room. Cutting them off from the rest of the Revenant, attempting to isolate them with his posture.

The hum of conversation began to soften, eyes turning toward Cindy. The looks she received were very different from those directed at Enid. Curiosity, approval, and desire all aimed at the gilded woman seated across from Enid at the Queen's left.

232

"Surprise," Dimitri whispered in her ear.

Anger flared as Dimitri lifted his glass toward the couple. Her hands shook so violently that Enid had to clench them in her lap.

"Marcus," he murmured in greeting. The other man nodded in response before leaning into Cindy and whispering. Cindy turned to him, glancing toward the other Revenant before shifting away.

A smiling woman in a pink dress with a full skirt brought a corked glass jar to the new arrivals. She poured thick red liquid into the glass in front of Cindy, giving a slight curtsy and backing away, before she handed the bottle to Marcus. As she left, confusion filled her delicate face. Marcus glared at the woman's back, the arm over Cindy's chair tense.

Cindy remained indifferent, refusing to meet any eye— including Enid's. That stung because Enid couldn't seem to tear her eyes away from the sight of her friend. She could only stare. Fighting the burn of threatening tears.

The soft murmur of voices cut off suddenly.

Every eye moved as one toward the door as the Queen walked in, fashionably late and obviously set to make an entrance. Her clothing was nothing more than a thin sheet of silvery fabric clinging to her curves. The straps delicate silver chains. A circle of silver sat around her head from which silver strands and crystal beads dangled in the black waves of her hair. She was a startling contrast of dark and shimmering light. A radiant night sky.

She moved with the same dangerous grace of all of their kind, only more pronounced as if she expected every eye in the room to be upon her. And they were. The Revenant were all frozen before her, staring in exaltation at their Queen. Only Cindy's eyes flicked toward Enid's as she looked around, before catching herself. She stared at the Queen, tense, forced. Nothing like the other Revenant.

The Queen stopped next to her seat as the attendants pulled her chair out, settling her into it lovingly before moving back to either side. They were crimson garbed shadows at her back, only moving when given some unspoken command to address the Queen's needs. Her glass was filled, the attendant curtsying and backing away after doing so. She ate nothing. A plate not even set before her on the wooden table. Once she had taken a drink of the thick red liquid, licking the ruby drops from her lips, did she turn her attention to the group. A motherly smile upon her face.

"Thank you, my dearest ones, for being here today as we welcome new arrivals to our family." She motioned to either side of her. "And a joyful reunion between our newest addition, and a prospective one. Once the Enforcer fails in his trials."

Cindy and Enid locked eyes over the table to a chorus of soft laughter.

"Eat, drink, and rejoice over our continued growth and prosperous blessings."

The Revenant cheered at that declaration, and the talking and laughing continued as though a silent order granted it.

"Enid, sweetheart," the Queen said, a bright smile upon her lovely face, "you must be so happy to see your friend. She wouldn't be here if it weren't for you. We thought you might be pleased."

The Queen acknowledged the couple on her left. Cindy's eyes flashed bitterly before they lowered to the empty plate before her.

"My Marcus has been so very accommodating," the Queen continued.

Marcus's hands clenched on the table. Cindy took it in hers, a silent solidarity passing between the two. With her other, she lifted her glass to her lips, trying to hide the shaking as she took a hearty gulp. Enid's eyes widened as the thick, red liquid was swallowed. A flush crept onto Cindy's cheeks when she noticed her alarm.

"Marcus and Dimitri have always been two of my favorites," the Queen spoke as though unaware of the tension among the group. "I do hope you understand when I call them to fulfill their duties. We do have obligations in our community. They can't always remain by your side."

Her eyes narrowed dangerously, the full weight of them on Cindy. The veiled threat obvious despite her sweet tone. There was a story there. Enid was certain. Marcus brushed his fingers along the skin of Cindy's arm. As though it was a secret signal, Cindy's attention snapped toward the Queen with a bright smile.

"Of course, my Queen," Cindy assured, her voice sweet and bright. "We are ready to serve."

The Queen smiled proudly, her shoulders drawing back as though preening.

"Please, call me Isis."

Cindy lowered her head in feigned meekness. "Yes, Queen Isis."

Satisfied, she turned back to Enid. "You do not seem pleased, my dear."

Enid tore her eyes away from her friend. Attempting to reign in her volatile anger. She could almost feel her cheeks blazing with heat, the fiery burn of it in her chest.

"Why would I be?"

The Queen's eyes narrowed. Dimitri's hand found the curve of her thigh, squeezing in silent warning. Enid twisted toward him, allowing him to see the full face of her fury.

"My flower," Dimitri soothed, "hasn't our majestic Queen been so very generous in throwing us this wondrous celebration. We are all so lucky to be at her mercy." His bright eyes met hers meaningfully as he emphasized the last few words.

Enid froze, her anger washing away as she realized her error.

The Revenant were all silent. They stared intently at Enid as though ready to tear her from limb to limb at a command. Cindy's eyes were wide. Marcus appeared indifferent, but his body tensed as though prepared to protect the woman at his side. Cindy gave a subtle shake of her head as she picked up her glass again, watching Enid over the rim as she took a deep drink.

"Of course," she said, turning back to the fuming Queen. "What I meant was, why wouldn't I be? Your majesty has been very…magnanimous."

The Queen stared. Enid squirmed beneath that hard glare. Unconsciously, her hand moved to the bracelet Vidar had given her. The smooth dome of the green jewel warm and comforting beneath her fingers. The Queen relaxed.

"Quite," she finally replied.

Conversations continued, the tension evaporating. Dimitri's hand left her thigh with a slow, lingering caress of fingertips against the exposed skin. He picked up her wine glass, lifted her hand in his and delicately kissed her fingers before he wrapped them around the stem.

"Drink," he whispered. Her hand trembled only a little as she pressed the cool glass to her mouth, gulping the sweet, honeyed wine.

"The Enforcer put on a very entertaining show," Marcus said, his free hand moving to fill his glass with blood. "I hear he is recovering very well from his wounds."

Enid's head snapped up at that statement. His eyes met hers briefly before he gave a nod so slight she couldn't be sure of the movement. He took a deep drink from his glass before continuing his survey of the room.

"Yes," the Queen sighed, "I do enjoy such a bloody display. It is too bad the Enforcer is beneath my consideration, or I may be tempted to help him heal that poor, battered body. I might even let him enjoy it, given the amount of blood he spilled tonight."

The Revenant tittered with laughter. Enid didn't trust herself to speak. She could feel Dimitri's stare. Could see the vibrant blue from the corner of her eye. Refusing to meet his ardent gaze, she instead kept her focus on her plate. Taking in the hammered, gold detailing around the rim as if it was the most interesting thing she had seen. Vidar was okay. He was healing. That was a welcome relief.

***

After that awkward dinner, in which Enid barely ate, Dimitri took her for a walk through the tunnels. She wanted to talk to Cindy, but she and Marcus disappeared without a word. Enid would need to find time alone with her friend—if at all possible. She needed to tell her how sorry she was, how she never meant for any of this to happen.

There were many features of the Revenant sector that reminded her of the human world above. Torchlight sconces lined the walls—the flickering orbs of fairy light far more infrequent. There were also many decorative embellishments like clay vessels filled with fragrant flowers, and hanging brass bowls with the soft mist of perfumed incense drifting lazily from their open mouths.

Tapestries hung along the walls of fantastical beasts—unicorns and griffins. Momentarily she wondered if they were some of the real creatures she now lived among. She had yet to wander across either. Flowing swaths of gem-colored fabrics hung along the walkways. The shops and small cafe spaces decorated like an exotic bazaar. The sound of running water lingered around each bend. Some sort of fountain, either standing or wall mounted, resided among the different floors of the annex. Their clock, while beautiful, depicted the sun with a rage-filled, demonic face.

The Revenant, with their human faces, made her feel as though she could imagine this as some sort of large market in a far-off land. The only differences among them were the variety of race and complexion, and types of dress. As though a melting pot of nations united to form a vast cultural trading hub, and she was a fortunate spectator to the splendor of its existence.

Dimitri stopped at different shops every so often to push upon her some sort of delicacy. Bottles of fragrant perfumes were wrapped for her to take. Chocolate that melted in her mouth like smooth butter. A silken scarf that accentuated the color of her eyes.

At one shop, he spoke to a dark-skinned revenant whose face was flushed from the coals of a nearby spit. Flanks of meat turned over the embers, globs of fat and juice falling every so often to sizzle in the low flame. The smell was mouthwatering. A morsel of the delicate meat was given to him.

"You must try this," Dimitri said softly as he held it up to her lips. He refused to let her take it with her fingers.

Cautiously, she opened her mouth, watching him warily. He only chuckled, flashing her a curve of a smile as he delicately placed the meat between her lips, the tips of his fingers grazing them seemingly on accident. Though, the heated look he gave her spoke otherwise.

She narrowed her eyes in annoyance, but then the flavor burst upon her tongue. It was heavenly, the meat perfectly seasoned and flavorful, coated in a sweet and savory glaze. It was decadence. Dimitri slowly licked his fingertips clean as he watched her, that smirk upon his face knowing and suggestive.

"It is delectable, yes?" he questioned.

She rolled her eyes. "It is acceptable."

Dimitri laughed loudly then, his eyes lighting up in amusement.

"Come, my flower, do not let your irritation of me cloud your judgment."

Enid groaned. "Fine," she admitted. "It's amazing."

He continued laughing as he took the bags from her and pulled her exuberantly down the winding pathway to the story below. She found herself smiling softly at his cheerfulness. From the expressions of the other Revenant, all mystified and confused, she was sure this was a side of Dimitri rarely seen.

He chatted amicably, pointing out his favorite food stalls, and the stores with the best spices. There was a place that sold books, and others that sold clothing of both modern and more vintage design. Though he was quick to tell her that if she needed anything he would introduce her to his favorite seamstress. Enid nodded along, half listening to him as her mind drifted aimlessly to thoughts of Vidar.

"One more stop, my flower, and then I will take you to your room," Dimitri promised. He pulled her into a doorway to one of the winding tunnels between floors. Up they walked through the levels. When they reached a doorway of a familiar color, she realized he had taken her to the annex her rooms were in.

Curiosity filled her as he led her through the now familiar winding catacombs. They entered the chamber containing the frozen body of Vidar's father, and down the subsequent hallway, past her door, to Vidar's. It was then that Dimitri stopped and stepped to the side.

He gestured toward her. "You wanted to make sure he was ok. As a human you are able to enter without an invitation," he said, his voice low.

"Why are you doing this?" Enid asked.

He looked at her, his eyes full of emotion. Want and hurt clearly written within the softness of his gaze. "I promised you that I only wanted your happiness. That I would do whatever it took to make you feel joy." His throat bobbed. "I am keeping my promise."

She stood in shock, uncertain what to do. This was unexpected.

"Thank you," she said softly. She reached for the doorknob.

"I will be here when you are done. To walk you to your rooms," Dimitri murmured.

"You don't have to do that," Enid replied, looking over her shoulder. He frowned at the ground, shoulders tense.

"I will make sure you are safe," he replied stubbornly, shaking his head. "I will walk you to your door."

Enid nodded and reached her hand out to touch his arm. He looked up at her then, hope flaring in his eyes.

"Thank you," she said again. Then, turning the handle, she stepped into Vidar's room.

CHAPTER

27

The only sound that met her was the ticking of a clock. There was no fire in the stove. No sign of life. Fear quickened her steps as she rushed through the cozy living space and ducked through the hanging fabric to the bedroom.

He lay upon a platform bed, large frame barely hidden by the sheet thrown over his waist. One leg hung over the edge of the mattress, bare to his hip. His upper body lay exposed, displaying the dips and curves of firm muscles, and the red stained, white gauze wrapped around his injury.

Not wanting to wake him, but desperate to touch him, to know he was alive and well—Enid crept quietly to his side. His dark head lay against a pillow, his arm curled beneath. The other at his side, hand open in relaxed sleep. Dark lashes fanned across the pale skin of his cheek, chest rising and falling in a gentle rhythm. Her heart melted at the sight of him. Lips slightly parted, face beautiful and slack as he slumbered.

It wouldn't be terrible if she kissed his forehead before she left, right? Quickly, so as not to wake him. As her body neared his, her mouth pursed, eyes closing, she suddenly felt the firm grip of a hand at her throat.

With a startled gasp she was dragged over the top of Vidar's body and pressed to the mattress, the sharp edge of a blade at her side. Eyes wide, she stared in shock at Vidar's angry face.

Realizing it was her, the fury faded to horror.

"Enid, I'm so sorry," he rasped, releasing her.

Tossing the knife aside, he searched for injuries. Large hands sliding along her neck and the soft silk of her dress with gentle thoroughness. The feel of him touching her so intimately had her breath catching, a flush breaking out along her skin. In his panic, he didn't realize the effect he was having.

She sat up on her elbows when he knelt back and ran a hand over his face, seemingly convinced she was ok.

"I shouldn't have snuck up on you," she replied, "I was just so worried. I needed to make sure you were ok."

Those gray eyes met hers and he froze. Desire and need mirrored her own within the stormy depths as he looked down the length of her. Any more words she may have said died in her throat. When he reacted, it was suddenly. Like a breaking damn unleashing a torrent of otherwise restrained desire.

An arm wrapped around her waist, firmly tucking her against his hard chest. While his other hand found the back of her neck, weaving beneath the soft waves of hair. His lips crashed against hers in a searing kiss. She responded instantly, mouth opening to receive him. It was everything she expected, everything she longed for. Soft, urgent, and full of unexpected passion.

He held her vice-like against him, his fingers teasing at the edges of her silk dress, exploring the bare skin of her lower back. She moaned, pressing herself closer, her arms wrapping around his shoulders, fingers thrusting into his hair. Only when he flinched in pain did she stop, pulling back in alarm.

She realized she was straddling his naked lap. The thin fabric of her dress the only barrier between them. Her legs were wrapped around his waist—pressing right against his injury. She jerked away.

"I'm so sorry!"

Instead of complaining, he held her in place, his forehead against hers. They were both panting heavily. The need to kiss him once more was so strong that Enid had to force her body still.

He is wounded. She chastised her carelessness.

He chuckled softly, the sound deep and erotic.

"No, I'm sorry," he replied. "Only, I promised myself if I saw you again, I was going to kiss you. Like I've wanted to for

241

so long, completely and properly." His nose trailed along hers, his hand firm on the back of her neck.

"Was that, okay?" he whispered. Uncertainty colored his voice.

She smiled, her resolve melting as she closed the space between their lips for another scorching, passionate kiss.

"What do you think?" She murmured, stopping to catch her breath.

He groaned, his lips brushing hers as he spoke fervently against them. "I think that, injured or not, you are going to have to tell me if you want to keep this dress, because otherwise it will be in shreds."

Her back hit the mattress as he hovered over her, ready to claim her completely. She bit her lip, heart hammering, unable to speak. Unable to do anything but feel as a calloused hand ran up the length of her thigh, sliding the sleek fabric of her dress aside. The touch slow yet firm as he took his time to explore. She sighed, arching into the sensation. The weight of his palm shifted higher, exposing her hip to the cool air, fingers poised to rove further. His tongue moved in slow circles along the nape of her neck, tasting and teasing with just the right amount of pressure.

"Vidar," she moaned, her head dropping back to give him better access even as she gasped, "We can't."

The words left her reluctantly. She shivered as the hand at her hip slid around the curve of her bottom and then froze. He sat up, looking her in the face with confusion and worry. She touched his cheek.

"I want to, so much." Her hand ran along his chest, her eyes dropping to admire the view, hating herself. Not wanting this to end. "So very, very much." She took in a deep, shuddering breath. "But Dimitri is right outside, waiting to walk me to my room."

Darkness clouded his face as he turned a narrowed glare toward the doorway. As if he could send his hatred through the stone to kill the unsuspecting Revenant.

"He brought you here," he grumbled, his voice full of loathing.

Enid nodded.

"I am surprised," he growled. "These next few days are reserved for him to get to know you, while I prepare to risk my life in the next challenge."

"Don't say that," Enid gasped.

"I can't help it," he replied in a hushed tone. "I have spent the last few days teaching you. Preparing you for a life in this world, and all the while wanting you desperately, but trying to keep you at arm's length. Thinking I would win this for you, and then I would let you go, to be human. To have a normal life hidden away somewhere safe. I've been a fool."

The mattress shifted as he lowered himself atop her once more. His mouth hovered over hers, moving along the curve of her jaw, up to her ear as he spoke.

"It would be easier for me to stop breathing than let you go. I can't take the thought of letting you walk out of my life and never seeing you again." His breath puffed lightly within her ear, his tongue darting out briefly nibble the lobe.

Enid shuddered, her eyes rolling back into her head.

"I could sooner cut out my tongue than never be able to taste the sweetness of your skin." His hand twisted into the back of her hair, gripping it hard enough to tilt her head back, his lips skimming the curve of her exposed neck.

Her hands trailed lower down his chest as she moaned, wanting more of him. His words were ragged and heavy. Body trembling with restraint.

"I would rather go deaf, than never again hear the sound of your laughter. The way you speak my name."

Slowly, he caught her lips with his. She couldn't get enough of his kisses—sensual, intimate, profound. She melted, giving herself over to that feeling completely. When he pulled away, they were both breathless. She was dizzy, as though she could float on air.

"I will win this for you, Enid. Then I will claim you. And, if you will have me, we will be bound. I will spend all the rest of our days making you feel how worthy you are."

A tear slipped down her cheek. He kissed away the salty drop.

"I swear it," he murmured urgently.

***

Moments later, Vidar stood with her at the door. A pair of sweatpants low on his hips, a fresh gauze patch on his side. Enid had insisted on helping him change it. Wanting to see with her own eyes that he was healing. The stitching was crude, but held. There would be a scar. Carefully, she had helped to dab the fresh blood away, verifying that it had stopped leaking before securing the tape around the clean gauze. He watched her as she examined it, pressing a kiss to her forehead and lips when she finished.

Grudgingly, he walked her to the door, pressing a book into her hands before she left. "To continue your education, while I am forced to stay away," he murmured.

She placed a hand over his heart, feeling the strong, quick beat beneath her fingers. Stepping on her toes, she reached for him once more. Granting one last kiss. He lifted her against him, her feet leaving the floor, pressed chest to chest as he claimed her mouth thoroughly before releasing her.

When she opened the door, Dimitri stood on the other side, leaning against the opposite wall. He pushed away from it as she stepped out, his eyes slowly taking her in, a frown upon his face.

Enid felt herself blushing. Were her lips as red and swollen as they felt? Could he see that her hair was tousled? Pulling her shoulders back, she turned and walked down the hall toward her room. She would not be ashamed. Not of Vidar, and not of what she felt for him.

Stopping only when she realized Dimitri wasn't following, she turned back to find him. He was still outside Vidar's room, the two men glowering at each other through the opening.

"Dimitri," she called. Eyes still burning into Vidar's, he reached down and grabbed the shopping bags before following. The soft click of Vidar's door reached her ears, the sound creating a twinge of pain in her heart. Two more days before she could see him again.

Dimitri remained silent. When they reached her door, she stepped into the safe confines of her room. The tension easing in her sanctuary. Dimitri held the bags out, waiting patiently for her to take them. As she did, he grabbed hold of her wrist as it slid past the threshold.

"I can make you happy, my flower," he insisted. "I will do everything within my power to give you everything you desire."

"I know Dimitri, you would do your best."

She couldn't stand there and look at the pain and wistful eagerness bright in those vibrant eyes. Gently, she pulled her hand away, taking the bags with her into the security of her room.

"I will not give up," he warned.

She did look up then, showing him the full depth of sadness and pity she felt for him. He took a step back, as if to withdraw from the weight of emotion in her face.

"I know," she whispered.

He stood in the hallway, that startled, sorrowful look on his face as she slowly pressed the door closed.

CHAPTER
28

Enid awoke to the sound of soft knocking. She sat up groggily, her entire body stiff from exhaustion. She barely slept. Tossing and turning for hours, itching to go to Vidar. In the end, she knew she needed to keep her distance. An agreement had been made between them, an agreement she would respect. Not to mention, the fear of distracting him, of causing some sort of mishap to occur during the trial because he wasn't focused, ate at her. She would never forgive herself.

The knocking started again, slightly louder, a little more persistent. With a groan, she pulled herself from the billowy cocoon of blankets and pillows, and trudged to the door. The fairy lights slowly came to life around her as she crossed the room. Dimitri stood in the hall, a steaming coffee in one hand, a napkin wrapped, flakey pastry in the other. A charming smile stretched across his lips.

"I thought you might like some breakfast, my flower," he said, holding the items toward her proudly. Enid cleared her throat, her tired mind struggling to interpret what was happening. Slowly, she took the items. The smell of rich, spicy coffee tantalizing her senses.

"Thank you," she muttered. She stood there a moment, unsure of what to do.

Thankfully, Dimitri didn't take long to pick up on her insecurity.

"I will wait out here for you to get dressed. I want to take you somewhere, but we will need to be quick. Dress comfortably."

He gave her another sure smile, before turning to lean against the wall. She closed the door with her foot.

"Here we go," she sighed to herself, before taking a bite of the buttery pastry.

***

Dimitri took her to a deep level of Dokkalfar. She recalled Vidar explaining to her that these sectors housed the group of Fae referred to as Underlings. The darker, more dangerous of the water fae lived here, along with the tunnel loving gnomes and golems, among others.

The central annex was cavernous and quiet. The busy shops and bakeries on the other levels did not exist here. Instead, there was only the quiet rush of a waterfall as it fell from the top of the chamber, evaporating into a cool mist before it reached the bottom.

There were far fewer lights. The ones that existed were covered over in so much of the creeping vines that the shimmer of it barely peeked through. Above the waterfall, the large clock ticked. Its face carved from dark ebony. No sun graced its façade. Only darkness and the pattern of waves beneath a full moon.

The tunnels here were shorter and narrow. Not as grand and sprawling as the other levels, but still tall enough to allow the larger fae to walk through without having to stoop. As they wound through the halls, a sense of unease stole through her. Dimitri only smiled in reassurance, holding up a lantern of fairy light to keep the shadows at bay. At least no other fae appeared to be wandering about. The sun was still up in the world above, and so the world below slept.

After a few minutes of walking, the sound of trickling water reached her, and the hallway seemed to brighten. As she rounded a bend in the tunnel, she halted in surprise. A distance away, light filtered in a green haze through a layer of hanging moss and vines. Water dripped down the lush curtain, pooling in a small, shallow puddle. Enid blinked, unused to the brightness of sunlight after all these days in the glow of fairy orbs. Dimitri stayed behind her, sticking to the safety of the shadows.

"It is a bit too early for me, my beauty. I must wait. I thought you might like this though. I am sure you are anxious to see the light of day after so long."

Delighted, she walked alone up to that sheet of greenery, grasped the edge and gently lifted it to the side. Tucked behind the vines sat a pool of water within a wide, cavernous mouth in the mountain. Light streamed through a gap in the top. A golden beam sparkling in the water drops that cascaded from the vines and roots clinging to the rock, spilling into the pool below. Rocks glittered beneath the clear surface. Seeing no one else around, she stepped through, her hand shielding her eyes as she adjusted to the brightness of it all.

The crack that allowed in the sun started high above her, continued down the curve of the mountain face, and ended at waist level on the other side of the large, domed space. The opening widened there, showing off the view like a mountainside private deck with a swimming pool.

The covered space around the pond was surprisingly dry. Drawn to the view of tree covered mountains, she ignored the water, going straight to the opening.

The view was sprawling. A sea of green as far as the eye could see. The soft light of the setting sun hovered above the rolling surfaces, touching the highest points with golden light.

She watched in wonder, sinking onto a curve of stone at the lip that made a perfect bench. As the light faded, the colors transitioned from a soft, dusty pink to a deep, russet orange streaked with purple and bright pink hues. Enid sucked in a breath, drawing her knees to her chest, her head resting against them as she stared out at the scene. Trying to burn every color, every facet of the picture into her memory.

When the sun was no more than a hint of orange between the curve of the hills, she felt Dimitri beside her, lantern in hand. He hung it upon the wall and sat next to her. Wiping a tear from her cheek before he noticed, she lifted her face toward him. The orange of the sun faded away to the dark purples and blacks of the star lit night sky.

"Why did you show me this, Dimitri? Why would you give me a glimpse of something that I could never have again if you were to claim me? While lovely, and I am grateful, this does not help your cause of making me Revenant."

Dimitri leaned against the rock wall, resting his arm along the lip of the massive opening. Fingers drawing circles on the edge.

"That is what I wanted to discuss," he said cautiously. "I understand, there will be things you hold dear, that you would miss if you were made Revenant. So, I propose that, when I claim you, I will allow you to remain human, provided that you agree to be bound to me."

Enid paused, surprise and irritation flaring through her. "You mean *if* you claim me," she clarified.

His eyes narrowed into icy slits. "I mean *when*, my flower. I will wait for all eternity if need be."

She glared.

"A binding is a permanent vow, Dimitri. They are not easily broken."

Dimitri cleared his throat, his eyes hardening with determination.

"A binding, when with the right person can be invigorating and powerful, but with the wrong person is as though wearing chains. I promise to never chain you, Enid, my flower. I will be your strength, and you will be my empathy. You will soften my jagged edges and help bring me back to my humanity, as I will be your protection, your defender, your servant in all things."

Enid looked out over that star speckled sky, recalling the image of the golden sunset.

"Once there is an outcome to the challenges, I will think about this. If Vidar wins, it will be a moot point. I will be bound to him."

Dimitri flinched.

"I wanted you to know what I am willing to do, Enid. To help you understand what you mean to me."

"Thank you, Dimitri," she replied.

They sat for a few moments in silence, looking out over the sea of stars. The sounds of night echoing through the valley of trees below. Finally, growing impatient, Dimitri stood and held a hand out to her.

"Come, my flower, there are other things I would like to show you before we must prepare for dinner later."

"Will this be another dinner with your family," Enid asked, trepidation filling her at the prospect as she took his hand and stood.

He removed the lantern from the wall, and guided her back to the catacombs within the mountain.

"I am afraid so, my flower. The Queen is quite insistent that we provide you full hospitality. Do not worry though. It is not every night we gather like this. Only special occasions, and if the Queen is feeling particularly bored or in need of company."

As he spoke, he held the lantern high, continuing to light the way for her, through these much darker hallways. The stretches between light were much longer here, as though the creatures that called this space home were meant to see in the dark. Dimitri's own eyes flashed with a greenish hue in the low lighting, the reflective surface reminding her what lurked within him, what he really was.

"Our Queen leads a very lonely life," Dimitri explained. "Her binding to King Fenri is one of convenience and political gain. She fights for our freedoms and needs among the fae. We are often looked down upon for the fact that we were once human, and that we populate much quicker than other fae."

Enid listened to his story as they walked, the tale helping to distract her from the darkness, and echoing splash of water in the too quiet tunnels.

"There was a great war between our people, and we lost many on both sides. Then, our Queen and King Fenri came to a compromise, to join our people through their union. Since then, we have experienced a tenuous peace, but our poor Queen suffers a heavy burden for the good of our family."

Enid's eyes narrowed suspiciously. He sounded strange as he spoke about his Queen, as though fed the lines from some external source. She was considering this, when he suddenly stopped, his head tilting to the side. From somewhere in the darkness, there was a soft singing. The tune was sweet, but sad.

"What is that?" she wondered, taking a step toward that mournful song.

Dimitri grabbed her shoulders, the lantern crashing to the ground. "Cover your ears," he insisted.

Surprised, she complied, slapping her hands over them firmly. Blocking the sound of that compelling tune. He whirled, pressing her behind his back. His focus on someone or something she couldn't see in the murky shadows.

Slowly, the feminine curves of a woman melted into view. Her eyes shone silver in the dim light. Her dark hair hung in shimmering waves along the length of her body to her shapely thighs. She appeared to be wearing no clothing. That soft, shining hair covering the more intimate parts of her. A smile curved her lips, turning that sensuous beauty dangerous and feral.

Siren, Enid realized with a start.

The woman's lips moved, words passing between her and Dimitri. Only the vibration of Dimitri's back against her side gave her an indication of when he spoke. Then he was turning toward her, his hands gently taking hers and pulling them from her ears. The woman looked on in amusement as Enid glanced toward her nervously, reluctantly letting Dimitri move her hands.

When she spoke, her voice was soft and delicate, the sound a silky purr.

"You used to be so responsive to our song Dimitri. What has changed I wonder?" Those pale, unnerving eyes moved once more to Enid, assessing her like a cat observing a mouse. "Is it this one? The one the Enforcer has laid claim to?"

Dimitri growled low in warning.

"*I* have laid claim to this woman. She is protected," he hissed.

The Siren ignored him, appraising Enid quizzically.

"Yet you are not the one facing the challenges for her."

Her hands ran along the length of her hair as she remained focused on Enid.

"I am warning you, Siren," he snarled.

Her eyes shifted to his in surprise.

"I never thought I would see the day that you would be so unwilling to share one of your claims. You usually enjoy watching such things," she smirked. "Why, only yesterday your sister was down here with her new pet. He was quite… receptive," she sighed meaningfully.

"My sister's business is her own," he said, dismissing the statement with a flick of his hand.

The siren's head tilted quizzically, her expression exaggeratedly thoughtful as she hummed.

"Yes, well, it seems that your sister has a lot of business in the lower levels lately. Namely, on behalf of your Queen."

Dimitri shrugged. "Our Queen is eager to make allies among all the clans of Dokkalfar."

"Hmmm. Yes, but after what she did to my clan, it is going to take a lot more than a shared meal to win us over," she snapped, apparently unconvinced as her gaze drifted to Enid once again. "Do not worry, bright one." The siren's eyes softened as she smiled at her. "No harm will come to you among my kind. My sisters and I have sworn a vow."

Dimitri stiffened. "What vow?"

The softness and teasing left her as she hissed, baring her teeth at Dimitri.

"That is none of your concern, Revenant," she sneered.

Dimitri snarled in return, fangs snapping into sight. The Siren rolled her eyes, looking past Dimitri to the concerned face of Enid.

"You are welcome down here. The water nymphs and merfolk will also give you safe passage. Beware the golems though. I am uncertain where their loyalties lie."

She walked away then, dismissing Dimitri with a shake of her head before she melted back into the shadowy passage.

"Who was that?" Enid asked in a hushed whisper.

"Esmelial," he grumbled. "A siren. Her clan and ours have had a… tumultuous relationship since the last fae war. They blame us for their hunting rights being suspended after we lost. Now meals have to be brought in to them. They are not pleased."

Dimitri didn't stop again until they were back in the Revenant sector. Only then did he cease his brooding, his demeanor relaxing and pace slowing to a normal gait.

***

Dinner that evening was much the same as before. The Revenant gathered in their glittering finery. Voices hushed in conversation. Eyes moved over Enid as though she was a bug pinned beneath the eye of a magnifying glass.

She sat awkwardly, the green, velvet dress she was given barely covering her breasts, the neckline plunging uncomfortably low. Her legs were mostly hidden, unless she moved, the dual slits at either side of her skirt shifting to expose them. Curling tendrils of her hair floated along the nape of her neck from the elegant updo her hair had been twisted in. She felt like a doll, dressed and displayed for the Queen's pleasure. All of them were, she realized. Each creature here part of a gleaming collection.

The Queen smiled, the gesture more fierce than consoling as she inquired about her time in their realm, half listening with a bored expression to the response.

Cindy remained as silent as ever, avoiding Enid's eyes, and the other Revenant altogether as Marcus, ever her protective shadow, fed her cues and signals. Her full, curly hair was pulled back into a sleek bun on top of her head, displaying her neck and shoulders in a strapless red gown. Her matching red lips were drawn in a perpetual frown.

Dimitri plied Enid with food and drink which she barely touched, his exuberant conversation hollow in her ears.

Finally, the Queen stood. Her attendants rushing to move the chair and fluff the puffy skirts of her gold satin gown so they flowed around her gracefully. Her face turned toward Enid. "I am going to turn in for the night. Tomorrow should be fun." Her lip curled cruelly.

Enid's face paled.

"Dimitri," the Queen snapped. "When you have escorted this one to her room, come to my chambers. I have something I require of you."

"Yes, my Queen," he said adoringly.

As she exited, the other Revenant began to drift away, suddenly tired of the paltry display. Cindy and Marcus stood to leave. Enid jumped to her feet.

"Can we talk, please."

Her friend's wide brown eyes shifted to hers.

"I have nothing to say."

"Cindy," Enid pleaded, "you have to know I had nothing to do with any of this. I didn't know this was going to happen."

Cindy turned on her then, her chin lifting as she glared down at her, making her feel small and insignificant with that one fiery look.

"You had everything to do with this," she hissed. "I would still be human if it weren't for you. I would still have my life."

Marcus flinched, hurt flaring across his face before he gently put his hand on her shoulder, squeezing softly. The anger within Cindy dissipated as she melted into his arms, her satin dress whispering quietly as they embraced. His lips went to her ear, moving fervently. Cindy nodded, her eyes dropping to the floor.

Enid could only stare in stunned silence as her friend turned her back on her, and walked from the room. Dejected, she stood there, tears pooling as the rest of the Revenant left. Dimitri and her alone remained. The only sound was that of the water flowing into the pond against the far wall.

Dimitri's body was firm at her back. Gently he turned her to face him. He lifted her chin with a finger, his eyes full of sympathy.

"She will come around," he reassured, his voice soft.

Enid shook her head sadly, tears slipping down her cheeks as she did so.

"She hates me," she gasped, her voice breaking as her throat clogged with misery.

Dimitri lifted her hand to his lips, placing a delicate kiss there.

"She doesn't know what she is feeling right now," he murmured against her skin before he allowed her to pull away. "When we first become Revenant, there is a flood of emotions. Things are confusing—intense." His hands moved to the tops of her arms, rubbing them gently before giving a slight squeeze. "It will pass, and then she will understand. She will remember that she loves you, and you will be reconciled."

Enid only sobbed, unable to hold back the flood of tears.

"Come," he said. "Sit with me a bit longer." He pulled their chairs out, easing her down onto hers before he leaned down, his hands on the table, flashing that charming smile.

"What can I do to please you?"

Enid looked up at him, tired and unsure.

"Tell me about when you became Revenant," she said finally.

Dimitri frowned. "Are you sure, my flower? It is not a happy tale."

"Yes," she said, her curiosity getting the better of her once again. "I would like to hear it."

Pacing away, he put his hands on his hips and then moved the sleeves of his black shirt further up his arms. Fidgeting as though to postpone the telling of the story.

"I suppose," he said slowly, "that I became Revenant for my sister. We are twins, did you know that?" He spoke quietly, almost as though he was worried someone else might hear.

"My sister was not always how she is now. She used to be kind, innocent, curious about everything—much like you." His blue eyes burned into hers, filled with an openness she had never seen from him. It was mesmerizing. "She did not; however, have your strength, or courage."

He walked closer, his head down, expression thoughtful. Enid wondered how much of his story he was willing to tell. From the way he bit his lip, and the softness of his voice, she wasn't sure if it would be much at all. He seemed hesitant, contemplative, his words slow to come.

"My father ruined her. Beat the hope and compassion right out of her. Twisted her and broke her spirit, body, and mind." His hand ran through his hair, brushing the longer strands on top away from his face, eyes moving to the ceiling as he pressed his hand into the back of his neck. Finally, he faced her, a look of determination hardening his masculine features.

"We both were much changed because of the actions of our father. It is strange is it not, how the decision of another can so dramatically alter the course of our own paths?" He chuckled darkly. "Though I suppose you understand that concept very well, as you yourself have been put upon your path because of the actions of my sister and I. Perhaps you will understand, once

I tell our story. Perhaps you will see it and hate the man who set me on my path to you. Maybe then you can love me." His voice lowered, faltering softly at the end of his sentence as if afraid to voice this hope.

Dimitri sat next to Enid. "Do not judge me too harshly, my flower. Do not hate me for pulling you into this dark place. You cannot blame me for reaching for your light. Please."

Enid swallowed thickly, tamping down the emotion that flared within her at his open vulnerability. She willed her heart to maintain its steady rhythm. She would not give him any reason to falsely believe she would accept him.

Part of her would always hate him for taking away her freedoms, her simple life, but part of her was grateful for this place as well. She had found a joy she didn't think was possible. There was a sense of normalcy here, no disease, no curse hanging over her. No reason to hide. And it was all thanks to him. For bringing her to this place, and introducing her to another world, despite its dangers.

"Tell me your story Dimitri," she simply said.

He nodded, giving her a small smile of gratitude. Then he sat back and began to speak, looking into the distance as though seeing through the years to that moment in time.

CHAPTER

29

Dimitri didn't remember much of his mother, or their life before her death. He remembered that she was beautiful, with hair the color of a raven's wing, and eyes the pale blue of a glacier in icy waters. She was a laundress, and worked hard to feed the family. She had to, since their father did nothing but drink himself into an early sleep every night. He remembered the tears that his mother used to hide from him. The bruises that covered her beautiful face on the days his father was in a particularly foul mood.

One night his father was so angry. The beating was terrible. Dimitri and Lania cowered beneath their beds. Small bodies huddled into the furthest corner. The next morning their mother did not wake up.

She was given a simple funeral. Barely more than a hole in the ground. Her children tearfully shivered in their threadbare clothing at her graveside, tears streaking their dirty cheeks. Her husband merely nodded at the priest before placing his hat on his head and wandering off to the nearest inn for a drink.

Dimitri tried his hardest to find work, to keep their bellies fed, but it was hard for someone so young, especially when every coin was immediately wrestled from his hands the minute he came through the door. Mainly, it was the pity of the other villagers that kept them from starving.

As they grew older, it became apparent that Lania would be gifted with the same beauty as their mother. It wasn't long before his father noticed how the other men would look at her, and not much longer after that before he used it to his advantage.

The first time his father brought a man to their house, Dimitri and Lania regarded him warily. Their father never had time for friends before, but then her father took Lania aside, whispering to her, and Lania began shaking her head. Her expression was of terror. It was when her father and the man began dragging Lania into their room, screaming, that Dimitri rushed to her aid.

He was too weak. Too slow. The large man disappeared into the room, the door slamming firmly shut behind him. Dimitri threw himself against it, only to meet the solid fist of his father. The force of the impact sent him sailing backward. His ears rang. His eyes wouldn't focus. The taste of blood filled his mouth as he dizzily attempted to sit up.

"You'll stay down, if you know what's good for you," his father growled, fists at the ready for another blow, should Dimitri choose to defy him. From behind the door, came the muffled sounds of his sister's screams.

That soon became the norm. Dimitri would try to protect his sister in vain as, night after night, one or more men would find their way to her bed. After the first few months, she no longer fought and screamed. After a year, she no longer smiled or spoke. She pulled into herself, locked away. Only going out at Dimitri's urging for fresh air, for a walk, or to pick flowers. She would stare off into the distance, her eyes bleak as they wandered, her fingers plucking at the flowers in her hands. A trail of battered and bruised petals scattered in their wake. She only seemed to come to life when one of the men wandered by, her body stiffening in fear, her eyes wide as she tried to avoid their gaze.

They no longer starved and, other than the daily fights with his father, he was not abused, but life was by no means easy for Dimitri either. The men of the village sneered at him, calling him weak, and the women would laugh in his face. However, many of the women who regarded him so callously in the open, were quick to soften to him in the confines of a private corner, or beneath the shadows of a secluded stairwell. His good looks and charm drew the eye of many women in his village, despite how improper it was considered to be seen speaking with him.

One girl in particular he became enamored with. Irina. With hair the burnished gold of wheat at sunset, and eyes as blue as the sky in summer. Many times, when he had been booted from the cottage, bruised and bleeding, he would seek comfort in the warmth of her arms and the soft honey of her lips.

Standing at the edges of the market, the old women casting him furious glances, he would wait. Then Irina's golden head would come into view through the muted browns and greys of the village. A beacon of warmth and light. Cautiously he would follow, stalking her at the edges of the crowd, waiting until that moment when her bright eyes would fall upon him. All it would take was a look, a shift of the head, and they would find themselves in a tangle in some hidden corner. A frenzy of stolen kisses, firm caresses, and swallowed moans.

"We can't keep doing this," Irina would gasp as his fingers blazed a trail beneath her skirts, lifting them to plunge into the secret treasure they contained. She never let him go any further than a touch, never allowed them to fully lay together as he so desperately desired, but he understood. He didn't want her frivolously. He wanted her completely.

"Be my wife, Irina," he would moan against her skin as she bucked against his hand. The sweet wetness of her coated his fingers, driving his desire to a frenzy that quickened his strokes. A gasp fell from her full, soft lips. He swallowed the sound hungrily with his kisses, savoring each moan and breath that broke free.

"I cannot, Dimitri," she murmured in response, always. Dimitri would pull away then, his heart shattering in his chest. He shouldn't be so hurt after so long. How many months had they done this dance? Each time she would refuse him. Each time she would plead for him to understand. He had no prospects. He was from a family plagued with rumors of shameful notoriety. His father a drunk murderer, and his sister a whore.

He backed away, leaving her standing there—beautifully disheveled. Lips red and full from his eager kisses.

"Dimitri," she said, her voice full of pity.

"Don't," he replied.

One day while out at the market with his sister, Dimitri was haggling with a particularly stubborn baker over the price of bread when the sound of raised voices drew his attention. A few stalls away a woman stood over the shivering form of Lania, a meaty fist raised, face mottled in fury. Forgetting the bread, Dimitri rushed over.

"KEEP AWAY FROM MY HUSBAND, FILTHY WHORE," the woman yelled out, her fist connecting with his sister's frail body. Lania flew to the ground with a pained shriek.

Dimitri grabbed the woman's wrist, keeping her from raining blows down upon his sister.

"How dare you hit my sister," he spat, voice dangerously low. He released her wrist, fearful that if he continued to hold on, he would snap the bone in his grip. Rage had his fists curled at his sides.

"You tell her to leave my husband alone. He denies it, but I know he goes to that house of yours. I know he lies with her. Giving her money that should be used to feed my children."

The woman turned back to Lania, spittle flying from her mouth to land in a slimy wad in Lania's raven hair.

"Find your own husband to bugger, you harlot."

A crowd had gathered by that time. Women looking on with hard, hateful faces. The men casually attempting to avoid looking at all—some in indifference, others with guilt. They pressed their families on, pushing wives and daughters away from the scene.

Lania sobbed from the ground.

"I don't want... I don't..." her voice cracked and wavered, her words an unintelligible blubber.

Dimitri shoved the woman back, kneeling and gently lifting his sister to her feet. Pulling his handkerchief from his pocket, he cleaned her up and gently led her away from the murmured whispers and loathsome glares.

Lania refused to go outside after that. She would only stare blindly out the window—regressing into herself. A beautiful, expressionless doll. That woman's husband still came several times a month. Though he had the decency to avoid Dimitri's hard stare. Shame coloring his cheeks as he walked by, coins clutched in his grubby hands.

The same dance again, Dimitri shoved out the door as his father slurred a greeting to his customer. Lania at the window, her blank gaze landing on Dimitri as he rolled across the ground, lip bloodied. The door closed behind the men, and slowly she backed away, shuttering the window to the outside world. Dimitri shouted his rage. No one acknowledged it. No one cared.

With a curse he stood to his feet, and wandered to the village. The sun had begun to set, casting shadows among the buildings. Animals were being shepherded into their small rooms to settle. Most people were fearful of wandering at night, afraid of the creatures and spirits that wandered aimlessly in search of hapless victims, but not Dimitri. Dimitri relished this time. When he could move about without worry of catching a distrustful eye, or sharp word. When no one noticed the haggard son of the drunkard. The brother of the whore. Worthless. Disgraceful.

"Dimitri?" The voice cut through the negative slurs racing around his head. Usually that sweet, melodic sound would have sent his heart racing, but tonight he was not in the mood. Still, he stopped and looked.

Irina stood in the doorway of her father's house. Her bronze hair aglow with the light of the fire behind her. Worry creased her lovely features. Casting a quick look over her shoulder, she stepped out, closing the door soundlessly before tiptoeing through the shadowy garden.

"What is it?" she whispered, once they were safely hidden behind a copse of trees.

"What is it always?" Dimitri hissed angrily. Irina put a delicate hand to his cheek.

"Why do you stay, Dimitri?"

He pulled away from her touch, angry and frustrated, but also drawn to the way her lips parted when she looked at him with those eyes. How the setting sun seemed to catch in her hair like spun gold, lending a warm glow to her velvet skin. She was invitingly distracting.

"I can't leave," he grumbled, trying to look at anything but her. "I cannot abandon my sister."

"Why not?" she scoffed. "She has chosen to be what she is."

Dimitri stilled, turning toward the woman he thought he loved in shocked disappointment.

"What did you say?"

His voice was low, dark. It trembled with warning, with the promise of violence. Irina either didn't notice, or didn't care. A sneer twisted her usually pretty face into an unrecognizable, unpleasant mask. Disgust filled Dimitri at the sight.

"If it were me, I would have taken a knife to myself, rather than allow my body to be used in such a way. Your sister has chosen to be a whore. You owe her nothing."

She reached for him then, her face softening into the one he had so fervently watched glow with rapture in his embrace. Now he only felt revulsion. He stepped away, her fingertips grasping empty air.

"How could you say such a thing?"

"You know it is true," she said, a hardness in her voice he had never heard before. "Life for you would have been much easier if she had."

"You know nothing of life, Irina," Dimitri growled. "You are one to talk, throwing yourself at me in the hidden corners of the market. Allowing yourself to be touched and fondled in the shadows. In secret." He closed the distance between them, his hand gripping the spun copper of her hair roughly, pressing her against the solid trunk of the tree at her back.

She cried out.

Through gritted teeth, he spoke, "Should I take you now, Irina? Right here? Force you as my sister has been forced each night? What would you do then? Would you finally deign to marry me, or would you bury a knife between these supple breasts of yours out of shame?"

His free hand squeezed her breast painfully before sliding down her side, shifting to lift her skirts, inching them up slowly. Irina wiggled helplessly against him, attempting to push him away.

"Would you like it, I wonder? Would you become my whore?" He hissed into her ear.

Irina managed to pull her hand free from the crush of his body. The sting of it connecting against his cheek stopped him, clearing the fog of anger. He let her go and stepped away, watching the wild look of fear slowly fade from her face. Reaching into her skirt, she pulled something out and threw it at the ground at his feet. The metal edge of a blade gleamed in the fading light.

"Go. Give this to your sister. See what her choice would be."

With that she turned and fled. Back to her father's house. Back to warmth, comfort, and safety. Dimitri plucked the knife from the ground, and wandered away in the opposite direction.

He wasn't sure how long he drifted, or what time it was when he made his way back to their cottage. Only that the stars were bright in the sky, and a full moon cast a faint glow over the fields and meadows. A fire still burned in their hearth, the smoke spiraling lazy and white before fading into the expanse of starlight. The front door opened, throwing an orange rectangle along the dirt path before it, and out wandered the same large man who had entered earlier in the evening. His balding head glistened with sweat in the firelight as he lifted a brawny hand in farewell. A satisfied grin showing the spaces of his missing teeth.

Dimitri stopped on the lane, instinct pressing him back into the shadow of the brush that lined the way to his home. His hand drifted to the waistband of his breeches where he had tucked the dagger for safe keeping. Without thinking about why, or what he planned to do, Dimitri watched the man wander past before stepping out to silently follow him at a distance.

As he walked, the man whistled cheerfully, relaxed and happy as he made his way through the dark to his home. Blissfully unaware he was being pursued. When he reached a particularly secluded alley, Dimitri made his move, stepping into his path. The surprise and fear that shone across the man's face sent an unexpected thrill through Dimitri. The knife in his hand felt heavy and cool.

"Wait!" the man shouted.

He didn't.

The sound of his voice broke the restraint Dimitri held so precariously. The voice that had most likely whispered in his sister's ear as he defiled her. Dimitri lunged forward, the knife flashing seconds before it was buried within his fat neck. The man gurgled, reaching sluggishly toward the wound in surprise. Warm liquid spurted over Dimitri's hand, causing the knife to slip from his grasp. Backing away, he watched as the man fell heavily to his knees, clutching at his neck before slumping over. A quivering gasp interrupted the silence, and then he was still.

"Well," came a sultry voice from the depth of the shadows. Dimitri jumped in fright. "It's not every day you wander upon such a delicious kill. And so efficient."

From the darkness came the most beautiful woman he had ever seen, with skin the color of a starless night, and eyes that could peer into his very soul. Never before had he seen her kind. She was a wonder, and a terror all at once.

Dimitri shook his head, panic beginning to set in over what he had done.

"I didn't...I haven't...I didn't know." The words tumbled out of his mouth in a confused rush. His mind attempted to grasp what he had done. The blood on his hand was starting to get sticky. Frantically he wiped it on his coat.

"You didn't?" The woman questioned moving forward to look at him curiously.

"I mean, I did... but I- I don't know," he stammered.

"Poor boy," she murmured, her hypnotic eyes holding him in place as she ran her hand gently along his cheek. "Was this your first kill?"

Dimitri nodded, his head hanging in shame. The woman shifted to catch his eye.

"And what made you do it? Money? Fear? Desperation?"

Tears pricked the back of Dimitri's eyes.

"He was violating my sister," Dimitri choked out.

"Ah," the woman said with a sigh, "Love." The sound of understanding in her voice made it even sweeter to his ears.

"You are a champion," the woman said with a smile so bright and glorious that it drove the very breath from him.

Suddenly, he wanted nothing more than to do anything for her, *be* anything for her.

"What if I told you, my sweet boy. That I could make it so no one would ever hurt you or your sister again." Her hand drifted down to his chest, delicately touching above his heart.

264

"I could make you invincible. Men would live to fear you, and women would live to love you."

Irina's bright blue eyes, filled with disdain, flashed within his mind.

"What must I do?" he murmured.

The woman smiled.

***

The sound of screaming echoed in the darkness of the night. Clouds had rolled in at some point, blocking the face of the moon from the massacre that occurred beneath its unseeing gaze. Lania twirled in circles in the road before him, face lifted to the sky in ecstasy. Her dressing gown dark and sticky with blood.

"Isn't it wonderful, Dimitri," she exclaimed, taking in a great breath of air before releasing it.

Her eyes shone with a merriment he hadn't seen in years. Her cheeks were flushed with excitement and happiness. It made his heart leap with joy to see her so exuberant. Since the moment he had broken down the door of their cottage and torn their father from limb to limb, she had been smiling. Now, standing in the road, covered in the blood of the men who had used her over the years, she looked like an avenging angel. She licked at the fangs in her mouth, her eyes wandering restlessly.

"Dimitri, I want to find another. Finish yours and let's go."

The Queen melted from the darkness then, her ebony eyes shining as she smiled at Lania.

"Such wonderful enthusiasm," she purred. "But I'm afraid it's time to go. We have a distance to cover before the sun comes up, and this village has been depleted. Another victim of a terrible plague I'm afraid."

Dimitri looked down at the body in his arms. Red marks and bruises covered the pale skin of his victim, indeed giving the appearance of some horrible plague rash. The Queen lovingly ran a hand down Lania's hair, placing a tender kiss on her forehead before turning to Dimitri.

"Are you ready to go?"

He cast one last, lingering look over the body. Blue eyes, glazed in death, stared sightlessly at the sky above. Hair the color of gilded wheat hung limply between his fingers, soaked in blood.

"I'm ready," he said, allowing the body to slip from his arms and hit the ground with a solid thump. He stepped over Irina without a backward glance, and followed Lania and his newfound goddess into the great nighttime wilderness beyond.

***

"We were changed that night. For the first time in our lives, we were no longer meek and afraid, starved and beaten. We were powerful and beautiful. We could have whatever, or whoever we wanted. It was all within our grasp. So, we took it. We took it all."

Dimitri's eyes were blazing with ferocity, his face bright with exhilaration. He was frighteningly beautiful as he recalled the justice he delivered. Enid's heart fluttered in fear at the curve of his smile as he raised his chin, looking down at her with a haughty expression.

She couldn't help but feel for him, for what he had been through. She could empathize, to be beaten, hurt, made to feel unclean and used. She understood. Had felt that way before, and had relished her freedom. Only, she was still powerless, still vulnerable. What would she become were she to be given that kind of assurance? If she had the strength to never allow another to hurt her again. Would she become like him? Like Lania? She couldn't say.

His gaze locked onto hers, unbridled desire shifting within his eyes. Slipping an arm around her waist as he moved closer, his fingers gripping her chin and lifting it so they were eye to eye.

"It wasn't until that day in the alley, when you were begging me to spare you, that the glimmer of that memory returned to me. Others had pleaded for their lives before, but it never connected until you came along, already bruised and beaten, desperate for escape. Suddenly, I was reminded of the girl my sister had been before my father brutalized her. I remembered the boy I had been, hopeful, desperate to make a better life for myself and my loved ones. So… human. I had forgotten what that meant, how to feel."

He was so close, his nose grazing hers, lips hovering he spoke, lidded eyes staring into hers. Enid's heart raced, her mouth went dry. Delicately, her tongue flicked out, wetting her parched lips. Unable to comprehend her emotions, she could only hold still, watching him—waiting. His eyes followed the movement of her mouth eagerly, and then he was closing the distance, his lips claiming hers. He gave her one sweet, long kiss and then he pulled back.

"You saved me from myself," he breathed.

Enid was so confused. Want and fear fought for purchase within her. He had kissed her with such gentleness. Her mind told her she couldn't give in, but her heart was warming. Slowly, she put her hands against his chest, her eyes closed, the feel of his kiss still lingering upon her lips, and she pressed him back.

She opened her eyes, seeing the way his teeth pulled in his bottom lip, slowly releasing it while he stared at her. Raw with need. She cleared her throat.

"Dimitri, I cannot make you any promises."

He closed his eyes. When he opened them, he seemed more relaxed, in control.

"Come," he said. "I will walk you to your room."

She nodded, standing and smoothing the skirts of her dress before turning to walk toward the door. Suddenly, Dimitri had hold of her wrist, and with a slight tug, whirled her around to him. One arm wrapped around her waist while the other released her wrist to grasp the back of her neck. His grip was firm as he pulled her tightly against him. Hungrily his lips crashed against hers. Without thinking, she felt herself responding, her lips parting, chest heaving. Her arms remained at her sides, her brain not functioning other than to kiss him back, her body melting into his.

Groaning, he pulled away, panting as he looked down at her flushed face. Her body limp and yielding in his arms.

"Yes," he said, his voice deep and heavy with need. "That is what I expected. You will be mine, Enid. You belong with me."

***

The walk to her room was quiet. Dimitri stopped trying to pull her into conversation. A contemplative smile etched his face as he snuck glances at her, hands in his pockets. He carried himself with more confidence than usual, relaxed and self-assured. When they stopped at the door to her room, he leaned over, lips buzzing against her ear.

"I enjoyed our time together. I hope you did as well."

Enid nodded numbly. Her only response a sharp inhale when she felt his lips hovering over the side of her face, tracing along her cheek, grazing upward as though relishing every inch of skin. Softly he pressed an intimate kiss against her forehead.

"I will see you tomorrow, my flower," he whispered.

He remained in the hall, that proud look upon his face as she softly closed the door, retreating to her private sanctuary.

Enid leaned against the thick wood slab with a heavy sigh. Her mind was a twisted mess, and her heart was no better. Vidar was what she wanted, what she needed. She knew that. But something about Dimitri wouldn't leave her alone. Some pull she couldn't explain. She abandoned the fruitless reverie, ready for comfort and rest.

Halfway across the room, she stopped. A bouquet of roses sat on the small table next to the chairs. The deep red flowers within a sparkling crystal vase. There was a card perched against it, her name inscribed upon the cream envelope in a sophisticated hand.

The only other person with access to her room was Vidar. Her heart pounded as she pried the note open, her eyes greedily taking in the words on the page.

My Dearest Enid,

I shouldn't be writing. I have given my word that I will give you space while you spend time with the Revenant, but I can't stand going into this challenge tomorrow without leaving you at least a few words. These weeks of getting to know you have been more of a gift than you will ever know. You give me hope again.

Hope that I am worthy of love. Hope that there can be brightness, and light even in this dark, lonely place.

I will be giving this challenge everything I have, so that I can come back to you. My reward will be having you in my arms once again. If anything happens to me, remember my gift to you. Use it to escape this place, and use the knowledge you have learned to exist and survive outside of these treacherous walls.

Forever yours,
Vidar

Enid pressed the letter to her chest, tears flowing freely. She didn't even bother undressing or unpinning her hair. Kicking her shoes off, she tumbled into her bed, curling up within the warmth of her blanket. Her fingers stroked the twisted bracelet. The metal warm against her skin as she cried herself into a fitful sleep.

CHAPTER

30

The tick of the clock was irritatingly noticeable, more so tonight than usual. Enid paced the length of her room, attempting to drown it out, and failing. Each rhythmic click reminded her that time was running out. Soon the next trial would be upon them, and she would sit and watch while Vidar fought for both of their lives. Any minute now she would be called to bear witness.

Every time she tried to sit down the waves of anxiety would come crashing around her. This was worse than the night of the first challenge. This time she wouldn't be able to see Vidar until he was done. Couldn't hug him and wish him well, or beg him to save himself. The knock at the door had her jumping, her heart nearly clawing its way up her throat. She flung the door open, slamming it into the wall in her haste to answer.

Lania and Charlie stood within the hallway, a bright smile upon the small woman's face, a scowl etched across Charlie's. Enid stopped before she crossed the threshold, taking a large step back. Lania cocked her head to the side.

"Come now, sister. I will not harm you," she reassured. "My brother would be very unhappy were I to do that, and I will not disappoint him."

Enid looked over her shoulder toward Charlie, making it clear where the source of her unease lay. Loathing filled his dark eyes. Lania twisted around, noting the angry glare upon his face. She rolled her eyes, giving her back to Charlie as she leaned toward Enid.

"Do not worry about my pet, sister. He knows better." She spoke in a low conspiratorial tone, as though Charlie couldn't hear, or was incapable of understanding. She perked up again, holding out a cup of coffee, and a small paper bag. "Coffee cake?"

"Where is Dimitri?" Enid questioned.

Lania shrugged her shoulders. "Our Queen requested him. I have been sent to bring you to the next challenge."

Hesitantly, Enid reached out and took the offered coffee before stepping into the hallway. Lania smiled brightly, and began to walk away, chattering about anything and everything she saw. She was like a child in the way she spoke and reacted, attention jumping from one topic to the next so quickly that Enid had a hard time keeping up. Charlie merely walked beside her, a silent and indifferent companion to the constant stream of babble.

Enid couldn't help but examine him from the edge of her vision. Charlie as a Revenant was completely different than the Charlie she had known. She couldn't help but wonder how much of that was due to the change, and how much of it was Lania.

It wasn't long before they were joined by other groups of fae making their way to the challenge. The flow of the crowd became thicker as they wound up the passageways to the top most levels. The King's guard were dispersed among the crowd, keeping peace and directing the flow of traffic as it became thicker. The sight gave Enid some peace.

They reached the opening to a complex looking arena, when Lania gave an excited squeal and bound over to a lovely fae with shining waves of golden hair. As the lively, dark-haired woman was distracted, Enid felt a hand grip her wrist and yank her roughly into a corner. Charlie pinned her against the wall, hiding her smaller body with his large one. His hand covered her mouth, keeping her cry muffled.

"You don't think you've gotten away from me yet, do ya darlin'?"

Panic rose within her as he released her wrist, pressing her against the rough wall with his body as his hand traveled up to twist into the waves of her hair, yanking it back firmly so she was forced to look into his cold, angry eyes.

"One way or another you will pay for all this."

Then he was gone, and she was standing against the wall, alone and in shock when Lania came skipping up, her pale blue eyes wide, her face flush with exhilaration.

"Come sister," Lania gushed. "The fun is about to begin!"

Enid allowed the petite woman to pull her along to their seats.

***

The roar of the crowd rang in Enid's ears as she stared across the expanse of the open pit before them. Stationary and rotating platforms shifted and moved in no noticeable pattern. Along those shifting wooden panels, and throughout the rest of the arena, dozens of winged creatures were stationed. Some of them were so small that they appeared to move with all the speed of a hummingbird, their tiny bodies merely a blur to the eye.

Vidar stood at the other end of the void studying the layout. Each path was carefully calculated, the risks measured as those stormy eyes took stock. Anxiety thrummed within Enid as she watched him prepare.

A railing circled the entire pit with only two openings. One where Vidar was positioned, and the other exactly across from him where another platform jutted over the expanse. The chair she was escorted to sat directly behind that platform, giving her a full view of the arena and its dangers.

Beside her, Dimitri leaned forward, elbows on his knees, pale eyes twinkling as he smirked at Vidar. If Vidar noticed, he didn't let it show, that steadfast gaze locked on the task before him.

At his hips hung a belt with a grappling hook attached to a bit of rope, some carabiners, and a white cloth. The only tools he was allowed for this challenge. He tightened the belt, adjusting its weight on his hips as he paced back and forth, concentrating on the different avenues before him.

Below the gauntlet of ropes, ladders, and platforms there stretched only darkness. A chasm of unknown depth from which there would be no return even for the mightiest of fae. Enid shuddered as her eyes were drawn into its gaping mouth.

A hush settled over the crowd as the King and Queen appeared. Their seats, as usual, were stationed on the upper ring surrounding the abyss—overlooking all. The Queen stood, her hands going up. Dimitri became rigid, leaning toward her with unbreakable focus.

Throughout the crowd each of the Revenant reacted the same way, as though they were one mind, and their Queen was the one pulling their strings. The other creatures were respectfully quiet, but did not give the same amount of concentration as the Revenant. Around the curve of the pit, Enid saw a subtle shift of movement and turned to find Cindy looking at her. Her large eyes filled with sadness. As their gazes met Cindy turned her head, her stance mimicking that of the other Revenant—her attention on her new Queen.

"Today, we stand witness to the second challenge of the Elemental. Air!" The Queen shouted, lifting her hands as she motioned at the pit before them. There was a roar of applause. The King merely leaned back in his throne, no enjoyment visible upon his stern face.

Enid felt the familiar creeping guilt wash over her. Vidar was a good man. Her lips moved in a prayer, willing him to come through this trial unscathed.

Protect him.

The applause died down as the Revenant Queen motioned for silence.

"Vidar Halvarson, once again we implore you. Do you wish to continue with the challenge, to win the claim of the human woman, Enid Washbourne." Her voice was clear as a bell, carrying over the silence—echoing over the chasm with ease.

"I do!" Vidar shouted, his response ringing through the chamber, into the pit. Enid warily eyed the darkness, an eerie feeling of dread filling her as the sound of his voice resonated within the depths.

A shiver ran down her spine.

"And do you give your oath that you are here of your own free will to face this challenge. That you understand the risks and are willing to accept them?"

"Yes!" Came his reply.

273

Enid looked at him, longing and fear battling within her. The brawn of him was emphasized by the form fitting gray tank top he wore, and the black pants that were tucked into his boots. His broad shoulders were pulled back confidently. Their eyes locked across the gap. She pleaded through that look, her eyes insistent.

Please. I'm not worth it.

The narrowing of his eyes in return was the only response she got.

Yes, they said. *You are.*

"Very well, then. The challenge ends when you reach the opposite platform across the chasm. You may use what you have at your disposal, as well as what is contained within the pit. Once you reach the other side, your challenge is complete. You may begin." The Queen sat down on her throne, eyes alight with exhilaration.

Vidar looked to his King. There was a brief nod between the two. Enid wondered at the meaning behind that gesture. Was it a salute, a request to proceed, or simply a goodbye. Either way she wouldn't find out until she was able to ask him at the end of this. She filed that away for later.

At the Queen's command, the winged fae in the arena began to flap their wings in a seemingly coordinated pattern. Baffled, Enid watched, unsure of what was happening until she began to notice the swinging and swaying of the ropes, ladders and platforms.

The wind created by the swift beat of the fae's wings whirled about, a small gale escalating within the confines of the arena. As if that wasn't enough, a small cyclone began to take shape. The forms of several of the small fae swirling within it as they fed its creation, sending it flying around from one rickety terrace to the next. Enid gasped.

"They are quite remarkable creatures, yes?" Dimitri said, gesturing out to the winged fae. "There are many such enchanting discoveries for you to explore within your new home, my flower. I have many more wonderful things to show you."

Lania leaned over from his other side. "There are also many terrible things to see as well, dear sister."

Enid stiffened at that statement. Dimitri's hand found her back, rubbing small reassuring circles along it.

"Do not frighten her, Lania," he scolded.

"You are no fun anymore," Lania pouted, her body slouching in her seat like a child throwing a tantrum.

Charlie reached over, stroking a hand along her thigh. Lania leaned into the touch with a purr, her bad mood forgotten. His brown eyes met Enid's over her dark head, gaze full of promise. Enid turned her attention back to the arena, and Vidar. Fervent prayers for his safety upon her lips. Her hands steepled in front of her mouth as she stared across the chasm of storm filled chaos, toward her captivating champion.

As a gong resounded through the chamber, Vidar snapped into motion. Wrapping the white cloth around his hand firmly, he stepped back as far as he could on the slab of wood before taking a running jump, arms and legs pumping through the air. Enid felt like time slowed as he hung suspended. She held her breath. And then he was snapping back through the space, having successfully grabbed a rope with his cloth wrapped hand.

She could barely watch as he went swinging toward one of the swaying platforms where a particularly nasty looking puck waited. The dark abyss below gaped ominously. Wicked, curled horns shook from side to side on the creature's large head as it glared at Vidar. Hooves stamped, causing the unsteady structure to shudder perilously.

Vidar swung onto the platform, and without hesitation, propelled himself off the railing and around the back of the puck. The rope clasped within his hands looped around its neck and Vidar yanked hard, pulling with the weight of his entire body. The puck's eyes bulged, hands scrambling and pulling in vain at the rope straining around its thick neck. Vidar wrapped the rope tighter around his hands and leaned further back, constricting the rope, the muscles in his arms jumping from the tension. The puck's face turned red, water streaming from its eyes before they suddenly rolled back. It slumped to the platform with a solid thud.

Enid's hands went to her mouth, stifling the gasp of shock. The horror of it all made her feel sick. She stared at the body of the fallen creature. Dimitri put an arm around her, his hand rubbing her arm soothingly. The slow rise and fall of the creature's back assured her that he was only knocked out, and she sighed her relief. She couldn't fathom being responsible for the death of another being.

Her eyes moved away from the puck, gazing out among the cheering, gleeful faces of the crowd. It was a frenzy of excitement all around her. This was the world she was forced to be part of, where violence and destruction were occasions for merriment.

Further up the rise of the seats opposite her, two sets of familiar eyes stared back. It felt as though all the blood drained from her face as the ghoul and the minotaur, her aunt's caretakers, gave her small waves. Sick smiles stretched across their inhuman, vindictive faces—filled with the promise of pain and torment. She shrank into Dimitri's arm. The smile he flashed her was spectacular as she turned away from those monsters and gave in to his soothing touch.

A shocked gasp from the audience snapped her attention back to the challenge. Vidar dangled from a rope. By one hand. Somehow the twister of turbulent air and fae had caught him, whipping him around mercilessly. The small winged creatures pelted him, and the larger fae, with their bird-like wings, gathered around. They kept the maelstrom within the circle of their feathered appendages, that funnel of air concentrated in an unforgiving frenzy of lashing wind.

His teeth were gritted, eyes closed as he struggled to keep the rope within his grasp while pressing a hand to his side. Each time a wing slapped him, he winced, welts raising along his skin. His side was red, the unhealed wound having broken open— blood spreading along the cotton fabric beneath his fingers.

Enid let out a bloodcurdling scream as his grip faltered and he slid to the end of the rope, legs dangling over the waiting chasm. With pronounced effort, he grabbed the rope with both hands and pulled himself up, his shaking arms barely able to hold him. The wind fae still pelting him mercilessly.

Swinging the bottom of the rope up, he gripped it in a loop, creating a foothold and securing it with a carabiner. His arms trembled with the effort it took to complete before he got a foot in the loop. The extra purchase allowed him to take the grappling hook from his belt, his hands now free to hold it while simultaneously maneuvering the rope. Enid clapped her hands. He was breathtaking.

Dimitri hissed in annoyance. A frown on his face.

Vidar swung the hook expertly, assessing each of the winged creatures. One by one it struck out, quick as a snake, hitting each in the head or a wing. Enough momentum was created that he was able to swing away from the small fairy cyclone as it came by him. Coordinating the rope's circular swings in time to the movement of the mini tornado.

The larger winged fae fell back, each landing upon a distant platform to tend their wounds. The wind began to dwindle significantly as they retreated. The twister dissipated next, the smaller fae scattering with high pitched screams as his focus turned to them. And then he was swinging away from the rope, landing safely on the next ledge.

A hanging rope bridge lay between him and the next platform. He scaled it easily, though Enid couldn't help but worry at the paleness of his face. The sheen of sweat upon his brow showed his strain. His side obviously bothered him as the blood began to drip from his shirt, small drops painting the surface beneath his feet.

He vaulted from a wooden platform, twisting through the air over the top of a Dryad—the tree nymph bearing bark- like skin. Landing behind it, he kicked out his leg, sweeping the tree fae off of its feet before hopping up and leaping to another ledge that swayed side to side before the final platform.

Enid smiled brightly, her body shifting to the edge of her seat. Only a simple jump remained to the finish. Enid could make it herself easily. Vidar locked eyes with her, his mouth tilting up in a small, victorious smile. Next to her Dimitri fumed.

Vidar leapt.

Enid was nearly bouncing in her seat in excitement. Then a blur of movement caught her eye. One of the small pixie creatures rushed toward Vidar, a large circular ring in their tiny arms. As Vidar's leg stretched toward the last platform, the creature snapped the circlet of metal around his wrist. His eyes widened in surprise, and his head jerked toward Enid. Horror filled her as she looked down at her own wrist. The bracelet of metal that was there only a few hours ago was gone. The circlet now fastened securely to Vidar's wrist.

She jumped to her feet, reaching in vain as the pixie smashed against the glass bubble. A flash of light blazed from the green circle as it burst. A gust of air shoved the crowd back. Enid covered her eyes against the glare of light and the flurry of wind as she was thrown backward into her seat.

When she looked up again, Vidar was gone. The platform that marked the end of the challenge remained mockingly empty. Whispers and shocked gasps filled the arena. The King shot to his feet, barking orders at the nearby fae to send out a search party. Calling for the one who had used the bracelet to be brought forward.

It was all a distant rumble in Enid's ears, her eyes still staring at the blank spot. He had been so close. Only a fraction of space between him and victory. Now all that remained was empty air, and a single, solitary drop of blood on a wooden plank.

Dimitri roared in celebration, standing and pulling her up against him. The air felt suddenly hot and stagnant. She couldn't breathe.

"You are mine," he shouted. He pulled back, looking her in the face, his hands gripping her arms. "I will make it worth everything," he insisted. "I swear it."

Enid couldn't respond. Still searching that empty space in vain. He was gone. And with him every hope of a normal life, of the feelings that had begun to evolve between them, and, despite Dimitri's claims, her humanity.

Dimitri's hand gently turned her face toward him, his eyes examining her worriedly. His mouth moved, but she couldn't process what he was saying. The chaos of the arena was nothing more than the far-off buzzing of bees.

I'm not worth it, her brain insisted, repeating those earlier doubts and fears. Distantly, she realized tears were raining down her cheeks. Dark spots danced before her eyes. She felt herself falling. Then, nothing.

CHAPTER

31

A deafening, thunderous roar drew her forth from the dark embrace of oblivion. Fury and sorrow filled the sound. The thick sense of danger had her instantly alert, her body's response forcing her into vigilant consciousness. A crashing noise followed, the tinkling of shattered glass driving her upright.

King Fenri paced an unfamiliar room. Glass and broken bits of furniture crunched beneath his feet. He whirled as she sat up, eyes blazing with a golden glow as he stalked over. The skin along his face and arms rippled, thick tufts of hair beginning to emerge. He stooped low, his hands gripping the back of the couch at either side of her head, trapping her between them. His face nearing hers as a low rumble built in his chest.

"What did you do?!" Fenri snarled, teeth bared.

"No-Nothing!" Enid stuttered, panic clouding her mind.

She screamed as he jerked her up by the throat, lifting her high, the sound stopping abruptly as her breath was cut off. Fenri was irrational, his face twisted with an inhuman rage. The animal in him took over completely. Enid could only watch as his golden eyes narrowed up at her, the flash of sharp teeth snapping. She kicked wildly, her sight fading at the edges.

As terror overwhelmed her, something in her responded, a new, but somehow familiar, sensation flooding her senses. Instinctively, she felt herself relax into it, her body going limp, her vision white, as the feeling of floating in an abyss, of weightlessness, came over her.

Endless possibilities lay before her, each one an attainable future. One particular string called out to her, flashing among the tangle of filaments. She recoiled, reluctant to reach out and see what could become, reluctant to feel that loss of control. Unwilling to hold the weight of that many fates all dictated by the millions of actions around her. Flickering in and out of existence with each new decision. It overwhelmed her, an endless sea she couldn't navigate.

It was terrifying.

With extreme effort, Enid recoiled from the tapestry of strands, and struggled into awareness. Fenri was blinking up at her, the anger having dissipated from his face. Carefully, he lowered her to the floor and released his grip on her throat. The shifting of his skin vanished, the hair receding back into his arms.

"Your eyes changed just now," he growled, examining her closely. "What did you see?"

Confusion fluttered through her as she gulped in air, her hand at her throat.

"Changed?" she rasped. "I didn't see anything."

Doubt crept into his voice.

"Your eyes went blank, completely white," he said, gesturing toward her face. "Vidar was right, wasn't he? You are important, and more powerful than you realize."

He frowned, his shoulders sagging, hands tugging through the unruly locks of his hair. She eased back onto the couch, no longer afraid for her life now that Fenri seemed to regain control.

"I don't know what you're talking about."

He ignored her, turning away to pace once again, obviously lost in his thoughts.

"Not that it matters much longer," he grumbled. "Not when the Revenant get their hands on you."

"Dimitri promised me he wouldn't make me into one of them. He said I can stay human."

That was the only decision left to her at this point. The only hope she had left to cling to. Vidar was gone. Their time had been so short. Pain flared within her.

"The Queen will never allow that. Is that why you betrayed Vidar?" The King asked sharply, rage once again shifting along his features. "Did you strike a bargain with the Revenant?" His hands fisted at his sides.

Enid shook her head.

"I would never betray Vidar," she hissed in outrage, the anger helping to ease the bitter pain of grief. Her hand rubbed absently at her wrist, feeling the loss of the missing bracelet.

"THEN HOW—," he yelled, his voice cracking with sorrow. He paused, his voice becoming softer as his sadness overcame him. "How did they get it?"

Enid ran through her memories, recalling this morning when she was getting ready, how she had fidgeted with the bracelet. She had spun it along her wrist while she paced within her room. After that, she couldn't recall. Lania and Charlie had shown up and—Charlie. Enid gasped, shooting to her feet.

"Charlie," she said. The King lifted a brow in question.

"This morning, he threatened me. He grabbed my wrist and pushed me into a corner. He must have slid it off when he did."

The King growled low in his throat, stalking back and forth in the room as though trying to dispel nervous energy.

"Lania's new play thing. He must be trying to gain favor and move up in the ranks. Isis would go to any length to have what she desires. She must have plans for you, or she wouldn't have taken the time to go through all of this."

Enid looked toward the flustered King.

"Where did Vidar go?" she asked, tears filling her eyes. "Do you know?"

He stopped his frantic march.

"No," he said. "Only Vidar knew where it went, but I do know that wherever it was, it would be full of daylight. Where none of the Revenant would be able to go for many hours." Enid's heart felt like it was breaking all over again.

"He said this might happen," she sobbed, tears freely flowing down her face. "He said he could end up like his father." With those words her legs gave out from under her.

She fell onto the couch and wept.

There was a hesitant knock at the door. The King stormed over, flinging it open. One of the guards stood on the other side at rigid attention, face pale.

"I told you not to bother me now," Fenri barked. The guard gulped.

"I'm sorry, your Majesty," he stammered. "The Queen is insisting the woman be brought to the Revenant now for the claiming."

Enid sank further into the couch as though making herself smaller, less noticeable, would save her from the Revenant Queen's clutches. Fenri glanced over his shoulder, his face softening.

"The human has suffered a terrible loss and is distraught. I am granting her a period of mourning. When she has recovered, she will be brought forth to the Revenant for resolution."

The guard bowed respectfully before leaving to deliver the King's decree.

Enid breathed a sigh.

"Thank you," she said gratefully.

"Don't thank me yet," the King said ominously. "I am only postponing the inevitable."

***

Enid was escorted to her room by two guards a short while later. Dimitri waited in the hall, hair slicked back from his troubled face. When the door opened, and she stepped out, he brightened. Enid held up a hand as he came toward her, and the guards at either side of her shifted, blocking her. He growled in warning. Neither sentry seemed intimidated by the display.

"Dimitri," Enid sighed, drawing his attention. She lifted her head, allowing him to see the sadness there—the pool of tears in her eyes.

"I need you to give me time. Just a day or two. Please."

Slowly he nodded and stepped aside.

Enid heard him mumble as they passed, "I will be waiting, my flower."

When they reached her room, the guards waited for her to cross the threshold before they retreated—leaving her to her own devices. Everything was as she left it that morning. The flowers from Vidar sat in their vase, his letter on her dresser. Tears fell in an unending stream as she took them in, dripping from her chin onto the rug strewn floor. The books he gave her sat upon her desk.

She sank down, curling into a ball on one of the soft wool rugs. Her hand went to the ache in her chest, clawing at it as if she could tear the pain away. He was gone. The man who had so fully loved this place, despite their prejudices of him. Her protector. The Enforcer of Dokkalfar.

What would happen now? What would become of her? When would the Revenant come to take her? What would she become without her humanity? She knew Fenri was right when he said the Queen wouldn't let her keep it.

The questions came faster and faster—a floodgate of doubt. Her mind reeled.

Pressing her fists to her temples, she screamed out her frustration. The pounding of her head beat in time to her heart. When she couldn't stand it any longer, when she thought she might come apart at the seams, suddenly there was silence.

The world went white.

Ash rained down, falling onto her face like delicate butterflies. The flakes breaking apart where they landed. The slow flutter frightfully beautiful in the soft glow of lamp light. The dark was deep and all consuming. It filled her with comfort. In the distance a shriek split the night, sending a shiver of delight along her skin. Lifting her nose, she took in a deep breath. The coppery tang of blood was heavy in the air.

From the shadow of a nearby alley there was a sob. With her keen sight, she saw the huddled form of a woman cowering in a corner. A hand muffling the cries that so desperately needed to be voiced. She stalked forward, eager to assist those screams. Anxious to hear them join the melody of terror that rent the night.

Enid jerked, her vision clearing, the fairy lights on the ceiling coming into view. Sweat dampened her forehead and neck, the throb in her head slowing. She lay on the floor, unable to move. Afraid that if she did, it would call forth another vision. She didn't want it. The very thought of becoming that thing, a creature that found joy in pain, disgusted her.

Turning her head, her eyes landed on Vidar's letter. What would he have done? The bracelet was gone. That means of escape stolen from her, along with Vidar. The King had given her a few days. That would have to be enough time to come up with something. Even if it was just a way to delay a while longer. Maybe Dimitri would keep his word, at least long enough for her to figure something out. Though, given the vision, that wouldn't be a permanent solution. At some point she would be turned if she went with him.

Vidar would want her to fight. Slowly, she lifted herself from the floor. Her hand shook only a little when she picked up his letter. One phrase instantly stood out on the page.

Use the knowledge you have learned.

She turned to Vidar's books.

***

Enid was exhausted, but sleep refused to take her. Not that she would have entered its embrace willingly. There was too much to do, too much at stake. It felt as though it had been days. Days that she had languished within the confines of her room, sadness overwhelming her. Instead, it had only been hours. She read and reread Vidar's letter. Her eyes pouring over the curves and lines penned onto the paper with his own hand.

The books he had given her sat open. The drawing of the labyrinth at the top of the stack. The ancient paper slightly brown at the edges, ink vibrant despite its apparent age. Enid had stared at it until it lost all shape, tracing the lines of the path through the turns and twists over and over until she could no longer focus her eyes. He couldn't be gone. She couldn't accept it, wouldn't. Something deep within her, the part of her that saw things she used to think couldn't be real, wouldn't let her.

She lifted the ancient book carefully, moving over to her bed, needing sleep, but unable to part with the last reminder she had of Vidar. As she stood, a parchment of paper fell from its pages. She stooped to pick it up, glancing over it curiously. Her name stood out, written in Vidar's neat, curving hand. Lines drifted from it, question marks popping up randomly, fae names scrawled hastily alongside them. One in particular caught her attention, a large circle drawn around it.

Enid's head shot up, the flicker of an idea passing through her like an electric current. Her eyes drifted toward the door.

Without giving herself more time to think, time in which she may come to overturn this incredibly stupid decision, she threw on her shoes and rushed out into the hall. She was taking a big risk, but if she could pull it off, it would be a way out of the Revenant's grasp. She would need help though.

The hallway outside was empty. Dim sunlight drifted through the hole above the frozen body of Vidar's father. She almost stopped to stare, thinking that somewhere out in the world above, Vidar was in the same condition. A beautiful, sad statue. Pushing the thought away, she continued, making sure to keep alert.

Following the same path Dimitri had taken her a few days before, she hastened along, her mind going through the plan in her head. Words forming and reforming themselves as she considered. According to the giant clock, the sun was high in the sky at the moment. Those who couldn't handle its blistering rays were safely asleep. Others were busy tending their gardens, preparing for the coming night, or above ground tormenting would be victims.

The lower levels were eerily quiet as usual. Enid kept to the shadows, allowing the distance between lights to help hide her frail, human form away from the predators that lurked within. She knew it was in vain. All it would take was one small scrap of bad luck to become someone's next meal, but she pressed on. Only when she heard the soft fall of water, and saw the glow of light around the bend, did she sigh in relief. She made it.

Outside, the day was as dreary as she felt. Rain fell hard through the gap of the mountain, splashing into the shallow pool below. The rocks beneath the surface obscured by the constant agitation. Enid walked around to the viewing point, and stood in the cool rain. It drenched her thoroughly as she stared out into the hazy wilderness before her. Thick clouds of fog hung heavy among the evergreens. Looking out at that view, she stood and waited.

The light of day had begun to bleed from the cloud covered sky when the rain finally stopped. Her hair hung in a limp sheet around her. Her long sleeve shirt and loose pants stuck against her skin. She shivered a little, the fading light pulling away some of the heat. If she wanted to get warm soon, she would need to venture back into the mountain. Still, she waited.

Finally, when the light of day was no more than a memory. When only the sound of dripping water behind her remained to guide her toward the entrance to the tunnel, did she hear it. The sweet, inviting song melted from the darkness, wrapping itself around her in a tantalizing rhythm. Enid ground her feet into the rock below. Her fingernails dug into the flesh of her palms, anchoring her as she began to feel the effects of the tune. A low hum echoed over the pool of water, louder now, its source hidden within the deep shadows.

"You put yourself in great danger, beautiful human. Coming out here, so alone, without your over protective Revenant, and the Lord Champion dead and gone," the voice murmured softly.

"You made a vow."

A mirthless laugh echoed along the wet rock, sending tremors of fear spiking through her.

"Not to you."

"I need your help," Enid whispered, her voice rebounding oddly in the half-covered cavern.

"Why should we help you," the voice hissed, closer now and to her right. Enid stood her ground, resisting the urge to flinch away. "You who are about to be Revenant," it snapped at her ear. Anger filled that otherwise melodious voice.

"I don't want to be Revenant," Enid insisted. She stood her ground as she felt the brush of a body against her back. It was gone just as fast. Swallowing heavily, she continued, willing the fear from her words as she spoke them. "I have something else in mind, but I will need help. I have come to make a bargain."

There was a long silence. For a moment worry and dread engulfed her. Finally, there was the clatter of rock and the quiet, eerie sound of intrigued murmuring from multiple directions. That voice came out of nowhere next to her.

"We are listening."

CHAPTER

32

King Fenri sat upon his marble throne, head in his hand, a tiresome expression upon his gruff face. Queen Isis marched before him, hands waving heatedly as she spoke. The long train of her wine-colored dress wrapped up beneath her feet. Her red garbed attendants buzzed around her worriedly, as she kicked at it angrily, only to shy back as she shoved them away. Enid stood at the base of the dais, listening to the Queen rant. Beside her, a stricken look upon his handsome face, was Dimitri.

"There was an agreement," the Queen screeched. "You were aware! And now you want to go back on that!"

Enid gave a quiet sigh. She was prepared for this—understood there would be backlash.

"I'm sorry, your Highness," she said. "But that agreement was between Vidar and Dimitri. I was given no choice in the matter. Now that I have had time to acclimate to this life, I am making my own claim. I wish to choose a clan on my own."

The Queen stopped her pacing, turning to glare down at her. "I don't believe you truly understand what it is you are asking, human. In our world the only option is to conquer, or be conquered. If you cannot stand up for yourself in your own right, then someone does it for you." Her gaze ran up and down Enid, her mouth twisting in a sneer, teeth bared. "You wouldn't survive."

Undeterred, Enid merely shrugged.

"I am willing to prove my abilities. I will take on the Elemental Challenges."

King Fenri raised an eyebrow in amusement. The Queen scoffed.

Enid continued before anyone interrupted.

"If I fail, I am willing to then become Revenant and be claimed by Dimitri."

She glanced over at Dimitri, frowning when she noticed the displeasure evident on his face.

"If you fail," the Queen said in exasperation, "you will be dead, and completely useless."

"With all due respect, your highness," Enid said, "but if I am made a Revenant, I will be dead anyway." Her arms crossed in front of her chest, uncomfortable at the idea of dying. "If I have been told correctly, all that is required for my conversion is to willingly take the blood and be killed thus allowing the blood to override my human immune system and turn me Revenant."

The Queen raised her chin, glaring down at her. "And?"

Enid shrugged. "Then I will take the blood before the challenge. If I die, then I will automatically become a Revenant."

The King frowned, his eyes narrowing in displeasure. The Queen became contemplative, her onyx glare shifting to Dimitri before sliding back to Enid.

"And what, exactly, is keeping us from making you Revenant now, dear?"

Behind her, King Fenri cleared his throat. "I'm afraid I am, *my dear.*"

Queen Isis whirled, her long, intricately braided hair swinging around her hips.

"What?!" she shouted. "You know our rules, you yourself insisted there must be a claim."

The King smirked, his hand rubbing absently at his beard.

"I believe I said if she was willing to give up her human life, and immerse herself within our world, that I would honor her rights as fae. If the girl passes the challenge, it will prove to our people that she is capable of handling herself in our world."

Nostrils flaring, the Queen's hands fisted at her side.

The King followed the movement, his eyes sparkling with mirth. "If I didn't know better, I would think you have some ulterior motive in mind for the woman. You wouldn't be planning something vile, would you wife?"

Isis crossed her arms over her chest.

"I care for the well-being of my children," the Queen said, her eyes shifting to Dimitri. "The girl plays with one of my favorites as though he is no more than some expendable toy."

Enid turned to Dimitri, watching as his shoulders sagged, face lowering to the floor.

"It's not like that, Dimitri—"

"DO NOT SPEAK TO HIM!" The Queen shouted, her eyes twin slits of fury. "You don't deserve him."

The King leaned forward, elbows on his knees as he looked at Dimitri. "Does the Revenant wish to absolve his claim?"

"NO," Dimitri hissed. He gave Enid a cursory glance, pain flaring through it before he turned away.

"I maintain my claim," he muttered.

"Very well, then," the King declared as he stood. "Enid Washbourne will partake in the Elemental Challenges, should she fail, she will immediately be reborn as Revenant. The first challenge will begin tomorrow."

Enid's head shot up. "Tomorrow?" she gasped.

Fenri arched an eyebrow. "The Labyrinth is still set from Vidar's challenge."

Enid swallowed, feeling suddenly so small and delicate.

He clapped his hands and rubbed them together. "Now if we can be finished with this, I am starving." With that he turned, leaving through the small door at the back of the dais.

Enid swayed a bit on her feet. She should be happy. She had done it. Only now a sense of dread came over her as she realized how soon she was going to have to face the first challenge.

The Queen looked down on her from the dais. "This was unwise," she said.

Enid couldn't respond. She might be right, this was rash, but there wasn't much of a choice.

The Queen turned on her heel and stormed out of the room, her attendants fluttering nervously as they ran after her.

It was just her and Dimitri now. Silence hung thickly around them.

"I will take you to your room," he said, his voice so full of emotion that for a moment Enid felt regret. Not for what she felt she had to do, but for the fact that in the process she had hurt him.

"Dimitri, I'm so—" He held a hand up, quieting her.

The walk back to her room was uncomfortable. Dimitri didn't even look at her, his pace quick, his footsteps heavy. Many of the smaller creatures scurried out of his way, sensing the storm brewing within. When they reached her door, she tried once more to say something. To apologize, for how things were developing. To explain.

Before she could open her mouth, his large hand gripped her by the throat and pinned her to the stone wall. A startled *eep* passed her lips, her shocked gaze on Dimitri's face. He scowled at her, his face hardening as he leaned down.

"I gave you everything you wanted, everything you could ever need or desire. I bared my soul to you. I moved heaven and earth to bring you here to me. Was willing to allow you to keep your humanity. I *groveled* at your feet. And this," his grip tightened, thumb pressing a line along her skin. "This is how you repay me. You reject me, discard me as though I am worth nothing. Treat me as though I am lower than mud."

Fingers laced through her hair before yanking hard, forcing her to look into his enraged face. She couldn't speak, couldn't think, only stared with wide eyes. The severity in his face both terrified and startled her.

His lips crashed against hers—demanding and authoritative. The grip around her neck released. His hand moving instead to the side of her face, holding her still as he forced his kiss upon her. Her hands shot out, slapping, pushing, punching at him uselessly. Grabbing her wrists, he pinned them above her, chuckling darkly.

"I can make you want it, my flower. You seem to forget that. It would be as simple as a kiss, and you would yearn for me. You would beg me to unleash your hidden desires." He ran a hand slowly down the length of her body, fingers probing indiscreetly among the private curves and valleys of her flesh. She whimpered. "To unwind this proper, uptight girl from her shell, and really discover the naughty little vixen I know hides beneath." His fingers dipped between her legs.

Enid seethed in fury.

"You could try, Dimitri, but you and I both know you would have to force me to take your blood. You would be no better than your father," she bit out.

That statement hit harder than any slap. Dimitri went rigid, his nostrils flaring. He released her, but she wasn't going to stop now that she had his full attention. The fear and fury fueled a rant of epic proportions, her weakness against him driving her to lash out in the only way she could.

"You know if you make me Revenant, you would grow to resent me. You would hate the creature *you made* me become. Deep down, you would feel responsible for taking my humanity. My compassion, my kindness, everything you say you love about me, would disappear, and it would be all your fault. Just like your sister." Her voice shook with the depth of her anger. She took a step toward him, her chest pushing against his. "You tarnish everything you touch," she snapped.

Defiantly, she scowled at him. Daring him to refute her.

Jaw ticking, a crazed look in his eye, Dimitri grabbed her arm. She couldn't look away, terrified that if she did, he may kill her. His other hand found the knob to the door, and thrust it open. He yanked her closer, making her realize just how much pain he could inflict, before he shoved her through the opening. She sprawled along the floor of her room. Safe now in her sanctuary. He loomed in the doorway. Hands pressed against the frame.

"Yet, you force me to make you Revenant," he ground out, voice low. "You'll never survive the challenges." And then he was gone, storming off down the hall.

CHAPTER

33

Anticipation kept her from sleeping. Even a hot bath did little to ease her discomfort. When the time finally came to travel down into the depths containing the labyrinth, Enid felt woefully unprepared. Dimitri's angry face came back to her. His parting words from the night before on a loop in her mind.

You'll never survive.

She already knew the route through the intricate maze. The book still sat open upon her desk. Her fingers had walked it that morning before she stepped out. The King's guards gave her worried looks, but remained quiet as they escorted her to the maze entrance, where Fenri already stood, waiting. His rugged face seemed even more weary with the flickering light from the torch flame throwing shadows across it. Enid nervously stood her ground—ready to receive her instructions.

He grunted a greeting, his hand motioning to a small table on which sat a few weapons. A crossbow, which she didn't know how to use. A slingshot, she knew would be useless with her aim. A sword, which was too heavy for her to carry. The last item was a small dagger. At least this she could hold. Unfortunately, it would require close contact to be of use. She prayed it didn't come to that.

As she picked up the dagger, Fenri shook his head. He scratched at his beard before placing his hands on his hips and squinting at her curiously.

"I haven't decided yet if you have a death wish, are stubborn, or incredibly stupid," he grumbled.

"Or," Enid said softly, "maybe I'm tired of everyone trying to control me. Perhaps it was time for me to make a choice for myself. I should at least have the opportunity to choose my own path."

"I can respect that," the King said, giving her a nod of approval.

"It seems to me all of your choices were taken off the table the minute you decided to entertain this idiotic endeavor."

Enid turned toward the sound of the Queen's voice as she walked toward them with a sneer.

She didn't respond. Focusing instead on pulling a leather belt around her hips, the small dagger sheathed at the side. Her scarlet hair had been pulled back into a braid, but even now tendrils of it fell out around her face, getting in her eyes. She was doomed. Hands shaking, she yanked at the belt in an attempt to tighten it. It slipped down the curve of her hip ineffectually.

Gentle hands covered her own and tugged the belt into place for her. Hesitantly, she looked up into Dimitri's impassive face. His touch was light as he deftly secured the belt at her hips. His emotions unclear to her for the first time since he brought her down to this dark world.

Tears pooled within her green eyes, and she blinked them away. Now was not the time to fall apart. His gaze flicked to hers, giving away nothing.

"I'm sorry. I think I understand," he said, so quietly it was hardly even a breath. "And you were right."

Their eyes remained locked for half a second longer, and then he was backing away. The Queen took his place in front of her, eyes cold in the torch light.

"You have squandered a rare opportunity, human."

Enid merely stared straight ahead, ignoring the snub.

"No matter," the Queen sighed. "The challenge is the same as before, only instead of three Minotaur, you will have two to contend with in the Labyrinth. We will go easy on you, since you are, after all, so very fragile." She leaned toward Enid, her voice dripping with venom. "I always get what I want. Don't forget that." Standing upright, she plastered a pleasant smile on her face.

"Good luck," she sang and gestured toward Dimitri. "Give her the blood, then come take your place in the stands," she ordered, not bothering to stay to verify he complied.

"Yes, my Queen," Dimitri said obediently.

King Fenri leveled the Queen with a look of pure disgust before turning to Enid once more, features softening.

"Wait for the gong, and then enter. The quicker you are, the more of a chance you stand in evading the Minotaur. They are not very fast. Just get to the other side."

Enid nodded, attempting to hide her shaking hands by clasping them firmly together. The nervous glance the King gave her proved it was a futile effort. He turned and walked down the hall, guards close behind.

Alone now, Enid faced Dimitri, uncertain about what would come next. What these first steps into that labyrinth would truly mean for her.

"I did not want this," Dimitri murmured, stepping close. "I offered you your humanity."

"I know," Enid responded. "And I am sorry. I really needed to try to do this for myself."

For some strange reason, she trusted Dimitri. She knew he would protect her. However, she did not trust his Queen, and the control she seemed to have over her people. So, she kept her vision to herself, not feeling secure enough to give him any information the Queen could use against her.

"I will be waiting for you at the end, no matter the outcome," he said.

Enid closed the distance between them, throwing her arms around his neck in a firm hug. His arms encircled her, holding her close while she shivered. Tears streamed down her cheeks. She knew she should be angry at him, should hate him. But he was all she had right now, and she was so very scared. In need of the comfort of another.

"I'm afraid."

He stroked her hair. "No matter what happens, you will be okay. The blood will help with your fear, but it will make it hard to focus. Your thoughts will drift to me. You must fight it and concentrate on the labyrinth. I will be watching." He leaned back a bit so he could see her face.

"May I kiss you one last time, without the blood's influence."

Hesitantly, she nodded her approval. She was heading straight to her death. If this didn't go right, then she would need him to get through the transition, as painful as that would be.

He bent toward her, lips soft as he pressed them to hers. She responded, tasting, searching, feeling him let go of the tension he held as they melted together. Dimitri pulled away, his eyes searching hers. His fingers traced the curves of her face as though dedicating it to memory, and then his eyes darkened as he took her head between his hands and urgently captured her mouth in a searing kiss.

Enid's heart fluttered as the kiss became more passionate, desperate. It was then that she tasted the familiar coppery, honey taste of his blood in her mouth and she was lost. Reluctantly Dimitri pulled away, peppering kisses along her cheeks and nose.

She reached for him, not wanting to let him go. Needing him beside her. He shook his head, shattering her heart. What could she do to make him happy? If he asked it of her, she would stab the dagger at her side into her heart and become Revenant right then and there. He took her hand in his, and she exploded with happiness at the touch.

"Go, focus on completing the labyrinth. Finish this challenge and survive. I will be waiting on the other side."

Enid smiled, squaring her shoulders with determination. Her love needed her to do this for him. This would make him happy. Only, he didn't seem delighted as he frowned—sadness and disappointment in those piercing blue eyes. Then he was gone.

Only when he faded out of view around the corner, did she turn toward the entrance. There was something she was supposed to remember. A gong. There would be a gong, and creatures she must avoid. Minotaur. Wasn't that what the King said? The memory was fuzzy. Dimitri occupied those thoughts now. Dimitri. He said he wanted her to focus. Needed for her to get to the other side of this maze.

Focus, Enid. Focus.

There was a touch at her back. Dimitri? She whirled. It wasn't him.

She frowned at the siren who stood looking at her curiously. She gave Enid a slight smile.

"We don't have much time," Esmelial said in that sultry voice that always raised goosebumps along Enid's flesh. "One of the Minotaur within the labyrinth is willing to help you. He is imprisoned by his clan because he is sympathetic to humans, and refuses to harm them. You will recognize him by the scar over his left eye. There will be a collar around his neck. It is set to a remote to electrocute him if he does not comply. You must get it off of him or he will be forced to kill you or die."

"How do I get it off?"

"There is a latch recessed within it. It requires a special key." Esmelial held up her hand, a small metal spike with a hook on the end within her fingers.

Enid smiled. "How did you get this?"

The siren merely shrugged. "I can be quite persuasive."

Enid nearly laughed out loud as she took the key. Dimitri would be pleased. Her body warmed at the thought.

Fingers snapped in front of her face. Enid started.

The siren's lip curled in disgust. "You've been given the blood already."

"He said I must win. I must survive. He will be happy if I survive."

Enid looked toward the labyrinth longingly. Dimitri waited for her. She felt the eyes of the siren watching her with barely contained intrigue.

"Interesting," was all she said before she melted away. "Good luck."

The large door before her showed nothing of the labyrinth beyond. The eyes of the carved snake watched, sharp teeth biting into its own tail. Was this what Vidar saw when he stood in this very spot? A flicker of sadness welled up within her at the thought of Vidar, pushing aside her infatuation of Dimitri for a short time. What would he do if he were here right now? She looked down at the small key within her hand, tightening her grip on it.

She needed to do this.

A loud, ringing bong reverberated around the walls of the labyrinth. It was time.

Enid lurched into the twisting hallways of the maze. Above her there was nothing but cavernous darkness. The silence was terrifying. An illusion, she knew. High above would be the snarling, raucous audience of creatures. All jeering and taunting, eager for her demise. And Dimitri. He would be watching.

She rushed through the turns, her mind slipping to that picture of the labyrinth. Her feet following the path set in her mind. Listening intently for any sounds, she went as fast as she could. She was coming upon the center of the maze when she heard the first footfall of another being.

Silently, she slipped behind a bit of fallen stone. The crumbled rock large enough to hide her from view. There was a huff of breath. Heart pumping, she inched around the jagged rock. Trying to catch a glimpse of the creature beyond. Its back was to her, head moving in the air. Sniffing for her scent. Around the massive neck gleamed a metal collar. Nervously she stepped into sight. Turning toward her, the Minotaur narrowed its large, brown eyes.

No scar.

Enid's blood ran cold, her eyes widening in horror. Everything happened in slow motion. The beast roared in triumph, sharp horns taking aim for her. It darted forward, gaining momentum, barreling at her like a freight train.

At the last minute, Enid reacted and thrust herself to the side. The creature rammed into the stone, shattering the boulder to fragments with a resounding crack. Debris rained down on her. A shrill scream tore itself from her lips. She scrambled to her feet and ran, pushing herself as fast as she could through the passages.

The turns were quicker here, which worked in her favor. Behind, she could hear the sound of the Minotaur, his bulk crashing into the wall at every tight turn. She knew she was going to be in trouble soon. Another turn and there would be a long, straight spot. He was sure to catch up to her there. She pulled the dagger out of its sheath as she slid around the final corner.

Far ahead, another Minotaur stepped around a corner. A long scar ran down his cheek from his left eye. She didn't stop.

Couldn't. Lest the creature behind her catch up to her and gore her back. The Minotaur in front began to run at her, his horns lowering. Behind her a furious bellow split the air. The other one was gaining.

When she was close enough, it gave a downward motion with its hand. She threw herself to the ground, her body slamming against the stone, the dagger clattering away from her. The Minotaur sailed over the top of her as she skidded along below him. There was a sickening crack as the two slammed into each other.

Enid stood to her feet shakily and looked around. One of the Minotaur lay on the ground, motionless. The other was climbing to its feet, stumbling a bit as it did so. When it turned toward her, she almost slumped in relief at the sight of the ragged scar. Then it was running toward her. She began backing up, confusion and fear making her clumsy as she nearly tripped over her own feet. Her dagger was gone. Only the key remained, clasped tightly in her sweaty palm.

The Minotaur grabbed her arm and lifted her off her feet. Its breath huffed in her face, sending the tendrils of hair snaking down from her braid fluttering. Her eyes were directly in front of the thick metal collar at its neck. The key in her hand felt remarkably heavy as she realized what he was trying to do. Her eyes fastened onto the tiny recessed hole where the locking mechanism was. Quick as a flash, her hand darted forward, the key locking into place and turning easily. The collar clattered to the floor. The Minotaur threw her over his shoulder and ran.

She braced her arms against his back, trying to keep from bouncing. As her fingers found purchase, there was the dizzying feeling of falling through space and white light flooded her. Threads of opportunity flew before her, several of them flickering frantically. She didn't back away this time. She reached out with both hands, and grabbed a glimmering tendril as it floated by. A sequence of events unfolded before her. In one the Minotaur rescuing her was captured, his death brutal and horrific. In another, he escaped, disappearing into the tree mist fog of the mountains.

The vision was fading when she became aware of the Minotaur running through the large exit. The opening still splattered with blood from Vidar's challenge.

He set her down in the tunnel, large hands shaking as he glanced around. He still had freedom to run for.

"Thank you, human," the Minotaur was saying in his deep, booming voice. He turned to leave.

"Wait!" she called out. He hesitated. "Take the right tunnel, not the left. Go up a level, and stay to the right. The climb down will be tricky, but you will make it."

He seemed surprised for a moment, but recovered quickly. There was no time to waste.

"You have my gratitude," he said before he turned to run.

Enid gave a heavy sigh when she saw him turn right at the end of the tunnel. She sank to the floor and leaned her head against the wall. Her heart still thumped wildly from the adrenaline. She looked over to the carved snake around the door.

She was through. It was over.

With a sigh of relief, she closed her eyes.

The sound of footsteps came from down the passage, and she opened her eyes to see Dimitri rushing toward her. Her heart skipped a beat at the sight of him, but she wasn't overcome. The thrall was wearing off. She smiled tiredly as he dropped next to her, checking for injuries.

"You did it!" he exclaimed. "You are amazing."

His accent was thick as he spoke. Excitement and relief evident as he lifted her from the floor and cradled her in his arms, standing to swing her around.

There was the sound of a single person clapping and the King walked up, his guards flanking either side of him. Enid urged Dimitri to set her down, her footing only slightly unsteady now.

"That was quite unexpected," the King said, a small smile peeking through the scruff of beard. "I will admit I am impressed."

"Thank you, King Fenri." Enid gave a shaky smile.

"Tonight, I am holding a dinner in your honor. A celebration of your victory."

"That's really unnecessary."

She wasn't sure she would be able to stand much longer, let alone attend a dinner.

"I promise not to have you out too late. You will have the opportunity to get plenty of rest before the next challenge. And it will also give you the chance to meet with other clans. You will need to choose one to align with if you successfully complete the challenges."

Enid shifted nervously. She only completed one challenge so far. Everything was happening so fast. The King was right though. It had to be done. She mumbled a quick acceptance. Dimitri shifted beside her as the King walked away.

"What am I going to do?" she said quietly.

Dimitri glanced over at her, his jaw ticking. "Survive."

CHAPTER

34

The dinners she sat through with the Revenant were nothing compared to the one hosted by the King. Many of the clans were in attendance, gathered in clusters. Enid was shuffled from group to group on the arm of the King himself. His normal dress of casual pants and t-shirts replaced with a black tux. Scruffy hair combed and gelled. Beard neatly trimmed.

If he was uncomfortable, he didn't show it. Enid couldn't say the same. The gold strapless dress wrapped tightly around the curves of her body, cascading in a ripple of shimmering fabric to the floor, made her feel like an ornament for display. A goblet of dandelion wine was placed in her hands. She sipped at it thankfully, allowing the sweetness to calm her jittery nerves.

While some clans were aloof and tense, such as the Minotaur who glared at her in silence, most were kind. The Sirens greeted her openly. Their barely clad bodies draped in nothing more than what appeared to be shimmering nets. Knowing looks passed among them, each giving her a long hug. The pixies drifted about her happily, some in vibrant colorful, gauze gowns. Bashful nymphs smiled shyly, their flowy dresses seemingly made of the very flowers and trees they so loved. Fauns, pucks, and a lone centaur were grouped to themselves, chatting amicably. They gave her appraising looks as she was introduced.

The cluster of merfolk surprised her the most. Their hair a variety of colors ranging from common wheat to a more unusual vibrant lilac and a deep blue. Beautiful shells were woven into the lustrous locks. Their clothes were nice but much more casual, as though the fact they wore clothing at all was enough of an effort. She was amazed to see they walked on two legs. When she questioned King Fenri about it, he gave a booming laugh.

"When they are in the water," he explained, "the tail will appear, but when they are on land, they can call legs at will."

"Wow," Enid breathed in amazement. "The best of both worlds."

The King chuckled. "Don't let them fool you. Their ways are as odd as any of the clans here. The women tend to be more independent and adventurous, while the men are prone to seek a life of domestication. Their main goal is to impregnate their women so they can raise children. In fact, if it weren't for the sole drive of the men to procreate and rear as many children as possible, their kind would have died out long ago. It is very rare to find a compatible couple for conception among them. Among any of our kind, really," he mumbled as an afterthought.

Enid's eyes widened as one of the handsome mermen came up to her, his tan skin accentuating the vibrancy of aqua eyes. Long, golden hair hung in waves down his broad shoulders. A loose-fitting white shirt that was barely buttoned displayed the contours of a muscular chest. Lifting her hand delicately, he left a lingering kiss.

"You are a rare beauty," he whispered admiringly. "Our children would be beautiful."

Enid gasped, yanking her hand from his. The King roared with laughter as she stuttered out a thank you. The merman winked at her. A charming smile on his chiseled face as he melted back into the glittering group.

Next were the ghouls and golems. Vicious creatures who lurked within the lower, blackest levels. They eyed her hungrily. Enid glared back into beady eyes. Her own fierce smile meeting the thin-lipped sneers. The ghoul from the asylum smiled the largest. His hooked nose quivering as he sniffed at the air, searching for her fear. She threw him a scowl worthy of Vidar himself. The golems were larger creatures, muddy in color and complexion. Eyes that appeared to be no more than polished stone stared at her blankly.

"A necessary evil, I'm afraid," the King explained after a brief introduction. She hated turning her back as they walked away, still feeling the sneers and hungry stares. "They enjoy the taste of dead flesh, and tend to be sent out to clean up some of our more grotesque incidents."

"I am not joining that clan," Enid said in disgust.

"That will surprise no one," the King smirked.

Lastly, he escorted her to a group of human-looking fae. The only indication that they were anything but human was revealed in the flash of their predatory eyes, and the animalistic way they carried themselves.

"These are the shifters," the King explained. "Most of us are wolves, the most common type, but there are a few of the rarer species, such as bear, or cheetah. Raj here is a tiger shifter." His hand clasped the shoulder of a tall man with large amber eyes, and skin the color of burnt umber. He flashed her a genuine smile that she returned warmly. She recognized him as one of her escorts on a few occasions.

"Congratulations on your victory. It was quite riveting." His deep, melodic voice held the barest rumble.

Enid mumbled a brief thanks, already tired of the praise. She'd gotten lucky, and had help which no one could know about. Shifting uncomfortably, she began searching the room, attempting to look anywhere but at the eyes upon her.

A woman by herself against a far wall drew her attention. Her long, waist length hair was pure white and twisted into a thick braid. She didn't wear a gown or glittering jewels. But was dressed in the black combat gear of the guards. Her red-orange eyes were sharp as they skimmed the room. Eerie against the whiteness of her skin and hair. Enid instantly recognized her. It seemed like an eternity when she stood next to Vidar, watching this woman intimidate the minotaur and ghoul.

"Who is that?" Enid asked.

The King glanced in the direction of her nod.

"Ah," he said. "That is Dagny," he whispered. "She, like you, had no clan. A daughter of the great goddess Danu, or so it is said. She can't seem to remember and neither can anyone else but, she is the last of her kind. A banshee. She joined the shifter clan several decades ago, and is one of our best warriors. She tends to keep to herself. Her temper is...easily invoked. Vidar worked closely with her, but he was one of the few with the same tenacity for battle."

At the mention of his name, she felt that sting of pain and a flash of jealousy. She pushed it aside. She couldn't let herself grieve right now, to think about Vidar being gone.

"Danu?" Enid questioned.

Fenri nodded. "Our first Queen. She ruled for many centuries in solitude, when our people first recall coming to this realm. Before humans discovered us and began to both worship and fear our kind. That is what the myths say, anyway."

Curiosity quickened within her. She made a mental note to look through Vidar's books for any mention of these events when she had a moment. For now, she needed to concentrate on her own survival.

A sudden rise in hushed conversation drew Enid's attention toward the door. Walking into the great hall, head high, a golden circle upon sheets of glistening hair, was the Revenant Queen. Every head in the room turned toward her as she walked by, long legs flashing through the fluttering skirts of her soft pink gown.

She stopped before the King and Enid, a smile on her lips. Behind her Dimitri followed, with a look of ambivalence that, to Enid, seemed forced. Cindy and Marcus trailed behind. The Revenant men as always wore their black, the women standing out in comparison.

Enid's eyes met Cindy's hopefully, only for Cindy to look right through her. Marcus put his arm around Cindy's waist, his hand sliding along the yellow silk of her form fitting dress soothingly. His face, however, remained as unexpressive as ever.

"Husband," the Queen purred. "It is pleasant to see you entertaining, and making an effort with your appearance, but this all is a bit much isn't it? We do know that the chances of the human being successful are very slight, even if she did somehow pass the first challenge."

Her head tilted toward Enid. "How did you manage that? It looked to me as though you somehow got that Minotaur to help you. Though I have no idea how you were able to achieve such a feat."

Enid looked away. "I'm very lucky," was all she said.

The Queen hummed thoughtfully. "Dimitri, why don't you entertain our guest of honor. I'm sure my husband is weary of the company, and I have some things to discuss with him."

The Queen's long fingers reached out, pulling the King's opposite arm toward her. King Fenri glanced at Enid apologetically, his face hardening as he looked to his wife.

"Let's go, *dear*," he grumbled.

Dimitri stepped closer, his eyes raking over her.

"Have you eaten?" he asked softly.

At the mention of food her stomach twisted painfully.

"No, but I could eat," she replied.

He led her to the table piled with an assortment of various meats, cheeses, vegetables, fruits, and breads. She was plucking roasted vegetables and meats onto her plate when Esmelial found her.

"You were quite successful tonight. Are you ready for the next trial?"

The siren tossed a look of contempt at Dimitri before focusing back on Enid.

"I hope so," Enid said. "I'm incredibly nervous after what happened to Vidar."

Esmelial's eyes softened with sadness. "What happened to the Enforcer was unfortunate. He was a good fae," she stated wistfully. "Do not worry too much, human. I have a good feeling." She gave her a meaningful look and slowly walked away. Hips swaying beneath the glimmering net material that barely covered her.

Dimitri escorted her to a seat where she was able to sit and turn her mind away from the efforts of mingling among the clans. She nibbled at her food, attempting to shrug off the exhaustion of today's events. Dimitri offered nothing more than a comfortable silence.

Enid was staring into space, relishing the peace, when a creature she didn't recognize stumbled into the table. A mostly empty bottle of dandelion wine in its furry claws.

"I know you," it slurred. Large teeth protruded from its bottom jaw. Spittle flying from its mouth as it drunkenly spoke.

Dimitri hissed at the creature. "Leto, you have had too much to drink."

Leto wore a tiny suit over the mass of fur that covered his body. His tie hung loosely around his neck, the top three buttons of his white shirt undone. Due to the shortness of his stature, his chilling, scarlet eyes were directly level with her own as she sat. He would have appeared quite ferocious if he wasn't making such strange faces as he attempted to focus his sight. Shrugging Dimitri off, he turned once more toward Enid.

"I've seen your nightmares. They. Are. Delicious."

Enid focused upon the little creature. "What?" she asked, confused by his ramblings.

"Alright, Leto, that is enough," Dimitri growled, yanking him back by his shirt collar. "My sister will be here shortly. Why don't you go prepare yourself?"

"Lania's pet invited me into the house. I was only doing what you asked," the creature slurred. "But I really wanted a taste. Her nightmares…such delicacies."

Dimitri snatched the hairy creature up by his tie, strangling the fae with it as he snarled in his face.

"Enough, Leto."

He let go, letting the poor, drunk thing slam to the ground in a heap. Lurching to its feet, the creature hiccupped and wandered off, mumbling to itself. Pitching from side to side and bumping into other beings, it meandered through the crowd.

"What was that?" Enid asked.

"Leto is a Mare," Dimitri explained with a casual shrug taking a sip of his blood.

"A Mare," Enid said softly. Her mind wandered back to the night outside of her mother's house. Charlie had mentioned something about dreams, she had forgotten. How could she have forgotten?

Dimitri nodded, his eyes drifting around the room. "They can enter people's dreams and give them nightmares, or terrors. They feed off of the energy released by the fear."

"You sent him to my mother's house. Him and Charlie. To make me come to you willingly. You were trying to drive me to you, weren't you?"

Thoughts of her mother brought a sudden throb of pain to her head. She winced, her hand going to her forehead. Dimitri watched her, brows lifted, a frown on his handsome face.

For some reason she felt betrayed. Seeing the Mare brought to mind all of the schemes Dimitri used to lure her there. With the pounding in her head came the urge to push the thoughts away. The desire to forget washing over her. This time, she latched on. Holding firm to the thought even as her head ached in protest.

He manipulated her, seduced her, took her from friends and family. She would never set foot in her home again. Never laugh with the people at the diner. The emotions hit her hard. She was angry. Angry at herself for how easily she had forgotten. How she allowed herself to depend on the very person who kidnapped her. She had felt she should be grateful. Her mother must be so worried. She was alone, and Enid had been gone for weeks. For all she knew, Enid could be dead.

"How could I have forgotten? How could I not think?" she hissed in frustration.

Dimitri's eyes darkened. "You forgot because I asked you to. The night I brought you here. When I gave you my blood, I used the thrall to make you leave your human life behind, the people you held dear. I told you to dismiss any thought of your family from your mind the moment the memories came up. I asked you to come here to my world, to give it and myself a true chance, because despite what you may think you can never go back. You can never leave. And I am *sorry*. I'm sorry. But you needed to forget, to make it easier for the transition." His hands were clenched into fists on the table. His jaw muscles ticked. "I can't let you go. Not ever. Especially now."

Looking down at her plate, she suddenly couldn't touch another bite. Her appetite vanished as quickly as the thoughts of her mother had every day since she got to Dokkalfar.

She knew she couldn't go to the human world again, but she never thought that she would leave everyone behind. Never thought at all, because he used his thrall on her. Kept her naïve, compliant. She stood from her chair, her head aching, eyes full of tears.

"Where are you going?"

She couldn't answer, couldn't speak.

"Away," was all she said as she rushed from the room, her feet carrying her down the now familiar corridors.

"Enid!" Dimitri called behind her.

She didn't stop. How disconnected had she allowed herself to become? What else had she forgotten? Not until she was in her room with the door shut, did she allow herself to fully explode. She shrieked in rage, tears streaming down her cheeks. A fist pounded on the door.

"Enid!" Dimitri shouted. "Let me explain!"

"GO AWAY!" she screamed.

It felt like something within her had broken. She was terrified and furious. Faces flashed within her mind. All of the people she lost. Her mother, her friends at the diner, Cindy, Vidar. All of their lives altered forever, or destroyed because of the actions of one selfish individual.

And she had given in to him, felt bad for him. She had apologized to him for hurting his feelings. Allowed him to kiss her. Had allowed him to take her from her life, and the people she held dear. Why?

She thought back to her time here. The moments she started to recall her old life, her family, her friends, and how quickly it had passed out of her mind. The splitting pain in her head until it had.

The pain was there now, intense, insistent. But the wall had fractured. As she pushed the thoughts of her family and friends to the forefront, it shattered to nothing, leaving only the ache of loneliness, the hurt of loss, and a fury for the one who took it all away so thoughtlessly.

"Irina, please!" He called. The pounding stopped.

Before she even considered her actions, she stomped to the door and threw it open. Dimitri was frozen on the other side, his eyes wide as he realized his mistake.

"I'm not her, Dimitri," Enid said firmly. "If that is what all of this has been about, then you have failed. I will never be her."

He opened his mouth. Her hand wrenched back and flew through the air. It wasn't until she felt the sting of the slap against her palm that she realized what she had done. Of course, he didn't even flinch. The only movement that showed he felt the slap at all was the closing of his mouth, and the widening of his eyes.

They stood staring at each other like that for a few ragged breaths until she slammed the door, refusing to look at his face any longer. She would win these challenges, she would claim her own life, and she would find a way to fix everything. To hell with what anyone else had to say about it.

CHAPTER
35

The void of the pit mocked her from where she stood observing the chaotic course. It was quiet here, for now. Her stomach was in knots. Anger and stubbornness kept her upright, propelled her along the path that led to the platform over that bottomless chasm. She wouldn't let the Revenant win.

Esmelial was beside her. The Siren's face relaxed and unworried. It did little to ease Enid's fears. Fingerless gloves were strapped onto her hands to protect the delicate skin from the ropes, and to help her grip. One of the perks of being human. They made the challenge "easier" for her. Though, looking out at the winged creatures showing off their skill with mighty bursts of wind, Enid was sure she would need all the help she could get.

The King chose that moment to walk in, his casual clothes and normally scruffy appearance a welcome sight. He looked better this way. More at ease than he did in the tux the night before. Stopping next to her, he turned to look out at the arena, his arms crossed. She was still studying the course trying to chart the easiest path. Something with smaller jumps, less wind, more stability.

It wasn't looking good for her.

Thankfully, there were no creatures on the platforms themselves. The large winged fae were the only creatures present, their short bursts of air ready to blow her off course, and send her sailing into the abyss.

"Don't think about it too much. You will cause yourself to panic," the King said. He scratched at his beard. "Just…react. Trust your instincts."

Enid nodded. It was actually good advice. Advice she should consider using outside of the challenges as well. She had spent too long ignoring her instincts.

Ull handed the King a belt before offering her an easy-going smile. Though she did notice the apprehension that swept across his features. Fenri held the belt up for her to see before tying it around her waist. Carabiners, a grappling hook, a white cloth. The same as Vidar.

Her hands ran over the items, familiarizing herself with them, and wondering if these were the very ones Vidar used. She shook her head, dismissing the thought. Of course they weren't. He was wearing his belt when he was transported to his death. Blinking away a haze of tears, she mumbled a quick thank you to the King before he left.

Enid once again nervously checked herself over. Her boots were tied. Olive cargo pants tucked into the top of them so they wouldn't snag. Her black tank top was tucked into those, and her belt hung snuggly at her hips. She had braided her hair back out of the way, tighter than usual so hopefully it wouldn't be flying in her face. On her arm she had written the names of her friends, and of her mother. Reminders, for when she was given Dimitri's blood, of what he had cost her.

Esmelial leaned against her arm, drawing her attention.

"When the gong sounds," she said so softly that Enid had to bend closer. "There will be some of the invisible little air pixies around you. Friends of Vidar's. They will help you through this challenge. Don't do anything too big to mess up or it will not go unnoticed." The Siren smiled up at her cheekily. "Last I checked, humans don't fly."

Enid chuckled. "We do not."

Relaxing a little at the thought of the pixie's help, Enid once more looked out toward the arena. She could do this. She had no choice.

Her spine stiffened as Dimitri stepped up next to her.

"Can we please talk?"

Enid rolled her shoulders. "I'm a little busy," she replied coldly.

Esmelial patted her arm lightly, throwing the Revenant a narrowed glare as she walked away. Dimitri tugged his hand through his hair. Shifting back and forth on his feet, his mouth opening and closing. He lost the battle to keep silent within seconds.

"I was different then. I didn't know what I know about you now."

"That doesn't make what you did ok, Dimitri. You murdered people I cared about. You made me forget them, forget my mother, as though they didn't matter. What if someone made you forget your mother?"

His face sparked with anger. "I did forget her, for centuries. It made things easier. Deep down you know that it made things easier for you too. That's why you allowed it for so long."

Enid whirled on him. "Excuse me?" she hissed. "What do you mean I *allowed* it to happen?"

Dimitri's lip curled, his eyes icy slits. "You shook my thrall off easily. Quicker than anyone I've ever seen, yet you allowed that little bit of influence to linger. You needed it to happen, admit it."

Rage filled her. Rage and a little fear that what he said was true. It had been easier for her to forget her past life, her friends, her family. To avoid facing everything that happened because of her. Tears began to fill her eyes. She couldn't give in. There was too much at stake. Her hands shoved at Dimitri's chest ineffectually.

"Give me the blood and go away," she said bitterly. Dimitri grabbed her arms, pressing her against the wall.

"You know I speak the truth, and yet you still continue to hold on to your anger."

"And I will continue to do so until I am no longer angry. Now do what you came here to do and leave me alone!"

They stared at each other. Dimitri obviously wanting to say more, while Enid refused to say anything else. Finally, he bit his lip and bent toward her. Turning her head, she pursed her lips together.

"Not like that," she declared. "Not anymore."

He licked the blood from his lips, the wound healing immediately. His eyes were hard. With a growl he bit into his wrist holding it to her mouth. Squinting at him angrily, she put her mouth to his wrist and took a small amount of blood. Before she could allow herself to feel the effects of the thrall, she pushed at him.

"Go."

He backed away as she turned to the arena, her eyes focusing on the words written across her wrist in the black ink. *Mother.* Pleasant thoughts of Dimitri began to creep into her head. Forcefully, she pushed them out, her eyes on that word. Allowing her anger to burn away the feelings of tenderness. *Remember and focus.* Squaring her shoulders, allowing no further contemplation, she stepped into the crowded arena and took her place.

Creatures of all clans flooded the space. The rings of benches filled to capacity. To her right the King and Queen sat upon their dais in their wooden thrones. She stopped in the middle of the platform over the seemingly endless void and looked around timidly.

The King stood to his feet. The crowd went silent.

"Today we gather to witness the second trial of the Elemental Challenges. Air! Our new human has surprised us all, I must say. Let us see if she can do it again!"

At this the crowd around her began to roar, clap, and hoot. The enthusiasm was shocking.

"Ring the gong!" King Fenri shouted.

The deep, bell-like sound reverberated throughout the space. The vibrations echoing from within the chasm. Her body felt rigid, her muscles frozen. Below, the blackness stretched endlessly. The shadows seemed thick enough to reach out and snatch her into a cold embrace.

In her ear she heard a small voice, and felt a slight breeze at her back.

"Stay to the left," a pixie whispered. "That part of the course is going to be much easier."

Enid looked to the left, her eyes tracing the path to the end. The pixie was right. Though there were longer drops, the obstacles were much closer together on that side. With a deep breath, she backed up and took a running leap toward the first platform.

She landed squarely in the middle, the wood shaking as her weight fell upon it. The crowd roared around her, some cheering, others booing. Tuning out the sound so it was only a dull rumble, she fixed her attention straight ahead.

Directly in front of her was a swinging rope, easy to reach. She took hold of it, making sure her grip was tight before propelling herself forward to the next wooden ledge. It was a steep drop. The momentum of her landing jarred her a bit. Teeth slammed together within her skull. Her knees screamed in protest. Shaking it off, she focused on the path, weighing her options.

To her right was a second rope swing, with a climb up to a scaffold above her. Beyond that she couldn't see. To her left was the wall of the pit, with a rope net attached to its side. She could climb that to a swaying wooden dock. The blackness stretched below her. A shiver ran up her spine.

"The left, the left," one of the pixie's buzzed in her ear. With a quivering breath, she turned, grabbed hold of the netting and stepped on. It swayed alarmingly. Bit by bit she crept along, trying not to look down into the gaping nothingness beneath her feet. Nothing but her grip on the net kept her from plummeting to her death. The pixies continued to urge her on. Tiny voices and the soft flutter of wings pressed her forward.

A sudden gust of air had her clinging tightly to the rope. She was only a couple of feet away from the edge. As the wind became stronger the swinging platform slammed into the side of her legs, knocking her from the netting. She let out a scream as she began to fall only to land directly on the solid planks of the structure as it started to rock away.

There was no time to feel ease. As the deck began to swing backward, she realized her foot was caught within the net. Her back grated against the wooden slats as the platform pulled away beneath her. Furiously she scrambled for purchase, her hand catching on a bit of the rope holding the structure aloft. Her arms shook, keeping the upper half of her body on the platform. She couldn't hold on for long. The weight of the platform was too much. She wiggled her foot desperately as it continued to swing back, stretching her body over the pit.

A flurry of the pixie wind slowed it long enough for her to kick her foot free. Gasping, she dragged her dangling body up, the edge biting into her waist. The grappling hook tore free from her belt. She watched, transfixed as it fell down into the depths before scrambling all the way to safety.

Violently trembling, she knelt on hands and knees, shifting back and forth with the movement of the scaffold. She wasn't sure if she could continue, if her legs were strong enough to hold her. She took deep, gasping breaths, trying desperately to get her bearings. If the grappling hook ever hit the bottom, if there even was a bottom, she couldn't tell. There was no noise. Only silence. Silence and the unending darkness.

One of the angelic fae gave her a sympathetic look. Their large wings lazily flapped back and forth. Subtly the creature turned a fraction, directing the breeze away from where she swung. The pendulum-like rocking slowed. Mouthing a thank you to the fae, Enid took a moment to gather herself.

The pixies at her sides pushed at her, urging her to her feet. Shakily, she stood, her hands latching onto the rope railing on either side to brace herself. Thankfully her legs held. She wasn't sure how long she could hold her nerve. She already felt herself beginning to unravel.

Another square bit of decking hovered below her, held up by four pieces of rope stretched horizontally across the shaft. It appeared to be anchored into the wall by large eye hooks. If she could make it there, then all she had to do was jump to a rope and swing herself to the finish.

With a deep, steadying breath, she waited for the platform to swing closer and launched herself into the air. Her arms and legs wheeled through empty space and then she hit the slab hard. The ropes flexed beneath her weight shooting her up. Her heart was trapped within her throat as she floated weightless above the wooden square.

When she came back down the side of her face hit roughly. Pain lanced through her head. Her arms and feet grasped the sides, holding herself in place as the platform continued to bounce. Tears fell from her eyes, falling in circular spots along with the bright scarlet of blood on the freshly hewn wood.

The rope was agonizingly close. All she had to do was stand and reach for it, but each movement of her limbs had her tilting precariously. Slowly she inched her arms in, attempting to push herself up. There was a sudden shift to her right. Her body pitched dangerously. She froze. The platform stilled.

"You must get up," a soft voice squealed in her ear.

"I'm trying," she whispered.

The crowd was in a frenzy. Her face throbbed. Carefully, she began sitting up again. As she did, she felt a gentle push around her, like a steady breeze helping to stabilize her. Right hand shaking, left arm held out to keep her balanced, she slowly reached for the rope. Her fingers grazed the coarse fibers. Suddenly, the slab shifted beneath her feet and she was falling.

Without thinking, her fingers snapped out and latched onto the rope. Thrust forward by the downward force she went swinging over the final bit of the chasm. A shriek tore from her as she soared through the air, propelled by her fall and the rush of air from the pixies. Tears were swimming in her eyes, but even so she could see her feet were directly over the final cantilevered structure.

She let go of the rope.

Her body slammed down, her vision blurred as jarring pain shot up her right leg. There was a split second of stunned silence, nausea threatened at the sudden agony, and then the crowd let out a roar so loud that she felt the tremor of it through the wood beneath her.

"Thank you," she breathed softly to the invisible little fae. She felt the lightest of touches on her cheek and hair before there was a breeze, and she knew they were gone.

Tears dripped from her eyes. When she went to wipe at them, her fingers came back streaked with blood. There was a cut above her eye. Unable to care at the moment, she closed her eyes and let her hand fall to the side as she caught her breath.

Footsteps came up beside her forcing her to open her eyes. She was greeted with the lopsided smile of the King. His booming laugh filled her ears.

"Need a hand?" he inquired, offering his.

Taking his hand with her gloved one, he pulled her to her feet. Enid's ankle gave out, and she nearly collapsed. Only the King's firm grip kept her upright. She gritted her teeth, biting back the yelp of anguish that wanted to break free.

"Looks like you'll need a healer." He waved over a few of his men. "Take our champion here to the infirmary. Make sure she's taken care of."

Raj smiled as he took her right arm, throwing it over his shoulder.

"Another resounding victory." She returned his smile with a small one of her own, a grimace replacing it as she attempted to put weight on her foot. Ull moved quickly, wrapping an arm around her waist as he positioned her left arm over his muscular shoulders, helping to release the burden.

"Keep this up, and you'll be the first human in history to pass the Elemental trials." He gave her an encouraging smile.

"If I keep this up, every bone in my body will be broken," she replied.

They chuckled, and began moving her carefully from the arena. Her eyes connected briefly with Dimitri's as she was escorted away. A look of concern on his face. She felt his eyes on her all the way through the arena and down the hall.

CHAPTER
36

The infirmary was not what she expected. Instead of natural rock walls like the rest of the underground city, the walls and ceiling in the clinic were pure white and smooth. The floors were the same with a subtle slope running to drains in the middle. Four beds were positioned on the far side of the room, all empty and made with military precision.

Opposite the entrance was another door marked office. Whose she couldn't be sure. There was no name plate to indicate. She found out soon enough. Ull and Raj were lowering her onto one of the beds when out stepped a Centaur.

He wore a pale blue scrub shirt over his very human torso, and nothing on his horse bottom half. She tried not to stare at the unusual sight of him. This large, bulky creature in a clean, sterile hospital environment. Pulling on a pair of gloves, hooved feet clicking on the smooth floor, he stepped up to her. The hair on his head matched the color of his body, the silky chestnut locks clipped above his ears. Though it hung long enough in front that it barely grazed the edges of his large brown eyes.

"Hello there," he greeted. "I suppose it was only a matter of time before you ended up here."

She gave a small, polite chuckle, though she didn't feel much like laughing. The ache in her leg was becoming more unbearable as the excitement and adrenaline from the challenge wore off. Raj and Ull gave each other looks before quietly excusing themselves.

"You're in good hands," Raj assured her with a pat on her shoulder before he left.

The centaur held out his hand.

"My name is Milentorius, but everyone calls me Miles."

She took his hand, giving it a brief shake.

"Enid Washbourne," she replied softly.

"Did you just get done with the second Elemental challenge, Enid?" he asked as he examined her ankle with surprisingly gentle hands.

Enid winced and nodded, not trusting herself to speak lest she cry out.

"Seeing as you are alive, it looks like congratulations are in order."

Enid didn't respond, other than a flinch as he found a tender spot. Loosening her boot as much as possible, he carefully removed it. Her ankle was purple on the side and a bit swollen. Expertly and efficiently, he wrapped an ice pack over it. Lifting it onto a pillow before he started cleaning the cut over her eye.

"You had Revenant blood when this happened?" he asked.

"I did," Enid replied.

Eyebrows furrowed, he leaned back and really seemed to look at her.

"Unusual," he murmured.

"Is it?"

"The Revenant are creatures with unnaturally quick healing abilities. With Revenant blood in your system, these wounds should have begun to heal almost immediately."

Enid frowned. "It did feel different this time," she said almost to herself.

"Different how?" Miles inquired as he placed a butterfly bandage over the cut.

"I'm not sure. I was so angry, and really anxious about the trial."

Miles only smiled. "Well, Enid Washbourne, you will live. You will need a few days with the ankle. Even then you will need to take it easy. Though I understand the next challenge will be soon. I hate suggesting it, but you might need a bit of that Revenant blood to help heal."

Enid shook her head.

"I'm only taking it as part of the agreement for the challenge. Otherwise, I won't have anything to do with them. You don't have a way to somehow—magically heal it?"

She almost expected him to laugh. Instead, he leaned back, his hands lacing behind his head as he stared up to the ceiling with a faraway look.

"There was a time I could, not that long ago. Only about a hundred years have passed since the last time my hands healed."

He held his hands in front of him. Fingertips rubbing together as though trying to recall the feeling.

"Unfortunately, that time has passed. The old magics are fading." He gave her a friendly smile. "We adapt. I've learned a great deal about human medicine over the years, and I can still diagnose with a touch. Some magic lingers within me yet," he said with a wink. "For now, I suggest rest, ice, and elevation for the ankle. Try to stay off of it. When you get the blood tomorrow it may heal. I will be there in case it doesn't, and I may be able to push for a postponement of the challenge."

A thank you was on the tip of her tongue when the door to the clinic opened, drawing their attention. In walked Dimitri, followed closely by Lania, and Charlie. Enid narrowed her eyes, her arms crossing over her chest.

"What are you doing here?" she grumbled.

"I have come to check on you, and help you to your room, my flower."

"I don't want your help."

Her lips nearly pulled back along her teeth, baring them fiercely. The fae were beginning to rub off on her.

"Do you plan to hop to your room on one leg from here?" Dimitri asked with frustrating calm.

Enid groaned in irritation, but reluctantly acquiesced. He scooped her up easily, taking care with her ankle.

"Don't get any ideas," she hissed, her arms still crossed angrily before her.

"I wouldn't dream of it, my flower," Dimitri purred.

Charlie opened the door for them as Dimitri carried her out of the clinic. Lania skipping along behind.

***

When the door snicked shut behind them, Miles stood staring into empty space for a moment. A hand absently rubbing his jaw. The door to his office opened, revealing the lean, petite frame of the banshee, Dagny. Her amber eyes met his.

"Well?" she inquired, her white brow arched.

Miles considered for a moment longer before he finally gave her a nod of confirmation.

"I'm afraid it is as you said."

Dagny looked toward the door. A look between sadness and fury danced across her youthful face.

"Then this is it. It's the end," she whispered.

"You don't know that," Miles said, reaching out and placing a hand upon her shoulder despite knowing better. She shook him off, her eyes flashing dangerously at the offending appendage. Miles didn't react. He wasn't fazed. He understood the response, was probably one of the few who could.

"She's the last, and she's here. Undertaking the Elemental challenges no less. What do you think is going to happen?" Dagny slung her thick braid behind her back before stomping toward the infirmary door.

"I think she might surprise you," he replied. "I think she might surprise us all."

Dagny tossed him a slight hopeful look. One that only he could read. And then she was gone.

***

Enid worked hard to avoid looking at Dimitri, her body stiff in his arms. If he noticed, he didn't seem to care. His demeanor was calm, relaxed, and respectful—as much as she hated to concede anything positive about him.

Lania buzzed with excitement, chirping merrily about the trial.

Enid ignored her.

321

Charlie drifted along behind. The dutiful little pet Lania claimed him to be. However, when Enid's eyes would unintentionally drift his way, there was a terrifying gleam of hunger that gave away his true impulses. That look made him difficult to ignore—the urge to keep the obvious danger within plain sight deeply ingrained.

Murmured congratulations and praises of bravery were given as she was carried by. Though occasional looks were thrown her way by fae eager to make her their next meal, their next toy to enjoy and break.

When they reached her room, Dimitri set her down, keeping an arm around her waist as she struggled to maintain her balance on one good leg. Usually, whenever he was this close, she responded to his touch, even begrudgingly. However, as he held her, his firm arm bracing her with ease, she felt nothing. No dizzying sense of desire. No flutter of her heart, or nervous butterflies in her stomach. No lingering side effects of the thrall. In fact, after she had his blood, she couldn't recall there being any thrall. What could this mean?

The centaur's words came back to her. The blood should have healed her. She should have been under its influence. Yet here she was, completely unaffected and slightly broken. She would have to be careful from now on. If the blood wasn't reacting with her the same way as normal, who could say if it would even turn her Revenant if she were to die.

She looked down at the names written on her forearm. The letters slightly smeared from sweat and tears. Charlie was leaning against the wall by her door. His indifferent mask breaking for a moment as he caught her looking at them. He chuckled.

"So, he finally told you." He smirked, words dripping with mirth.

Enid glanced at him sideways.

"Told me what?"

Dimitri stood rigid, glaring at Charlie long and hard. Lania elbowed her pet in the side. He looked away from Enid, that blank mask over his features once again.

"Nothin'," he muttered.

Enid considered pushing the issue, only to change her mind. Something told her anything Charlie said would only serve to upset her, pushing her further toward certain destruction. Instead, she did what she had started to become very good at. She ignored him.

Swinging her door open, she stepped away from Dimitri, hobbling into the safe confines of her sanctuary. She felt silly, hopping on her good leg, hands gripping the walls and then her door for purchase. Every so often she put the slightest amount of weight on her hurt ankle to maneuver.

"I will bring you food this evening," Dimitri said.

"No," Enid stated.

He looked ready to argue, but closed his mouth and nodded in resignation before turning to walk away. Lania watched her brother disappear around the corner. Once he was out of sight, she turned an icy stare at Enid.

"You will regret hurting him." Her voice was low as she spoke, the threat within clear.

"I regret a lot of things about Dimitri," Enid responded.

Lania hissed, her fangs peering out from her lips, her eyes narrowed slits of blue ice. Tugging on Charlie's arm, she whirled and stormed away. Charlie smirked at Enid before he followed after. Lania's dutiful little puppy.

Enid shut the door.

CHAPTER

37

A few hours later, there was a knock. She shuffled out of bed, easing her throbbing ankle from the pillow it was propped on. At least with the tight bandage it felt a bit better. She was careful not to jostle the books strewn around her, several of them open to pages of interest. Using the desk chair to help slide herself across the room, she opened the door, peeking out into the hallway.

Esmelial was waiting with a few of the pixies fluttering above her shoulders, a covered plate in her hands. Behind them lurked the hulking figure of a minotaur. Enid's eyes widened. Artemis. She wouldn't forget the way he toyed with her at Northspire. The feel of his tongue scraping down the side of her face. The siren followed her gaze, glancing back over her shoulder at him.

"He said he needed to speak with you. I didn't sense a threat, so we allowed him to follow." She shrugged her shoulders indifferently. "We also brought you some food. You were so furious with the Revenant, I didn't think you would let him feed you. You must keep up your strength."

Thanking her, Enid set the plate on the chair next to her.

One of the pixies flapped their wings, as though shaking them off. Long silky hair flew around it, as pale as the strands of a spider's web. A fluttering dress of gossamer, light as the breeze the tiny fae was so adept at imitating, draped over its delicate body.

"I am so sorry you were hurt today." It looked over at the Minotaur as though it wanted to say more, but couldn't.

Enid smiled warmly.

"I am only thankful that it wasn't any worse." The pixie nodded, a bright smile lighting up its face.

"We will see you at the challenge tomorrow. Get some rest," the Siren said before walking away with the pixies in tow.

The Minotaur huffed, shifting from foot to foot as she turned her attention to him. Only the fact that he couldn't touch her while she was in the safety of her room kept her confidently in place. His arms crossed over his chest before uncrossing and hanging awkwardly at his sides. Enid tilted her head, watching him as he appeared to think about what he needed to say. Finally, he cleared his throat, his deep voice unusually soft.

"I wanted to thank you," he started. The words were obviously hard for him. He seemed to almost choke on them as they passed his lips. "You saved my brother from imprisonment in the Labyrinth."

Enid started. The Minotaur who helped her that day was his brother.

"He saved me too," was all she managed to say in response.

"Yes well, he is happy now and living the life he always wanted. Free to be himself. We went hunting for the first time together in a very long time. Deer meat isn't so bad...I guess. Though their fear is...tangy," he grumbled.

"If you don't mind my asking, why was your brother put in the Labyrinth to begin with?"

The Minotaur looked away then, breath puffing around his brass nose ring. "He is not the same as most of us. He never enjoyed the taste of humans, and is more...open to cohabitating peacefully with other creatures. That tolerance in our kind is not natural. He was shunned by our father, and made an example of by our people. Conform to our standards and beliefs, or suffer. My brother has always been stronger than our father gave him credit for."

"That's terrible," Enid said softly. "I am glad he is free to be himself."

"Yes, well," the Minotaur shifted on his feet again. "That is all I had to say." The words came out rushed and loud. He turned to leave and then stopped, looking back, those large eyes surprisingly kind.

"You have my gratitude, and my allegiance. If ever you require my assistance, I will answer the call."

Enid's mouth dropped open in shock. The Minotaur huffed once more, and then was gone. Footsteps echoing down the hallway well after he was out of sight.

Shuffling with her chair over to the table before the wood stove, Enid sat with her covered plate. She was overwhelmed. The Minotaur's words pulled something tight within her. A feeling of camaraderie, of belonging she'd never thought to find here. She found herself sending out a silent prayer to the universe. *Please let it be true.*

Her stomach rumbled hungrily. Grateful for the warm plate of food, she lifted the silver lid. Resting atop the shredded roasted meat, next to buttered potatoes and fragrant beans, was Vidar's twisted metal bracelet. The lid slipped from her fingers, clattering to the floor.

Lifting the bracelet, she studied it closely. The green gemstone was gone. An empty oval now lay in its place within the corded strands of metal. Her hands trembled. This bracelet should have been lost. Attached to a statue-like corpse.

Where did it come from? Did Esmelial know where his body rested now? Clutching the bracelet to her chest she allowed the flurry of emotions to flood out of her. Her body now filled to the brim and unable to contain them.

CHAPTER

38

The next morning found Dimitri outside her door, insistent on escorting her to the trial. Unable to fit her now very swollen ankle within her boot, Enid reluctantly agreed to being carried. Especially when she learned the challenge would be held several levels below, where the Underlings lived.

It was no surprise that the water challenge was held there. Most of the water within the mountain fed into an underground river network. In fact, the waterfall within the center hub of their levels fed into the main channel, which flushed out of the mountain into the nearby river. Once more, she was grateful for Vidar's books.

The excitement was palpable, even in the darkness of the lower levels. The room she was carried to wasn't as large as the previous arenas. Boulders lined the exterior of the room where a few fae sat in clusters. But for the most part it was standing room only. The Sirens all came, along with many of their cousins such as the Merfolk and the Selkies.

Enid took extra care not to make eye contact. The persuasion held by most of the fae currently present could be produced simply by a look. Gratefully, Vidar's books included lots of information on the water fae.

As there wasn't much room for a large crowd, many of the fae were turned away. Enid was surprised to hear that the results of the event would be announced within the public areas of each sector, allowing for everyone to be included if they could attend or not.

Dimitri carried her through the throng of creatures and set her next to a river that ran along one side. Glowing algae grew along the rock wall and the bottom of the water giving it a bluish glow, illuminating enough that Enid could easily see. The gently flowing water ran into a small, dark hole lower in the wall where the visibility disappeared. Enid stared nervously into its depths. She prayed the challenge wouldn't require her to be underwater in that darkness. Somehow, she didn't think that prayer would be answered.

As he promised, Miles was there. The large horse part of him prancing nervously. The crowd automatically moved out of the way for the Centaur as he walked through. Only Dimitri gave him a hard look which Miles met unflinching before leaning down to look over her ankle.

"Still looks pretty tender. Have you tried standing on it?"

Enid nodded, trying not to hiss as he gingerly touched the bruised area.

"No luck, huh. We will see what the Revenant's blood does. If it isn't helpful...well, we will talk to the King about that," Miles glanced around as he spoke. He nodded over at someone, and Enid followed his gaze to see the white-haired banshee leaning against the far wall.

Dimitri's hand went to Enid's back as Miles walked away.

"I know you are angry at me, my flower, but you must accept me. You must let me help you."

Enid glared at him.

"Why do I need to accept you for it to work? Shouldn't it just—work?"

She turned, watching where Miles stood by the banshee, Dagny. He was whispering to her. Red eyes met Enid's, evaluating her from across the room. Enid looked away quickly. Fenri mentioned Vidar and Dagny had worked together. Maybe the banshee knew something about his current whereabouts.

Dimitri huffed. "Normally, yes, but something with you is...different. Maybe it is your immune system starting to react against the blood. Maybe you developed a tolerance and require more, or...you have turned your will against me and somehow shielded yourself."

Enid scowled. "That's a little bit on the nose, don't you think?"

He flinched.

She leaned forward, her hands pressing into the stone beneath her, stare burning into his.

"Why should I give you any chance to weasel your way in again? After all the manipulation, the scheming, the threats you used to get me here."

He leaned toward her, his voice soft as he spoke. "I am changing. What you are mad at, the Revenant who took you, who betrayed your trust, is gone. All because of you."

Tilting his head, he shifted closer to speak in her ear. She almost backed away, but stopped when she accidentally met the gaze of a selkie behind him. The beautiful fae's wide, black eyes were hypnotic. Enid froze, unable to look away. The selkie's mouth tilted in a smirk as she held Enid in her sway.

In her ear, Dimitri's voice whispered.

"Let me love you. Let me protect you. Let me heal you, as you have healed me."

Enid felt the words sinking in, their command locking in place as she stared into those hypnotizing eyes. "Heal," she breathed.

"Forget the pain," Dimitri's smooth voice continued. "Accept me. Let down your walls."

Bit by bit, she felt herself relaxing into him. She felt those words as if they were tangible. Their silky fingers threading into her brain, loosening her anger, her resolve.

"Accept," she sighed.

"All I want is to be yours, and for you to be completely mine," he said, his voice vibrating along the soft, downy hairs of her skin.

"Mine," she echoed.

His lips grazed her earlobe in the barest of touches. The effect was immediate. Her entire body quivered.

"Kiss me," he hummed.

Then his lips were on hers, soft and firm. There was the now familiar taste of his blood on her tongue. She melted into it.

Dived into the depths of the taste and the feel of him. His hands were in her hair, holding her as his mouth devoured hers. She accepted him. He was hers, and she would be his. She could give in. Would give in. He would love her and they would be together for all eternity.

Arms wrapping around him, she pulled him tighter, not caring that they were surrounded by other fae. The pain in her ankle was forgotten, gone. Whatever walls she had in place shattered, crumbling to dust.

White light filled her vision and before her was a stream of images. Dimitri holding her lovingly in his arms, his hand caressing her cheek. Him standing behind her as she looked into a mirror, a dress of pure white silk molded to her body. A flash of light as a strange stone door opened and they were pulled through, hand in hand. The earth gone dark, blood and ash raining down. Isis wearing a crown of onyx and rubies, laughing from a throne of bones.

Dimitri jerked, shock and awe written across his face. "What was that?" he whispered.

"What are you doing?" a loud voice called out behind them.

Reluctantly, she pulled her gaze from Dimitri, turning to the angry figure of the King. He seemed so disgusted, and her addled brain couldn't understand why. Dimitri pulled her legs onto his lap, undoing the straps on the single boot she managed to get on that morning.

"We are preparing for the trial, your highness," Dimitri explained with a smug smile. Enid watched the movement of his lips with rapt attention. She wanted to tip forward and capture them again, to drown in the taste of him.

"You have given her the blood already," the King growled. "She doesn't even know what she's supposed to do yet and now she can barely concentrate."

Dimitri turned to her, rewarding her with a brilliant smile. "I will make sure she understands. Her ankle was hurt. I needed to heal her."

Enid's eyes moved to the King. "He will protect me," she said. Dimitri's words, slipping from her mouth effortlessly.

King Fenri frowned.

Dimitri helped Enid stand onto her bare feet, ankle completely healed. She leaned into his side, not wanting to be even an inch from him. Sudden shouting drew everyone's attention.

Dagny stood in the middle of the room, a dagger in her hand at the throat of the dark haired selkie. The banshee was whispering harshly to the fae who had started to turn toward her attacker. At the banshee's words, the selkie's eyes shot to the ceiling, her head yanked back as Dagny grabbed her hair roughly. They left the room, Dagny dragging the selkie by her hair, the edge of the dagger pinned to her delicate throat. No one dared interfere.

Esmelial watched them pass, anger clearly written upon her face. Those burning silver eyes found hers. Enid nearly jumped into Dimitri's arms. The intensity of her rage felt as though it could sear her skin.

"Listen up then, Revenant. If she fails this test because of the thrall, I will take it out on your hide."

Dimitri clicked his tongue. "My Queen would never allow it."

King Fenri stepped forward, so close they were chest to chest. Dimitri shifted Enid behind him. A low growl rumbled from the King as he gave Dimitri a feral smile. "She wouldn't find out until after I've had my fun." An eerie glow flashed across the King's eyes for a split second. Long enough for Enid to know the King meant what he said, and he was more than capable of backing up his threat.

Dimitri kept his mouth blissfully shut.

"Pay attention," the King snapped. "Within this river there are several chambers. You must find the chamber containing the wishing pearls of Aphrodite. Bring one back here and you will pass this portion of the trials. Just know, some chambers hold creatures who are a bit less...social."

What was that supposed to mean, she wondered.

Enid frowned and looked around. Esmelial was gone, and the King merely observed her with bitter disappointment. The water awaited, louder now that she knew what she needed to do. The sound called her to her doom.

She was handed a head lamp.

"It will be dark in most places. This will be your only source of light. Do not lose it. Also…" The King sighed heavily, concern filled his face as he looked at her as though she were already lost. "…there will be places where the air will be no more than a few pockets, or where you will have to hold your breath for some distance. Conserve it wisely. Move quickly. Be aware."

Enid swallowed thickly, nodding her head. She could swim, but she wasn't the strongest of swimmers. Her hand found Dimitri's. She was scared. She didn't want to go. He could protect her, look after her. Couldn't she stay here with him? Accept her fate. She was his and he was hers. Those words ran on a loop in her mind.

"Bring me back that pearl, my flower," Dimitri whispered into her ear. "We will wish ourselves into a life of happiness."

Enid's eyebrows furrowed, her mouth curving into a slight frown. He wanted her to go. She looked around once more. Miles still stood against the wall watching with interest. His tail flicked against his flank. All the faces around her were staring. Mouths moved in hushed tones. Coins passed hands. All calculating her chances, weighing the odds.

She put on the head lamp, making sure it was tight as she turned toward the water, shaking out her body as though she could cast off the nervousness. Dimitri grabbed her arm, holding her in place. His fingers caressed her cheek. She sighed into the touch.

"Either way, you are coming back to me," he promised. Enid bit her lip. Uncertainty warred within her despite his words and the blood she felt racing through her veins.

She looked toward the King. He gave her a single nod, his eyes pleading with her to come back alive and in one piece. For a second, she was transported to the moment he gave Vidar the same look. Right before he started the air challenge and vanished to his death. Dread flooded through her so cold that when she hit the river beside her, she could barely feel the chill from the water. There was no going back now.

Even though the current was gentle, the wall came at her faster than she would like. With a deep breath she dived under, allowing the river to carry her as she clicked on the lamp and swam deeper into the underground channel.

There was no light here, no glowing algae to keep the darkness from suffocating her. The headlamp was a welcome tool. Swimming as fast as she could, she kept her eyes up for any shimmer of an air bubble. The current helped propel her, helped to keep the panic at bay, to keep her heart rate steady. She was thankful for the yoga pants and long sleeve shirt she wore. The fabric was quick drying, and clung to her like a second skin, keeping her movements unencumbered.

Just when she was beginning to worry, when her lungs began to feel the first small burn from the need of air, she saw it. A slight, silvery sheen along the rock above her. Pressing to it, she broke into a pocket of air big enough to allow her face to peek from the water. Taking a large gulp of air, she dove back into the current, swimming quicker now.

The walls were rough, but blessedly wide. It helped to keep the feeling of claustrophobia from overcoming her, inducing a deadly panic attack. She swam as quickly as she could, her eyes alert, lungs burning. It felt as though she swam for miles, but she knew better. She had about sixty seconds between breaths. There was no way she could hold her breath any longer.

The burning feeling was beginning to return. The ache in her chest building as she looked around for an air bubble, an opening. Anything. A faint hint of green light shone up ahead.

Swimming toward it, she found a hole in the wall at her right, the light of glowing algae filtering through the water. Fire was building within her. She pushed through the opening and into the chamber. Propelling herself upwards with a shove of her feet against the rocky bottom, she burst above the water into sweet air. Gasping, she filled her lungs over and over, relishing the feeling of them expanding and retracting as her heart rate slowed.

"Well, I'm surprised you made it this far," came a familiar voice from a rocky ledge at the back of the chamber.

Enid swirled toward the sound, her arms splashing the water as she nearly jumped out of her skin.

"Esmelial," she gasped. "What are you doing down here?"

The siren shrugged her shoulders. Her hair plastered along her body like a wet suit of silk threads. "I took advantage of the commotion you made with your Revenant. I'll have to give it to him, he is clever. Using the selkie to amplify his persuasion over you. Tricky little bloodsucker."

"He healed me," Enid heard herself saying, surprised with how defensive she felt.

"He's trying to trap you," Esmelial hissed, her teeth flashed in the green glow of the algae as she bared them.

"He loves me!"

Esmelial wheeled back as though struck. Her head tilted to the side as she studied Enid. The water around her was feeling a little more frigid, or it was the scrutinizing stare of the siren. She couldn't tell.

"I'm disappointed," the siren said softly. "I thought more of you."

Enid paddled to the ledge, pulling herself up and laying on the rough stone. Not able to speak at the moment, she only stared up at the algae covered ceiling. Shame burned within her, but so did anger.

"How are you going to meet your end of our bargain, if you allow yourself to become one of those leeches?" The siren continued.

"What's the point? Vidar is gone. Dimitri is here, and I cannot survive in this world without someone to protect me. What use is a bargain with a dead woman?"

"Gone?"

Something in Esmelial's tone made Enid sit up and turn to her fully. Her attention focused solely on the siren.

"Is he still alive?" she whispered. "Is that how you got the bracelet?"

Esmelial offered her only silence. It hung in the air between them.

"I think you need to meet someone," Esmelial finally said. "She's in the next chamber, further down the channel and to the left." Her silver eyes met Enid's again meaningfully. "Be Cautious. She has lost her mind."

"Who is she?" Enid asked.

"She is all of us. She is who we will become if you do not succeed." Esmelial looked away, but not before Enid saw the sadness that crossed her face. The glimmer of tears that threatened to fall.

"Go. I will wait."

***

There were more pockets of air through this part of the channel. Enid was easily able to make her way without alarm. A flash of something unusual in the beam of lamp light caught her attention. Scratched into the rock was a strange looking symbol. An x stacked atop another with a line drawn straight down the center of them. Underneath an arrow pointed left.

Following the direction of the arrow, she turned to see an opening. Nothing but blackness showed from the other side. The dark so intense it was almost an entity in itself. Carefully she swam forward, the lack of air forcing her onward despite her apprehension. The beam of light did nothing to cut the dark. It wasn't until she had broken the surface of the water and could hear the echo of her ragged breathing that she realized she was in another cavern. Slowly, she swept the light around, looking for anything to help orient her. There was nothing.

Her nerves were getting the better of her. She considered swimming back, but that sad look on Esmelial's face haunted her. So, she pressed on. Paddling in the direction she just came, she finally located the wall of the chamber. The shadows were so thick, she was nearly upon the wall itself before her light revealed it.

There she found more markings etched into the rock face. A pattern matching the one she saw at the entrance interspersed with other various designs. Runes of some sort. Taking note of the etchings at this section of the wall, she followed the rock face around. The strange markings covered nearly every surface she discovered. Finally, she reached a ledge and was able to pull herself up, allowing her body to rest as she cautiously watched the shadows.

Rotating her shoulders, she rubbed at her aching arms. The light refracted off of the dark surface of the water and the rune covered walls as she rotated her neck. She paused for a moment, mid-stretch.

How was she able to so easily see the water and the walls now? Only moments before she had crawled her way here due to the unbearable darkness.

The hairs at the nape of her neck began to stand on end. Her whole body flushed with adrenaline. Turning her head slowly to the right she was met with a wall of solid, black shadow. As she stared into that mind numbing blankness it suddenly shifted. A faceless dark head appeared right in front of her. Enid screamed, rearing back on instinct. Her body slammed into the rock wall painfully.

The shadows rolled and compacted until a female body accompanied that blank face. Long wisps of hair floated from it on a windless breeze. Wings peeled out from its back, flecked with holes and ridged edges. Ripped and shredded pixie wings. Finally, it stood there, a fully formed shadow of a winged woman. Faceless and void of any characteristics. Only a shapely form pulled from the darkness.

A voice floated from it, soft and sad.

"Are you lost too?"

Enid stared for a moment at that figure, her brain processing the words that came from its mouthless face.

"I-I'm not lost," she stuttered. "I was sent down here as part of a trial. To retrieve a pearl of Aphrodite."

She allowed her body to relax a bit, cautiously sliding off the wall, but not stepping any closer toward the mysterious creature.

"Are you lost?" she asked.

A low keening wail came from the shadow fairy as its body twisted around, appearing to look for something.

"I can't find my way home," the haunted voice whispered. "It was there, through the veil of the realm, but now I can't see it. *I can't see*. The way is blocked."

The wail began to grow louder as it peered around, the sound echoing around the chamber. The faceless head turned back to her.

"WHY CAN'T I SEE?!"

Enid jerked, her arms coming up defensively as the figure lunged at her. When she felt no impact, she slowly opened her eyes. It sat there staring at her, only inches away. Fear rippled through her, and she choked back a sob. Her instincts screamed at her.

Danger. Run. Hide.

"We are different than we were before," the dark pixie said. It leaned toward Enid so all she could see was the never-ending blackness. The sound of its voice an echo in the space around her.

"We weren't always like this, you know," that voice whispered. "We are in the wrong place. It's the *wrong place*. This isn't how we were meant to be."

A finger of shadow traced a line down her cheek, gently at first, and then harder. Enid let out a shrill cry as the point of that dark finger punctured her skin. A line of crimson breaking open along her cheek. The figure flinched in shock, head canting to the side. Those long strands of hair drifted around it. Then, its wings stretched out, shivering menacingly, the sound like a hiss. The arms of the creature drew up, its fingers lengthening into talons of shadow.

Enid stepped away from the wall, moving to throw herself into the water and swim away from this place as fast as she could. The creature jumped on her first. Talons tore into her arms as she threw them up to protect her face.

"IT'S ALL WRONG! WRONG! WRONG!!" The voice shrieked over and over. The words bouncing around them in a cacophony of anger and fear. Enid felt those claws scrape down the side of her ribs.

She screamed and screamed. The sound tearing out of her, unable to do anything more.

"I CAN'T SEE!! I WANT TO GO HOME!! HOME!" The creature wailed, its claws slashing mercilessly.

"ENID!!" A man's voice yelled from the water.

The assault stopped as both Enid and the shadow fae looked over. Within the water, a glowing strand of beads around his neck, swam the merman with the honey-colored hair and aqua eyes.

Taking advantage of the distraction, Enid thrust the fae away and rolled into the water. The shadow howled in rage, her figure breaking apart, and the room flooded with darkness. Enid searched frantically, trying to find the merman, looking for the way out. The light on the headlamp couldn't break through the mass of shadow. Then he was in front of her, pulling her close.

"Take a deep breath," he said in her ear.

She complied and they ducked beneath the surface. His strong arms encased her, keeping her close as he swam out of the chamber with incredible speed.

The water rushed past Enid faster than she was accustomed. The pressure so intense that water attempted to rush past her lips and up her nose. She tucked her head into his chest, keeping the life-giving air within her lungs as long as possible. Even still, it wasn't long before the fire rose in her chest. The burn clawing its way up her throat. The small amount of air she had left began to leak out. Bubbles trailing behind them through the water tinged with the swirling red of her blood.

She tapped frantically on the merman's chest. He slowed, looking down at her as the tapping turned into pushing and hitting. Panic overwhelming her. Lowering his face, his mouth pressed firmly against her own. She was stunned to stillness as air flowed into her lungs through a watertight kiss, bringing with it sweet relief. Enough that she was able to ignore the discomfort of such an intimate gesture.

His tongue flicked along her lips. She slammed them closed and pulled back—her lungs now full of air. He smiled before continuing on. Twice more he paused to administer those lifesaving kisses. Before long he turned through a small opening into a chamber flooded with light.

They broke the surface just in time. She wasn't sure how much longer she could go on. Dizziness and exhaustion overtook her. She nearly fell back into the depths of the water, but for the arms holding her up. She felt herself being lifted and a hard surface under her. Her eyes fluttered open. She was met with beautiful shades of turquoise as the merman examined her. His hands making quick work of finding the worst of the wounds.

"Don't move," he said. "Thankfully, you had the Revenant's blood or you may not have survived. You are already healing, but I will put some pressure on the deepest wounds until they've had time to seal."

Pain flared at her side as he pressed his hands against the gouges. She cried out. Her body shook. Nausea rolled her stomach.

"I know, I'm sorry," the merman comforted. "It won't be long. Try to hold still."

Enid focused on not moving instead of the pain that consumed her. His hands were warm and firm against her side. As her focus shifted, she felt the world crumble around her, the brittle edge of it peeling away. Then she was standing in a brightly lit cottage.

The windows were open. The smell of the sea drifted in on a breeze. At a small, yellow table in a bright kitchen sat the merman. His long, flaxen hair in a ponytail. A loose-fitting cotton shirt covered his chest, the sleeves rolled up along his forearms. Shorts showed off legs that were well muscled and tan. He cooed over a bundle in his arms. A small, chubby hand reached from the blanket, stretching towards his face. Laughing as tiny fingers grasped at his mouth, he peppered them with kisses.

A woman walked in from another room, a flowing sundress barely hiding her curves. Enid started when she realized she recognized her. It was her mother's assistant, Jane. No longer timid and demure, she gazed with love at the merman. Crossing the room, she draped her arms around his shoulders. Joy and happiness radiating from her pretty face as she looked down at the bundle. Her usually mousy hair was a shimmering mass of wavy chocolate. Impossibly large, amber eyes flecked with gold. Enid had never noticed how beautiful she was.

With a gasp, she was back in the damp chamber. The merman looked down at her with curiosity.

"I saw them," she said softly.

"Saw who?" He asked as he examined her wound, carefully removing his hand. The bleeding had stopped, the skin stitching itself together slowly.

"Your wife and child," she replied.

His head snapped up.

"My wife, and child? I will find a mate?"

Enid nodded as she started to sit up. "I know who she is."

He laughed, throwing his arms around her and lifting her in a tight hug. She flinched in pain that slowly faded. Another feeling taking its place as she fully healed. He stood on strongly toned legs, his tail nowhere in sight, with her gripped against him.

"What is she like? Is she beautiful? Is she kind? Will she love our child?"

Enid was frozen, her face pressed against his chest and flaming scarlet.

"Um, are you naked?"

He stopped and looked down between them.

"I had no clothes with me," he said simply.

"Can you put me down, ah—what's your name?"

He gave her that bright smile, his aqua eyes shining with humor. "Adrian," he replied.

"Ok, can you put me down Adrian?"

He lowered her feet to the ground, and she backed away, keeping her eyes up as she did so.

Adrian laughed loudly. "I always find it funny how modest humans are about their bodies."

Enid nodded nervously. "Well, I suppose that someone who spends most of their time in water with no clothing would think that way."

Trying to look anywhere but at him, she took in the cavern around them. The walls were layers of colored rock of red, white and beige. They reflected the light from above and below. Directly above the cave was a pure white, large fairy orb casting a bright glow. Below, an iridescent rainbow shimmered deep in the depths.

Adrian followed her gaze.

"That is where you will need to go to retrieve the pearl."

"All the way down there?" she breathed. The bottom seemed so far.

"I will give you air, should you require it. And it is not deep enough that the pressure will be much of an issue," Adrian promised. "It will only make you a bit uncomfortable."

Enid looked at him warily. "Now that I know who your wife will be, I feel bad about having your mouth on mine. Besides,

Dimitri would not like it." As she said his name, her mind drifted back to him, sadness and longing blooming within her.

The merman crossed his arms over his chest.

"I haven't met my mate yet, but I know that she is going to be an understanding woman, especially if she knew your life was on the line. Also, despite what the Revenant might tell you, he does not own you. Though I have heard how strong their thrall can be."

"You don't know anything about him," Enid hissed defensively. The merman shrugged his muscular shoulders.

"No, but I can sense your power. It is strong. I can also sense the persuasion used to bend your mind and entrap you. I can break it, but it will be slightly distressing for you."

Enid stepped away from him. "Don't. Dimitri is trying to protect me."

Adrian looked at her again, longer this time. His eyes flicked from her face, to the light below the water. Finally, he spoke, "Esmelial told me how important you are, what you are going to do for our kind." She only watched him warily as he continued.

"The fae trapped within that cavern back there, her name was Amaris. She was one of the more playful of the Shadow Nymphs. When her mind began to splinter, I was part of the group who had to prepare that chamber to help contain her."

He looked away then, sadness filling his face. "I cannot entrap any more of us in a dark, lonely prison." Those turquoise eyes met hers again. "Please," he whispered.

"What do you need to do to break the thrall," she said softly.

He stepped up to her, staring at her with those bright eyes of pure aqua.

"You worry about getting that pearl. I will worry about the thrall."

***

The water was warmer the deeper she swam. Glowing oysters lay before her along the rock. Their prismatic shells cast small rainbows that lit the water with an ethereal shimmer. Enid nearly ran out of breath staring at the clusters.

Adrian slipped up to her, his tail the same stunning blue-green as his eyes. Pressing his mouth to hers, he breathed air into her lungs. Fingers lingered through the scarlet strands of hair that came undone from her braid. His lips grazing along hers as he slid away. Her heart skipped, confusion one of the many feelings messing with her at the moment.

Turning her attention once more to the oyster bed, she swam forward, kicking toward the closest cluster. Her head lamp had been left at the ledge above, unnecessary in this light filled pool. The shells were surprisingly sharp. Pain stung her finger as she pulled at a particularly stubborn oyster, blood blooming from the tips in red clouds. Adrian took her hand in his, shaking his head as he pointed to the oyster she was trying to pry out of the bed. He pointed out toward the rest of the bed and then patted his hand over his chest.

Enid looked out among the bed of oysters, drifting over them, trying not to touch the blade-like edges as she searched. Only, she wasn't sure what she was supposed to be looking for. She turned toward Adrian, shaking her head. Bubbles rose from her mouth as she shrugged helplessly. He pulled her close, her chest pressed against his as he once more lowered his face toward hers.

The air filled her lungs, his hands drifted down her back toward her waist, her breath hitched. As she began to pull back, he stopped her, slowly but firmly kissing her. His warm hands traced the curves of her back and waist. A real kiss that sent a flurry of butterflies erupting in her stomach. His hand went to the back of her head and he pressed the air back into her lungs before releasing her.

Then she felt it, a steady thrum from within the bed of oysters that beat in time to the racing of her heart. It pulled her to it, that steady vibration within the water. As her heart rate slowed, so did that pulse. When her eyes landed on a large oyster in the bed, its colors swirling and twisting along the shell, she knew. This one was hers.

As soon as her fingers touched it, it slowly opened. The shell within was black with rainbow swirls of color. A pale oyster lay upon the dark background, and tucked at the edge of it was a large, perfectly round, black pearl. Gently she plucked the pearl from its membrane. The oyster shell closed.

Adrian smiled at her brightly, took her hand, and guided her toward the surface. Enid threw her arms around his shoulders when they were back above the water.

"Thank you, thank you, thank you," she said, holding the pearl before her. Rainbows swirled like slick oil over its dark surface. It was large, about an inch in diameter. She clutched it firmly in her palm, triumph rushing through her.

"How did you know the kiss would help me find it?" she asked as she let go of him and swam toward the dry ridge of rock. She was ready to retrieve her head lamp and complete the challenge.

"The pearls of Aphrodite react to passion and lust, the pheromones that are released while in those states. It chose you when you reacted to the kiss. Plus, I had to break that pesky thrall," he said with a chuckle.

Enid stopped at the ledge. Now that he mentioned it, she did feel different, more herself. She thought of Dimitri and didn't feel that all-consuming need she had moments ago.

"You broke the thrall with a kiss?"

A sheepish look flashed across his face as he looked over at her. "I've actually been working on it since I took you from Amaris's cave. It was the most stubborn case of persuasion I've seen. I've never had to push out so many pheromones in my life. I'm actually a little concerned about being around anyone until I've had time to let them dissipate."

Enid laughed as she pulled herself out of the water and sat on the edge of the rock.

"What are you going to wish for?" Adrian asked, leaning his arms against the ledge next to her, his tail moving lazily in the water.

"I don't know," she murmured. "Can I wish for anything?"

"Of course," he said, "though, don't be upset if it doesn't come true. The magic hasn't worked in a very long time. His hand went to the string of pearls around his neck absently. "But, if what you say is true, and you know my mate, then one of mine may be coming to fruition very soon."

Happiness brightened his face.

Enid took his hand in hers, giving it a squeeze. "Jane is going to be a very lucky woman."

His eyes widened.

"Jane," he whispered reverently.

Enid gazed at the pearl in her palm, her heart aching. She wanted that feeling. Suddenly, she missed Vidar greatly, and her mother. If only she could see them again.

"I suppose," she said softly. "I would wish that Vidar was alive and well, and that I could see my mother one last time. At least to say goodbye." Her eyes closed, a tear sliding down her cheek.

The pearl within her hand gave off a pulse. As it burst out, a tingling sensation set every small hair on end. She felt the vibration push past her and out through the walls of the cavern. Then everything was still.

She opened her eyes.

Adrian was looking at her with his mouth open, the knuckles of his hands white where he gripped the ledge.

"What was that?" Enid asked.

Adrian swallowed. "I think your wish was granted."

CHAPTER

39

Adrian took Enid as far as the chamber where Esmelial waited. The siren was pleased to see her clutching the pearl, without the influence of the thrall clouding her mind. Once Enid promised Adrian that she would find a way to introduce him to Jane, the merman swam off through the underwater tunnels. It was time to finish this challenge.

Esmelial stood with her, looking toward the exit. "You will make it," the siren promised. "You have come this far."

With that, Enid was back in the water, following the curves of the tunnel. Swimming against the current was a little more difficult. By the time she made it to the finish, her lungs were on fire and her muscles burned, but she made it.

Gasping and sputtering, she swam toward the row of rock along the water. Hands grasped her, pulling her to safety. She sucked in breath after breath of air and collapsed against the nearest stone as a warm, dry towel was draped over her shoulders. King Fenri stood over her, patiently waiting as she caught her breath.

"Well?" he finally asked. "Did you find it?"

Enid dropped the towel as she reached trembling fingers into the small pocket at the waistband of her pants. The pearl rolled into her fingers and she held it up for the King to see. Hushed voices murmured in excitement around her. The King smiled widely.

She felt Dimitri beside her, touching the torn edges of her shirt where the shadow nymph attacked her.

"I'm ok," she said, pulling the towel back around her, covering the shredded fabric. He smiled, his hand going to her cheek. She forced herself not to move away. Worried that he would resort to further measures to keep her in thrall to him.

"What would you like to wish for, my flower?" he asked, those glacial eyes peering into hers.

"I already made my wish," she said. Looking down, she made a show of wiping her face with her towel.

"What did you wish for?" Lania questioned, bouncing with enthusiasm.

Enid covered her face with her towel, thinking quickly. Better to give half-truths. She could not let them know her thoughts still drifted toward Vidar.

"I wished I could see my mother one more time, to say goodbye," she said softly. She lifted her face toward them. Lania's eyes were wide.

A scoff drew her attention. Charlie.

"Well, that's going to be impossible," he muttered. He spoke low, but her ears still picked up the words.

"Excuse me?" she said as she stood, the weariness in her limbs fading to the background of her mind.

Charlie rolled his eyes and looked away, his blank stare going to a wall.

"Come, my flower," Dimitri said beside her. "We will get you some food and dry clothes."

Enid pushed him away.

"No," she said, her focus solely on Charlie. "What do you mean by that, Charlie?"

Lania glanced between them nervously, her hands clasped together. Charlie looked at Enid with an air of indifference.

"Because she's dead," he stated.

Enid staggered back at those words. Her heart stuttering in shock.

He continued, a malevolent gleam in his eye.

"Killed her myself," he said. "The night that you left, I showed up at the door, beggin' her to speak with me. Of course she let me in, the heartbroken, former almost son-in-law."

Tears streamed down her cheeks.

"She died a slow, painful death," he continued, a smile stretching wide across his face.

Before she could react, Dimitri was in front of him. His hand around Charlie's throat. He lifted him into the air before slinging him into the rock wall above the flowing water. Charlie's body hit with a loud crack, dust and pieces of rock splashing loudly into the river along with him.

"Dimitri!" Lania gasped as Charlie's unconscious body floated along the water and was pulled through the opening in the wall, disappearing from view.

"He was being rude," Dimitri explained to his distraught sister. He clicked his tongue and scoffed. "Your pet will survive. He is Revenant, he cannot drown."

Lania mumbled under her breath, arms crossing as she pouted. Dimitri turned to Enid. Before he could touch her, she held up a hand.

"Don't."

Her tears fell onto her already damp shirt. Then the King was beside her, pulling her along with him as they left the chamber. The crowd parted. Dimitri remained where he was, agony written across his face.

***

She was numb. Blankly, she looked around. A fire crackled in the wood stove. Distantly, she wondered when it had started. Her clothes were dry now, but it couldn't have been that long. She barely recalled entering the room and sitting down.

There was a knock at her door. Enid only looked over at the slab of wood. She was uninterested in whoever was on the other side. Most likely Dimitri. And she was in no mood to see him. This was all his fault.

The knock persisted.

Muffled whispers had her frowning toward it, but still, she did not move. Someone made a loud shushing noise, and there was silence.

The knock came again, slightly louder this time.

She continued to ignore it. The whispers became louder, more frantic.

"She's not here."

"She is."

"We need to hurry. I can't be caught here. I'm not going back."

"We know, you've only mentioned it twenty times."

"Everyone be quiet, you're going to get us caught."

"You be quiet."

Enid rolled her eyes and walked over to the door, flinging it open. Grouped in a cluster, Enid was surprised to find the two Minotaur brothers, Esmelial, and two pixies.

"Finally," Esmelial hissed.

"What do you want?" Enid asked. Her voice held no warmth. She was too tired for this.

"You need to come with us," Esmelial replied.

"Why?" Enid crossed her arms in front of her. "So I can fulfill another bargain? So someone else I care about can die?" "Why should I do another thing for any of you?"

"Because we are going to get you out of here, insolent human," Artemis grumbled. The other elbowed him, the scar over his left eye more prominent as he glared at his brother.

"What?" he mumbled. "She is insolent."

They both looked at her. "You saved me from the Labyrinth. We have come to save you from this place."

One of the pixies flew in front of her, those spider silk threads of hair wafting around her as she spoke in her high-pitched voice.

"Vidar is waiting."

Enid became instantly alert.

"Let's go," she said.

ACT III

EMBRACING DESTINY

CHAPTER

40

The night air was shockingly cold. After so much time spent within the mountain, she felt exposed out in the open. Stars freckled the dark expanse of sky, seeming even more numerous due to the new moon.

The Minotaur led the way, bickering as brothers tend to do. Hector, who she helped escape from the Labyrinth, snorted at his brother, Artemis, as the gruffer of the two kept making snide comments.

"If you are going to persist in being obtuse, brother, you are more than welcome to leave."

Artemis only huffed in return. "I gave my promise. I will fulfill it. I did not vow to be pleasant in the meantime."

He turned away, searching the night—fully alert.

"Besides, we both know at this point that I will no longer be accepted in the clan if we are caught. My fate will be the same as yours, brother."

At this statement the arguing ceased. The party continued with little conversation.

Before long absolute silence descended upon the mountain forest. The shadows were thick in the canopy of fir and pine towering above them. Not even the crickets chirped. Esmelial stilled, as did the other fae. Enid followed suit—alert for any disturbance in the dark forest.

To her right the shadows seemed to roll, and two glowing, coal-like eyes blinked open. Enid gasped and jumped back, her heart pounding in her throat. The fae turned toward the noise, the pixies skittering away behind a tree. From the dark fog stepped the Shadow Man.

"Anu," Esmelial sighed. The pixies peeked out from their hiding spot.

He gave a wide grin. His fingers gripping the brim of his top hat, which he tipped in greeting. Then, placing both hands—one on top of the other—on the cane in front of him, those burning eyes turned to Enid.

"Have you found what your role is meant to be yet, my dear?"

She shook her head, unable to speak.

"Perhaps we can help you make up your mind."

He held his hand out, waiting patiently. Hesitantly, she reached out and took it.

Without warning the shadows engulfed her and she was pulled through air so thick it felt like it was pressing against her, attempting to keep her in its gloomy folds. She couldn't move, couldn't breathe, but the grip of the Shadow Man's hand in hers was strong. It yanked her through that heavy, glutinous atmosphere.

Next thing she knew, she was in a large, open meadow. The Shadow Man and her friends were nowhere in sight. Tall grasses swayed, lit by the glow of light from a nearby cabin. A well-worn path led to the porch through the grass and flowers.

Quietly, she stepped onto the dirt path. The porch creaked. The light from the window darkened as someone passed in front of it. Enid's heart hammered and she froze. The moonless night did little to help her vision, but she knew. She felt the truth of it even as her mind railed against the thought. Too afraid to give in to hope, but hopeful none the less.

She had already lost so much. It left her apprehensive. Yet, as she got closer, the light from the cabin revealed what she had hoped. What she yearned for in her heart all along. The reason she pressed to claim her independence. The reason she made the bargain with the Sirens. The memory of him was all that kept her going—pushed her to be a better version of herself. Only now she didn't have to rely on memory alone.

Before her, whole and unharmed, was Vidar.

She rushed forward, throwing herself into his arms.

"Enid," he sighed into her hair.

He squeezed her tightly against him, and she clung to him in return. Her body trembled as sobs broke from her. Emotions from everything she had learned and experienced over the last few days compounded in a tide of tears. As he held her, for the first time in a long time, she felt truly safe.

When she was all cried out, she looked once more up at him. Her hands traced the lines of his face, brushed back the wavy strands of black hair. She soaked in the sight. The curve of his brow, the fullness of his lips. Stubble grew along his jaw, giving him a slightly more rugged appearance than usual. The intensity in his face had her catching her breath. Sharp edged and barely contained, so dominant, so *him*.

"How are you alive?"

Vidar gave a slight smile. "Apparently being half human is a blessing. When I arrived, it was late but the sun was still up. It felt like my skin was on fire, and then nothing. When I came to, I was lying in the field in the dark. My skin burned all over like I had been boiled alive and all around were shards of stone."

He pushed a strand of hair behind her ear as though he needed to find an excuse to touch her.

"I was so weak that I could barely move. Anu and Pythia were standing there, waiting. They've been here this whole time. Pythia is like you. She saw what was going to happen. Where they needed to be to help."

Enid turned to find Anu standing behind them with Esmelial, Hector, and Artemis.

"I hate to break up the reunion," Anu said in his deep baritone. "But there is much to discuss, and less time till daylight."

CHAPTER
41

The cabin was not built for the number of creatures it now contained. The Minotaur brothers hadn't even bothered trying to squeeze through the front door. They sat on the porch, listening to the conversation from the open doorway.

Enid shivered from the cold, even sitting next to the sparking fire. She clutched the edges of Vidar's jacket closer. After spending weeks in the moderate temperature of the underground city, she was having a hard time adapting to the frigid cold of this place. No one else seemed bothered.

Outside a dusting of snow had begun to fall. The pixies rushed out at the first sign of snowflakes to play. Every so often the wind carried their delighted bell-like laughs to her through the open door.

Pythia remained bundled in a comfortable chair next to the hearth, which was where Enid found her when they walked in. The older woman intimidated her. As they were introduced, she immediately grabbed Enid's hand in her frail one, staring at her intently as though waiting for something. Now, she only looked at her with hopeless disappointment. Unfortunately, it was a look Enid was getting used to receiving.

"You haven't told her about the prophecy. This whole time," Esmelial spat as she paced in front of the fire, her glare targeted at Vidar who returned it with a stern look of his own.

"She has had a lot to deal with. Learning about fae, acclimating to Dokkalfar, the trials. I did not want to burden her with another thing too soon."

She scoffed. "Males. Overprotective, dim witted— You can't just keep her in bubble wrap and expect her to get strong enough not to break."

"I do not need your lectures."

The siren lifted a finger, ready to lay into the large fae.

"What prophecy?" Enid asked, again.

The question that started the argument was the one that ended it. Pythia remained silent, letting the fae sort out their business, waiting for them to finish arguing so she could continue to explain to them why she was here. Enid only sat, confused and growing impatient.

Esmelial turned toward her, the scowl replaced with a gentler look. "There is a prophecy that you will destroy humanity."

Pythia snorted. "It's not as simple as all that."

Everyone turned toward the old woman.

"You know it?" Esmelial asked.

"Know it, ha. I'm the one who received it." Everyone stared. Pythia sighed. "In my vision, I saw you," her bony finger pointed to Enid. "You stood on a precipice, flanked by two shadows. If you choose one, you would become the Queen's puppet, bringing on the downfall of this realm and all those connected to it. If you choose the other, then the Queen will fall and the way to the Realm of Fae will open to those who have been lost to it."

"Two shadows?" Enid watched the older woman with rapt attention.

Pythia's finger lifted again, this time directed at Vidar.

"Him, and another."

Enid clenched her teeth. Vidar and Dimitri. The two fighting to claim her.

Esmelial sucked in a breath. "What do we do? How do we open the door?"

Pythia's cloudy, brown eyes snapped to the siren. "You want a road map? Visions don't work like that. It's not a step-by-step guide. The way will open." She huffed, mumbling under her breath.

"Well, how do the Revenant know about the prophecy?" Esmelial pressed, undeterred.

"That would be my fault," Anu said from the kitchen as he prepared a pot of tea. "I was there, in the beginning. When the deal was struck, and Isis, the first Revenant, was created. She was different back then. Vengeful, yes, but who wouldn't be after... Anyway, Pythia had the vision, and I went to Isis, as a friend, asking her what she knew. What the prophecy meant. She didn't know, of course. But ever since then, she has hunted for the one who would fulfill it. She sees it as her destiny, her birthright. She will do everything she can to make sure you are one of hers."

"Three of the four challenges are done," Enid said through the chatter of her teeth. "If I pass the last one, then I can claim any clan that I want. I won't need to worry about the Revenant."

Pythia chuckled, shaking her head in exasperation at Enid. "That is a very naive statement. Have you learned nothing from your time in the Underworld? The Revenant will not let you go. Their Queen will not allow such a valuable tool to slip from her fingers."

Esmelial hummed in affirmation. "The Queen was absent at the last challenge. No doubt she has other plans in motion. You cannot underestimate the Revenant. I agree with Pythia. They will not give you up. I think this whole thing with the trials has been a distraction."

"A distraction for what?" Enid asked.

"You think if we knew, we would be wasting our time talking about it," Esmelial muttered.

"But what would her end goal be, what else could she possibly want? She's the Queen of all the fae."

At this statement Pythia shifted in her chair, leaning forward to catch Enid's eye. "The world, young one. She wants the whole world. Everything that has been denied to her for centuries."

"This would not be the first time she has attempted to do such a thing," Anu said. "That is how we were exiled from Egypt." His thick white dreadlocks swayed as he shook his head sadly.

"Why would she need me for that?" Enid countered.

"Because," Vidar said from his place at the small table opposite the fireplace, "if what Pythia says is true—"

"Of course it's true," Pythia snapped.

Vidar only glanced at her with a raised brow before turning back to Enid.

"Then you will be the most powerful seer the world has seen. If you are Revenant, she will have you in her full control. She can use you however she likes."

Enid shifted in her chair, remembering the blank stares on the Revenant faces anytime their queen commanded their attention.

Anu brought a cup of tea to Pythia, placing it lovingly in her hand before offering some to the others. Enid took a cup from the tray Anu held, her hands relishing the warmth.

"We must try to find out more of the Revenant's plans," Vidar murmured, his gaze thoughtful.

"I can help with that," Esmelial replied with a smirk.

"It does not matter!" Pythia shouted in frustration. Her voice came out in a wheeze as she attempted to raise it. It seemed to take a lot out of her. "We are talking semantics. What we need to focus on is preparing Enid. She must hone her gift and complete the bond. That is the only way to bridge the veil between the Realm of Faery and the Realm of Mortals. All of this will be for nothing otherwise."

Pythia began to cough, her tea spilling over her hands as she did so. Anu rushed to her, taking the cup gently and setting it to the side.

"We must go, my love," he whispered. "You have pushed yourself too far."

Pythia looked to Enid, her eyes watery, each breath harsh with effort. "We will be back tomorrow afternoon, while it is still daylight. There is much to do."

Enid only nodded in response as she cast a nervous glance to Vidar. This was a lot to set on her shoulders. She couldn't blame Vidar for not telling her sooner. Though a heads up would have been nice. She could have easily already fallen into the Revenant's hands.

"I know you have seen what is to become of this world if we do not succeed. You must not fail." With that statement

Pythia turned to Anu, the shadow man lifting her in his arms before they were gone in a swirl of wind and shadow.

Esmelial set her cup down. "I will try to buy you as much time as possible. Your mother's loss was a tragedy, and for that I am sorry, but I will use it to our advantage. Surely the King will give you a few days of leniency before the last trial. By then I hope things will be …clearer."

Muffled argument from the open door drew Enid's attention.

"Well?" Hector said, clearly upset with his brother. Artemis rolled his eyes.

"I am sorry I did not mention it sooner. Things were different, this was before—" he huffed. "Your aunt is dead."

"What?" Enid whispered. The Minotaur looked toward Vidar.

"The Queen went to Claeg, the ghoul I worked with at the sanitorium, shortly after the human—I mean, Enid, came to Dokkalfar." His eyes flashed back toward Enid. "She wanted to get rid of any ties you might have with the humans. There really weren't that many."

A tear fell down Enid's cheek. The Minotaur suddenly looked very regretful.

"I am sorry for your loss," he said, sounding gentler than she had ever heard.

The jacket around her shoulders wasn't enough comfort, the tea cup shook in her hands. She set it on the nearby table. Vidar closed the distance between them and lifted her into his arms before he sat, shifting her so she was on his lap. He wrapped her in his reassuring embrace.

The Queen had ordered the deaths of her mother and aunt. But why? Even if she had control of her gift, why would the Queen be so desperate for it? Why would she be so willing to bring an apocalyptic nightmare to the world?

"How?" Her voice broke as she spoke the word, barely able to get it out of her mouth.

"It is best you do not know," Artemis replied.

Enid pressed her face into Vidar's chest, unable to look at anyone. There was a shuffling sound and Esmelial's voice drifted from the door. "I will inform the King that Enid will need some time to grieve. We will wait for Anu outside." There was a moment of silence and then the Siren spoke again.

"If it is any consolation, they may be gone from this Realm, but the Realm they are in now, I have heard, is free from any pain for the innocent. For ones such as them, there will be peace and happiness until they are ready to make their return. And for the ones who have done them harm—they will earn their punishment." With that the door squeaked to a close, and footsteps clamored down the porch steps.

She remained tucked against Vidar, her quiet sobs the only sound except the crackling of the fire.

CHAPTER
42

Enid woke from a deep sleep in an unfamiliar bed in a room with no windows to the smell of cooked bacon. She could almost pretend that all was right in the world. Outside that door was her mother, alive and well, making breakfast. But that wasn't her reality. That image of a perfect morning didn't fit even when her life was normal. Not that it ever was.

When she stepped out into the main room, she found Anu scrambling eggs on the stove. Pythia walked about with the silver handled cane usually found in the Shadow Man's grip. Her ancient body hunched as she moved with a cup of coffee to the small table.

With a nod of greeting, she went to claim a cup for herself. It seemed so strange, going through these motions. Awake with the sun up. Having coffee with the smell of breakfast in the air. Even if it was past noon. She peaked behind one of the thick curtains covering the window. A light dusting of snow lay on the ground, slowly melting under the heat of the sun. She squinted at all that light. It was so bright after so much time in the dark. Letting the curtain fall back into place, Enid took a seat next to the seer.

The first sip of the hot, steaming liquid was making its way down her throat when Pythia reached out and snatched her wrist in her withered hand. The older woman's eyes turned white, her mouth went slack, and suddenly Enid felt something within her tug.

Her vision went white, her stomach sank. Pain splintered between her eyes. So sharp that she nearly screamed, her teeth clenching to keep the sound in. It was as though a great space hovered at her fingertips. Like when the visions came upon her, only this time harsher, forced. It was Pythia. Taking her deeper than she'd ever been, and with surprising strength. Past the threads of fate, to the very center of that wide cast tapestry.

Light was all around her. Bright, white, and unending. And that's all there was, nothing else. Nothing except Pythia. She stood tall and proud, moving with ease as she smiled at Enid and gestured her closer. Age and physical capacity seemed to have no bearing here.

"What is this place?" Enid asked in a hushed voice.

Pythia looked around. "This is where everything begins, but has yet to happen. A place of endless possibilities. Here, there are no distractions. This is where you will learn to control your power."

Enid shifted uncomfortably. "What do I do?"

Pythia stepped up and took her hands. "You must understand what is at stake."

Shapes began to take form in the white nothing, the scene breaking through the fog. Pythia stood beside her as the familiar events unfolded. Around them was chaos. Ash rained down from the sky. Creatures of all types walked about attacking and killing humans. The very worst of the dark fae.

"This is the vision I saw when I met Anu. When he opened the block. This was the first thing that came to me."

Pythia's white hair swayed as she nodded. "This is what will come to pass if you choose the Revenant. This is what we must stop."

From the shadows she stalked the night, slaughtering and killing. The Queen watched over it all with delight, feasting as tributes were thrown at her feet. Enid was at her side, whispering into her ear. Secrets and desires. Things yet to happen and future possibilities. All for the Queen's entertainment, her greed.

"How are we going to be able to stop this?"

"It will not be easy, but the decision that affects the outcome has yet to be made. The future remains unclear. We must find that point. The moment of deciding, and since you are the one to make it, you will do the seeking." The grip on her hands tightened as Pythia took a deep breath, seeming to steady herself, her eyes staring into Enid's.

"Reach through the vision, follow the thread to the moment when you feel the shift, when it splits. There you will find the choice and you can prevent it from coming to pass. You must open yourself up to your magic. You have spent so much time walling it off."

Enid focused. Within the confines of her mind, she reached out, searching. Pythia, a firm presence at her side, helped, guiding her as she teased the edge of the vision aside and gripped the thread. It thrummed in her palm, warm and seductive. Suddenly, she could see.

She could see the thread woven into the pattern, and how it spread out, shooting off in different directions—the moment of choosing. Carefully, she followed it back to another thickly woven web of threads and stopped, letting the image fan out before her.

The scene unfolded, slipping into place with a hazy appearance. This path was uncertain. She stood within a ring of fire. Lava bubbled from within pitted rock. Dimitri stood next to her, his hand clutching her arm.

Pythia's voice was low in her ear—gentle yet firm. "Not here, you must go back further. Find the pivotal point, that is where the choice must be made."

Concentrate, she told herself. Sifting through the tapestry she went back, back. And there. A rift. Seemingly so small, so insignificant, but from it several large clusters of thread spun off in various directions. Pushing herself to that point, it burst forth.

Vidar and she stood within the meadow, right outside the cabin. A crescent moon hung above, the stars a glittering masterpiece in the sky. The comforting sounds of the night a gentle symphony in the background. There was no snow, but it was still cold.

Enid stood within a thick coat, her breath puffing from her in a white mist. Vidar was silent next to her, looking up into the swath of the milky way. A sad look upon his handsome face. Longingly, she gazed at him, her eyes following the lines of his face.

She was telling him how she could not bind herself to him, to anyone. Not yet. He nodded, he understood. Of course he did. He would. She herself had thought this a hundred times. She owed it to herself, to figure out what she wanted. It made sense. Deep down she knew all along this was where she was headed. This was the decision she had made. Knowing what she knew now though...

It wasn't fair. She was finally putting herself first, and it was the wrong move. Smothering a sob, she hung her head.

"It could be worse, my dear," Pythia stated next to her. "Let me show you how it could be, if the Revenant win." Her hands went to Enid's temples. The vision around her faded back into the white mist. And then there was searing pain within her skull as an image was shoved into it.

A different version of her stood next to Dimitri. They were in New York. It was dark, but it was not night. She wore all black. The freckles on her nose stood out starkly against the alabaster of her skin. Her eyes were vibrant, her hair a darker shade of auburn as though shadow itself colored it. A vicious smile graced her blood red lips. Beneath her a woman cried as life drained from her body.

From the sky, ashes rained down like snow. Other Revenant were out with them, roaming the city as they slaughtered. Fae as well, terrorizing, murdering, goring themselves on flesh, blood, terror, and death. The constant wail of sirens like a broken record on a loop. As she stood from her kill, Dimitri pulled her into his arms with a hungry look. They shared a deep kiss, tasting the blood of each other's victims.

Out on the street her Queen strode through the city. Delighted laughter ringing like music into the ash-streaked sky. Enid was pulled toward the sound, desiring nothing more than to please her Queen, her reason for being. As she reached her goddess, she was rewarded with a bright smile. Her glorious Queen beckoned her forward. Graceful, soft fingers cradled her face. Tenderly, she gazed into the ebony pools of her mistress's eyes.

"None of this would have been possible without you, my love," the Queen purred before her lips caressed Enid's. Their arms wrapped around each other in a tight embrace as the kiss deepened.

With a gasp Enid jerked herself away from Pythia's hands.

"All those people," she sobbed. Part of her still felt how she relished the way their lives slipped away in her hands. "No."

Pythia coughed, fatigue seeming to wear her down. "That is what will come to pass if you do not heed my warning."

"But… if I am bound to Vidar, there is a chance to stop it from happening."

Pythia looked at her with sad eyes. "It is a dangerous thing, to look too much into your own fate. It incites fear, causes good people to do terrible things in order to avoid it. The only reason I show it to you now, is to stop the destruction of this realm."

Enid nodded thoughtfully.

Pythia began coughing harder. Enid reached for her in concern when the woman stumbled to her knees. With a jolt Enid was rocked backward in her chair. She blinked. They were in the kitchen. Across from her Pythia was slumped over the table. Anu bent over her, fussing worriedly. His blazing red eyes met hers.

"That is all for now," his deep voice stated. A dark shadow swallowed the room, and they were gone.

***

Hours later, Enid stood outside in the meadow. The night was as cold as the one before. Her breath fogged in the air around her. The snow had disappeared, melting beneath the rays of the sun during the day. Above her, the clear sky, littered with twinkling stars and the hazy streak of the milky way, suggested there would be no snow this night.

Fortuitous that Pythia helped her see a vision of this moment so quickly before it was bound to happen. She shook her head at the thought. No doubt this was all part of her grand plan. Enid didn't doubt the ancient seeress knew much more than any of them were aware.

There was a rustle behind her, movement shifting through the long grasses. Then Vidar was there, his gaze, like hers, locked onto the expanse of sparkling sky. She had been out here longer than she cared to admit, thinking. It was rather remote. All she had seen was a clear stream in a rocky bed, and the mountains around her with the towering trees and sounds of wildlife. It was peaceful. If only they could stay out here, away from everything that threatened them. But it was useless. Actions were already in motion that would spell certain doom for thousands of people, if not the world.

She glanced over at Vidar. His profile was strong, stoic. He stood silently. Patiently waiting for her to gather her thoughts. That made her smile. He never pushed her to do anything, and for that she was grateful. Especially when it seemed that is all anyone ever did, but she needed to know what he felt. This didn't only affect her. He was as much a part of it.

"So, apparently, for the fate of all mankind. For the fate of several realms, actually, you and I should be bound together for all eternity."

He didn't say anything. The silence was grating. She glanced over.

"Nothing to say about that? No input, no feelings about any of this?"

He turned his head toward her, a slight frown at the edges of his mouth.

"You know how I feel. I think I made that pretty clear the night I had you pinned beneath me in my bed."

Enid's face flushed at the memory. A warm pull low in her abdomen at the thought of that night. She looked down at her feet, unable to meet his eyes.

"I'm not taking this decision from you, Enid."

He put his hand on the side of her neck, his thumb beneath her chin tilted her face to his once more. Holding her gaze intently, he stood before her, demanding and unrelenting.

"Look at me when I tell you this. I need you to know I speak nothing but the truth."

She swallowed, her eyes widening at the sincerity she saw staring back at her.

"I would let the realms burn if it granted you happiness. If it kept you from making a decision you weren't comfortable with, I would let them all go to waste. I have no qualms about that. I would throw gasoline on the flames." His grip on the side of her neck tightened as he pulled her closer. "You don't know what torture it has been, keeping my distance, watching the Revenant with you. How badly I wanted to tear his arms from his body every time he touched you. But I would endure it again, and more, if that is what you needed from me. I will not make this decision for you. I will not take your freedom. Only, tell me what you want of me and I will do it, I will be it. For you."

This time the silence was hers. They stood together, locked in the fragile moment. This was the turning point. The decision to be made. The world held still with them in a quivering bubble of anticipation. A held breath that would break only when that silence fell, when she said the words. Only...she couldn't find them. The words wouldn't come. There was only him, and the feeling of his hand on her neck, the weight of his declaration settling over her. But she knew. At that moment it clicked into place for her. Without waiting for the words to reveal themselves, she shifted, reaching for him. He met her, lips crashing with an urgency that sped her already racing pulse. The bubble burst.

***

There was a knock at the door of the cabin. Enid sat up with a groan. Next to her Vidar rolled over, untangling his legs from hers and the sheets. With a flash of a smile, and a last, long kiss, he stood, pulling on clothes. Enid followed suit. A blush crept along her cheeks as she replayed the last hour within her mind.

She wasn't quite sure how they made it from outside to the bed. Only that there had been a frantic rush of movement. Hands and lips hectically searching and tasting as they stumbled into the cabin. The door was barely closed when Vidar lifted her body to his, pushing her against the solid wood. Her legs wrapped around his waist as she pushed his coat down his large arms.

The small table had been next, the lantern nearly tumbling from the surface as Vidar tore her coat off. Then they were in the bedroom, the last bits of fabric littering the floor. It felt right, complete. Like the buildup of the last few weeks had finally come to fruition.

As they came together, something within her locked into place, a sense that she was where she belonged. Never before had she been so complete, so safe, so... whole. Vidar wasn't just a companion, or a lover. He was the other piece of her she didn't know she was missing until that moment. For the first time in her life, she felt at home.

She smiled as she walked into the main room and watched him open the front door. Pythia and Anu stood on the other side, knowing looks upon their faces.

"Well?" Pythia asked as she shuffled into the cabin, "Some of us don't have time to waste."

Enid looked over at Vidar who wore an amused smile.

"We've agreed to the binding," she told the older woman, heeding her words and getting straight to the point.

"About time," Pythia huffed, holding up a cord. "Where are we going to do this?"

CHAPTER

43

They gathered in the meadow. Hardy wildflowers shifted in the breeze created by excited pixies. More of them had shown up when Anu returned with Esmelial, the Minotaur brothers, and Adrian. No one else knew of their secret or could be trusted to keep it.

Enid stood facing Vidar, their eyes locked as the significance of the moment hit them. She couldn't help the slight tremor in her hands. Vidar clutched them, thumbs rubbing soothing circles over her skin. Before them Pythia held the braided cord of black silk above their joined hands.

"The color of this cord represents strength, power, wisdom, vision, and success. May these traits be bestowed upon your union. I will bind this cord around your hands three times, binding your mind, body, and spirit together as one. At each circle I will tie a knot, locking in the bind and your vows to each other."

Pythia turned to Vidar. "Do you bind yourself to this woman, Enid Washbourne, of your own free will and volition, promising to fulfill your vows to her with a clear mind and open heart."

"I do," Vidar said, his eyes never wavering from Enid's as he spoke clearly with no hesitation. Enid shivered.

Next, Pythia turned to her. "Do you bind yourself to this man, Vidar Halvarson, of your own free will and volition, promising to fulfill your vows to him with a clear mind and open heart."

"I do," Enid replied. The air around them seemed to still as though the very earth was listening, bearing witness to the sanctity of the ceremony.

Pythia placed the cord over their hands and wrapped it around, tying a knot within the loop as she nodded to Vidar. He took in a breath before he began, his voice solid as he spoke his vows.

"I vow to be your sword and shield, your protector and champion. I will be your guide through the realms and all the places between. I share with you the gifts bestowed upon me at my making. I vow to be loyal and faithful in all our endeavors. This I vow to you, Enid Washbourne, before the witnesses here, and all the Realms within creation."

The cord around their hands warmed, a flash of gold shimmering along the strands as the knot was sealed. A wave of warmth flooded her, his promise a physical touch along her skin.

Enid gasped.

Pythia wrapped the cord around their hands again, before looking to Enid with a nod. She took a deep breath, squaring her shoulders, and froze.

She went blank. What would she say? What could she vow to this man? He deserved so much more than her. As her panic began to take her, she felt Vidar squeeze her hand gently, his face calm and reassuring. The words came to her, automatic, unbidden, and truly from her heart.

"I vow to be your light through the darkness, your support and comfort. I will be your guide through our future within all the realms that we may travel. I share with you the gifts bestowed upon me at my making. I vow to be loyal and faithful in all our endeavors. This I vow to you, Vidar Halvarson, before the witnesses here, and all the Realms within creation."

She felt the knot as it tightened, locking in the vow. The cord once again warmed. She didn't see this time if there was a light—her focus solely on the face of the man before her. His gray eyes darkened, a promise of heat and passion that made her core clench. His thumb brushed against the skin of her hand underneath the bindings. She tucked her bottom lip against her teeth, and those steely eyes narrowed at the movement, his throat bobbing as he swallowed.

Pythia wrapped the final loop. "May your bond be everlasting, may your vows never waiver or break, may no being ever come between you. Your destinies are entwined as this cord has entwined your hands. As this final knot slips into place you may seal it and your vows with a kiss."

Complete silence settled around them. Enid pressed up on her toes as Vidar leaned down. Static tingled through her as their lips met, the kiss deepening. The knot tightened into place on the cord and she felt the heat from it as it slid over the both of them. A pulse lashed out from deep within her, jolting between them like they were a live wire, connected by the electric cord that simmered around their hands. It rushed out in a burst, a wave of power pouring into the night.

Her hair blasted back. Pythia stumbled into Anu's arms. Esmelial, Adrian, and the Minotaur staggered. The Pixies were blown away, tumbling through the air before they fluttered to a stop.

"So mote it be," whispered Pythia, her voice trembling in the silence that followed.

As Enid and Vidar continued to look at each other with wonder and awe she realized that their connection was really there. A physical, tangible bond that she could feel within her. Fingers grazed against her cheekbone, Vidar's eyes tracing the line with perfect accuracy. She looked down at their still bound hands. A smile tugged at his lips as he watched the confusion dance across her face. Amusement bloomed within her. It felt different, stranger than usual, the emotion was disconnected— like holding a hand that wasn't your own. She felt it but knew it wasn't hers.

I can feel that, she thought, looking up at him—realizing it was his emotion she was sensing.

Can you feel this? His voice came from inside her head. She nearly jumped when she felt the touch of lips on her cheek.

"Yes," she gasped—out loud this time. Vidar chuckled, pulling her closer, his mouth at her ear.

"Let's keep this to ourselves. I like the idea that I can tease you whenever I please, without anyone else being the wiser."

Enid felt herself blushing, suddenly thankful it was so dark. "How is this possible?" she whispered back.

It seems, his voice came from in her head again, *that if we focus on the other, and push our thoughts and emotions through this connection, that we are able to transfer them. I thought of touching your cheek, and it felt as though I did.*

This is amazing, Enid whispered to him in the privacy of their minds.

***

Even though it was a secret, rushed ceremony, there was still a party after. The pixies had brought dandelion wine from Dokkalfar. Esmelial and Adrian had pulled together a bit of food and some sort of sweet honey cake. The Minotaur gathered enough wood to keep a fire burning in a circle of stone for the remainder of the night. And Anu and Pythia had carefully gathered their binding cord, placing it in a carved wooden box that Enid slid under the bed for safe keeping.

Pythia assured her that the power of the binding was within them. The cord only helping to invoke the symbolism of the bind in a physical way. Enid still wanted to save it. A keepsake to look back on in their hopefully long and happy future together.

The fae told stories and anecdotes about their long lives throughout the night. Enid found herself laughing more than she thought possible. A few times she thought of her mother, her aunt, her best friend, all the people she wished could be there sharing the moment with her, and her heart would ache. In those moments she would feel Vidar reach out to her. His arms encircling her body both physically and mentally, words of reassurance and warmth whispered into her mind.

A few hours before the sun came up, the fae all took their leave with words of congratulations. Even Artemis gave Enid a hug, his bulking frame surprisingly gentle before he and his brother stumbled off after Anu. The last of the fire was stamped out, and it was just the two of them.

Vidar swept Enid off her feet, cradling her within his arms.

"This is something humans do, right?" he asked with a mischievous gleam in his eye as he carried her over the threshold of the cabin and straight to bed.

"Better make sure we consummate this thing. Make sure it really takes, right?" Enid teased.

"That is true. I think it would be unwise of us to risk it," Vidar murmured.

His hand curled within the hair at the back of her head, pulling her mouth toward his. Swallowing her moan, he teased and stroked her tongue with his. She gave in completely, her arms around his neck, fingers twisting into his hair. It felt as though his lips were everywhere. Kissing down her neck, flicking against the pebbled peaks of her breasts, dipping between the cleft of her legs. Her body shuddered at the sensation. Vidar chuckled, pulling back to watch the heated look on her face. She bit her lip, severing the cry that ripped from her.

Then she was tossed through the air, landing with a shriek and a thud on the bed. He stood before her, gray eyes dark and stormy as they trailed over her body. Slowly, he pulled his shirt up over the chiseled contours of his stomach and chest. Enid's breath caught, watching the ripple of muscles as his shirt was tossed carelessly to the side. His hands moved to his pants, the button popping free before he pushed the edge of his waistband down a fraction. He was teasing her, moving excruciatingly slow.

Unable to hold herself back any longer, Enid imagined her fingers scraping along his chest and stomach, tracing the patterns of muscle beneath the smooth skin. Vidar's eyes widened. His body rigid. She smiled innocently, using the bond to create the sensation of her tongue following the trail of fingers, tasting the slight saltiness of his skin. Her teeth nibbled gently.

Vidar's head dropped back with a deep groan. She watched from the bed, her legs dropping to the side as she felt and saw him tremble through their bond. Allowing herself to push him further, she focused on the large bulge straining against the fabric of his pants. Her tongue licked a line from root to tip.

"Gods!" Vidar cried out.

His head jerked forward, eyes hungry. Before she could blink, his clothing was gone, banished to the wooden floor, and he was on top of her. Her clothing disappeared just as fast.

Enid relished the feel of his skin on hers. The way his strong hands caressed and probed her curves. His skin was hard and smooth under her touch. She took her time exploring every soft and firm inch of flesh. With the bond, she reached for the silky, rigid length of him. Physically, she wasn't able to take him fully within her mouth, but with their bond, he slid down into the back of her throat easily.

"Enid!" he gasped as he stiffened above her. His eyes rolled back into his head, and then it was her turn to cry out as she felt tongue and teeth exploring the delicate folds between her legs. Pressure pulsed around the sensitive nub of her clitoris.

Writhing beneath him, she pushed and angled herself, frantic to feel him within her, desperate for more friction. At her silent urging, he pressed his tip to her dampened core. Grasping her hands in his own, he pinned them above her head. Slowly, bit by bit, he slid into her.

Their eyes locked, her wide green ones staring into the depthless gray storm of his. Her hands gripped his harder, her legs wrapping around his waist, locking him in place as she encouraged him further until he was fully seated.

She gasped as a white light flashed before her vision. She stood in front of a doorway—nothing more than a rectangular shimmer in the air. A dusty lavender sky lay beyond, an alien landscape she had never before seen. Next to her Vidar held her hand, mouth open in wonder at the scene before them.

Vidar pulled out and thrust in, breaking the vision. Enid gasped, the feeling snapping her to the present. Her breath was ragged as she savored the sensation of him filling her. When she thought it couldn't get any better, he began to roll his hips with more force. Sliding in and out in long, unhurried strokes, deeper and harder.

"Fuck," he whispered.

Enid only whimpered in response as she felt him throb. Her legs tightened around his hips, shifting to accommodate the new angle. Wave after wave of pleasure flushed through every inch of her as she lifted to meet him, matching his rhythm. She was consumed with the feeling. The sensation all she could focus on, all she knew.

She felt him use the bond to press his mouth to her firm, erect nipples—pulling and teasing them with teeth and tongue. His dark eyes were ravenous, his mouth tilting up in a satisfied smirk as he watched the euphoria on her face.

Enid thanked the bond as she screamed out.

The palms of her hands tingled where they clutched his. The slow, steady pace became more urgent. The long, gentle thrusts hastening into short, hard bursts. He sat up, pulling her on top of him, and pounded into her with the single-minded intensity only he could give her.

She bucked as the orgasm crashed over her, pushing her into mind numbing ecstasy. Only his hands on her kept her grounded against him, anchored her in place. A deep, possessive growl vibrated through his chest as she pulsated around his member, his features blanketed with raw hunger. Suddenly, he froze.

Enid whimpered as he held her still, only the tip of him within her, his face pressed against her chest. His back moved up and down beneath her hand as he fought to control his breathing. Through the bond she felt uncertainty, fear, desire, and carnal passion raging within him. Delicately, she stroked along his back, her fingers trailing up his neck and into his hair. He shivered at the touch, a low hum slipping into the now silent room.

"Vidar, what's wrong?"

He shook his head, squeezing her tight. Even that small movement had him throbbing within her. She groaned at the sensation, and Vidar moaned in response. Confusion erupted through her. She could feel his need, his desire, but there was so much fear there as well.

"Vidar, look at me," she pressed.

"No," he whispered.

Tightening her fingers within his hair, she pulled, forcing his head up. Mouth clamped into a thin line, he allowed the movement, but wouldn't open his eyes. She could see the tension in his body, feel his worry through the bond.

"Vidar," she whispered. "Please, don't hide from me."

His nostrils flared as he fought himself. She could feel him clinging to his control, wrestling it into place. Holding back from her. This was unacceptable.

Grabbing his hand in hers, she pressed his fingers to her lips before slowly sliding them down her neck to her chest. A rumble sounded in his throat as she slid them over her breast and down her stomach.

"I am yours," she murmured. "And you are mine." Their joined hands reached the place between them where he was still barely sheathed within her. Her breath rushed from her in a broken gasp.

Vidar's eyes snapped open, inky blackness fully covering the entirety of them. Enid smiled. There was no reason for him to fear her response. They were bonded. Fear was not an emotion she would feel—not toward him. She pressed that encouragement down the bond.

Her fingertips grazed the little hairs at the nape of his neck. The very tips of his ears now had a slight point that hadn't been there before. Her hands moved up to explore that tip before tangling into his hair. His chest seemed wider as it rose and fell in time to his harsh breathing, his dark eyes full of hunger and need.

Slowly, she leaned forward and pressed a kiss to his lips. Reassurance flooding through them, she felt him begin to relax, though uncertainty still kept him hesitant. Gently, he returned the kiss, slow and tentative. Only then, when her tongue finally parted the tightly clamped line of his mouth, did she feel the sharpened points of fangs. Drawing his bottom lip into her mouth she sucked at it. A low growl rumbled through him and she was finally able to see, as he panted with desire before her, that his canines were fanged points. Smaller than a Revenant's, but fangs nonetheless.

He looked up at her with those bottomless black eyes. "I've never felt like this before," he grumbled. "So full of hunger and desire—uncontrollable. You bring out the beast within me. Only in the heat of battle have I felt such a loss of composure."

The tang of his fear licked down her spine, sharp and sudden. He really felt like he could lose himself, that he may hurt her. Enid pushed it aside. That was his worry, not hers.

Smoothing that panic away through the bond, she bit her lip, wiggling her hips a bit to slide another inch down onto him. Groaning, he caught her, holding her in place.

"I am not afraid of what you are, Vidar. You are mine. That is all that matters."

She leaned back, allowing him to take in her body as she trailed a hand down her chest to her navel. "Now claim what is yours."

With that, he finally let go and rammed her down hard on the thick length of him. It only took a few deep strokes. Her legs quivered and she threw her head back, gasping as she came undone around him—his breath harsh against her exposed neck.

The firm muscles of his chest heaved against her as he held her tight, the rhythm of his movements frantic as he neared his completion. She could feel the beat of his heart, solid, strong, and fast.

A compulsion she couldn't ignore crept over her.

Pressing her mouth to his neck, she found the spot where the pulse was strongest. Her lips parted, and her teeth sank in. Vidar shuddered. There was the white-hot feeling of his fangs in the crook of her neck, and then a blinding, uncontrollable flush of pure rapture.

Entwined together, they throbbed in unison, ripple after ripple of sensation washing over the both of them. Enid was almost worried it would never end, the feeling pressing down over her—drowning and lifting her again and again. Could a mind shatter from endless orgasms? She wasn't sure, but she was certain she was on the brink of finding out.

She laced her fingers in his, her other arm wrapped around his neck as she held onto him for dear life—riding out those waves. She could only focus on the sensation of him within her, against her, and those cresting surges of pleasure. Her hand tingled, a prickling sensation that was barely noticeable.

They weren't sure of how much time had passed, or what time it was when they finally collapsed from exhaustion against each other. What they did know is they never wanted this feeling to end. Enid knew without speaking, without a single shade of doubt, that Vidar loved her. And that somehow in the short amount of time she had come to know him, she had fallen so deeply in love that she was willing to risk her very life to keep fighting for him.

CHAPTER

44

Sleep weighed her down. She sat up, the warmth and comfort of the bed enticing her to lay back in its billowy embrace. The clock on the nightstand read ten p.m. It was well past night fall. She had slept later than usual. Though, given last night's activities, she was not surprised. Vidar was nowhere to be seen. His side of the bed felt cool under her palm. As quickly as she could, which wasn't very with the way her head was pounding, she began to dress in some of the warmer clothes Esmelial brought for her.

Something caught her attention as she was pulling on her shirt, a flash of color from the corner of her eye. On the back of her hand, a pale mark stood out, stark against her skin, like a white tattoo. It was circular, an intricate, woven design. Stars were scattered within the center of the knotted pattern, and lines of varying thickness sprawled out from the center, cutting the circle into four uneven sections.

Hurriedly getting dressed, she slammed open the bedroom door, searching for Vidar.

He stood before the fireplace, shirtless. A blazing fire already raging within the hearth. His fingers absently stroked a symbol along his chest, the same pale, intricate design she had on her hand on the back of his. She could feel his confusion through the bond, reflected in the look of contemplation upon his face. He was just as lost as she was.

Gray eyes flicked to her, reading her face even as her emotions trickled down the bond. They were an open book, each to the other.

Crossing the room to stand in front of him, she examined the symbol on his chest. Fingers tracing the pattern of swirls over his left pectoral. The lines twisted and turned in hard angles upon itself, creating sections of four equal quadrants. It looked similar to a shield. He took her hand in his, examining the symbol there, his fingers tracing a constellation among the stars.

Curiously he grazed the neck of her shirt. Without a word, she pulled the fabric to the side, revealing the pale, white lines twisted in three interlocking loops above her breast. As she had done, he traced the pattern under his fingertips. Tingles erupted along her skin where he touched, causing her to shiver involuntarily.

Dipping his head, he kissed her shoulder. She sighed, leaning into the contact, a rush of delight soothing away the tension. Moving the fabric back into place, he pulled her close, wrapping an arm around her back. She leaned her forehead against him, below the strange mark that now adorned his chest. Their eyes closed simultaneously.

"What does it mean?" she whispered.

It took a moment for him to answer. When he did, she was not surprised to realize she already knew what it would be.

"I have no idea."

CHAPTER
45

The Enforcer had been good to his word before his disappearance. Esmelial and her sisters had no issues getting their visitation paperwork. Though, the attention they received at the checkpoints was more than thorough. She expected it. Over a hundred years had passed since they were last allowed hunting privileges. Though the king did emphasize it was on a trial basis. Still, Esmelial was pleased as they passed through the shimmering portal. They weren't having to sneak out this time.

The alibi Esmelial gave the King for Enid was met with some uncertainty, but he took it anyway. The Revenant's Queen was less than thrilled. She would apply pressure. There wouldn't be much time. She was going to have to get information as quickly as possible. Hence the little hunting party. Her sisters were eager to help. Impatient as they were to drink deep from the desire of the youthful, wanting flesh they would soon encounter.

They stepped out in an empty alley not far behind the Revenant owned nightclub. Already the sound of music vibrating the air reached her sensitive hearing. The smell of prospective prey, primed and teeming with lust, wafted to her as they walked around the corner and spied the line of humans.

They didn't bother with the wait. A male at the front of the line started to protest, only to stop when Deanthia pressed a gentle kiss to his mouth. Passion flared, the male ran his fingers along the smooth chocolate of her skin. Her green eyes winked.

"See you inside," she whispered. He whimpered in response. Esmelial smirked as the bouncer looked up from his clipboard with a bored expression and opened the rope, allowing them to pass.

Her sisters giggled, moving into the warmth of the club with palpable excitement. It had been too long since they last hunted all together, the four of them. The smell of bodies and hormones flew at them from every direction. Esmelial took a deep breath, releasing it with a satisfied sigh.

With a nod, the others scattered about the room, each pulling as much attention to themselves as possible. It wasn't difficult. The humans, and even some of the fae, flocked to them. The temptresses put on a performance, swaying and humming to the music. Taking small sips of pleasure from unsuspecting victims.

Esmelial watched for a moment before she took the stairs to the upper floor. The guard at the bottom waved her on with a nod of confirmation. They didn't even make it difficult anymore. Fucking arrogant Revenant.

A rough hand on her arm stopped her as she stepped onto the landing. A human male with a cocky grin and, from the smell of him, too much alcohol in his system. She shoved aside the irritation, keeping her face pleasant as he leered at her.

"How about you and I get to know each other better?" the male slurred, pulling her closer. She smiled, splaying her hand upon his chest.

"Maybe some other time," she purred as she pressed him away. She didn't have time for this. Not to mention, in his state, it wouldn't be much of a meal.

Anger flushed his face as his grip tightened.

"Do you think you're too good for me, bitch?"

He kept his voice low, jerking her roughly against him. Esmelial gritted her teeth as he pulled her against his lurching body, breath hot against her face. Uninhibited, his hands wandered. Stupid, disrespectful, arrogant jackass.

"You want to have some fun?" she hissed, "Fine. We will have fun."

"That's right, baby. I knew you'd come around."

Esmelial grabbed his head, pulling him close and, with a deep breath, latched her magic into his already eager body. He went rigid, eyes widening. As she took that breath, she reached into him, his life force pulsating, rushing out so fast it made her dizzy. His face turned red. His body began to quake. The essence that made him began to dim and pain took its place. It was all he was, all he knew. Unending, soul crushing, pain. Before she took too much, Esmelial released him. In the fear filled reflection of his eyes she saw herself. Silver eyes so bright they lit up her face.

He staggered back and dropped to the floor coughing and sputtering. Two more humans ran up, lifting him and patting his back in concern.

"Your friend has had too much to drink," Esmelial sneered before turning away.

"She tried to kill me," the human gasped.

"Dude, she's five foot nothing. You're drunk as hell, come on."

She smirked as they carried their friend down the stairs, his head bobbing. William's office door was already open. The Revenant leaning against the frame, watching the departing humans with a scowl, his arms crossed over his chest.

"You always know how to make an entrance," he said as she walked by. He shut the door behind them, reclining against it with hands in pockets as he took her in from head to toe.

"Did you miss me?" she murmured, stepping closer, fingers stroking the buttons of his shirt.

He smiled, standing so they were chest to chest.

"What do you want, Esmelial," he said. "You didn't come here for a hookup. You already got permission to hunt freely." He left her standing there, moving over to his desk where he pulled out a couple of glasses and a decanter of dark alcohol. "Your girls are already out filling themselves as we speak."

He waved his hand toward the window before taking a seat at his desk and gesturing her toward the other glass. The liquid within caught the light as she lifted it and took a sniff. Whiskey. She set it back on the desk, untouched.

"Can't a girl just come to visit an old friend," she said as she stepped behind him and draped her arms over his shoulders.

She put her mouth against his ear, her voice humming in question, weaving the tone with suggestion. William sighed and took one of her arms, directing her around the front of him to his desk. With a smile she arched against the edge. He didn't seem fazed. A slight frown tugged at the corners of his mouth.

"How about this time you just ask me outright what information you're looking for, and we skip the song and dance." He gulped his drink down in one swig.

Esmelial blinked, frozen in place.

"What?"

William spun the glass in his fingers. "You think I really forgot all those times like you told me to? You think I don't know you've been playing me this whole time?" He sat the glass on his desk with a solid thunk and stood to look back out the window, hands in pockets once again, dismissive, distant. "Sweetheart, I lost my human life getting played. I know when someone is trying to pull the wool over my eyes."

She crossed her arms over her chest, anger flaring. "So why give me the information? Why not lie about it? Why pretend you didn't remember?"

He was silent for so long that Esmelial was certain he wasn't going to answer. She stood, her hands fisting at her sides.

"I was brought up to believe that family was everything," he finally said.

She stilled, head cocking to the side.

"You never turned against family, always helped them when they needed it, always stayed loyal. Then, I got played." He looked over his shoulder at her with a smirk. "My own uncle turned me in for something I didn't do. Said I was expendable. So next thing I know, I'm at the harbor getting fitted for a set of cement shoes by a rival gang. The queen herself was the one who saved me, and offered another family. A better one." He slowly crossed the few steps that separated them. "You do everything you can to keep your sisters safe. You break rules, lie, steal." His fingers reached up and touched her lips gently. "Seduce." He dropped his hand. "Not even the Revenant, for all their talk of family, know what it truly means to sacrifice the way you have. They don't understand the real meaning of the word."

Surprise would be an understatement for how she felt at that moment. All the time she spent with the Revenant, he was nothing more than that. Revenant—untrustworthy. Prettier than most, sure. But now, hearing all this, he seemed…more. William. For the first time she felt like she really saw him for who he was, instead of one of the creatures she had grown to hate.

"Now," he said, "tell me what you need."

Esmelial swallowed. "I need to know what the Revenant Queen plans to do with the human girl, and what the final challenge is."

William swore, then reached over the desk and picked up her abandoned glass of whiskey, draining it. He ran a hand over his face, sighing deeply. "I may have a nice face, and a head for business, but that won't keep Isis from ripping it right off my shoulders if I give you that information."

"Please, William," Esmelial pleaded.

He froze, eyebrows shooting up to his hairline. "You've never asked me nicely for anything before." The empty glass clicked back onto the table, his jaw ticking as he looked her over. The silence was nearly suffocating as he seemed to think over what he could say. Testing words and rejecting them before coming to a conclusion.

"Did you know there is a forgotten annex in Dokkalfar that no one knows about? Not even the King. It was discovered a few decades ago, sealed up at the end of a long hall with a dead end. The Queen hid it, and has been using that annex for her own personal exploits. Keeps her rejects down there. There's even talk that it goes further, a whole abandoned city right beneath us."

"How do you know this?" Esmelial had never heard of such a place before, and she had been around far longer than the Revenant.

"The Queen's attendants are horrible gossips and flirts," William muttered.

Esmelial frowned, not liking the dark look that passed his face at that statement. She shook it off. Why should she care?

"I suppose that is all the information you can freely give me?"

He gave a single nod, his jaw muscles flexing as though he wanted to say more, but physically couldn't. His lips pulled into a tight line.

"Nothing is done for free. What do you want in exchange for this information?"

He seemed to contemplate her for a moment.

"A kiss."

Esmelial bit her lip. "I think I can handle that."

She leaned into him, her hand drifting below his waist. He grabbed it in his, the other going around her throat. Esmelial froze at the sensation. It wasn't unpleasant the way his hand rested there, not squeezing, just leading. He backed her into the nearby wall, watching the expression on her face. Moving slowly so she could pull away if she wanted. When her back hit the wall, he released her hand. The thumb at her throat stroked her neck, remaining in place as he dipped his face closer to hers.

"Only a kiss," he murmured.

With that his grip tightened incrementally and he pulled her lips to his. His other arm snaked around her waist, lifting her against him. Tongues, teeth and lips melded in a slow, sensuous dance that she had never felt the likes of in her hundreds of years. Her legs weakened, the arm around her supporting her. Never had a lover evoked this depth of emotion before. Never had she felt so much, so completely. And all of it with a simple kiss.

When the kiss ended, she swayed against him. Her eyes still closed. She felt the soft graze of fingertips along her cheek, and the lingering brush of his soft lips along hers, and then he shifted away. Setting her down on unsteady feet.

Her eyes fluttered open, her hand going to the wall for support as she watched him walk to the window, staring down into the crowd below. She swallowed, her hands smoothing down her dress despite the fact it had not even one wrinkle. Her heart thrummed within her.

"You should go," William said, his back to her.

She didn't bother saying anything. There were no sarcastic quips or meaningful parting words to be found. So, silently, she walked out of the office and back down the stairs. Her sisters found her quickly, grouping around her with flushed, excited faces. Before they walked out into the night, Esmelial risked one last look up to that darkened window. She couldn't see through the tint, but she knew, could feel it like a caress along her skin. The feel of William's eyes on her.

CHAPTER
46

All good things come to an end. That is what they say anyway.

As Enid stood in the field of wildflowers and grass, looking out at the very spot where they completed their bond only the night before, she had an eerie feeling that she was going to miss this moment.

Pythia scowled from a chair set by the fire.

"You must keep trying!" she demanded. "Open your heart, your mind, your emotions! Feel the energy around you! You have spent your life behind a wall of your own creation, burying your gifts. You must break them free!"

With a sigh, Enid closed her eyes and reached out with her mind for Vidar. She could picture him clear as day. Could feel the bark of the tree at his back, the hardness of the earth where he sat. Through his eyes, she could see the ferns surrounding him.

That's right, Vidar's voice whispered through her mind. *Once you have a grasp of where I am, imagine you are there. Like stepping through a door, just pick up your foot and go through.*

Lifting her foot, she held that vision in her mind and then stepped forward. Her eyes opened.

Pythia glared at her from her chair.

Enid's head fell forward, her breath blowing out in exasperation.

"We've been at this for hours. I don't get it. I can sense everything about where he is, but I can't get there."

"You must keep trying. I know you can do this! I've seen it!"

The older woman began coughing, her breath labored. In a flash Anu was next to her. Pythia looked lovingly up into the face of her shadow man.

"My strength fails me." Her voice was frail as she spoke, a wheeze within the measured words.

"Nonsense," he murmured, his hand tracing the planes of her withered face, his eyes soft with adoration. "You are as virile as you have always been."

Pythia's face softened, her hand settling on top of his as she leaned into the touch.

"I have done all I can. Our time runs short. There is nothing more for me here." She looked toward Enid, her eyes full of fear. "You must discover what you need on your own."

Enid swallowed, her mouth opening and closing soundlessly. There was nothing she could say. Delicately, Anu walked Pythia into the cabin, helping her to traverse the perilous stairs to the door.

Enid's shoulders sagged, the weight of the realm heavy upon them. They had been at this most of the night. Vidar was delighted when they first started. Connecting with his mind had been easy, like sliding into a favorite hoodie. Trying to connect to his abilities had proven more difficult.

After getting over the shock of the symbols etched magically upon their skin, they sat down to talk. The markings had him contemplating the ancient lores, which had him reminiscing over his lost abilities. That led to him trying to explain what it felt like to walk between places.

It was a gift he hadn't had access to for years. As he described the feeling of it, they were both shocked when he disappeared from within the cabin only to reappear on the front porch. Enid felt his joy as he howled with excitement. Bursting back into the cabin, he rushed over and lifted her in his arms, spinning around and around.

Enid had laughed in delight at his reaction. Vidar's face shone with happiness, his laugh wild and carefree. Then he pulled her in and kissed her deeply.

"Thank you... thank you," he murmured when he stopped to breathe.

"For what?" she asked, attempting to speak as he pecked at her lips. "I...didn't do...anything." Finally, she pulled back with a giggle.

"Oh, but you did, you wonderful woman. I haven't been able to use that magic in so long, and you've brought it back. It's all because of you."

"But I really didn't do anything," she insisted.

"You didn't have to," he replied. "It's just being around you. Everything has gotten stronger, like you've jump-started a dying machine. Haven't you seen it? The abilities? Our markings? It's all because of you. You are a magical, amazing woman. You even got the Sirens on your side, to swear a vow to you when they would rather use you for food. Something in you calls to our kind. You are a miracle."

When Pythia heard about Vidar's gift returning, she insisted they start working on tapping into each other's abilities. Now, Enid wasn't sure at all if any of it had to do with her, or with the bond, or anything. She only knew she was tired, and frustrated, and feeling utterly useless. Pythia was so desperate that she needed to save the world, but she didn't have the first clue how, or where to start. She could feel the older woman's despair.

Enid was staring off into the distance when she felt the presence of the Shadow Man at her side.

"I've failed her," she choked out, staring straight ahead, unseeing.

"No," he said. "She is tired. She has walked this world longer than most of her kind. She will not for much longer."

"What will you do?" Enid asked.

"Where she goes, I follow," he said simply.

"Even to death?" she gasped, looking at him incredulously.

He turned to her then, his eyebrow arched in amusement.

"There are other realms than these, and I have known for a while that our time in this place is drawing to a close." His voice

389

lowered conspiratorially. "Hel personally showed me our names written within the golden book."

"I'm so sorry," Enid said sadly.

"Why?"

"Aren't you sad?" she asked.

He laughed out loud then, his gaunt form shaking with merriment. "Do you weep when you move to a new house or city?"

She thought for a moment, startled at the comparison. "Sometimes," she admitted.

Smiling broadly, he examined her thoughtfully, his head tilted to the side. "Perhaps we may weep, then, when the time comes," he mused, his focus shifting to the distant landscape. "Mostly though, we are exhilarated at the prospect. A new adventure in a new realm, with our youth and vitality restored to us." He drew in a deep breath as though already testing out a youthful set of lungs. "We are ready."

"I thought that a human bound to a fae lived forever," Enid said, confused.

He chuckled, clicking his tongue. "Even the fae do not live forever," he explained. "I am a creature of darkness and shadow. I have lived for thousands of years. The darkness has reached out to me for some time now, beckoning me home to its black embrace."

He sat down upon a nearby stone, his face faraway and wistful, his hands resting on the top of his cane. "The first time I felt it, I came home to Pythia, eager to share with her. That was the day we found her first gray hair." He shook his head. "Death comes for us all someday." A beat later, he looked toward the sky, considering. "Well, most of us."

Enid was once again overcome with the realization that the dark man before her was older than she could contemplate. As old as Pythia appeared, her shadow was far older. Even so, when she and Vidar had questioned the pair about the sudden appearance of their marks, Pythia had been as confused as them. The shadow man seemed contemplative, but remained silent on the matter.

Enid had the feeling he knew more than he was letting on, but wouldn't say. She let it be. There was no telling if what he knew had any bearing on their situation, or was merely a myth passed on through time. The true value lost over the millennia.

They were both sitting in silent reverie, when there was a woosh of air, and Vidar came walking out from the darkness between two trees. As he stepped up to her, she leaned into his muscular frame, seeking comfort. Looping an arm around her, he drew her closer.

"I have an idea for something we can try," he said soothingly. "Do you trust me?"

"Always," she whispered, staring up at him. He smiled down at her, dark strands of hair falling over his forehead. Her heart ached at his beauty.

Taking her hand, he led her into the forest. "When I say now, hold tight to my hand, take a deep breath, and hold it."

"Okay," she whispered.

As they stepped between the trees, he gave the word. "Now."

Enid took a deep breath, holding it tight as she clamped down on his hand. There was a furious gust of wind around her. It was chaotic and maddening. Like the pull of waves in a storm from a great distance. There was so much space it was difficult to tell which direction any of it came from, if any. Before she could fully grasp her surroundings, they were standing in the mouth of a cave overlooking the forest. In the distance she could see the smoke from the cabin drifting in a white cloud through the star filled sky.

The air broke from her in a rush, and she sucked in another in shock. Vidar's hand was on her back, circling it soothingly as she bent over, her hands on her knees. She felt like she might vomit. The feeling was unexpected, disorienting. It was as though her body forgot which way was up.

"That's what I've been trying to do this whole time?" she gasped. "What was that—all of that...wind?"

"That was the veil between all things. It can be confusing at first. Imagine it as the space between atoms. It is not as large as it seems, but also endless. It connects everything and is connected to nothing, all at the same time."

Enid threw him an exasperated look that had him chuckling as she stood up, feeling better now.

"I'm never going to get the hang of any of this," she murmured.

"Why don't we rest for a bit," he suggested, sitting on a nearby rock and pulling her in front of him. His arms wrapped around her shoulders as she leaned into his chest. They sat like that in silence, looking out at the stars over the dark treetops until Enid couldn't stay quiet any longer.

"I feel like I've been running for hours, and I haven't gone anywhere," she sighed. Vidar hummed, his head resting against the top of hers.

"Maybe after you've experienced the transition a few more times, it will get easier. You didn't know what to expect before."

"I wish that were it," Enid replied. "But I'm having difficulty tapping into my own ability as well. It comes to me when I least expect it, or when Pythia pushes me to it. But I can't seem to call it at will."

"Then let's work on that. It will be easier to reach your own gift, and I will try to tap into whatever you see."

"Ok," she said with a sigh. "I'll give it a shot."

Relaxing into his arms, she closed her eyes and tried to clear her mind. Since they were pretty certain the Revenant were behind the disaster that was going to happen, she turned her thoughts to them. She opened her mind, sinking into the vast realm of possibility—that blank space where everything had yet to be determined—and tried pushing aside the fabric of time before her. At first, she didn't feel anything, only Vidar's arms around her, the stone beneath her.

She thought back to what she felt whenever she was within the web of fates. The sensation that the world was brittle, that the fabric was shifting, changing, evolving. Her mind reached out once again for the edges of the current path fate was taking them down, and this time, she felt it. A gentle pulse in the air, calling her toward it. She held it, the thrum swelling in recognition, and then she was racing forward, toward that endless web of interconnecting fates, until she stood in its very center.

Halfway there, she thought. Now she needed to focus her intention. What plans did the Revenant have? What were they going to do to her? To the world? Dimitri popped in her mind. Did he have any idea what was going on?

Focus, she scolded herself. She needed to see the Revenant Queen's plan. Their future. She needed to think of what the Revenant were as a group. Maybe then she could hone in on them. The Revenant never changed, never evolved. They were steadfast, frozen in time, locked within themselves.

A tug pulled within her chest. Fate urging her to look, to seek what she so desperately sought. Keeping the thoughts of the Revenant within her, she pulled back at that tug, forcing the vision forward.

Around her the mist faded and she was standing outside, in a graveyard, in the rain. A woman stood in a blue raincoat, soaked to the bone. Enid stepped next to her, wanting to see who she was. Before them was a gravestone.

Isadora Marie Washbourne
Wife, Sister, Mother, Friend
Born October 21, 1973 – Died October 10, 2024

She didn't know she was crying until she felt the tears on her cheeks. This was her mother's gravestone. She was so intent on it she almost didn't notice the other figures surrounding them until it was too late.

They wore all black. Black clothing, large black coats with hood and hats, gloves, and face coverings. Revenant, outside in the day, protected from the sun by the storm, and their layers of clothing. The woman jumped as she noticed them surrounding her.

"Enid?" An unfamiliar voice questioned over the rain. The woman lifted her head, startled as she realized there were other people with her. Enid gasped.

Jane.

"Wh-who are you?" Jane asked nervously. Her glasses were covered in raindrops. Wet strands of hair stuck to her face, her lips nearly purple from the chill.

"We are looking for Enid Washbourne," came the reply.

Jane shook her head. "She's missing. No one knows where she is. She didn't even show up to her mother's funeral."

Jane's voice was sad, reserved, but also frightened and cautious. The woman seemed to shrink in upon herself as she stood in the center of the masked figures. The black cloaked

Revenant hissed in frustration and looked over at one of its companions. There was the tilt of a head toward Jane, and a nod of understanding in return.

Enid cried out as the other Revenant jumped on top of the delicate woman, knocking her to the ground before tearing into her neck. Jane screamed and screamed, until there was a gurgle, and the screaming stopped.

Enid couldn't stop though. Her voice tore from her in a high wail, useless, unheard, and unheeded as the shy, quiet girl was shredded to pieces. Then the Revenant walked away, muttering to themselves.

She fell to her knees next to the mutilated body of her mother's former assistant. Jane's thick framed glasses had been knocked from her face, her lifeless amber eyes staring blankly up at the clouds. A phone had fallen out of her pocket. The date and time read October 29, 2024. 2:16 pm. The day after tomorrow.

Closing her eyes, Enid pushed away the vision. Her knees gave out. Vidar's arms around her were the only thing keeping her from hitting the ground. A sob broke from her as she held onto him. His arms a life raft in the waters of her sorrow.

"I'm so sorry," Vidar whispered.

She lifted her head. Words failed her. He smoothed her hair back.

"I saw," he said with a nod of his head. "You don't have to say anything."

"We have to stop it," she gasped, the words breaking as they tumbled out.

"We will."

CHAPTER

47

There wasn't much time to go over a plan. Enid wanted to get to her mother's as soon as possible to intercept Jane before she could go to the cemetery. Obviously, her mother's affairs had been taken care of. She had known there was a will, with fully detailed instructions set for everything. Her mother had made sure of it after the passing of her father. What she didn't know was what arrangements were made for her aunt.

Sunrise was in a few hours, and Northspire would be closed to visitors during the night. So, the only time she had to go would be during the next day. Vidar assured her he would be able to get her into the building. It would require walking them into a stairwell, safely away from any sunlight. From there she could find out about her aunt's remains before they made their way to her mother's. It left little time to do more than ask the pixies to get word to Adrian and Esmelial. Thankfully the little sprites loved the grassy meadow in front of the cabin, and were often found frolicking among the wildflowers.

Pythia gave a stern glare. "You should be working on the control of your abilities. The life of one human isn't worth sacrificing the whole of the realm."

Enid returned the glare with a steady, unwavering gaze.

"This is something I have to do. I don't expect you to understand, but I can't let another person lose their life because of me. I will continue to do everything I can to help the realm, but I will do it my way, starting with this one person. It's important to me."

The ancient seer gave her a brittle smile, her watery gaze turning to Anu.

"It is time."

Enid looked between them in confusion.

"We will only be gone a couple of days."

Pythia sighed. "I have no more days left to give you. My visions have ceased. Most have come to pass, and I can see no further. I have been looking forward to this day for a very long time now. Go. Save your friend. Perhaps this act will give you what you need to also save this realm."

Enid hesitated. "But—"

Pythia huffed. "But nothing. Go. This will not be the last time we see each other. Save your goodbye for then."

Anu came up beside Pythia with a chuckle, his hand resting on her shoulder. "Go to your destiny, Enid Washbourne."

The light bled from the room, and just like that, they were gone.

Sleep didn't come easily. When it did, it felt like only seconds before she was shaken awake again. They readied themselves within the darkness of the small cabin. The dangerous sun barred by wood and stone.

"Only a few quick walks," Vidar reminded her as she groggily pulled on her clothes. "Once to the institution and then back before we go to your mother's. The distance will be draining. It's been too long since I've traveled this way. I forgot how much it takes out of me."

He finished lacing up his boots. Sitting back in his chair, he ran a hand through his tousled hair, stretching his arms and back. Enid couldn't help staring as she watched the black shirt strain over the contours of his chest. If it weren't for the fact they had to leave soon, giving Vidar enough time to rest after, she would have pulled him back into bed and stripped that thin cotton fabric from his body. Time was short, though. Instead, she stepped up between his legs, wrapping her arms around his neck.

"Thank you for this," she murmured. "I know it will be exhausting."

He flashed her a smile, hands gripping her waist as he pulled her closer. Need, desire, and some other emotion that she couldn't place drifted through the bond. Was that love? Enid had never been in love before. She had known infatuation. But this deep, intense feeling that ached within her now, that she wasn't familiar with. She only knew it was the same emotion she felt every time she saw Vidar. The same feeling that bloomed and grew whenever they touched, whenever he laughed with her. It was a persistent flame in her heart that burned only for him.

His hand cradled the side of her face. His lips pressed to hers, exploring them gently and thoroughly before backing away, leaving her panting and ready for more.

"If we don't leave now, then I won't be able to pry myself off you." Voice low, eyes dark, his hands traveled to her hips where they tightened incrementally as if he didn't want to let her go. His mouth hovered over hers, ready to claim it again. Reluctantly, she slipped away. Disappointment flared from both sides of their bond.

"Let's go," she sighed.

***

Enid pictured the stairwell to Northspire in her mind. The building itself with the ominous, gloomy atmosphere. The sterile hallways with their locked doors.

"Focus on the stairwell," Vidar whispered.

She nodded, closing her eyes and gripping the leather of his jacket tightly—her own coat zipped up securely to her neck. She took a deep breath, preparing for the vortex of the veil between. The image of the stairwell popped into her mind, the smell of the stale air, the feel of the metal railing beneath her hand.

Vidar held her tight. "Now," he murmured. As one, they took a step.

Shock jolted through her when she hit air, her foot falling before slamming hard against the edge of concrete. She gasped as it slipped. Vidar yanked her back, pulling her to her feet before she could tumble down the steep flight of stairs.

"Shit, I'm sorry. Sorry. I didn't mean to drop us directly on the stairs." He waited until she got her footing. "I'm a little rusty."

Enid gave a slight laugh, her hand on her chest as the racing of her heart calmed.

"It's ok. I'm fine."

She glanced around, noting the numbers posted beside the door, the fine metal mesh within the narrow window.

"You did it," she said with a smile that quickly turned to concern as she looked into Vidar's face. A sheen of sweat sat upon his brow.

"You might as well sit and rest," she said. He was so tired already. She could see it in the way his shoulders drooped. Feel the sudden drain with the bond. "The sun is out. You won't be able to go anywhere else. I'll take care of what I need to for my aunt and make my way here. If I can't, I'll get a cab to my mother's and meet you there." He nodded.

"I wish I could help you through this," he said as he sat down on the step wearily, his eyes drifting uneasily toward the door.

She sent a caress through the bond, her fingers grazing the side of his face and weaving through his hair even as she walked down the stairs to the doorway.

"You are," she murmured. She looked back over her shoulder, her eyes meeting his meaningfully before she stepped through the door.

Thankfully, it was quiet in the hall. All the doors were closed, like the last time she was here. She walked over to the metal doors at the end and peered through the small slit of a window. The room beyond was bright with sunlight from the garden, and also blissfully unoccupied. She hadn't expected it to be this easy. Maybe luck was finally on her side.

Careful and alert, she walked through the halls until she reached the door leading out to the lobby. Peering through the window, she could see the receptionist at her desk, her small hands flying along her keyboard. As quietly as possible, Enid pulled the door open a fraction, and reached into her coat pocket. A ball of cotton and a large bandage sat in her hand. It was all she could find in the cabin at short notice.

Keeping an eye on the receptionist, she tucked the cotton against the door latch and secured the bandage over the top. Now when she slid the door close, it would shut without latching. Hopefully, this would give her a way back in, and no one would come along to find it.

The phone rang at the desk and the receptionist twisted away from her to answer. Before she could turn back, Enid made her way into the lobby, letting the door slide shut behind her. The woman's brunette head dipped below the counter as she opened a door to her side. Enid sent a thank you out to the universe as she took the opportunity, crossing the distance to the front of the desk before the woman came back up.

"Oh!" she shrieked, her hand pressing to her chest in shock as she sat up to see Enid standing before her. A shaky laugh bubbled from her throat. "I didn't hear you come in."

Enid smiled broadly, hoping she appeared relaxed.

"I'm so sorry I frightened you."

The receptionist waved it away as she finished up her conversation on the phone, laughing with whoever was on the other side about her little jump scare. When she hung up, she turned to Enid, a broad smile upon her face.

"Now, how can I help you?"

"I'm here to talk about my aunt. Aislinn Worth?" Enid replied.

The receptionist's eyes widened, sadness and pity overcoming her expression. "Oh, yes." She turned to the computer, tapping at the keyboard. "We have been trying to get in touch with someone regarding her personal effects." She looked toward Enid then, water lining her eyes. "I understand you also lost your mother recently."

Enid nodded, attempting to push the ball of emotion that choked her aside.

"I'm so sorry," the pretty brunette whispered.

Enid almost told her it was ok, not to worry, but it wasn't. It wasn't ok. So, she only nodded numbly, lowering her eyes to her clasped hands on the desk as she blinked back tears, unable to trust herself to speak.

Something wet splashed across her face. Dark, ruby specks flecked the skin of her hands, the dots vibrant alongside the white stars on her mark. Her head shot up.

The receptionist stared at her with wide, surprised eyes. A blood coated blade protruding from the front of her throat. Behind her, Claeg's red eyes glittered triumphantly. His green hand clutched within the receptionist's glossy brown hair. Yanking the knife from her throat, he released his grip, and her body slammed heavily onto the desk before sagging to the floor.

Enid's breath came out of her in the same instance that her brain began to work again.

Run! Vidar yelled through their bond. His anger and distress helped to break her from the shock. Her sneakers squeaked along the tile floor as she rushed back toward the door. Back to the safety of Vidar.

Claeg reached her before she made it past the sun-soaked room outside the garden. His arm clamped around her, and he yanked her off her feet. Through the small windows, she could see down the long hallway. Vidar stood outside the stairwell door, face full of rage as he stared the ghoul down.

"This was unexpected," the ghoul chirped, his foul breath next to her ear. "The Enforcer is alive, and I have his little plaything in my grasp. It was worth the wait. Days spent wandering this place in the hopes you would show up to claim your aunt's remains and here you are."

"You aren't supposed to be here. You were forbidden from leaving Dokkalfar."

The ghoul cackled. "The King will get what he deserves. I don't fear his wrath. Just like I don't fear the Enforcer." His black toothed smile flashed in the corner of her eye, foul breath warm on her cheek.

Down the hall, Vidar turned, his solid frame disappearing into the shadows of the stairwell. The door slammed shut behind him. Enid whimpered, fear gripping her with a tight fist as he vanished.

The ghoul clicked his tongue. "The half-breed wouldn't have stood a chance anyway, even without the sunlight. In case he decides to get creative, let's you and me go outside, shall we? I can show you where I killed Aislinn."

He used her body to slam open the doors, her shoulder and head hitting the glass so hard it made her dizzy. Claeg dragged her over the patio, up the grassy knoll overlooking the garden beneath the massive oak tree. He threw her down on the bench before leaning over her, his beaked nose trembling in excitement.

"A beautiful place to die, right? That's what your aunt thought anyway."

He sat next to her, bony arm encircling her shoulders as though they were two friends enjoying a sunny day on a bench.

"You know, they found her body in her bed. I had to be careful with that part. Have to leave the bodies and make the deaths look accidental. Well, most of the bodies. There were a few choice pieces I was able to reserve for myself. I have friends in the morgue," he explained with a wink. "But I killed her right here, right where you are sitting." His solid, red eyes were expressively joyful.

Enid looked at him in horror, her stomach twisting violently in disgust.

"Why did you do it?" she whispered. She shouldn't have asked, wasn't sure what pressed her to do so, only that maybe if she kept him talking then it would prolong the moment when he decided he was finished with her. She wasn't ready to die.

"Why?" A sneer twisting his lipless mouth over his blackened teeth. "Why?!" He repeated louder. He stood over her, his clawed fingers digging painfully into her shoulders. "Because for too long fae kind has been pressed into the bowels of this earth. We've hidden away, disguised our true nature, and curbed our hunger—starving ourselves. All because the precious humans are too fragile, too easily frightened and broken. Protected by powers greater than ourselves."

He slammed her down onto the seat of the bench, his hand pressing her head into the wood so hard she thought it would crack. She screamed. The blood covered knife appeared in his hand, flashing morbidly in the sunlight as he lifted it high.

"The Revenant Queen will put us in our rightful place, and humans will have a new role in this realm. They will be the cattle and sheep that nature intended them to be. Too bad you won't be around to see it."

The shriek that came from her was so loud that her throat felt like it was burning. The knife began to fall, rushing toward her face.

A gust of wind blew between them, and the knife flew from the ghoul's grasp, flipping away. He hissed and whirled. The wind whipped around him, blowing him back and forth, the sound of windchimes filling the air. Sprites. Enid gasped in relief, falling from the bench and starting to crawl away on hands and knees.

"Not so fast!" Claeg yelled, grabbing her ankle and yanking her back to him. Her fingers dug into the ground, tearing the grass in furrows. Swatting all around him, he fought off the tiny, invisible pixies that pummeled him. There was a loud crack as he made contact.

Enid gasped when a sprite flew into the oak tree. It hit with a sickening splat and the poor creature dropped to the ground. Its limp body angled unnaturally against roots and leaves.

The ghoul cackled before turning back to her.

"Looks like I get to have more fun killing you slowly."

Enid kicked and thrashed as she worked to break his hold on her. It was no use. Within moments he had her off the ground, his unusually strong hands squeezing around her neck. Behind him, the tree shivered violently. Enid's eyes widened, watching the trembling tree as Claeg dragged her back to the bench, throwing her down so hard the wood creaked in protest. A clawed hand drew back and then he gave a choked cry.

The ghoul staggered with a croak, his lifted hand now trying to reach behind him. Stumbling, he turned. It was then that Enid was able to see the dagger impaled deep in his back. From the doorway Adrian prowled forward, rage and hatred fixated on the ghoul.

Beside her, the tree groaned, the wood splintering and warping. There was a crack and a shower of sawdust rained down upon her. In place of the tree, there stood a beautiful woman. A nymph. She stepped from the divot of earth the tree had sat within, and knelt next to the twisted body of the pixie. Every creature stood frozen as she cradled the tiny body in her hands, her long brown hair littered with leaves. As she held the lifeless sprite close, the curtain of hair blanketed it from view. Her eyes turned to the ghoul, full of pain and fury.

She tilted her head.

From the now upturned dirt hole, the ground rumbled. A new tree began to form, twisting and heaving from the earth. Claeg dropped to his knees. Adrian halted in his advance, and Enid could only sit, frozen in place as the tree shifted and grew.

A face appeared within the trunk as it sprang up and up into the air. Twisted and knotted arms sprang from its sides, the ends of which creaked as they formed pointed, claw-like hands. When it towered high above them all, dwarfing the delicate nymph next to it, it turned to the ghoul, a gash of a mouth opening as it roared. The ghoul trembled, mouth hanging open.

The enormous tree creature stepped from the soil, limbs creaking and groaning as it stomped along the grass and stopped before the quivering green fae, who mewled pathetically in fear. It grasped the ghoul around his body, lifting him into the air like a doll.

"No! No!" Claeg shrieked, pushing on the large hand that held him aloft. The tree only watched with an angry sneer. The ghoul was screaming so frantically now, in such high-pitched wails that Enid had to cover her ears. That sound would haunt her. The terror and desperation within that scream heart rending. Claeg continued to squeal, beating on the wooden claw that held him.

There was a snap.

The ghoul's scream was cut short as his body flopped to the side, hanging limply in the grasp of the enormous tree-fae, red eyes glazed and lifeless. Huffing a breath, the creature gave the body a final, testing shake, and then turned toward the nymph. She smiled at the creature, offering it a small bow of her head, which it returned before lumbering slowly back to the hole it rose from.

It paid no heed to either Adrian or Enid as it slung the ghoul's body into the dirt and stepped in on top. The creature stomped in place, rooting itself into the ground, the body beneath it crunching. Then it twisted and morphed, stilling into a tree once more. An extremely warped, and abnormal tree, a face locked in sleep high up on its broad trunk. Its sagging branches hung leafless.

"Thank you," Enid whispered to the nymph. The fae only blinked at her before turning and walking away. The dead pixie still cradled within her hands. Enid stared after her until she felt Adrian rush up to her side.

"Are you ok?" he asked, looking her over for any injuries. She could only nod. Tears pooled as the adrenaline slowly bled from her, causing her to shiver uncontrollably.

"I came as quickly as I could. Vidar didn't have much time to explain what was going on when he popped up out of nowhere and grabbed me." Adrian stopped to look around briefly at the crooked tree, the torn grass, and the cracked bench beneath her. "Looks like you had everything handled."

Enid gave him an incredulous look, and immediately started sobbing.

"Oh, shit," Adrian said.

He helped her to her feet, pulling her back into the building and down the hallway. Vidar stood in the door of the stairwell, fingers white from how hard he gripped the casing. Shadows darkened his eyes. His skin was pallid and clammy. As soon as she saw him, she rushed to him. Slamming into his chest and holding on tightly, her body shivering—tears staining his shirt. He murmured soothing words, hands rubbing her back, his cheek pressed to the top of her head.

"We need to get out of here," Adrian said softly. She felt Vidar nod. He kept her tight against him with one arm, his other reaching out and grasping Adrian's shoulder, and then they slipped into the veil.

It was only a moment, and then they were back in their cozy, little cabin. Vidar began to wobble unsteadily on his feet. Adrian took his arm, helping to keep him upright, the merman taking the brunt of his weight as he and Enid guided him to the bedroom.

"Rest," he said as Enid unlaced Vidar's boots. Already he slept, his arms sprawled out at his sides. "I'll wait out here till nightfall," the merman whispered.

"Adrian?" Enid called softly. He stopped in the doorway, looking back over his shoulder at her. "Thank you."

Adrian gave her a smile and a nod before closing the door behind him. Enid dried the tears from her cheeks, and crawled into bed next to Vidar. The warmth of his body, the steady, slow rise and fall of his chest beneath her cheek soothed her—lulling her into a deep sleep.

CHAPTER

48

Silence. It was too quiet outside of her mother's house when they arrived later that night. Depressing and bleak. Like the silence that hovers around a tomb. The lights that were usually always on at night, showcasing the perfect landscape, were absent. Shadows and sadness filled those places in their stead.

Walking up the steps, she felt an involuntary shiver go down her spine. The spare key still sat in its hiding place beneath the fourth rock on the right. It slid into the lock with ease. As the door swung open soundlessly, she listened to the silence, to the sound of nothing. It felt wrong being here. The shadows of the foyer seemed to mock her.

She's gone. Dead. You did nothing for her. Failure.

Vidar's hand at her back silenced the voice in her head. With a deep, bracing breath, she took a step in. It was eerie, walking inside alone, in the dark. Never again would her mother greet her at the door. Never again would she feel the warmth of her hug. The faint smell of Chanel No. 5 wafted around her. The ghost of her mother. A tear slipped from her eye.

Vidar and Adrian waited patiently outside. Adrian had insisted on coming once she told him about her vision. Esmelial remained in Dokkalfar, pushing for more time and attempting to salvage the illusion that Enid was still in the city, isolated in her mourning. There had been whispers, apparently. Secrets are a hard thing to keep among the fae, and thanks to her vision, she knew the Revenant were aware she was gone.

A light was blinking on her left. The alarm. Automatically she pressed the numerical buttons and hit enter. The light stopped, the alarm shut off. Thankfully the code had never changed. Her broken heart fractured further.

Suddenly, she could no longer take being in the dark. She flipped all of the lights on. The outside porch, the exterior lights, the foyer lights.

Stopping long enough to invite Vidar and Adrian inside, she went room to room, turning on every light she saw. Banning the shadows. Banning the thought of death and loneliness that had enveloped this place, her home. Room to room as if in a frenzy. Even the small powder room beneath the stairs.

Tears blurred her vision, coursing down her face in a constant stream that dripped from her chin onto the floor. Little salty drops lay wherever she went, marking her path as she raced up the stairs and down the hall, flipping switches, throwing back the oppressive emptiness. When she reached her mother's study, she came to a sudden stop. The air left her body and she fell to her knees. Mouth open, eyes wide, she could only stare in shock until her lungs began to beg for air. And still she sat gaping, unable to pull in a single breath.

Distantly, she heard the thud of footsteps, far away, behind the rushing sound that filled her ears. Strong arms were around her, pulling her back, away. She fought it. She didn't want to go. She couldn't leave, but she didn't want to see either.

Among the pile of broken furniture and papers in her mother's study were stained streaks of smeared, diluted blood. As if someone had attempted to clean it, and couldn't seem to get it all the way clear. It painted the walls, the floor, was sprayed along the ceiling and bookshelves like some macabre art piece.

Vidar's voice in her ear pulled her back to herself, away from the rusted stains. Instinct kicked in and she loudly sucked in a breath, feeding the wail of anguish that rushed out of her.

***

She had passed out. That much she was aware of as she came to herself. It was dark and cold. The ground was rough. The ache within her was so strong it was all she knew, all she could feel. Not wanting to move, she lay there, allowing herself to be numb, unfeeling. She hadn't expected to see the blood, the destruction. It was too much.

A sound drew her attention.

"Enid?" Her name, whispered in question by the one voice she didn't want to hear right now. Dimitri.

Sitting up, she drew her knees to her chest.

"Go away," she said softly.

Her voice echoed out through the abyss, the sorrow within it apparent.

"Where are you, my flower?" Dimitri asked, his voice closer now. "Let me come to you, comfort you."

"No."

"You are grieving. I want to be there for you. Hold you. I can help you feel better."

He was beside her now. She felt him kneel next to her.

"I saw where my mother was killed today," she told him.

"I am sorry, my flower. I did not tell my sister's pet that he could do such a thing."

Enid snorted. He was delusional.

"You didn't tell him he couldn't do it either."

Silence.

"Did you know that my aunt was killed too?"

Dimitri's sigh came out of the dark.

"I am sorry," he whispered.

"Leave me alone, Dimitri."

"I cannot do that," he replied.

She felt his hand on her back. Fury rushed through her. In an instant she was up and away from him. Then, as though drawn to her by the force of her emotions, she felt Vidar's cool, calming presence at her back. Leaning into him, she closed her eyes and slipped into the safety of his mind.

The abyss looked different from his perspective. The darkness was not absolute to him. He could see Dimitri standing from the spot she had left. Anger and distress flashing across his features in equal measure. Vidar's right arm went around her protectively, his left fisted at his side.

"You are supposed to be dead," Dimitri hissed.

"Am I?" Vidar replied coolly. "I wasn't aware."

Dimitri's gaze went to her. "What have you done?"

"What I needed to do," she said. "Stay away from me, Dimitri. Stay away from my friends. No one else I care about is going to die."

He bared his fangs, his rage absolute.

"No," he said.

"No, what?"

"No, I will not leave you alone. I cannot."

"You can't, or you won't?"

"I CANNOT!" He yelled.

The rage Vidar kept so precariously tethered snapped. Stepping in front of Enid, he crossed the space to Dimitri and gripped him by the throat. Dimitri's feet kicked in the open air as he was lifted. He glared in hatred at his captor.

"You will leave her in peace. I have had enough," Vidar snarled. With that he threw Dimitri, sending him flying into the depths of the abyss.

"I'm surprised you were even able to pull this off, Dimitri. How did you do it? How did a Revenant create a pathway to Enid through the veil? What lies on the other side? The Realm of Dreams, I'm guessing."

Vidar stalked toward the Revenant slowly as he spoke. Enid could feel his curiosity, and a taste of dread, through the bond. But it was his anger, fiery and hot, that burned brightest.

"It is no business of yours, Enforcer," Dimitri snapped, fangs bared.

"Really? Tell me, why do you meet her in the Between, Dimitri? What lies within your dreams that you don't want Enid to see?"

Dimitri hissed, but he didn't respond. Guilt flickered within the bright blue depths that looked her way.

"You forget, Revenant," Vidar spat, "I am the Lord of the Between."

A roar of anger burst from him, and Enid felt a rush of power as he lifted a fist into the air and slammed it down onto the ground at his feet.

The darkness shattered.

***

Enid awoke with a start in her bed, Vidar at her side. Heavy blankets had been tacked up to block the doors and windows. He opened his eyes.

"It is still dark. The sun is beginning to rise. I wasn't sure how long it would take for you to wake. The Revenant won't bother you now, if you need to sleep."

She threw herself against him, his arms encircling her. Vidar captured her lips in a soft kiss. Reassuring calm flooded through their bond, helping to set her at ease. When he pulled back, he yawned. She could feel the exhaustion within him. Breaking the tether had taken a lot out of him. Dark circles hung heavily under his eyes. The use of his newly returned power *was* draining. He had done a lot of traveling through the veil in the last twenty-four hours, carrying people along with him at that.

"Now I am able to travel again, the Mares are going to be pretty pissed. They've been running rampant lately."

His eyes began to close. Enid leaned forward and pressed a kiss to his forehead.

"Sleep. The sun will be up soon. I'm going to make sure Adrian is ok and I'll be right back."

Vidar hummed in response, his breathe already evening out. The warm presence of him within her head faded as sleep stole over him. She walked quietly to the door, looking back just once to take in the sight, to make sure he was ok now that she couldn't feel him through their bond. Vidar on her bed, in her childhood bedroom, his feet hanging over the bottom edge. Her heart warmed at the sight. Softly, she closed the door.

Adrian was sitting in the kitchen at the small table. A glass of water in front of him, a far off look in his eyes. When she sat down across from him, he turned those worried, aqua eyes to her.

"I am sorry you saw that. It is one thing to lose someone you love. It is another to witness the scene of the event."

Enid turned her head away, looking out the window toward the lightening sky. She didn't want to talk about it, or think about it. Forcefully, she pushed the images out of her mind, and turned toward something she could help to stop.

"Jane was going to be at my mother's gravestone today around two. I don't have my phone anymore to call her, but she may be saved in the contacts on my mother's land line," she said. The phone sat on its cradle in the kitchen. A relic that her mother could never seem to do without. One that she was now grateful for, given the circumstances.

She hunted through the contact list, realizing she didn't know the quiet assistant's last name. Thankfully, there was only one Jane, and very few people actually programmed into this phone. Jane Euploia. Her eyes went to the clock. Seven in the morning. There was a good chance she would answer if she called now. Hitting the dial button, she uttered a silent prayer that this was the correct number.

After a few rings, the call connected. There was silence for a brief moment. "H-Hello?" came the soft, shaky voice on the other side. Enid recognized it immediately. She sighed in relief.

"Jane, thank goodness I found the right number."

"Enid," Jane gasped out. "Enid, I've been looking for you everywhere. Your mother–" Her voice tapered off. "You are calling from the house phone. Enid, the study. You didn't...you haven't–"

"I know Jane. I saw." Enid's voice cracked as the images came back to her.

Jane didn't sound any better. "I am so sorry! I should have called someone immediately to clear it. I tried to do what I could. There was so much and I was so afraid. I'll call someone right away. What was I thinking!?"

"Jane, it's alright. I understand."

"You should have never seen that!" Jane continued, her voice breaking. It sounded as though she were weeping on the other end of the line. Adrian drifted closer, his eyes full of sorrow and concern. "I will have it taken care of this afternoon. I promise."

"That's great Jane, thank you, but don't worry about it today. Instead, I was wondering if you could meet me

411

somewhere? I would like to have more information about what happened."

"Of course!" Jane replied. "There is so much to go over about your mother's wishes and the estate, and I'm sure you'll want to visit her grave."

"NO!"

Jane went silent.

"I'm sorry, I mean—I will, just not today. Could we meet at the coffee shop on Main Street, around noon?"

"Yes, of course. I will bring everything you need to sign."

"That will be perfect," Enid said, releasing a breath she hadn't realized she was holding. "I'll see you then. As Enid hung up the phone she turned to Adrian.

"She's coming."

Hope and joy brightened his face, seeming to light him from within.

"There's a guest room down the hall from my room. Try to get a couple of hours of sleep at least," she said with a small smile.

He tugged his jacket off and ran his hands through his hair, pulling it back into a loose ponytail.

"I don't know how I can sleep. What if she doesn't like me?"

Enid laughed at that. "From what I saw in my vision, she is going to love you."

"I have wished for this moment for so long," he whispered. His fingers reached up and touched the pearls around his neck. Enid smiled at the gesture. Remembering the look of wonder he held when her wishing pearl unleashed its power. The very sentiment he gave her then came spilling from her lips.

"Well, my friend, it looks like your wish has been granted."

CHAPTER

49

A few hours later, Enid sat in the coffee shop. Her eyes drooped from exhaustion. It had taken all her will power to leave the bed and Vidar, who slept so deeply even the kiss she pressed to his forehead before she left didn't cause him to stir.

Adrian was nearly thrumming with excitement as he set a coffee in front of her, and took a sip of his own. His mouth puckered bitterly at the paper cup which he promptly abandoned on the table. Enid smirked, her eyes drifting to the number the barista had scrawled under his name along with a little heart and the phrase 'call me' with an exclamation point. The merman paid it no mind, his gaze on the passing figures outside the windows.

Enid elbowed him, nodding to the door when she saw Jane's familiar head ducking into the shop. She had on the same raincoat and dark jeans she had been wearing in Enid's vision. The sight of her in those clothes was so startling that for a moment Enid only sat there and stared. The vision of Jane's beautiful blank eyes hauntingly clear. The brightness of her blood against her pale skin.

"Enid, I'm so glad to see you're ok," Jane said as she came through the door juggling a briefcase, her purse, and a cell phone. Her feet stalled, causing her to trip, glasses falling from her face as she plummeted toward the ground. Before she hit Adrian was there, catching her easily in his arms. He lifted her to her feet, still holding her close. Enid tried to hide a smile, noticing the instant spark between the two as their eyes met and locked.

"Jane," Adrian breathed as he stared into her face. "You are beautiful."

Jane's mouth snapped shut and she pulled away shyly, her face crimson.

"I-uh, I-" Jane cleared her throat, shaking herself as she stood straight. The formal, rigid assistant's poise coming back to her. "It's nice to meet you, Mr.?"

"Waterman," Adrian said. He took her outstretched hand in both of his, pulling it closer. "Adrian Waterman," he murmured, placing a kiss upon it. "Our children will be beautiful," he said with a white smile.

Enid put her hand over her face.

Jane jumped, yanking her hand away. "What?" she gasped.

"You'll have to excuse him," Enid said with a laugh, "he's European." She prayed Jane would write it off as a cultural quirk. No matter how feeble the excuse sounded.

Adrian picked up Jane's glasses, and handed them to her.

"Thank you," Jane said uncertainly as she took them. She removed her raincoat, her eyes drifting over Adrian, hands nervously smoothing out her gray sweater. Enid watched in amusement as she neatly organized the items from her satchel. Her glasses remained folded on the table top.

"Do you not need your glasses to see?" Enid questioned.

"Oh!" Jane said, reaching for them absently, her face still red. "I-I actually don't need them. They're not prescription. I wear them to feel more…professional," she said with embarrassment. Her hands fiddled with the glasses. "They make it easier to blend in," she murmured.

"A beauty like yours should never be hidden away," Adrian said as he sat in the chair next to her. Jane's flush somehow deepened as she put her glasses on, ignoring the handsome man who stared at her.

"Can I get you some coffee, or tea perhaps? Or both?" Adrian gestured to his cup, his eyes still on Jane. She frowned at the number and message scrawled on the side.

"No, thank you. I'll get it," she said.

"She hates me," he moaned, slumping in his chair as Jane went to the counter.

"She's shy," Enid replied. "Give her time, and don't push her so hard. Just be you."

"I am being me," he sighed.

"At least give her a minute to get used to you before you start talking about kids."

"Okay, okay," Adrian said, rubbing a hand over his face.

Jane came back a few minutes later, a coffee in hand. Adrian stood and pulled her chair out for her. She avoided his gaze, her cheeks pink.

They were there for what felt like hours. Enid signed many things, and was given the deed to the house, which she now owned outright—as well as a few other properties. She signed off on paperwork for the transfer of funds to her personal account, and to cover Jane's payment while she helped finalize the details. Wistfully, she looked at it all. All for nothing. These things would remain abandoned, but it kept Jane safe, being here instead of walking into some Revenant trap. Finally, Jane fidgeted in her chair.

"Another thing I wanted to discuss with you. In the final paragraph of her will, here," Jane pointed out the section with her pen, "your mother left me the beach house. I can't accept it."

"My mother wanted you to have it, Jane. You deserve it after all you have done, and I think it is absolutely perfect for you." Enid gave her a bright smile.

"But I couldn't—"

"Please," Enid interrupted. "It was what my mother wanted."

Jane swallowed and nodded. A tear fell from her eye. "Th-thank you," she murmured, her voice thick with emotion.

"Don't thank me," Enid replied.

"I need you to sign here and here, and we will be done."

Jane pointed out the carefully tabbed signature lines.

Enid signed, smiling at the thought of the assistant at the beach house with a merman for a husband. Maybe there was such a thing as fate after all. The coincidences were too perfect.

Adrian tensed as Jane packed up the paperwork, and Enid followed his gaze. Outside, across the street, stood a fae. A puck, huddled under a raincoat, glamour hiding his goat-like legs and curved horns.

"Excuse me," Adrian murmured, sliding from his chair and striding out into the rain.

The puck turned and ran around a building, the merman walking casually after.

"What an interesting man," Jane said as she watched him cross the road, looking for all the world like someone out for a stroll in a rainstorm. Enid nodded with a smile, trying to hide the worry that crept over her.

"I can see why you've been so difficult to reach, if that's who you've been with."

Enid's eyes widened. "Oh no. It's not like that. I'm actually seeing someone else. Adrian is only a friend."

"Oh?" Jane said, pulling her raincoat on.

"I think he really likes you."

Jane paused, shooting Enid a shocked expression. Enid glanced at the clock on the wall. One thirty. She needed to keep her occupied a while longer.

"What are you doing the rest of the day?" Enid asked, standing to put on her own coat as she followed the assistant out the door. Jane popped open an umbrella and held it up for the both of them to huddle under.

"I was actually getting ready to go to the cemetery to visit your mother's grave, if you changed your mind about going."

Enid was thinking over excuses, trying to find something else to keep Jane occupied when a van swerved up beside them. The door slid open as they turned to look. Two black clad figures jumped out and grabbed them, dragging both women inside.

Her screams were cut off by the hand over her mouth. Enid felt the van pulling away the minute the door slammed shut, and Dimitri's voice was in her ear.

"Why do you make me go to such lengths to protect you, my flower?"

Enid ignored him, her focus on Jane who was crying, her whimpers muffled. Charlie clutched her, inhaling deeply as his nose ran down her neck, fingers already pulling aside her hair.

"Leave her alone!" Enid shouted.

Charlie glared at her with a hiss. Maintaining eye contact, he extended his fangs and bit into the weeping woman. Jane screamed. Enid lunged forward.

"Stop!" She shouted as Dimitri held her in place, his arms securing her against him. She thrashed, bucking and twisting to get away.

The van swerved. "The Triton is here!" Lania cried out.

"Fuck." Dimitri murmured.

Charlie pulled away from Jane to look around, her blood dripping from his lips. She was pale, her eyes rolling back in her head as she went limp in his arms.

"Jane!" Enid tried to jerk herself free from Dimitri, tried to go to her, but he wouldn't release his hold.

A look of fear on Charlie's face told her something may not be quite right. It wasn't until a wisp of water drifted past her face that she stopped struggling. Several of the floating tendrils were working their way into the vehicle through the vents and cracks in the doors. She stared in awed confusion. Nothing in her studies told her about this.

Dimitri ducked away from one, dragging Enid with him. They found Charlie, latching onto him with more force than she thought possible. He began to cough and sputter as they worked their way into his nose and mouth, wrapping around his throat. Jane was gently pulled from his grasp and laid on the ground, the water caressing her carefully as Charlie choked and struggled.

Enid was shocked. Adrian. It had to be.

The van swerved again before slowing to a stop. A gurgling sound came from the driver's seat. The water had found Lania. Dimitri jerked around with a hiss. His sister was pinned to the seat, choking on the water that held her in place. A jet of the liquid hit the windshield hard, and the black substance, some sort of tinting they had placed there to protect from the sun, began to erode. Dimitri cried out as a beam of sunlight hit Lania right between her eyes. The hat and sunglasses she wore didn't protect her from sliver of sunlight. Potent to the Revenant even on a day as cloudy as this one.

Lania let out a garbled scream, her body drowning as she inhaled the water. She slumped over, smoke rising in the air.

Dimitri cursed. Charlie jerked up with a gasp, revived from the drowning. The tendrils lunged toward him again.

"Grab the girl, and throw her out!" Dimitri yelled as he threw a coat over Lania. Enid tried to yank herself away, but Dimitri wasn't giving her up that easily. He maintained the bruising grip on her arm.

Charlie slung the sliding door open, revealing Adrian walking toward them. He was less than half a block away, his arms out at his sides, eyes narrowed as he focused on controlling the streams of water that were only concentrated inside the van. The rain outside hovered like mist as it collected toward them. Charlie jerked Jane's body up. At the sight of the woman, Adrian faltered. The water fell with a splash. He sprinted, rushing to close the distance as Jane was tossed into the air.

Enid screamed as Jane fell, head first, toward the hard cement. Adrian's hand shot out, and a cushion of water formed, slowing her descent as he slid along the sidewalk below her. She didn't get to see if he caught her before the door was slammed shut. Dimitri had Lania out of the seat and Charlie took her place, covering the hole in the tint with his gloved hand as he sped away.

Lania groaned. Her face horribly burned, eyes swollen shut. Dimitri let go of Enid, pushing her into the far corner of the van as he knelt down to check his sister's injuries.

"Don't worry, sister," Dimitri murmured. "I will get you healed."

He pulled his mask off, eyeing Enid coldly as he leaned against the door of the van.

"You have disappointed me, my flower," he stated.

"The feeling is mutual," she snapped. He frowned at her. "Just, let me go, ok Dimitri. Don't do this."

"Do what, my flower?" Dimitri tilted his head to the side. "Love you? Walk to the ends of the earth to find you? Work ceaselessly for us to be together? Defy my Queen and face her wrath. ALL. FOR. YOU?!!"

He moved toward her as he spoke, getting right in her face. Fury evident in his tone.

Enid flinched as a hand went around her throat, the other fisting her hair. His eyes were glacial as she sputtered, searching for air, fingers scratching at his wrist.

"I have been ordered to bring you back, or I condemn myself and my sister to true death. My Queen has had enough of my defiance. I tried to be nice. I tried to be the good guy. Apparently, that is not what you want."

Tears filled her eyes.

He released her, and she gasped, pulling in a lungful of air that felt like glass shards as it passed through her raw throat. Enid turned her back to him, staring at the broken handles of the back doors. Tentatively, she touched her neck. She could feel the bruises forming. Speaking wouldn't do her any good right now. So, she leaned against the side of the van and closed her eyes. Silently praying Vidar would come find her.

CHAPTER
50

Lack of sleep had caught up to her. When she awoke, it was to the sounds of the door grinding open and voices. She was still processing where she was when a hand wrapped around her ankle and yanked her from the van with a hoarse yelp.

They were in a large, windowless, metal building. Other fae walked around, free of glamour. Not another human in sight. The keys of the van were tossed to a fae whose eyes flashed yellow. Shifter. Dimitri kept a firm hold on her, tugging her through the building. Enid didn't bother trying to escape. It was useless.

She was escorted to a door guarded by a lanky, brown creature with large, almond shaped, black eyes wearing a suit. Tufts of dark brown hair stuck up from the top of its head. She hadn't seen a brownie yet. Curiosity was cut short, when they were waved through. The door held open with a polite bow by the brownie.

Beyond lay a narrow, darkened hallway. It reminded her of the jetways to airplanes, but windowless. With dim, artificial lighting for those that couldn't see in the dark. At the end of the walkway was an open door above metal stairs. A train. Alarm bells blared in her head. Where were they going?

Another brownie greeted them as Enid was pressed up the stairs and onto the train car. This one had a head full of long, curly blonde hair. The color contrasted the dark, papery, bark-like texture of her skin.

"Good afternoon, sirs and madam," she said with a slight curtsy to the Revenant. Small, bright white teeth flashed from her cherub shaped face. Her gaze shifted to Enid. "Will you require a cleaning service?" she asked Dimitri with a pleasant smile. Enid felt like she might be sick.

"That will not be necessary," Dimitri said. "We will require refreshment, however."

"Of course," the brownie replied.

The train was elegant. Gleaming wood panels covered the walls and ceiling. Intricate molding graced the window frames and doorways. Black shades were drawn over the windows to keep the sun out. Red velvet covered seats sat in groups of four with a shining wooden table in the middle. Brass handles, knobs and buttons gave it an old-fashioned feel. The sconces, with their soft, electric lights, were the only visible modern touch.

They were led to a private compartment. Inside were bench seats in the same red velvet and a blackout shade over a large window. Dimitri pushed her down onto the bench roughly before taking a seat next to her. Lania sat across from him, her mouth a hard line, swollen eyes full of hate. Charlie was the only one that seemed amused. A wicked grin slid along his face before vanishing behind a neutral mask.

"Where are we going?" Enid whispered.

"We are going home. To Dokkalfar," Dimitri replied coolly. "You have a bargain to keep, a challenge to fail, and a death and rebirth to face."

"How are you so sure I'm going to fail? I've come this far."

He only smirked before turning to look at her with those emotionless eyes of ice blue.

"They are taking forever with those refreshments." He wound his hand in her hair, grabbing a fistful at the back of her head. Enid hissed as the pain. "I am starved," he purred.

His fangs flashed, and then he snatched her toward him roughly.

Agony. Burning, painful agony was what she felt as he tore into the soft hollow of her neck. He sucked greedily at the stream of blood that pooled to the surface, but still she felt it trickle down her back and chest. She cried, slapping at him ineffectually, begging him to stop. Finally, he released her. She was lightheaded.

Her hand went to the jagged tear in the flesh of her neck.

"Sister," Dimitri turned his attention to Lania, his face flush with her blood. "You need to heal. Here."

Enid was tossed, landing in the seat between Lania and Charlie.

The petite Revenant smiled at her brother widely before cradling Enid in a crushing grip. She bit into the skin on the other side of her neck, the pain more intense as her fangs sank deeper and with less mercy. Enid screamed.

"Charlie, you deserve a reward. Go ahead. You have my permission." Dimitri's voice was calm, remote.

Enid looked over at him with wide, pleading eyes. Tears streamed down her cheeks. Lania pulled harder at the gash on her neck.

"Thank you," Charlie whispered, a glint in his glee filled eyes. He leaned toward Enid, voice harsh in her ear, quivering with excitement. "This is only the beginning."

Then he lifted her arm, pushed her sleeve up, and sank his teeth into the bend of her elbow. His dark eyes watched her with wicked mirth as he drank greedily, biting over and over again.

Enid sobbed between screams. Begging them to quit, pleading with Dimitri to stop them. Mercy didn't appear to be on his agenda. He balanced his leg on his knee and picked an invisible fleck of dust from his black pants. Watching her with unfeeling eyes as she cried out again and again before she felt the life within her begin to flicker out.

"That's enough," he said quietly.

They let her body drop to the floor heavily, her head bouncing against the thin carpet. She felt sluggish. Couldn't think. Was her heart still beating? It was hard to count the slow, stumbling thumps. Around her the room seemed to shimmer in and out of focus.

Enid! Enid!

She felt herself being lifted. Dimitri's face wavered in and out of view.

"Enid," he purred, his lips curling into a smile. "You have lost too much blood."

Enid!

She couldn't focus. Was he still calling her name? What was he saying?

"Your wounds are still bleeding. You are going to die."

She moaned, her eyelids fluttering.

Enid, no! I can't reach you. You must live.

"What?" she mumbled.

"I can save you. You need my blood," Dimitri explained calmly. He bit down on his lip. A drop of ruby glistening on his lips. "You only have to come claim it."

A whimper fell from her.

Enid! Don't die! Please!

"Don't die," she muttered.

Dimitri smiled as he helped her sit up. Her head bobbed on her neck. There were cuts and blood all over her. Coldness clawed its way into her body. So very cold. There was a hand on her face holding her head still. She could barely breathe. It was so hard to see.

"If you don't want to die, all you have to do is come here and kiss me," Dimitri's voice whispered through the haze.

Her head lolled to the side. The very air around her seemed to shimmer. Black spots fizzled and popped at the edges of her vision. Distantly, there seemed to be some great, white light sparkling above her. It flared with a wild intensity, serene and full of joy to see her.

Live.

"Vidar," she whispered.

Dimitri chuckled. "The Enforcer can't help you now. We made plans for him."

As though she was feeling the faintest echo of a touch, Vidar was there. It was him. She could feel his fingers, his lips. A sob nearly broke through her in her relief but she was too tired to let it out. She wanted to tell him what was happening, to show him, but she couldn't string together the thoughts. Her mind was in shambles, and her eyes kept getting pulled toward that light. It was so beautiful.

I know, my love.

His voice was a soft caress within her mind.

I am coming for you, but you must live. Don't go to that light. You must open up to your magic. Let the Revenant heal you.

She was so confused.

Enid, Vidar's voice whispered through her. His lips caressed her tear-stained cheek. *You are dying. Open yourself up. Look with your gift.*

She felt his hand over her heart. Even the sporadic flutter of it, achingly slow, still skipped at his touch. Closing her eyes to that distant, twinkling star of light, she turned her attention within herself.

Pythia's words came back to her. How long had she spent locking herself, her power, away? How many times had she hidden it deep, pushing it down farther and farther? Now her very life depended on pulling it forward. On cracking that wall around her heart. It loomed there. High and wide, a barrier to protect, to contain. To imprison.

As she searched for her power, she felt Vidar there with her, helping her, guiding her. She allowed his warmth, his love to envelope her, to fuel her. Then slowly, like a leak through a crack, she felt it. Her power was vibrant and steady, an ocean behind that barrier. It surged as she called it forward. More and more it grew, frothing and bubbling as it rose forth, until it was an avalanche shattering the barrier she spent her whole life building like it was nothing more than a plate of glass.

Her eyes shot open.

Around herself, she could see an aura of white light flickering and fading, in and out. Within that light danced shadows, dying out as the light dimmed and flaring up as bright when it grew stronger. This was what her aunt saw when she looked at her. This was her power, her aura, her spirit, and the black flames that danced within were Vidar. They were right, she was dying.

The auras of the Revenant around her were dull, murky things. Red swirls of mist along with something else. Some sort of blackened tether that seemed to join them. Their Queen. She truly had them leashed to her. Did they know, she wondered.

Before her Dimitri smirked, waiting for his victory to be complete. The tether around him seemed to be more fragile, frayed. The bond to his Queen not as cemented as the others.

Live, Vidar had said. That swirling red mist held the key, and it was within Dimitri. She felt Vidar's hands in her hair, his lips grazed hers, encouraging her. The cut on Dimitri's lips had already healed. Shakily, she reached for the Revenant. He gave her a triumphant smile.

She parted her lips. Feeling like someone dying of thirst in the depths of the desert reaching for an oasis of water. Dimitri bit into the soft flesh of his lower lip once again, letting the blood well up. Still feeling the lingering touch of Vidar's kiss, Enid leaned into the dark Revenant's embrace and pressed her mouth to his, kissing away the ruby drops.

It burned. Jerking back, she cried out as the scorching fire seared through her. The red mist around Dimitri mingled with her light, trying to push back the dark flames.

"Nah-ah-ah," Dimitri whispered as he held her in place. "You haven't had enough."

He brought his mouth to hers, all teeth and hunger. The blood seemed to roast her from the inside, boiling her organs. Tears streamed down her face. The salty drops blended with the fiery blood on her tongue. Fighting the agony, she drew in a small portion of that red misted aura, letting it drift into the fading light of her own.

The burn began to fade.

When he finally released her, the wounds had healed over, leaving only patches of bruising behind. She would live. Enid shuddered. As the pain receded that red mist swirled within the now blazing light of her aura, like a pink haze. Where the haze moved, the black flames danced away, never touching.

"We have the ability to give intense pain as well as intense pleasure, my flower." Dimitri smirked. "Think about that the next time you decide to go against my wishes. The next time could be even more painful, or I could make you gasp and moan in pleasure right here."

He turned her face toward Charlie and Lania. "Or I could let Charlie make you beg him for his pleasure. What do you think about that?" His words were a breathy murmur in her ear.

Loathing coursed through her.
Charlie looked eager.
Lania giggled.
Through the echo of the bond, she felt Vidar's reassurance.
I am coming.

CHAPTER

51

The ground rippled and rolled. Vidar's hands and legs were pinned. He was defenseless. Deep in his mind he knew this wasn't the case. He knew he could control this place. Only his innermost fears and desires warped the landscape around him. Somehow though, he couldn't let go. Couldn't put the fear behind him and focus on what needed to be done.

Tall buildings stretched up into a dark sky, some of them crumbling, others on fire. Sounds of rioting and pillaging reached him. Screams and shattered glass split the air. So similar to a very real, but different night, long ago.

Enid needed him. He had seen that, had felt the flame of her life ebb away and nearly extinguish. It had taken everything in him to push through the confines of this realm and reach out to her. The bond was harder to feel from here. How had he been trapped in this place?

The effort it took to travel had drained him along with breaking the tether with the Revenant. That was the only explanation he had. Hundreds of years of not using his abilities had weakened him. Now he was trapped in another realm. Far from the woman he loved.

The evil, hissing laughter of the Mare echoed around him.

Defenseless, it taunted him. *Useless. She's better off without you.*

Ah, there it was. The reason for his paralysis. Already, as he reached out with his senses, he could feel the squat body of the hairy beast upon his chest. His physical body barred to him by its power.

Vidar growled in defiance. He was aware of the Mare's tricks. The creature would do whatever it could to plant a seed of doubt, to keep him confined here. He couldn't give up. Relaxing, he focused on what he desired. The ground stopped shifting. Gritting his teeth, he gathered his will, sending it out into the ether around him.

Large, glowing, red eyes hovered above him. The Mare. A giant of a creature within the Realm of Nightmares and Dreams. It hissed at him with rows of razor teeth. Vidar roared back, his fury breaking out of him like a shock wave as he yelled in determination. The bonds holding him in place shattered.

As he stood to his feet, he turned to look up at the giant, snarling beast before him.

"How long did you think you could really hold me here, Leto?"

The beast gnashed its teeth in frustration.

"As long as I need to, half breed," the demon spit out.

Vidar rolled his neck back and forth, his fists clenching and unclenching in anticipation.

"Then you better make this count, because it is your only chance."

The beast let out a mighty bellow, the sound rolling and echoing off into the distance, and then it charged. Vidar smiled in anticipation. He could feel the frenzy of the coming battle building within him. Fangs erupted in his mouth, his hearing became sharper as the tips pointed, he felt invincible—indestructible.

The Mare barreled down at him. Vidar shifted at the last minute, his clawed hands grasping the beast's throat. Red eyes flashed in fury, the creature snarled. He growled back as he channeled the power he held to maneuver between realms. On the mortal plane, he felt his body react, hand snatching out to grip the hairy throat of the creature above him. As one, within the dream realm and on the physical plane, the fae's neck snapped. It dropped to the ground. A true death.

Vidar stared down at the Mare's blank, glazed eyes. A winged shadow fell over its face. Vidar's head snapped up to see a form crash to the ground with an echoing boom, blowing wind and dust into his face. Black, feathered wings unfurled as the being stood. For the first time in a long time, Vidar recoiled in fear.

***

When Enid awoke, she was laying on a bed in a strange room. Candles burned all around her. The walls were bright red with the glow of flame. There was no faery light to be seen. Niches were carved into the walls, as was common in Dokkalfar, littered with carved, wooden figures and pieces of shiny rock. A large, oval mirror stood in the corner, next to a niche filled with clothes. Hanging beside it was a white dress of shimmering silk. Enid frowned, recalling a vision she had with Dimitri looking down at her wearing that dress. A different time, before she had made the decision to bind herself to Vidar.

Slowly she sat up, and nearly jumped out of her skin when she found Dimitri sitting in a chair next to the bed. His pale eyes bright against the darkness of the wall as he stared. Shrinking under that penetrating gaze, she looked away.

"You passed out on the train," he said as though she were looking for an explanation.

"Where are we?" she whispered.

"I told you, Dokkalfar," came his reply. Enid suppressed the rush of rage at his tone. Bitterness was clouding him. Stifling the urge to vent her frustration, she took a deep breath.

"And this is your room?"

He nodded.

Enid frowned.

"I would like to go to my room now," she said, standing from the bed.

"No."

"What do you mean, no?"

Dimitri stood from his chair, moving closer until their bodies were touching. Attempting to back away from him, she nearly fell onto the bed. Catching herself last minute, she steadied her breath and her feet beneath her, glaring up at him. His hands were in his pockets as though he didn't trust himself to touch her. That didn't stop his eyes from roving.

She shifted uncomfortably.

"You will remain a guest in my room until your final challenge is completed tomorrow."

Enid hissed a breath through her teeth, an edge of anger biting into her composure.

"I do not want to be a guest here. I want to sleep in my own room."

Dimitri leaned further. His slitted eyes bore hard into her wide ones. "Then think of it as imprisonment."

Enid stared in shock.

"What did you think would happen, my flower," he snarled, tilting his head to the side. "You left the city, without permission, without informing anyone. You were told to remain in Dokkalfar. The human world is no longer yours. You. Are. Fae. You will live as fae, and you will die as fae. That world no longer holds anything for you. If you cannot accept that, you will be executed." Dimitri straightened, his eyes running over her blood-streaked skin. "You will learn to accept it. There are no other options." He stopped, giving her time to let his words sink in.

Tears fell from her eyes unbidden. Dimitri's face softened at the sight.

"When I was sent for you, I was told to make the experience as unpleasant as possible. To teach you a lesson. If I didn't live up to the threat, then my sister and her pet were to step in and do the task for me. Her will is law. We must not forget that."

She was angry. She didn't want to die. She didn't want to be Revenant, trapped in the thrall of a demented Queen.

Dimitri jerked his head toward the door. "Come, you need a bath."

Reluctantly, she followed.

***

The Revenant were in high spirits. Glasses clinked and laughter rang out as she stepped into the dining hall, her arm locked in Dimitri's firmly. The chatter died as they entered, gazes turning to witness her return. She never felt comfortable here. The attention didn't help.

The white, silk dress offered no warmth on her chilled skin. The thin straps and low-cut cleavage left her feeling exposed. It didn't help that her hair was pulled back into a loose braid. She couldn't hide behind the thin, twisted tendrils that drifted around her face. She looked to the ground, attempting to avoid any of the Revenant's stares. There was a snicker from the back of the room, and the conversation continued as though it had never halted.

Dimitri guided her to their usual seats, pulling her chair out and sliding it in underneath her. Dandelion wine filled her glass. For what felt like the hundredth time in an hour she reached out for Vidar through their bond. Silence. Silence and darkness.

Where could he be?

Her stomach twisted within her anxiously, the small bites of food she managed to choke down threatened to come up. She relented to pushing the food around on her plate, as she contemplated tomorrow's events and the whereabouts of her mate. The slight scrape of a chair across from her drew her attention. Lifting her gaze, she met the wide, almond eyes of Cindy.

Head held high, she looked regal in a red jumpsuit, a wide black corset belt cinched in her waist, showing off her curves. The square neckline flowed into a high collar at the back of her neck. Her curls were smoothed back into a high bun with a red jeweled comb pushed artfully into the mass. She looked ready for battle.

Enid nearly fell out of her chair when Cindy looked her in the eye and gave her a subtle, red painted smile and a wink. Only shock kept her from returning it. Her friend seemed to be herself again. Life emanated from her in a golden glow of light that the others seemed to respond to. Enid took a sip of her wine, using the movement to conceal as she swept her eyes around the room. There was more going on here than the Revenant seemed to realize.

Cindy barely had her seat beneath her before her glass was filled. Many of the Revenant came over to murmur greetings. Praise over her outfit choice and beauty were spouted from across the table. She took it all in graciously, offering smiles and small phrases of acceptance to some.

Marcus sat next to her, her ever present protector, his dark eyes hunting for any signs of danger. A red fold of fabric was tucked into the chest pocket of a black blazer. He stood out among the males, the unbuttoned jacket over the customary black dress shirt. A jab of defiance.

Drawing her power forward, Enid really looked at her friend. Her aura was a golden light, flush with the red mist of all Revenant. Only, instead of the murky, swirling cloud that seemed to envelope the others, hers sparkled like glitter within the rays of light.

A golden tether connected her to Marcus, heart to heart. Other, smaller strands of light floated around the room. Wherever they touched the other Revenant, the aura of that creature lightened and shimmered. Those Revenant seemed particularly cheerful. They were the ones who sought Cindy out. The first to address her, the first to see if she needed anything, the first to seek her counsel. It was as though her light was a beacon of hope amid their misery.

A silent hush fell over the room as the Revenant Queen breezed in, surrounded by her red cloaked attendants. A princess style ball gown of red draped her lithe figure. She nearly stumbled on the way to her seat when she beheld Cindy. A frown pressed into the corners of her mouth before she smoothed it away behind a cold mask.

Her attendants buzzed to action as two of them pulled away her large throne-like seat, allowing her skirts to be arranged around her comfortably before pushing her closer to the table. A glass of blood was placed in her hand. Dark onyx eyes beheld Cindy disapprovingly. Enid didn't dare move a muscle. Cindy only smiled brightly.

"Your majesty," she said in greeting with a graceful dip of her head. The Queen arched a brow.

"I believe my orders today were that I was to wear red. In honor of our soon expanding family after tomorrow's festivities."

Cindy picked up her glass of blood giving it a slight swirl.

"Why yes, my Queen. I do believe you did say that." She took a sip of her blood, seeming to assess the flavor meaningfully.

Enid held her breath. She had seen this before. Cindy was notoriously calm and demure right before she really laid into a person. What had happened in the few days she was away?

"Then why, sweet Cindy," the Queen mused, "are you wearing red?"

The tension was palpable. The Queen's dark energy swirled around her viciously. The only sign of her anger was contained within the rolling miasma of her aura. The dark tendrils that connected her to each of the Revenant snapped and tugged in the wake. The Revenant cowered.

Except Cindy.

Cindy remained tall and regal under the icy glare. No connection tethered her to the volatile Queen.

"Why, your majesty, were we not all to wear red in honor of our guest and the dangerous trial she is to face tomorrow? Afterall, in my humanity, she was my best friend."

Cindy turned her attention to Enid, their eyes locking across the table. Gone was the bitterness and anger she had shown before. In that one look Enid knew she had her friend back. All was forgiven. With just that one look Cindy told her what she'd been hoping to hear all along. *I am here for you, my friend.* She gave a tiny smile. Her understanding relayed with a grateful nod that Cindy reciprocated. Tears pooled in her eyes, warping her vision. She blinked them away, taking a drink of her wine to hide them.

"I will use your lingering human emotions as an excuse for your blatant disregard of my wishes," the Queen hissed. "Do not let it happen again."

Cindy frowned as some of the other Revenant whimpered in pain, the angry Queen yanking hard on her invisible leashes.

"Why of course," she stated in the fake, sugary voice Enid only heard her use for particularly difficult people. "I meant no offense."

The Queen only glared a moment longer before she did what Enid was dreading the whole evening. She turned those big, hateful eyes on her, a vicious smile stretching across her painfully beautiful face.

"Welcome back, my dear."

Enid sat stiffly, her eyes moving down to her plate. In an instant the connection she had felt to herself, to her gift, to her friend, it all snapped shut within her. The wall came back up, each brick locking into place.

Danger, her mind screamed at her. *Evil*, her instincts warned.

Beside her, Dimitri took a deep drink of his blood. His aloof coldness leaving her feeling as though she were stranded in shark infested waters.

"I have to say," the Queen continued, "I am so pleased that you decided to break the rules and leave the city before your trials were completed."

Warily, Enid lifted her eyes to the Queen. A self-satisfied smirk adorned her face. A finger traced along the edge of her glass as she leaned against the ornately tall back of her throne-like chair.

"Not only are you now confined to our levels, which gives us so much more time to talk, but your final challenge is going to be much more… entertaining. In fact, we have control of the whole event. All part of the negotiations with my husband. You know, I don't think he ever expected you to attempt anything like this. He was so disappointed." Pausing for a moment, she took a long sip of her blood.

Enid felt like she might be sick. Her food looked less appetizing than it had before. Across from her Cindy wore a frown, her eyes cutting hatefully to the Queen while she wasn't looking. Marcus ran a hand along her arm. The Queen lowered her glass, those ebony eyes sparkling with amusement as they lingered over Enid.

"I cannot wait for you to see what I have planned."

The rest of the meal Enid sat rigid in her chair, unable to eat or drink. Within the turmoil of her anxious mind, she reached out again and again for Vidar. Disappointing silence met her each and every time.

For well over an hour the farce of a dinner continued on, with the Queen spewing taunting insults toward Enid as she picked and poked at the food on her plate. The dandelion wine had begun to make her head spin.

It finally came to a halt when two of the King's guard walked into the room, paying no heed to the hissed warnings of the Queen's sentries at the door.

"What is the meaning of this?" The Queen demanded.

"King Fenri has requested your presence in the throne room, along with that of the human."

The Queen's eyes narrowed dangerously.

"Why?" she asked. "He knows that the human is my prisoner now. It was part of our agreement."

The shifter was unfazed, even as the sentries crept closer, their sharpened weapons lowered in warning.

"There is a ... visitor, who has requested an audience. That is all I am at liberty to say."

The Queen tapped a nail on the side of her glass thoughtfully. Curiosity won out over her pride.

"Very well," she said, setting the glass down and motioning to her attendants. The throne was pulled away from the table.

"Dimitri, bring the human," she said over her shoulder as she stood and walked from the room. Dimitri stood dutifully, pulling Enid to her feet, and locked her arm in place within his. As though he were a gentleman taking a lady on a stroll. Only the tightness of the unyielding grip betrayed it for what it really was, captivity. She barely had her feet beneath her before she was pulled along, the Queen's red attendants surrounding them as they followed.

CHAPTER

52

Enid walked along behind the Queen, her eyes downcast. Dimitri propelled her forward, guiding her through the maze of tunnels.

The plainness of the King's throne room was a stark contrast to the Revenant's dining hall. It was no surprise to her now that she knew them. King Fenri loathed the ceremony and the frivolous pageantry that the Revenant Queen seemed to thrive on. This room was for necessity, not to show off might or power. The King prowled below the throne dais. His face contorted in rage and worry.

Casually leaning against the platform, unconcerned about the four shifter guards that surrounded him, was a man Enid had never seen before. He watched the King with a look of entertained delight. Power emanated from every fiber of his being. Enid didn't need her sight to notice the way the very air seemed to crackle around him.

She was reminded of the Greek statues she used to see in the museums with his full, wide mouth, strong nose, and square jawline. Long, wavy, midnight hair hung to broad shoulders. His eyes were the pale color of moonlight that flashed with light as they shifted around the room. Taking in everything with bored arrogance.

"Morpheus!" The Queen exclaimed, opening her arms in greeting.

"Isis," he replied with a smirk and a slight bow. "You are ravishing as always."

He took one of her hands in his, giving it a quick kiss. The giggle that came from the Queen took Enid by surprise. A flash of quicksilver was directed her way as the strange man took her in from head to toe, those strange eyes shimmering.

"And who do we have here?"

King Fenri stepped forward, his dark eyes narrowed.

"Enid Washbourne, this is Morpheus, King of the Realm of Dreams and Nightmares."

Enid shrank back as Morpheus came toward her. Dimitri released her arm, stumbling away as though pushed to the side. His face was strained as he tried to fight the movement, but couldn't.

The air around her snapped with electricity.

Effortlessly, she called forward her sight.

The aura around Morpheus was so large, it nearly engulfed the entire room. The others seemed to bend and shrink within it. Stars and small flecks of shimmering light rolled and swirled within the dark space of his aura like tiny galaxies. At his back arched the shadowy form of feathered wings.

The red miasma of the Queen's aura reached toward the darkness as though trying to attach itself to the spatial mass. It was pushed back each time, compressed. The Queen seemed oblivious that her deceptions were not working as she smiled brightly at the King of Dreams and Nightmares. King Fenri shifted, his body tense. Each time his dark gray aura was pressed upon he bristled, his eyes darting over to Morpheus. Enid couldn't help but notice the anxiety that lay within his gaze.

Only her bright white aura remained untouched. The edges melding and dancing along with the dark colors of his, lightening and shifting them into shades of dark blue, purple, and gold. Vidar's shadowy waves lingered within still, twisting from the colossal aura surrounding her. The only proof she had that Vidar was still alive, still connected to her.

"Enid Washbourne," Morpheus said slowly as though contemplating the syllables of her name. "It has been eons since I have seen a hybrid who is so...fascinating."

"She is soon to be one of my children," the Queen interrupted, stepping forward to place a hand on Morpheus's arm. He paid no attention.

Dimitri's hands clenched at his sides. He tried to move a foot forward, his face straining with the effort. A toe shifted, and then he was shoved back another foot. The Queen frowned.

"Is that true? You have chosen to be claimed by one of these creatures?" Morpheus asked. He leaned toward her slightly as though no one else in the room mattered. Like the conversation was private only to themselves. Enid felt her face burning from the attention.

"No, I have not. I have one last challenge to complete. If I pass it, then I am free to choose my own path."

"Is that so?" Morpheus replied. "And what path have you decided on?"

She looked around uncomfortably. "I wish to keep that to myself until I've won tomorrow."

That answer seemed to please him. A slow smile stretched across his face.

"Mysterious. And confident. How interesting."

Morpheus stepped away. Enid nearly let out a sigh of relief as the pressure around her eased. Dimitri rushed to her side. The Queen flashed her a dark look.

"Maybe you can help King Fenri and I out with a little issue we are having," Morpheus said as he made his way back over to lean against the dais. "One of his creatures has found its way into my realm and killed one of my subjects. We are deciding his fate."

With a flick of his hand an image shimmered into view.

Vidar.

He hovered unconscious in the air, hung from invisible chains. Enid gasped, instinctively stepping forward, her hand reaching. Dimitri grabbed her arm, holding her in place.

Morpheus smiled lazily, unsurprised by her reaction.

"I see," he mused. His eyes seemed to move all around her as though he was observing her aura the way she had his.

Enid only had eyes for Vidar. He was hurt. She could see claw marks along his chest, the blood barely oozing through the jagged rips in his shirt. His head was slumped to the side as

438

though in sleep, but the line between his eyes furrowed as he grimaced.

"Is he ok?" Her concentration remained on the image, but her pleading words were directed toward Morpheus.

There was a spark of static at her left, cracking against her skin. She jolted. Morpheus stood over her shoulder, looking down at her. One second, he was across the room, and the next he hovered right over her. A finger of fear tripped up her spine, sending a shiver in its wake.

"It would seem that the Mare put up quite a fight," he murmured.

He lifted a hand to her shoulder, the very tip of his finger tracing the curve of the triple loop mark under her collar bone. Enid paled. Dimitri growled in warning, his grip on her arm tightening as he yanked her closer to him. Morpheus' moonlit eyes flicked dangerously toward the Revenant, a sneer forming along his lips. Dimitri was once more shoved away. Shadowy wings snapped outward at Morpheus' back. She flinched. The movement drew his attention to her. Dimitri once again no more than a fly in the background.

"I was going to kill the interloper for his transgressions, but you have intrigued me. I will give you a chance to come to my realm and claim him. Until then, he will remain my prisoner, locked in an endless nightmare."

Enid drew in a sharp breath.

"You forget Morpheus," the Queen called out. "The girl will be one of my children come tomorrow."

"*If* she fails the final challenge," King Fenri grumbled, his massive arms crossed over his chest. The tension he carried stiffening his stance.

Morpheus remained looking at Enid. "I think she may surprise you, Queen Isis."

The Queen's dark eyes narrowed angrily. "She will not pass tomorrow's challenge."

"What are you planning, Isis?" King Fenri snapped.

The Queen chuckled. "It is of no concern to you, Fenri. We made a bargain. You cannot attend or interfere. The Revenant will manage the final challenge."

Morpheus raised an eyebrow. "Win this challenge quickly. Your bonded mate will not last long trapped within his nightmares. Even the strongest break within their terrors."

Enid faced Morpheus, her hands clasped in desperation. "You can't do this to him."

A shadow crossed his face. The very room seemed to darken as his wings flexed outward.

"I can do as I please," he snarled. "I alone rule in my realm. My will regulates its order and design. My orders are obeyed to the letter. My commands a decree. Only mortals have the luxury of free will. In my realm, my word is law. I have only to wish something into existence and it is so. Do not deign to tell me what I cannot do."

Enid trembled, stepping backward as Morpheus seemed to loom over her larger and larger as he spoke, his features darkening, twisting into a fanged nightmare. His eyes glowed, sparks shooting from them like lightning as they narrowed into slits. Those dark wings cast a blackness over her, isolating her from the rest of the room until all she saw was him. All she felt was his anger.

"Come find us, win back your love. If you can."

Absolute blackness swept over her and then her vision returned to normal. Only Morpheus was gone. Vanished.

"Wait!" Enid cried out. "How do I get to your realm?"

His disembodied voice echoed around them, fading away as though slipping through the cracks of time and space. "When the time comes, the way will open."

Everyone was silent for a moment as the final echoes of his voice melted away. Then the Queen whirled on Enid with a hiss.

"Do not even dream that you have a chance of succeeding tomorrow. You will not. There is no hope for you. You will fail, you will die, and then you will be mine."

Her attention snapped to Dimitri. "Take her away. Lock her in one of the cells. I don't want to see her face until tomorrow at the challenge."

"My Queen, I thought she was staying in my room."

"I CHANGED MY MIND!" the Queen roared.

Dimitri cringed, his head lowering in submission. He grabbed Enid's arm and yanked her from the room. The Queen's fury seemed to press at their backs as she was dragged along, barely keeping her feet beneath her in Dimitri's haste. It was only when they made it to the level below that he risked speaking.

"There isn't much time," he murmured, pulling her closer so that the low notes of his voice carried to her ears alone. "There isn't much that I can do except give you my blood to strengthen you. When the time comes, accept it. If you reject it, you will not live. This challenge is not what it seems."

"What is the challenge?" Enid whispered.

Dimitri's jaw ticked as he ground his teeth together, seeming to search for words. Pain lashed his face. Finally, he spoke, his eyes darting around as they marched through the spiraling pathway of the Revenant market. Few creatures littered the path. Still, Dimitri kept his voice soft, lips barely moving.

"I've been sworn to secrecy. I can't say."

Enid's mind whirled. For the first time, she had no help. No idea what to expect. The Revenant kept her locked away from the other fae. She had no idea where any of her friends were. The Sirens were nowhere to be found, not that she'd been given a chance to search them out. Adrian was hopefully taking care of Jane. Vidar was the prisoner of a powerful King in another realm. She was utterly, desperately alone.

Dimitri directed her to a hall she didn't recognize. The light was poor here. The walls barely shaped, the rock roughly hewn as though no care was spent to make them. Barred doors covered niches that were barely big enough for a single person to lay comfortably. He stalked to the farthest one, and opened the door.

Enid grasped the front of his shirt in desperation, pulling herself against him as he attempted to push her into the small space. He froze, body stiffening, eyes softening as they met hers. She had to try, for Vidar, for herself. She needed him to listen, to help.

"Please," she pleaded. "Is there nothing you can do? Nothing you can say to help me?"

Hesitantly, he reached a hand to her face, his thumb lightly grazing her cheek.

"I can't," he whispered, his voice cracking with emotion. "You chose the Enforcer."

441

"I did," Enid replied. "Is there no part of you that can forgive that? That can care for me as a friend? Are you so quick to dismiss me? To see me dead? Did you love me at all if you are so easily able to hate me now?"

Dimitri's eyes flashed with anger and he glanced down the hall before turning back to her. The hand on her face moved to the base of her neck and he pulled her closer, his lips hovering above hers.

"I do not want you dead. You should have been mine. I can't bear to see you with someone else, but that does not mean I hope for your demise. I only wanted your love." His words were rushed and soft.

"What is the point of warning me about this challenge if you can't help me?"

Dimitri's jaw clenched. "I needed to do something, anything."

"I am disappointed in you, Dimitri. I chose Vidar and I will not regret that. He is what I needed. You hurt me. You hurt me in ways that were cruel and vindictive. I know it was because of your queen. I understand that, but you are a coward for letting her so easily control and manipulate you."

Her hand uncurled from the fabric of his shirt and she laid her palm flat against the spot where his heart should beat. Pain flashed across his face, but he remained still.

"You have known nothing but pain and torment over the course of your very long life. The trauma of your childhood drove you into the arms of a Queen who twisted you into a creature that mirrored her own cruelty. But I've seen the good in you, the light that shimmers beneath. You are so much more than what she has made you. You can be so much more. Don't let her stamp out that goodness."

Slowly Dimitri's hands encircled her biceps. His blue eyes glued to hers. Gently he moved her back into the cell before letting her go and closing the door with a soft click.

For a moment they only stood there, looking at each other through the steel bars. Enid's words hung between them. Emotion seemed to war within Dimitri. His mouth opened, and then closed. A response he couldn't seem to bring himself to say swimming within the depths of eyes before he turned and walked away.

CHAPTER

53

Esmelial was seething. The Revenant were up to no good. Enid was back. According to Adrian she had been in Dokkalfar for hours. Taken by the Revenant. The merman confined himself to his rooms, his clansmen with him as they looked after a frightened and hurt human woman. Adrian murmured comforting words to the trembling female as the Siren stood in the doorway. The human's eyes widening at her nakedness.

"Clothes are too confining," Esmelial explained with a roll of her eyes as the female blushed and looked away from her. "You'll find our concepts of nudity aren't as modest as most humans."

The human didn't respond. Only leaned in to Adrian, whispering words she couldn't hear.

"I'm sorry. I will explain everything, I promise," he replied before he turned to Esmelial once more. "Enid is in danger. Do you think you can find out what the Revenant have planned? There is talk that no one but them will be allowed at the final challenge. One way or another, they will not let her walk away this time."

Esmelial nodded. "I will see what I can find."

She hadn't told anyone other than her sisters who her contact was. And even they didn't know the thrill and longing she tried to deny when she went to see him. The same feeling she had now as she made her way through the tunnels.

The Revenant levels were remarkably quiet. Probably at some dinner the Queen was holding. Her delicate sense of smell picked up what she was looking for, and she followed it. A voice caught her attention. Female, husky with desire.

"Come on, William. The Queen won't mind. What is the point of immortality if we don't allow ourselves to indulge in pleasures."

William's deep sigh reached her next. Esmelial edged closer to the wall, listening intently as she came upon a corner.

"I may be forced to give myself to the Queen, but that doesn't mean I'm free game for her lackeys."

"Forced!" The high-pitched voice colored with anger. "You are blessed to receive the honor of her ministrations. Her pleasure is our ultimate goal. You are favored, William. Do not make me change that for you. If you are very good, and please me, I will guarantee you a place at the Queen's side when she makes her final move."

Esmelial stilled.

"What move?" William asked.

"Come with me and find out," the woman crooned.

Esmelial had enough. She rounded the corner, taking in the sight of a red robed woman draped over William. They turned to look as she sauntered toward them. She sniffed at the air. The woman was coated in lust. William not so much. Not a hint of it lingered in his scent. That is until his eyes began to move along her as she crept closer. She smiled at him. The woman growled angrily.

"Do I sense a meal in the making," Esmelial breathed.

"Not for you, whore. What do you think you are doing down here?"

She pulled away from William, taking a step toward Esmelial. William yanked her back against him, his mouth at her ear.

"Don't waste your time on this one. We were just about to get to the good stuff."

The female smirked, rubbing herself against him with a hum of delight.

"Get out of here, Siren, or I may have to turn the Queen's wights on you."

Esmelial kept her face blank despite the disgust she felt at watching her writhe against William.

"Now, now," William murmured. "You know the Queen's rejects are immediately destroyed."

His eyes remained on Esmelial. The rejects. Wights. Esmelial paled. Oh gods.

"I'm sure the Siren has more important things to do," he continued. "After all, she isn't welcome here."

The Revenant was still glaring at Esmelial hatefully until William spun her around and pinned her to the wall with his body. "Now where were we?" His lips crashed against hers and she moaned, arms slithering around his neck as she returned the kiss with enthusiasm.

Esmelial was forgotten.

The Siren backed away, a part of her cringing at the sight of William so intimate with another. The other part of her laughed at herself. What was that about? She was a Siren, he was Revenant. Their arrangement was purely one of convenience. She'd had hundreds of males over the centuries, and there would be hundreds more. This one was of no consequence.

Still, her hands fisted, her teeth clenched as rage filled her and she rounded the corner, back the way she came. She was only a few tunnels away when a firm hand grasped her arm. Esmelial hissed, talons flicking out. William held his hands up.

"Shouldn't you be fucking that Revenant right about now?" Esmelial spat. William raised a brow.

"Is that jealousy, sweetheart?" He stepped closer. "Do you want me all to yourself?"

Esmelial shrugged. "It is no concern of mine."

His eyes darkened. "You shouldn't be here. This is dangerous, for both of us."

She looked around, her ears primed for any sound.

"I had to."

Without another word, William took her arm and pulled her along with him, walking briskly. After a few turns, they reached a door. "Come in, Siren," William said as he tugged her into the room. Esmelial stumbled inside. He turned and closed the door after them.

His room was neat. A made bed. A chest of drawers. A comfortable looking chair with a lamp and a small table. A decanter of his favorite whiskey in a nook with sparkling crystal glasses. And old, bound books. Shakespeare. Esmelial didn't know what she expected, but it wasn't this.

William was watching her with a look that bordered on hunger and frustration. He stepped toward her.

"What are you doing down here, Esmelial? You're lucky most everyone is at the Queen's dinner, or you would be toast right now." Esmelial stepped back as he advanced.

"I need to find out when the next challenge is." Her back hit the wall.

"That's common knowledge," he said. "Tomorrow." He braced a hand on the wall above her, leaning into her as he spoke.

"Where? What is it?"

He clenched his teeth. "I can't say."

Esmelial bit her lip in frustration. His gaze flicked to her mouth at the movement.

"It is like you told me in the club. The secret place that only the Revenant know. It's connected to this level, isn't it?"

He gave a single, pained nod. "Please don't ask me anymore," he whispered. He trailed fingers through her hair. "You have put yourself in danger by coming here and risked exposing me, as well. You've been a very bad girl."

Esmelial hummed. Desire radiated off of him. It was enticing. She inhaled the scent as she stepped closer, her hands running along his chest as she whispered in his ear.

"Are you going to punish me, William?"

"You would like that," he replied. "I don't reward bad behavior." He spun her around, her back to his chest as he twisted a handful of her hair in his hand, his other arm around her waist. Fingers caressed her side, sending tingles of heat along her skin.

Esmelial arched against him, lifting her face to the underside of his jaw. From his vantage point he could see the length of her. She used it to her advantage, her mouth trailing along his jawline as he stared down her body with dark eyes. Esmelial allowed her hands to wander, showing him all the places she liked to be touched. He hardened against her.

"That's a shame. I can be a very bad girl." She nipped at his neck.

William hissed, his hands quickly undoing his pants as he pushed the front of her into the wall. When he thrust into her it was with a deep, satisfied growl. Esmelial smirked, her hands planted against the hard surface as she pushed back against him with a roll of her hips. He cursed.

"Good girl," he moaned.

The words, paired with the tone of pleased dominance, struck a chord within the Siren. Her core clenched around him, her lower back dipping with a gasp. He released the fistful of hair, running his hand down the curved length of her spine before gripping her hips tightly.

"That's right, sweetheart. Give me everything you got."

Esmelial smiled wickedly, a silver glow reflecting off the wall.

CHAPTER

54

Enid wasn't sure how long she was in that cell when shuffling footsteps grabbed her attention. Hesitantly, she stood up as two of the Queen's attendants came into view, red robes swirling around their feet.

"Our Queen has asked for you, human," one of them said curtly, already unlocking the door.

The other reached in and grabbed Enid by her arm, pulling her, stumbling, into the hall.

"What does she want?" Enid asked. They guided her along, her feet barely touching as they dragged her between them.

"That is not for you to question," the angry one hissed, her short blonde bob swaying. "She asks, we obey. Do not forget that."

When they came upon a large set of wooden doors, the blonde let her go and led the way into a waiting area where they passed through another set of doors. These appeared to be recently made, the smell of stain and wood still fresh in the air.

In the chamber beyond there was a large hearth, a fire crackling within. On either side stood Cindy and Marcus, and before them, two leather chairs with a small table between. In the chair on the right, sat Isis, her back rigid, her hands delicately placed at the end of each arm. As Enid was thrust into the empty chair next to her, the Queen turned to her with a smug smile.

"Hello, my dear."

Enid frowned at her, eyes darting to Cindy and Marcus.

The Queen chuckled. "Since you arrived in our court, I have had so many issues. This one has become increasingly insubordinate," she waved a hand at Cindy, "and you...well, you're you." She leaned back in the chair, her fingers fiddling with the chain of the large ruby that hung there. "So, I have decided to kill two birds with one stone, as they say." She smiled wickedly. "You and I will have a little chat, and my newest subject will learn her place."

Isis sat up once more on the edge of her chair, snapping her fingers. When she did, Cindy went to a serving cart and poured blood into a delicate, crystal glass. This she presented, bowing as she held it out before her.

"That's not what I asked for Cindy, dear," the Queen warned, her tone light but firm.

Cindy dropped to her knees, shuffling forward. Delicately, so as not to spill a drop, she lifted the glass to the Queen's lips. She drank deeply, her onyx eyes sparkling. When she was satisfied, Cindy placed the glass on the table next to them, within easy reach. Anger flashed in her eyes, but she kept her mouth shut, her head lowered in submission.

"You missed something." The words were low.

Cindy was breathing deeply now, the rise and fall of her chest evident as her cheeks burned with fury. Slowly, she sat up, her eyes meeting her Queen's, fire within them, despite the fact she was relenting. A ruby drop of blood lingered on Isis's full lips. Cindy's hands went to the other woman's face, and she kissed that drop away. She kissed her like she would kiss a lover. A lover she hated.

Enid looked away from the sight, her own anger amplified by watching what her friend was forced to do. Marcus stared straight ahead, unblinking, unmoving. Acting for all the world as if he were oblivious to what was happening. Finally, Enid couldn't take it any longer.

"I thought you wanted to talk," she snapped.

The Queen pulled away, lips cleansed of the blood and swollen from the kiss. Cindy looked like she might be sick as the Queen waved her back to her place.

"Very well," the Queen responded. "Let me tell you a story."

Her gaze didn't turn to Enid as she spoke, but remained focused on Cindy and Marcus, almost as if she were telling the story to them—Enid nothing more than a casual observer.

"Once upon a time, there was a land ruled by mystery and magic. In this land, Kings weren't men, they were gods. Every aspect of life was done in servitude to these gods. Great temples were built, offerings were made, women and men alike gave themselves to the worship of these divine beings. And I was a lowly priestess in one of those great temples."

The Queen's eyes darkened.

"One day, our King, our god, came to visit the temple, to see what gifts he may glean, what offering he may leave for a successful battle the next morning. Now, this god enjoyed watching the priestesses work, and though it was forbidden for them to perform acts of a sexual nature in this temple, the god did not care. His appetite was insatiable. The other priestesses often warned each other to steer clear of the god when he would come to visit, especially on the nights when his bloodlust was high, such as on the eve of battle."

She stopped speaking then, her head tilting to the side. "Marcus, you look famished. Please, have some blood."

Marcus walked toward the table with the decanter.

"No, no, Marcus," the Queen called out. "Take it from Cindy."

Marcus stiffened, but turned, albeit reluctantly, and stepped up to Cindy.

"And Marcus?"

He lifted his gaze to her.

"Make it hurt." He frowned, his eyes widening.

"Now, where were we," she sighed as she watched Marcus bite into Cindy's neck. "Oh, yes. The god was crazed with his desire for the blood of his enemies, and so he went to the temple. I had heard the rumors, the stories of young priestesses that had the bad luck to be at the wrong place, at the wrong time. In the arrogance of youth, I truly believed such things would not happen to me. I was much loved, a favorite. My beauty and passion for the gods, for life, for worship would protect me. I was so very, very wrong."

She paused, examining the pained look on Cindy's face. Marcus continued to drink, standing at her back, cradling her in his arms. Occasionally, he would shoot a furtive glance toward the Queen, as though begging permission to stop. Cindy didn't utter a sound. The Queen merely watched. Enid felt the seconds tick by, her nerves fraying at the seams.

"It used to be," she finally continued, "that the fae were creatures of such magic, that they were regarded as gods, and occasionally appeared to us as such. In those days, their magic was strong. Their favorites were rewarded with gifts, or favors. One of the most revered magics was that of the mate bond. Back then, it wasn't the paltry thing it is today. Then, a fated pair only had to meet each other's eyes, and they would know, they would feel it within their bones, that this was their other half. That all changed not long after this fateful night. The night the false god stole into the temple priestesses' quarters and raped them, one by one."

Cindy was swaying on her feet, her face pale, Marcus's arms kept her upright. Enid couldn't take it anymore.

"Make him stop," she whispered, her voice trembling.

Isis tilted her head to the side. "Not quite yet." The smile she turned to Enid was full of malice.

"As I was saying, before I was so rudely interrupted, that night the King crept into my room, already having visited a few of the other priestesses, mind you. It wasn't until I felt him thrust inside of me, breaking the sensitive skin of my maidenhead, that I knew he was there at all. He was stealth incarnate, the epitome of the warrior he so desperately prayed to be. The demands he made of my body were harsh and insistent. I must have pleased him greatly, because he took me several times that night. My crying and pleading only seemed to further excite him. When he was finally finished with me, I was bruised and bloody—a beautiful, broken doll."

She stared at Cindy for a moment, watching her eyelids flutter, her body sag. "He called me as much when he stood over me and released himself one final time on my broken body. Then he leaned down and whispered, '*You have pleased your god this night. You may please me again in the future.*'"

A frown pulled at her lips as she invoked the memory. "The King won the battle that morning, and to celebrate, he ordered a great feast and visited the temple to make an offering of thanks. He was true to his word. I pleased him very much that night as well. I pleased him so well that it wasn't long before I was swollen with child." Her hand slipped to her abdomen, a faraway look in her eye.

"Alas, it was not to be. I was disgraced, forced from the temple. The King's wives discovered my shame and I was sent for. They looked down on me. Hated me for being pregnant with the baby of a god, when so many of them weren't able to conceive at all. So, I was kept under lock and key, and when the time came my child was taken and given to one of the wives to raise as her own. The child was not well cared for. It did not survive. I was lost in my grief, angry, and desperate for vengeance, and so this time I gave an offering to another. A goddess. She felt the purity of my pain, my hatred, and she granted me my desire. And so, I was made Revenant, and would go on to have many more children. After, of course, I drank my fill of the blood of my enemies. I bathed in it, gorged myself on it, until finally my anger was satiated."

Cindy went limp in Marcus's arms. The Queen frowned. "Lay her on the floor Marcus, we will continue her punishment when she awakens."

She continued her story. "Unfortunately, that apparent relief was short-lived. The anger still thrived within me."

She watched Marcus carefully lay his lover on the ground, eyes full of grief as he checked her over. A hint of a smile tugged at the corners of Isis's lips. Enid watched for the unbearably slow breaths that Cindy took. Her hands clenched so hard on the arms of her chair that her knuckles ached. Next to her, the Queen continued speaking, much to Enid's dismay.

"You see, the goddess stole something from me, when she made me Revenant. Something I would learn was dearly missed. So, I took my vengeance on her. In turn, she placed a curse upon me, upon all her children, and thus the prophecy came to pass. A way to break the curse."

The Queen's fingers found Enid's chin, twisting her face toward her.

"You, my dear, are the key."

Her attention drifted to Cindy and Marcus. Cindy pale and still, the light of the fire flickering along the contours of her face. Marcus on his knees at her side, his head hung in shame.

"My Revenant will forever be true to only me, or they will face the consequences. You will be one of them soon, bound to me until true death. You will help me take control of this realm. I am owed. For the cruelty of humanity, for the loss of my innocence and my child. I will bring this world to its knees."

Her face was cold and beautiful as she looked down her nose at Enid.

"Marcus, go get the others to escort Enid back to her cell, and be quick. I have other things I need you to satisfy before I sleep." Her smile was sinister as Marcus left the room. "Tomorrow you will face the final challenge and you *will fail*. It is for that reason alone that I have told you this much."

As Enid was dragged from the room between the two attendants, she caught a glimpse of Marcus kneeling before the Queen, her robe slipping from her lithe body. She thought she might vomit as she was dragged back to her cell and thrown inside. The woman, no, that *demon*, was truly demented. She had to be stopped. She shivered uncontrollably as she curled into a ball on her side, praying that Cindy would be ok. That the Queen wouldn't break her.

***

Enid didn't know how long it was before the first vestiges of sleep began to claim her. She knew that her legs were cramped and her back ached as she lay at the rear of the niche. The sun had to have long since been high in the sky in the world above. Slowly her eyes drifted close.

She was standing at the mouth of a cave, looking out onto a lush green forest. A single curl of smoke drifted into the bright, moonlit sky in the distance. Large, strong arms encircled her comfortingly. With a sigh she leaned back into the muscular chest.

"Vidar," she sighed, a smile playing upon her lips. She went to turn toward him, but his arms tightened, holding her in place.

"Don't move," he said, his voice strained. "It's taking all of my focus to be here right now." His words rumbled at the back of her head. She stilled, only moving enough to look up at him.

He was gazing down at her, eyes full of pain but also joy. "You have no idea how good it is to see you, even if only in the space between dreams."

"How can I help you?" she said. Her arms went to his, holding him tighter to her as though she could anchor him.

He gave her a smile, the dimple on his cheek showing. Her heart fluttered.

"You need to focus on your last challenge," he said. "I need you to survive." His hand stroked along her cheek lovingly.

"I don't know how. The Queen is up to something."

Vidar's smile melted away. "I wouldn't be surprised," he said. "However, you are stronger than you think. She underestimates you. You can use that to your advantage."

Enid frowned up at him, uncertainty flaring within her. How could a human, even a human with fae blood and a power she couldn't control, defeat a legion of Revenant?

Vidar stooped so that his lips grazed hers, holding her tight. Enid stepped on her tiptoes. Her lips tingled where they touched.

"Use your power, and mine locked within you," he whispered against her mouth. "Somehow you should be able to access it. It's there. It's part of you. Don't block it out. Embrace it."

"I have embraced it," she insisted. "I can see it. I can see everyone's aura, their power, swirling around them."

Vidar smiled brightly. "Good," he murmured. "Now you have to figure out how to guide it to your will. You are so strong. I know you can do it." His lips claimed hers.

Enid nodded when he pulled away, gasping. "I will do my best. For you," she whispered. "I will find you."

Before she could help herself, she twisted in his arms, and crushed her mouth to his. His arms tightened, and he returned the kiss with hunger and need. Enid lifted her hands to the dark locks of his hair, silky and soft beneath her fingers. She froze when she felt how long it was. The soft strands flowed to large, muscled shoulders. She pulled away. Morpheus looked down at her, a smirk upon his full lips. Lips she had been kissing. With a gasp she jerked out of his arms.

Morpheus clicked his tongue, wagging a finger at her shamefully as though reprimanding a small child. "That's not how this game is played, little one," he chastised with a smile. "Vidar is my prisoner, and I did not offer visitation rights." He reached out, running a hand down her arm. "Now, I'm sure such a thing could be negotiated," his eyes scanned her body, "for a price."

She snatched her arm away.

He put his hands behind his back, regarding her with interest as he shrugged his shoulders. "So be it. But that is the only interaction you will get until you free him."

He circled around her as though examining a puzzle.

"I will say, I am impressed. No one has ever cracked my defenses before. I'm going to have to keep a more careful eye on the two of you. Sneaking into the spaces between sleep and awake. Clever."

"Why are you doing this?" Enid asked.

"Because I can," Morpheus replied. His fingers reached out and grasped a tendril of her hair, rubbing it gently as though examining the texture. "There is little I find that doesn't bore me any longer. You most definitely do not bore me." He smirked.

"What can I do to convince you to let Vidar go?"

Morpheus lifted a shoulder and let if fall. He gave the strand of hair he held a playful tug before releasing it. "That is for you to figure out. I am merely an intrigued observer at the moment. I can't wait to see what you have in store for me."

He crossed his arms over his chest, a finger tapping at his chin as he looked her over. "For now, though, I do believe you should heed your lover's words, and focus on this pesky little challenge. Do you really not know how to access your gifts?"

Enid fidgeted beneath his stare. Embarrassment colored her cheeks. "I can ...sometimes." She looked away from Morpheus, the glitter of humor in his eyes infuriating her. She couldn't risk angering Vidar's jailor. Who knows what sort of torture he would put him through.

Morpheus put a finger beneath her chin, tilting her head so that she was forced to look back at him. "You've been shown the

456

way. Your power has been forced open for you before. You need to stop blocking it. You think you've opened up. You haven't. You keep trying to protect yourself. Don't you know it has to hurt before it gets better?"

With that he lifted a finger to the spot between her eyes. There was a flash of light. Enid blinked, the bright wash of light blocking her vision.

"You are incredibly frustrating…"

Morpheus' voice faded away.

With a gasp she sat up in the cell. She had been asleep, or halfway asleep she supposed. Her hand went to her forehead. There was an ache there. Her fingers came away clean. No blood. Still, her head throbbed as though someone had attempted to split it open. When she closed her eyes, orbs of light seemed to dance in her vision.

With a groan she laid back down, curling in upon herself as much as possible to keep warm. And she waited.

CHAPTER

55

That night, it was Dimitri who appeared to free her from her cell. Enid had slept fitfully, drifting in and out. Afraid to allow sleep to fully take her, lest the King of Dreams and Nightmares visit her again. When the sound of footsteps finally reached her, she was smeared with dirt. Her body was stiff from the hard floor, and her hair had fallen from her braid in places. Wisps of it coiled randomly around her. Without a word, Dimitri lifted her from the floor before covering her head with a black hood. And then they walked. And walked.

Sweltering heat seemed to come from every angle. Whispered voices and low snickers fell upon her ears. The acrid smell of sulfur stung her nostrils. Dimitri's firm grip was all that kept her upright as she stumbled along the uneven, rocky ground. The black hood over her head was stifling, causing sweat to drip from her forehead and the back of her neck. She wasn't sure how long, or how far into the city they traveled, but without her sight it felt like hours.

"You should lower your heart rate, my flower," Dimitri whispered. "Everyone is looking at you like food."

"How about you take the hood off of my head so I can see," Enid grumbled.

A deep chuckle rumbled at her side.

"It would ruin the surprise," he murmured in response.

"I think I've had enough surprises," she countered.

After a few more minutes of fumbling through unknown passages, they stopped. The hood was yanked from her head. Drawing in a deep breath, she instantly began to sputter and choke.

Hot, rancid air filled the room. A perfect circle of lava bubbled around her, giving off sulfur smelling puffs of cloud. Glancing over her shoulder, she saw a small walkway over the lava, with the Revenant forming a semicircle at her back. Fire blazed along the walls and in large metal bowls in the four corners of the room. Dimitri was at her side, staring forward, his expression forlorn. Fearfully she followed his gaze.

A blackened tunnel loomed beyond the ring of lava. The silence within deafening. Slowly, with her ever-dramatic flair, the Revenant Queen walked into her line of vision, around the circle of lava to stand in front of the dark, yawning opening. Two of her attendants took position on either side. A red garbed sentry at their backs, one eye on the tunnel, another on their Queen. Wary of whatever prowled within the dark depths.

Dread snaked its fingers through Enid's scalp and along her body, hair standing on end. Something lurked within. Something that waited patiently to hunt her.

A vision quickened in her mind, scratching for attention. It came to her easier than ever. Could this be Morpheus's influence? Before she could grasp it, the Queen raised her hands. The Revenant stilled. The vision drifted away.

Silhouetted by the firelight in the metal bowls, the dark figure of the Queen appeared more menacing than usual. Enid shifted uncomfortably. Both from the sinister smile the Queen directed at her and the blazing temperature of the room. Sweat ran down back causing the dress to stick uncomfortably. The slick silk did nothing to help ease the intensity of the heat.

Next to her Dimitri barely moved, a sad statue at her side. His attention riveted on his Queen, as was every other Revenant in the room. With one exception.

From the corner of her eye, she could feel Cindy's gaze upon her. It took every ounce of will not to turn to her friend. She breathed a prayer of thanks she was still in one piece. Dimitri's bruising hold on her arm centered her attention where it was required. On the dark queen.

"My children!"

Her voice rang through the room, echoing down into the tunnel behind her.

"Today we bear witness to the final challenge set forth for the human Enid Washbourne. The Fire Challenge!"

The fire blazed brighter within the metal bowls, sending sparks shooting up behind the Queen. The darkness seemed to tense in anticipation. Absorbing the words with keen interest.

"Enid Washbourne," she continued, "you will make your way through the tunnels behind me. Within these catacombs you will find an obelisk honoring the witches who have come before you through the halls of Dokkalfar. Carve your name along with the others, and make your way back to this circle of fire."

Enid waited in anticipation for more. The Queen merely stood there with a look of haughty amusement.

"That's it?" she finally blurted.

"Did you want more?" The Queen replied.

Enid's mind turned. This didn't make any sense.

"It's just that, the other challenges seemed a little more— difficult."

The Queen smiled darkly. "Nothing about this challenge will be easy."

Enid looked around. Cindy seemed as confused as she was. Marcus appeared uneasy. Lania wore a wide, toothy smile. Dimitri still refused to meet her gaze. His eyes instead focused on some distant spot. She looked back at the Queen.

"So, I only need to go find a pillar of stone, and scratch my name on it."

"That's right," the Queen purred.

Shaking off the foreboding that crept up her spine at the look of satisfaction upon the Queen's face, Enid nodded. With that, Dimitri finally moved, maneuvering her toward the walkway over the lava. His pale eyes raked over her as though taking her in for the last time. Sadness etched in them. Before she could blink it was gone, his face a mask of indifference as they turned fully to the crowd of Revenant.

Cindy gave a nod of reassurance that Enid returned as she passed. At least if she were to die today, she had the relief of knowing her friend was once again with her.

The Queen had moved to the side by the time they made it around the walkway. From here, the hot breath of the lava did nothing to assuage the cold air that bled from the passageway. Icy tendrils drifted around her ankles, blowing through the thin fabric stuck to her sweaty skin. She shivered.

"Be quick, my dear," the Queen whispered. "And remember my story. You will die this day. Know it will not be in vain. You will serve me in a purpose greater than yourself."

Her eyes seemed to peer into the depths of Enid's soul before they lifted to Dimitri. There was a subtle nod and Dimitri bit into the skin of his wrist deeply. She didn't fight this time as the ruby liquid was pressed to her mouth.

Looking at Dimitri, Enid wanted so much to convey to him the worry and fear she felt. Despite her anger toward him, despite what they had been through, she wanted him to know that she had seen him as a confidant. That if things had been different, they could have been friends. To remind him of her words to him the night before. His eyes flickered with emotion for barely a moment. He had things he wanted to say as well, but couldn't.

As his blood entered her, she felt rather than saw his essence blending with hers. She knew that if she focused her sight, she would see the red swirl of his power drifting through hers, along with the dark, smoky aura of Vidar that was always with her since their binding.

Interestingly, the thrall didn't appear. She anticipated it, waiting with a knotted stomach for the moment that would feel like a betrayal to her mate, but something stalled it, kept it at bay. Whether that was due to the bond, Vidar's aura, or her own ability manifesting, she wasn't sure. It was a relief though, to have her own mind.

Dimitri pulled his wrist away, the wound healing almost instantly. Closing her eyes, she reached out with her senses. Focusing toward that bit of Revenant aura, stroking and coaxing it closer. Calm came over her, and strength. She felt like she could lift a car if she wanted. The cold no longer reached her. When she opened her eyes, the darkness of the tunnel didn't seem as absolute. The slight pain of bruising was gone, her stiff muscles eased.

Shock thrummed through her. Had this been the key all along? Is this how she could focus and guide her power? She schooled her features, hoping that they mistook the sudden widening of her eyes for fear.

The Queen lifted her hands above her head, a smirk upon her lips.

"Let the final challenge begin!" she exclaimed in a clear voice that echoed around the room and down into the shadows. Her hands came together in a loud clap that reverberated through the tunnel.

Something within seemed to still.

With a final glance at the creatures behind her, Enid squared her shoulders and stepped forward into the gloomy passage.

CHAPTER
56

Darkness. That is all there was. Or all there would have been, had Enid not tapped into Dimitri's Revenant power. As it was, the tunnel she found herself traversing was difficult to navigate, despite her improved vision. She was certain some terror lurked within the blackness ahead, biding its time. The silence was unbearable. At least the cold was less formidable.

Her fingers dragged along the rough rock wall, more to help ground her shaky nerves than to help locate any openings. Experimenting with her newly keen senses, she remained alert, attempting to sense any sort of creature before they could take her by surprise. All she heard was silence. Silence so thick that even her own soft breathing was loud in her ears. The rush of blood in her body nearly as loud as a beating drum.

Step by step, she moved along on slippered feet, wishing she had been given the opportunity to put on more appropriate clothing. Maybe some boots. The floor was not as smooth as the other halls in Dokkalfar. While adrenaline kept the pain of the occasional jagged edge from bothering her too much, she found herself wincing at particularly sharp bits. After what felt like eternity, she stopped. The hallway continued straight. No apparent openings.

Something felt off.

Crouching to the floor, Enid placed her back against the wall and closed her eyes. She reached into the aura of her own power around her, allowing that room of dazzling white light to fill her vision. Frustration bit at her as it refused to come. Grinding her teeth, she steadied herself. Every time she had done this before, she had been pushed, led, or forced. The few times she managed to see on her own, it came unbidden. Unfolding around her like a play. She only had to draw back the curtain and watch.

The epiphany she had on the train, and earlier when she touched Dimitri's power did nothing to help her control her own gift. She was barely scratching the surface. It was useless. She banged her head against the wall behind her. Tears of fury glistening in her eyes.

A scratching sound broke her from her thoughts, drawing her attention down the tunnel to her right. She strained to listen, heart hammering. The noise came again. Louder this time as whatever caused it drew closer. Like the scraping of something along the floor, slow and long, as though it were being dragged.

Enid surged to her feet, her back pressed to the wall, eyes wide as she struggled to control the frantic racing of her heart. The scraping sound was punctuated by a slap against the rock.

Slap. Sccraaape. Slap.

It came closer and closer. Her hands twitched nervously, anxious for something to help defend herself. She had nothing. There were no loose rocks along the ground. No torches hung along the walls to grab. Wrapping her arms around herself, she wished fervently that Vidar was here.

At the thought of her mate, she felt the comforting strength of his aura. She pulled it closer to her, focusing until the shadows surrounded her body like a cloak. The hallway flickered.

Enid blinked. All at once she saw the halls the Sirens called home. Torchlight glowed along the wall. Within the pool of light, Esmelial squinted at her, bewildered. Stepping into the center of the hall, Enid reached for her. Another flicker and she was back in the darkened tunnel.

Slap. Sccraaape. Slap.

A dark figure lumbered around a bend in the hallway far ahead of her. She blinked taking a step back, her vision shifted and Esmelial was once again there, directly in front of her. Enid grabbed her hand. Esmelial's eyes widened, gripping her hard in return. A feeble attempt to hold her in place.

"Where?" The Siren asked briskly.

"A dark tunnel, beyond a ring of lava. There's something in here with me. It's coming."

A shrieked hiss, guttural and tortured filled the air, echoing as if from a distance. The Siren froze, her head cocking to the side as she listened, and then her eyes widened in horror. Enid's heart skipped within her chest. She didn't want to know what could incite such terror in a fae like Esmelial.

"Run," she gasped.

The hall went black. Instead of the pale, wide eyes of Esmelial, something else stood before her. The reek of decay hit her. A few dozen feet away the shuffling figure lumbered slowly forward.

Slap. Sccraaape. Slap.

In all appearances it seemed to be only a man dragging behind a hurt foot. But as the being moved closer, she realized it was a nearly emaciated, skeletal creature. Bits of muscle and flesh hung off its bones. Hair clung in stringy clumps along its skull. One yellowed eye bulged out of a socket of bone. The other squinted hungrily at her beneath sunken flesh.

It stopped.

The holes where its nose should have been lifted in the air and sniffed. A rattling growl vibrated from its bony body. Slowly, it opened its mouth. The rotting muscles allowed the lower jaw to hang abnormally wide, fully displaying the two long, sharpened canines. Enid gulped.

Revenant.

The growl evaporated into a hiss as the creature leaned back on its good leg. Taloned fingers flexed in preparation. In one swift movement, it flung itself forward, jumping toward her, hands outstretched.

With reflexes quicker than she thought herself capable, Enid flung herself beneath the creature. A furious shriek tore through the chamber as it scrambled in the air above her. Those yellow eyes watching her as it sailed overhead before slamming into the floor beyond and rolling to a stop.

Without looking back, Enid jerked herself to her feet and rushed as fast as she could down the hallway. Behind her, she heard the desperate struggle of the creature trying to come after her with its useless leg dragging. Even still, it was quicker than she thought. The scrambling noise inching ever closer.

Fear and adrenaline pushed her faster. She pulled the fabric of her dress higher, creating more room for her legs to flex wider. Rounding the bend in the hall, she bounced off the corner, propelling herself away as fast as possible. The rotting Revenant roared as she ducked from view, its movements frantic.

Up ahead she spotted a pile of rock. She scanned the pile, looking for one large and sharp enough to use as a weapon. Within seconds she had her pick, her legs burning as she focused on it.

The creature slammed into the bend of the wall, a shrill wail vibrating through the air. It was so close. Enid's heart hammered, gasping breaths burned her lungs. She was nearly there. She reached out.

It was right behind her. Harsh, frenzied breath reached her ears, a hiss raising the hairs at the back of her neck. She stooped, slowing long enough to scoop the large rock into her hands. Clawed fingers caught in the twists of her fraying braid. The tug was sharp against her scalp as she was yanked backward.

Verifying the smokey aura of Vidar's power was locked around her, she twisted toward her assailant, the rock held high. Strength she never felt before flooded her as the primitive weapon sailed in an arch through the air and slammed into the face of the cadaverous being. A loud crack echoed in the chamber as it made contact. The skeletal Revenant flew into the wall, releasing her hair and sliding to the ground.

For a moment it was still. Enid panted, a stitch in her side, her legs shaking as she stood and waited. Then, it moved, sitting up from the wall, and turning toward her. Its jaw hung from the rest of its skull. One side kept in place by a few strands of muscle and tendon. The left side of its skull had cracked apart, a gaping hole shattering its cheekbone. It shifted, lifting a hand as it struggled to right itself.

She didn't give it the chance.

Over and over, she swung. Lifting the rock high above her head before bashing it down on the creature. It took a few more hits with an edge before the skull completely smashed. Bits of brain oozed onto the floor. Finally, Enid stepped back, gasping for air.

The creature lay motionless. The rock slipped, dropping to the floor as she staggered and retched. Hands shaking, stomach spasming, until only bile remained. Finally, her stomach settled. Wiping a hand over her mouth, she stood and limped away from the broken body, edging around the pile of rock.

What sort of Revenant had that been? Nothing in the books Vidar gave her mentioned anything like that. She took ragged, calming breaths. Above the mound of rubble at her feet was a hole in the wall. It looked as though something had broken its way through. Drawing forward the Revenant power to sharpen her sight, she carefully climbed atop the fallen stone to examine the opening, stopping only to grab another jagged piece.

Peering around the edge, Enid was surprised to find a niche. The rancid smell of death drifted to her, forcing her to hold her breath lest she start dry heaving again. There was nothing within, and no opening led out, save for the one she stood at. Gouges and darkened streaks of dried blood etched the walls. Something had clawed its way through. She glanced over at the Revenant body, a shiver vibrating through her before she turned away.

Her eyes drifted along the walls of the hall, noticing for the first time the subtle differences in the rock at evenly spaced intervals. Smoother sections, wide enough for a door, as though someone had slid the rock into place purposefully. Moving over to the next section, she ran her fingers over it, feeling the difference. A loud thump came from the other side. Enid paused, and pressed her ear against the rock, using the amplified Revenant hearing to listen. There was a faint noise, like a mouse scratching from within. Then there was another thump. The wall beneath her fingers vibrated. A wail, desperate and hungry, reached her.

She jerked back.

There were more of those creatures trapped in the stone. Tightening her grip on the rock, her eyes moved along each of those makeshift doorways as they continued on down the long line of the hall, deep into the darkness. Thumping echoed from a few of the ones nearest her. As though something on the other side could sense her.

Enid ran.

***

When she finally stopped to catch her breath, it was only because her lungs burned, her legs screamed in protest, and the muscles within her thighs twitched. She wanted to collapse to the floor, but fear kept her shakily moving forward. Slowing her breath, she listened. No sound of breaking rock, or hiss of a Revenant corpse reached her ears.

There was another bend ahead. Slowly, she approached it. Her right hand was sore from where it squeezed the rock tightly. Switching it to her other hand, she rubbed her palm on her dress, attempting to soothe the blisters she felt forming.

A scuffle grabbed her attention. She was instantly on alert. Pressing against the wall, she glanced around the corner. A creature stood in the center of the tunnel, shifting from foot to foot. This one was less decayed. A soiled and tattered white shirt clung to a torso of flesh and muscle. Only the shifting gait, and confused lurching gave it away as something other than a fully formed Revenant. It turned toward her, nose testing the air.

Enid ducked behind the bend in the wall, her heart once again starting to pound erratically. She was unsure of what she saw, her brain unwilling to believe it. Because, as the face of the primitive Revenant turned toward her, she thought she recognized it.

No, she thought to herself fervently. Absolutely not. It couldn't be but, she needed to be sure.

Holding her breath, she eased to the edge again, her entire body trembling as she forced herself to take a quick look. Jason stumbled along the hall, a glazed, confused expression upon his face. The smallest sob broke from her lips before she even realized it had bubbled to the surface. Familiar, brown eyes snapped in her direction. She pressed her lips together, breath freezing in her lungs.

It was too late.

Jason opened his mouth, revealing a set of large, pointed fangs. With terrifying quickness, he ran toward her, bare feet slapping against the hard ground, arms pumping. It only took a few seconds for him to hit the wall opposite her.

A scream tore itself from her mouth and Enid pushed herself around the corner, sprinting further into the hallway. Instinct alone guided her as she jumped over a pile of rubble in the middle of the floor. She was preparing to hit the ground on the other side when she was thrust forward roughly. Something slammed into her, sending her sprawling, the rock still grasped firmly in her hand.

She twisted, lifting her arms to protect her face at the same moment sharp nails scratched at her, drawing blood along her forearm. Above her Jason's nose twitched, his eyes honing in on the crimson drops that welled from her broken flesh.

"Jason, it's me! It's Enid!" she pleaded.

No sign of recognition reached his eyes, only pure, undiluted hunger. With a snarl that exposed those dangerous fangs, he lunged. Enid jammed the rock into his mouth, lodging it in place. Feeling the strength of Vidar's power fill her, she reached her arm back and slammed her palm upward as hard as she could. Jason's head whipped back and he was launched across the hall. She scrambled to her feet, tripping over the frayed dress and catching herself against the wall.

No movement came from the body.

Slowly, Enid stepped toward him, ready for him to jump up at any moment. He remained inert. Dark brown eyes stared blankly at the ceiling. The rock within his mouth jammed back into the base of his spine, nearly severing the top of his head from the rest of his body. She slapped her hands over her mouth, gasping in broken sobs as she looked down at her friend. A friend she had murdered.

Her legs gave way and she hit the ground, a scream tearing itself from her. Shrieks of fury and misery tore from her over and over. She knew she should stop. Knew that the creatures within these walls would be in a frenzy at the sound, but she couldn't make it end. Couldn't contain the grief that fueled them.

Hot tears streamed down her cheeks. She hated the Revenant. Hated the Queen that ruled them. Whose cruelty ran so deep that she could do such terrible things to good people. Enid screamed her rage into the echoing halls. The answering cries of the entombed beings the only response.

She wasn't sure how long she remained like that. At some point she had stopped screaming. Blankly, she stared over at her friend's body. Exhausted and broken she sat against a wall, unable to go on. The banging of the creatures in their stone tombs had died down around her.

A vibration in the wall at her back broke through the numbness. Bits of dust and pebbles rained down from a crack. She gasped out a sob, weakly grabbing a nearby stone from the pile next to Jason's body. Fatigue and misery kept her from finding her feet, and she cried out as she hit the ground roughly after a failed attempt to stand. The wall shattered in a spray of rock. Enid lifted an arm to shield her eyes. Through the cloud of settling dust stepped the massive form of a minotaur. Behind him a smaller, feminine form came into view. Esmelial.

Enid dropped the rock, weeping in shock and relief.

The Siren rushed to her side as Adrian, Cindy, and Marcus filtered into the tunnel behind them. Cindy cried out as she walked over, finding Jason's body on the floor. Her shocked, tear-filled eyes met Enid's. Enid looked away, unable to meet the question within them.

Marcus leaned over the body, examining it clinically.

"Wights," Esmelial hissed in disgust.

"What?" Enid focused her attention on the siren, her voice raspy, throat sore from shrieking. She couldn't look at the body of her friend, or at Cindy's tear-stained face. It was Marcus that answered.

"Wights are Revenant that didn't fully complete the transformation. Something in them breaks and they become these shambling, rotting corpses. Their only drive is to feed their insatiable hunger. They will tear apart anything they come across, including each other." His eyes traveled down the hallway. "They are supposed to be exterminated as soon as possible. I don't know what this one is doing down here."

Enid cleared her throat, swallowing as she tried to control the trembling in her body.

"There are more. Trapped in the walls." Her voice was flat in her ears, barely a whisper.

Marcus stood, moving down the hall where he pressed his ear against a smooth spot in the rock.

He jerked back. "We should keep moving."

Enid was helped to her feet. Esmelial gripped her right arm, and Cindy her left, slipping it over her shoulders, a small reassuring smile upon her lips.

A tear rolled down Enid's face as she looked at her friend.

"Jason," she whimpered, her voice cracking.

Cindy silenced her with a soft hush. "I know, honey. Don't think about it, okay."

Enid nodded.

"You were lucky," Marcus said as he moved up behind them. "The spine and blood vessels to the brain were severed cleanly. A fraction less and he would have spat that rock out and ripped you to bloody pieces."

"Marcus!" Cindy hissed.

The big man didn't seem fazed. "Wights contain nothing of the humanity they had before being turned. Your friend was already dead."

Despite the coldness of his words, Enid was reassured. Jason was gone long before she ended the life of his physical body.

"Thank you, Marcus," she murmured.

Ahead of them, the Minotaur sniffed the air, his grip tight on what appeared to be a large sledge hammer. His bulking frame took up the majority of the tunnel. The scar over his eye wrinkled as he narrowed his eyes. "What now?" Hector asked, his deep voice rumbling in the silent corridor.

"Now, we help Enid finish the final challenge. Without being caught," said Adrian. He stood in the opening, dressed like one of the King's guards in tactical black. Sheathed daggers were strapped to his thighs, a sword at his back, a belt of throwing daggers across his chest. It seemed strange on him, but he moved with the assurance of someone well acquainted with weaponry. Behind him, a set of stairs led upward.

"How did you find me?"

Esmelial gave her a sly smile. "I learned from one of the Revenant that the Queen enjoys keeping a few wights in a secret annex of the city. It only took a little convincing to get the location. These two we ran into on the way down here, and this one insisted on coming to rescue you." She nodded toward Cindy with a look bordering between suspicion and interest. "She is very persuasive."

"If that psychotic bitch thinks she is going to kill another person I care about, she has another thing coming," Cindy said, her almond eyes flashing in anger. "I'll tear her damn head clean off of her bony ass shoulders."

Esmelial gave Cindy a slow smile. "I like you," she said. Her wide, pale eyes turned to Enid. "I like her."

A muffled screech came from behind the rock near them.

"Let's go," Marcus said.

As they walked, Enid filled them in on the details of the challenge. Calling forth the Revenant power within her, she felt her wounds heal, the cuts and blisters faded away and she was able to walk unassisted. The Revenant aura was fading. It wouldn't be long now before she wouldn't be able to use it.

"I have never heard of this obelisk," Esmelial muttered.

"Nor I," said Adrian, his brow furrowed.

"How is Jane?" Enid asked.

At the mention of his mate, a small smile flashed across Adrian's face. "She is well and safe within my room. No one can reach her there."

Enid let out a soft sigh of relief. One less problem to worry about.

"She has not had time to adjust to the situation, and I haven't been able to give her much warning other than to remain where she is. My clansmen are keeping an eye on her, but I am itching to get back," he admitted.

"I'm sorry you were pulled away from her because of me," Enid said with a frown. She remembered how confusing her first nights in Dokkalfar had been. At least she had some experience having seen some of the inhabitants of the city, albeit as a supposed figment of her imagination.

The merman shook his golden head. "I would not have found her were it not for you. I owe you. Besides, she insisted I come. She cares for you a great deal as well."

They continued down the tunnel. The bends were coming more frequently, always turning to the right. Enid realized there had not been a single left hand turn anywhere.

"The tunnel must be a giant spiral," she said. "The obelisk could be at the center."

"It's worth a shot," Cindy replied. "Better than busting any of those wights out trying to find it."

Hector held a hand in the air. Everyone stopped as he lifted his snout.

"Revenant," he whispered.

Adrian pulled a knife from one of the sheaths, handing it to Enid.

"A little better than a rock," he said with a crooked smile. "Go for the brain," he added, pointing a throwing knife at his eye with a jabbing motion. He twirled the knife in his hand before he stalked forward, following the Minotaur. Enid's mouth dropped open as she looked after him. Esmelial gave her a wicked grin.

"Do not worry, you may not need to use it. Adrian is one of the very best Tritons."

"What is a Triton?" Enid searched her memory for any mention of it. Nothing came to mind.

"An elite warrior among the merfolk. Guardian and assassin all rolled up into one dangerous package. Very few receive the honor of the distinction." The Siren clicked her nails together, her eyes glistening with dark thoughts. "This is going to be fun."

Hector stepped toward the bend in the passage with purpose, sledgehammer gripped tight in his massive hands. Behind him, Adrian moved with stealth, a knife in each fist. Esmelial sashayed after, her barely clad body containing no sign of a hidden weapon. Marcus remained behind Cindy and Enid, a watchful eye at their backs.

Rounding the corner behind the Minotaur, she stopped—realizing they had ceased their advance. Around the bulk of Hector's body, she saw Lania and Charlie in the hall. Each with a large mallet.

473

"Finally!" Lania exclaimed. "We have been so bored with the waiting. I almost went looking for your body." She smirked, a wistful look on her face. "The screaming. It was so poetic. So much misery."

Enid swallowed her anger. The Revenant bitch was baiting her. Lania continued, unconcerned.

"This is cheating, you know," she chided, her finger waving at the group around her. "Let us make it fair."

With that, she raised the mallet, and swung it hard into the wall beside her. It crumbled into a pile of rubble. On the opposite side, Charlie did the same. A Wight lurched toward Lania, springing from the niche with deadly purpose. With a laugh, the petite Revenant kicked it toward the group before moving to the next niche and slamming it open. Enid swallowed thickly as the Wights were pushed and thrown down the hall toward them, one after another. Her hand trembled as it gripped the hilt of the knife tightly.

Quick as a snake, Adrian leaned around the Minotaur, his hands twitching deftly. Two Wights dropped to the floor, each with a knife sunk deep into an eye socket. Hector took a few steps forward, his hammer swinging in the air at the closest Wight. The screeching creature's head popped like a pimple, trapped between the rock and the weapon's metal head.

As fast as the creatures were taken down, more were shambling toward them. Marcus crouched into a defensive position as a fervent Wight broke from its prison at their backs. Enid threw her back to the wall, knife held out with trembling hands.

Laughter came from her left. Esmelial sat on the shoulders of one of the Wights. A gleeful expression on her face as she snapped the creature's head from its neck like a flower from a stem. The body dropped and she skipped to her feet as she rode it down, slinging the head toward the two Revenant still breaking the Wights from their vertical stone coffins.

"Marcus!" Cindy called out fearfully.

Enid jerked her head to the right in time to see Marcus crush a Wight's head between his hands, only for another to jump onto his back. Before he could react, the Wight lunged, its fangs tearing into the flesh of his shoulder. Blood spurted along the walls.

"NO!" Cindy shouted.

Her hands flew out at her sides, a beat of power rushing through the air, and the Wight was thrown from Marcus. Enid stared in awe as her friend stepped forward, eyes narrowed into slits. The Wight clawed and struggled, its body shaking with effort. It was pinned in place, feet dangling. Cindy lifted a hand, trembling with fury. The Wight wailed. A sound of pain and confusion. Her hand squeezed into a fist that she sharply twisted. The tormented creature's head jerked around, neck snapping with a loud crack, and the body slumped to the ground. Cindy rushed to Marcus's side, using her hands to staunch the bleeding as the wound slowly stitched itself close.

"ENID!" Adrian shouted from her left.

A Wight flew at her. With a scream, Enid shoved the knife at the creature's face. Vidar's power flared within her, strengthening the force of the stab. There was a jarring sensation up her arm as the blade sank through the Wight's skull, and bit into the stone wall—impaling it to the rock. She stepped back, arms tingling from the impact. The Wight was fastened in place, a burst eye leaking down the pallid skin of its cheek. Enid had to look away to keep from retching.

"Damn girl," Cindy said, coming up behind her. "Looks like I'm not the only one who changed."

Enid gave her friend a shaky smile before turning her attention down the hall. Hector lowered his horned head and charged the passage, scattering Wights like bowling pins. Adrian ducked beneath a flailing Wight as it sailed through the air, yanking one of his knives from a felled corpse, and flinging it into the creature's brain before it hit the ground.

Further down the passage, around another bend, Enid could still hear the cracking of the mallets against stone. How long could they keep this up? The sound pissed her off. The Revenant were playing dirty, and they knew it.

Marcus and Cindy urged her along, stepping around the dismembered bodies littering the floor. Esmelial smiled happily. Hissing in the face of another Wight as she twisted its head around in one fluid movement and reached for the next. Cindy looked straight ahead, her face tight with focus as the Wights stopped mid attack, shifting away as though pushed by an invisible barrier. Her arm around Enid's as they maneuvered through the battle filled hall. Marcus had retrieved Enid's knife and was using it to decapitate the frustrated Wights one by one.

Enid's head swam with the carnage. Dizziness and nausea overwhelmed her. Her friends charged on, stabbing and tearing at the throng of creatures. Laying their lives on the line to help her reach her goal. If something happened to one of them, it would be her fault. Guilt and terror threatened her resolve, amplifying her anxiety.

A vision scratched at the edge of her mind. Eagerly, she called to it, the white flood of light blinding, the power comforting and warm as it washed over her. This was hers. It was right. She pulled it around her like a blanket, willing it to show her what she wanted to see. What was at the end of this passage?

As the light bled away, she found herself in a large, round room. Hector plowed through a crowd of Wights, stumbling in from the tunnel. A Revenant woman waited before a large stone obelisk in the center of the room. Lania and Charlie leaned against a wall at her back, smug looks on their faces.

The strange woman smiled, her eyes glowing with an orange light. Her hair, the deep burgundy of wine, began to float around her as a blistering wave of heat flowed out of her. The minotaur reared back as the woman lifted her hands.

There was no time to think, only react. So, Hector flung his hammer. The weapon spun end over end as it flew toward the Revenant Witch. Enid knew with sudden certain clarity. This woman was a witch, like her, turned Revenant to serve the bitter Queen. As the hammer was about to slam into her face, the witch caught the head of it easily in her palm. The metal melted. Dripping harmlessly to the floor.

With a smile, she pointed a finger at Hector and a blast of flame hit him, burning his body to ash in seconds. The same happened to Adrian and Esmelial, along with the final few Wights they fought, as they tumbled into the room. Enid screamed.

The scream echoed down the hallway as the vision left her, leaving her blinded by darkness. She knew without seeing that all her friends were looking at her. The Wights were still coming. She felt their unnatural auras of decayed death filling the air. A few blinked out as her friends killed them. Cindy was staring at her strangely.

"Your eyes," she whispered.

Enid nodded, waving her hand in the air to brush aside the comment. There wasn't time. The gesture reminded her of Pythia. Now she understood the ancient seeress's impatience.

"Cindy, we need to go first. Can you walk us ahead, and keep those things away?"

"I sure can," her friend said, confident as ever.

Enid pulled Vidar's aura closer, whispering through it a word of thanks and love to her trapped mate. An answering surge of energy met her in return. Her vision sharpened, and once again the dense, impenetrable darkness of the tunnel lightened.

They moved to the front of the group, stepping over dismembered corpses. Wights hissed and snarled as they came, pressed aside by Cindy's invisible barrier. The others made quick work of dispatching the undead beings, lessening their numbers as they went. No one questioned what she had seen. No one asked her to hold back. Instead nods of approval and encouragement greeted her as she passed each of her companions. She whispered her plan to Cindy as they walked. Cindy was attentive and thoughtful, offering suggestions. Soon, she was ready.

The timing was perfect. Because, it wasn't long before the glow of light colored the curve of the wall ahead of them. Bracing herself, Enid raised her chin and stepped into the circular chamber.

CHAPTER

57

"I've been waiting for you."

The witch leaned back against the obelisk, examining her nails as if overcome by boredom. Above her burgundy head, names were etched into the solid limestone pillar that nearly skimmed the rock ceiling. The names of witches.

A shiver ran down her spine. How many women like her had come down this same path? How many had been afraid of living among humans for fear of being put to death or incarcerated? And what of those that had suffered a terrible fate, burned at the stake, hung, drowned, lobotomized. All because of how they had been born. The things they knew. What they believed. Had she been born in a different time, she may have been one of them. How many had been innocents? Persecuted merely for the sake of a small-minded group of people, fearful of things they couldn't begin to understand.

The Revenant followed her gaze, a slow smile spreading across her lips as she stared up at the stone monument.

"Amazing, isn't it?"

Enid blinked, forcing her attention away from the names. The Revenant's amber eyes blazed with amusement and an eerie flame like glow.

"You know," she continued as she pushed away from the pillar and turned to look up at it. "You are very lucky. No," she said holding up a finger, "blessed. Blessed to be part of the epic story of our magnificent goddess. The world will tremble to behold her. Humans and Fae alike will line up to bow at her feet." She looked over her shoulder, glancing back toward Enid. Her eyes sparked with hints of fire. "And it will all be thanks to you."

Behind them, further back in the passage, Enid could still hear the echoes of her friends fighting through the horde of wights. Lania and Charlie stood on the opposite side of the room near a flight of stone stairs—mallets discarded. A wide, vengeful grin on Lania's face.

Heat began to radiate around them as the witch turned to face her fully, hands lifting at her sides. Fire danced upon her upturned palms, dangerous and mesmerizing as it fluttered and flicked in the air. As it flared to life, so did the torches lining the wall, igniting one by one. The flames lit up the dim walls, fully displaying the colorful Egyptian style artwork covering every inch.

It didn't take long for Enid to recognize the figures in the scenes. Each panel depicted part of the story the Queen had told her last night. The story of her conversion into the first Revenant. A figure of Isis before a white haired fae woman with purple eyes stood out among the paintings. Something about it was eerily familiar.

The witch chuckled darkly. "Don't worry. I'll make this quick."

Cindy gripped her hand tight. A reassuring squeeze as Enid felt her heart rate rise. With a smirk, the witch thrust her hands toward them, launching a stream of fire. Enid braced herself, turning away from the heat, holding her arm up as though it were a shield. A useless gesture, she knew.

As she took in another breath, she realized she was unscathed. The fire blazed harmlessly against a bubble of protection. Cindy glared at the witch with a smile, unflinching. Enid breathed a sigh. The witch lowered her arms. The flames extinguishing as she gave Cindy an assessing look.

"I will have to admit. I did not see you coming. I'm not sure what you are."

The sound of fighting crept closer at their backs. Lania and Charlie circled the room, each taking a side. Enid spared the

479

smallest of glances at Lania as she prowled closer. The Revenant's cold rage seared a target into her skin.

The witch continued to mock them, "Why are you fighting so hard to prevent the inevitable? You aren't leaving this city. You will serve our Queen, and if you would stop fighting it, you might learn to enjoy it." She turned to Cindy then. "And you," she hissed. "My Queen will reward me greatly for getting rid of you."

"If your Queen is so powerful, then why does she need Enid to do her dirty work?" Cindy folded her arms over her chest, her hip jutting to the side as she spoke.

The witch shrugged.

"The prophecy was clear. A witch with red hair will turn the tide and be the key to raising our glorious Queen to her rightful place. Now quit making things so difficult!"

"I may live the rest of my life in this city with the fae, but it won't be under Isis' thrall," Enid vowed.

More fire danced along the Revenant's fingers as she met Enid's hard look. "We'll see about that."

Enid didn't see it coming when Cindy slammed into her, throwing her to the ground. Charlie stood above them, mallet in hand. Enid had never even seen him pick it up. The witch had worked them perfectly, making sure they were distracted. Cindy was unconscious, blood trickling from her nose.

"NO!" Enid yelled as she reached for her friend. Before her fingers could so much as brush her, Lania snatched Enid away, sending her flying across the room. The impact against the painted wall was jarring. Her head spun as she dropped to the ground. Pain lanced up her leg from her ankle. Weakly, she lifted her head.

Charlie and Lania stood above Cindy's prone body. Muscles flexing, Charlie lifted the mallet high. Enid surged forward, raising a hand to ward off the blow. A roar broke the moment, and Marcus appeared from the darkness of the tunnel, slamming into Charlie and knocking him away before the mallet could fall. Esmelial wasn't far behind, her taloned fingers wrapping around Lania's throat.

There was no time for celebration, as a wall of fire hurtled toward her. Enid rolled away, throwing herself along the ground to take cover behind the obelisk. Her ankle throbbed in protest.

The fire didn't relent. It burned hotter, working its way around the large limestone column. The air sizzled painfully. Flame licked at her skin, painting it red where it touched. She flinched, jerking away. Panic was rising within her, threatening to carry her away on its cresting waves.

It couldn't end like this.

Another touch of the fire against her scorched skin had Enid leaning back against the cooler stone slab at her back, pulling her legs closer to her chest. The laughter of the witch echoed around her as a tongue of fire whipped out, searing another red lash in place, causing Enid to yelp. She needed to gain control of herself.

The woman was taunting her. Torturing her even. This could be over in seconds, but the witch would drag it on. Like all Revenant, she seemed to savor the sounds of agony that Enid couldn't hold back. Once more she reached out with her power, feeling for her sight, for a way out. There had to be a way.

The fire burned hotter. Horror overwhelmed her as the skin on her leg began to bubble. Jumping up, she squeezed tighter against the obelisk, favoring her hurt ankle. The flames grew, the heat so intense she thought it would suffocate her. There was nowhere to go and she couldn't take it anymore.

Enid screamed. Not any scream, but a shriek of such terror and torment that it felt as though her very soul shattered. The witch cackled in delight at the shrill note of panic. The flames abated.

"And you try to call yourself a witch," the woman chastised, clicking her tongue. "Shameful."

There was the slow click of heels and the Revenant came into view. Her dark red hair floated around her, seeming to dance and sway like the flames she so readily controlled.

"You should be proud, you know," she continued, watching the tears slide down Enid's dirt-streaked face with distaste. "You have the honor of meeting your end the same way so many of our ancestors did. This is history. Tradition."

The witch came closer, her head tilting to the side, eyes ablaze with dancing fire.

"Please don't do this," Enid pleaded.

The witch continued to study her like she was a bug under a microscope. Her mouth twisted with contempt.

"My Queen gave you many opportunities, and you spat upon each one. You had your chance. You don't deserve her sympathy."

Flame wreathed hands lifted toward her.

CHAPTER
58

Enid braced herself.

A wall of water flew in front of her, dousing the witch and her flames. There was a sizzle as the fire was extinguished and a rush of steam clouded the air. Enid blinked, unable to see through the fog. The witch screamed in frustration.

A hand gripped her arm, yanking her around the other side of the obelisk where she crashed into a hard chest. Adrian winked, his turquoise eyes bright. Blood was sprayed over his face, his golden hair now red from the amount that coated it. His knives were all gone, along with his sword. Possibly abandoned in the corpses littering the hall.

Hector lay on the ground, leaning against the entrance. His large frame covered in gashes. Esmelial had a hand against his side, holding a torn cloth over a particularly bad wound. Lania and Charlie were unconscious on the floor. Next to them, Marcus held Cindy. Her head limp against his shoulder.

"You are becoming increasingly irritating, little witch."

Stepping from around the statue, hair and clothes soaked with water, mascara running down her face, the witch hissed angrily. She flexed her fingers and fire engulfed her body, evaporating the water in moments.

"Then let me etch my name on this damn pillar, and we can leave you in peace," Enid replied as she limped away from

Adrian. Her hands twitched nervously as she faced the Revenant head on.

"Don't you see? That's exactly what I'm trying to help you do."

"What?" It took effort to hold still and wait for an explanation. Enough energy had been exhausted, and she wanted this over.

"It's a monument to all of the effort our Queen had gone through over the centuries in her quest to rise to power. Each of these names was a witch, a possible key. Each one failed. Until you. You will be the final piece she needs."

Enid took a step back as she looked up and realized that every inch of the stone was nearly covered in names. Thousands of names inscribed over the centuries.

Pointing a fiery finger, the Revenant gave her a sly smile.

"That is where your name will go."

Near the bottom of the obelisk was a blank space. Enid stared the Revenant down. Anger flared within her brighter than the flames the witch controlled.

"All of these women. What happened to them all?"

The Revenant shrugged. "They didn't work out. My name is here too." She waved a hand toward it. "I was supposed to be the key. Unfortunately, that is not where my power lies. I have been useful though. Unlike some of the others."

Enid glared at her.

"It was all a lie. The challenge. Has this been the plan all along? Bring me down here to kill me and force the turn? Why? Why all of this elaborate…bullshit."

"Oooh, someone's getting mad." The witch brushed a lock of stray hair from her face. "This all could have gone a lot easier if you would have let yourself be turned, but no. You had to play Miss Independent. Oh wait. You didn't do that either, did you? How is Vidar? Such a big man, with all that…muscle. I can see the appeal. Don't worry. If he makes it out of the Realm of Dreams and Nightmares, I'll be sure to help keep his bed *warm* for you."

The witch and Enid squared off against each other. The fury within Enid so white hot that a sudden calm came over her. Something ancient and predatory unfurled as though waking from a deep sleep. If she wasn't so angry, she would have been terrified. But now she welcomed it, coaxed it awake happily.

"I'm going to enjoy burning you alive slowly. Eventually I'll give you my blood to turn you, but if you heal from the burns or not…well, we will see," the witch snickered. "But first."

She turned toward the others, her arms lashing out as a burst of fire erupted from her like a flame thrower. Enid lifted a hand, stopping Adrian as he jerked forward, water already starting to pool at his fingertips. Before the inferno could grip her friends in its scorching embrace, it hit an invisible wall.

Gritting her teeth, the witch put more strength into her power. The flames burned higher, a roar echoing around the circular chamber, flaring uselessly against an unseen shield. Enid shifted on her feet, allowing her full weight to balance evenly on her now healed ankle. The burns and bruises on her body faded as she rolled her head on her neck. The witch dropped her hands, the fire dissipating as Enid stared her down.

"You?!," she hissed. "How?"

Enid shrugged. "Cindy thought it would be helpful if I took some of her blood."

Tilting her head to the side, she listened to Cindy's slow, even breathing. She was still knocked out, but she would be fine. When she woke up, she would have to thank her friend for her quick thinking. The walk through the tunnel was long enough for her to take a few sips and gain access to her power.

Hopefully, Cindy would forgive how easily she was distracted and let the barrier drop. Until the witch had tried to burn them and instinct kicked in, she wasn't sure it would even work. Now she felt the power whirling around her like a cool breeze.

The Revenant bared her fangs with a hiss.

"Bitch. I'll burn you both."

"Try it," Enid demanded.

Before the witch could react, Enid thrust her hands forward, pushing that power out of her like a giant hammer. It slammed into the Revenant, throwing her against the wall, her arms trapped at her sides.

Calmly, Enid walked up to her.

"You cannot keep me here, forever," the witch gasped as she struggled against Enid's hold.

"Let's see." Enid grabbed the witch's head as she reached for her own power, weaving it with Cindy's shield and Vidar's strength.

Images danced before her eyes.

"Let's find out what I see when I touch you. What my power is capable of."

Angela had been her name. Born to a witch in a small village in England. Taught to live and practice in secret. Hiding in plain sight. She never had any friends, was always alone, always picked on by the other children. Then she was a young girl, and a boy was nice to her. He came to see her day after day with a handful of wildflowers. Henry.

They would share secret kisses in the woods, explore lonely meadows and a hidden cave. Their secret space. They were going to be forever. She gave herself to him underneath the light of a full moon, safe within their cave. Huddled in the dark together after, he began to shiver with chill. She started the fire when she thought he was asleep. He saw.

Villagers came with pitchforks and sticks. Her mother was pleading, begging. She cried. Henry yelled the loudest, his hate filled eyes spearing her heart. That hurt worse than the stones they hurled at her. And when her mother burned, she screamed in fury and agony.

It was her turn. They tied her to the pillar of wood, right on top of the burnt remains of her mother. More wood was thrown against the charred scraps. It was Henry who set it alight, the torchlight reflected in the blue eyes she had so loved to gaze into. Those eyes that burned with hatred until she turned those flames around on them all. Then they filled with fear before they popped and sizzled down his blistered cheeks.

She was alone in a wasteland of burnt embers. Her Queen was impressed when she finally came to her with a promise of eternity and power. The centuries flew by in flashes of killing and flame—of blood and ash. Blue eyes looking back at her in fear, over and over, for all time. Blue eyes in anonymous faces, screaming. Always screaming.

Enid stepped away.

Angela shrieked, tears flooding her face, her head shaking back and forth as though trying to dispel the images. It would take only a thought. One thought and Enid could trap her there. Stuck within an endless loop of her memories. Rage pressed her onward. Rage at the Revenant, at the Queen, and the fire witch herself, for so callously harming her friends. It boiled within her, a red tide of fury. Lock her in her memories, in a prison of pain and torment. It was the least she deserved.

As she was getting ready to do so, power grasping at the memories, she stopped. Angela was weeping and pale. The horror upon her face shattered the rage, melting it away. She was so very tired, and no better than the Revenant if she gave in to that anger and harmed another.

Angela dropped to the floor with a thud as Enid released her, and turned her back. Instead, she looked over the group of people who had followed her into this hell hole. All appearing as tired as she felt.

Adrian gave her a smile that was strangely boyish and charming despite the blood that soaked him. Esmelial watched with a feral grin, no doubt ready to partake in any torture, despite the fact that her hands were busy holding Hector's blood within him. The Minotaur appeared to be unconscious, as was Cindy.

Movement from the corner of her eye drew her attention. Enid turned to see Dimitri racing down the stairs. A large double headed axe in his hands. Fury burned in his eyes. Enid froze at the sight of him, at the snarl that twisted his mouth.

She watched as he drew his arm back, the axe catching the light as he flung it forward. The sharpened blades spun around and around, twirling through the air. Enid lifted her hands in defense. Icy dread and shock filled her. She didn't expect this. Didn't see it coming. The axe made contact with a sickening thud.

Enid jolted.

CHAPTER

59

Angela stood against the wall. The head of the axe buried deep into the rock at her throat, hands still lifted toward Enid. The fire surrounding them died and they dropped limply to her sides. Slowly, her body slid to the floor in a heap, leaving her head staring blankly on top of the axe like a grotesque hunting trophy. Behind the gore was the painted scene of the Revenant Queen sitting on a throne, rows of creatures kneeling before her.

"Took you long enough," Adrian grumbled.

Enid tore her gaze away from Angela's disembodied head to give Dimitri a questioning look.

"I have been in Isis's thrall for hundreds of years. It takes time to break," he said with a shrug and a dismissive wave of his hand.

"You came to save me?"

Dimitri's indifference melted away as he turned the full weight of those ice blue eyes on her.

"I would walk through fire for you, my flower," he murmured, the emotion within those words pressing on her heart like a lead weight.

"Dimitri, I can't...." Her voice came out in a cracked whisper, the words choking her. Dimitri raised a silencing hand. Pain lanced across his face, and then disappeared.

"I know."

Esmelial and Adrian balanced Hector between them as they struggled to navigate his large body up the narrow steps. The minotaur looked rough. Horned head bobbing, eyelids drooping, a hand pressed to his side.

Cindy groaned against Marcus's shoulder.

"Did we win?" she asked softly. Enid rushed over to her friend, rapidly firing questions as she looked her over.

"Are you ok? How do you feel? Do you know what year it is? How many fingers am I holding up?"

Cindy chuckled as Marcus gently pushed Enid back with a shake of his head.

"She is not human anymore. Her healing has kicked in. She is young for a Revenant, and the kind of power she holds requires a lot of energy. She overdid herself, but she is strong." His eyes gleamed with pride as he looked at the woman in his arms.

"Ok, handsome. How about you let me stand up and we get the hell out of here before you start turning the charm on me."

Standing on shaky legs, Cindy launched herself backwards. Landing once again in Marcus's lap as she yelled out. Her eyes locked on the head staring blankly from the opposite wall. A trail of blood leading to the crumpled corpse.

"Who did that?"

"That would be me," Dimitri replied as he lifted his sister's limp body over his shoulder. "Marcus, would you grab my sister's pet? These two have a couple of cells waiting for them." He turned away, taking the lead at the foot of the stairway.

"Someone is going to have to fill me in on what I missed," Cindy muttered as Marcus lifted Charlie's prone body like a sack of potatoes.

"I will tell you everything, my queen," Marcus murmured, taking her hand and pressing a kiss to her head.

The stairway was regrettably long, especially for the two fae half carrying the minotaur up its spiraling steps. When they finally found the top, it was behind the room with the circular ring of lava.

King Fenri prowled around the outer edge of the bubbling liquid, tension and frustration vibrating from him. A group of the King's guard hurriedly gathered around Hector, carrying him off down the hall, most likely to the medical ward. Enid grasped his large hand briefly as they went by.

"Thank you," she murmured. He gave her hand a slight squeeze in response before releasing her. Enid watched them go until they were around the corner. The white-haired banshee followed along, watching Enid before she disappeared with the group. The limp Revenant were taken away also, off to a cell until a decision was made.

Adrian was murmuring to the King. Their heads bent in quiet conversation. The King stopped briefly to flag down a few of his guards, barking out rapidly fired orders. The group moved to the stairs, each checking over their weapons.

Her confusion must have shown on her face. Marcus stepped up next to her, Cindy leaning against his side. "They are going down to take care of the bodies, and any other Wights that may still be trapped down there."

"What will they do with them?"

Marcus shrugged. "Put them out of their misery, of course."

Enid nodded. She couldn't bring herself to feel any sorrow for the creatures caught between life and death. That was no way to live. Trapped in endless hunger. No end in sight. Only a shell of a body with nothing of the person that once possessed it. She shuddered at the thought.

King Fenri and Adrian finished talking and walked over to where Enid stood with the Revenant and Esmelial.

"I hear congratulations are in order," the King said, his arms behind his back, a smile peeking from the scruff of his beard. "We will have to have a celebration in your honor. The first human to complete the Elemental challenge. You will be the talk of Dokkalfar."

Enid smiled at the King, her anxiety relinquishing a little. But a sliver of doubt had her, once again, second guessing everything.

"I actually couldn't complete the challenge I was given," she responded with a frown. King Fenri gestured for her to continue. "I was told to etch my name on the obelisk, which I didn't do because it was a monument the Queen built to commemorate her rule over this realm. I refuse to be a part of that. So, you see, I couldn't complete the challenge."

King Fenri nodded, tugging at his beard lightly before he said, "I don't see any more of a fitting way to complete a fire challenge than by defeating a fire witch."

Overcome with sudden joy and exhilaration, Enid threw her arms around the King, hugging him tightly as she squealed with delight. "Thank you, thank you, thank you."

Her voice was high pitched and cracked with emotion as she spoke, but she didn't care. She had done it. It was over. Only—

Enid stepped back as King Fenri gently pull her away. He gave a small chuckle. Adrian stepped forward when he noticed the look on her face.

"Don't worry. The King won't snap your neck for hugging him without permission, this time," he gave a laugh, patting her shoulder affectionately. "Though he has been known to tear a limb or two off in the past, so maybe show a little more restraint in the future."

She gave a halfhearted smile in return. "I will, but it's not that."

She looked into Adrian's turquoise eyes, her own welling with tears.

"Vidar." She spoke his name in barely a whisper. Afraid she might crack open if she said it any louder. That the hurt would overtake her completely.

The King took her arms in his large hands, squeezing. "We all wish he could be here right now. Don't worry, Morpheus is true to his word. You will get him back."

"How?"

Worry flared in his eyes, and then he was shaking his head. "I'm not sure, but you will figure it out. Of that I have no doubt." He let go, folding his arms over his broad chest. "In the meantime, I do believe you have a clan to claim. Though, with your newly formed mate bond, that doesn't seem to be a necessity anymore, does it."

Enid glanced toward Esmelial. The siren who, until that moment, sullenly leaned against the wall as though bored, now watched intently. Her pale eyes bright with interest as she patiently waited.

"I have learned in the time I have been here that a clan is not just a group of the same type of creature." Enid looked around at the faces of her friends. Tired, covered in blood, and all watching with earnest, trusting faces. "It's a family. People you can rely on. Those that are there for you, and that you in turn are willing to put yourself on the line for. Every one of these people were willing to follow me into those tunnels today."

"People?" Esmelial scoffed, her nose wrinkling in disgust.

Enid rolled her eyes. "Sorry, beings, fae…I'm still getting used to all of this, okay. But what I'm saying is that each of you is my clan. My family."

Cindy moved away from Marcus and walked over to Enid. "I love you, E, and you will always be my family. I will always be there for you." She looked toward the King. "Enid will not be going near the Revenant clan." Her eyes returned to Enid's. "It is too dangerous. Especially now. The Queen won't stop."

Enid patted her hand. "I know. I will be careful."

Dimitri only gave her a nod as she threw an apologetic look his way.

"I planned to join the Sirens and Merfolk. The Sirens have done so much for me. And I would like to request a renegotiation on their hunting rights. They should have the freedom to hunt as needed, without overstepping the laws, of course. I know there were restrictions put into place after the last fae war, but I do believe they have proved themselves worthy of reconsideration."

"You said *planned*," the King commented, fingers scratching absently at his beard. Enid looked to her friends, the unspoken words hanging in the air. No one seemed surprised, or upset, only expectant. Waiting for her to say what they already knew.

"Vidar is my clan, my home. I'm going to get him, and bring him back. I belong with him. What we do when we get back, I can't exactly say, but we will be looking for a way to open the door to the realm of faery. To bring the fae home. Whatever that means."

Esmelial gave Enid a small smile and a nod of her head. Gratitude shining from her pale face.

Fenri nodded. "That sounds acceptable to me. Bring Vidar back. In the meantime, I will speak with the Sirens. I'm sure after a thorough discussion, and some thought, we will be able to come to an understanding."

"Even if it means going against your Queen?" Esmelial's voice held a faint tremble of anger that Enid had no problem picking up now that she had gotten to know her.

King Fenri looked over his shoulder at the glowering fae.

"It would appear that Isis has already implicated her wrong doing. She has disappeared. No one can pinpoint her location. She has a lot to answer for with what we have found today. This is a whole new section of the city I had no clue existed, and we have no idea how deep it goes. The abominations she has created and kept within its confines are being destroyed as we speak. The Revenant will all be interrogated. I will announce my final judgment on the matter once I have more facts." The King's face darkened ominously.

Esmelial's eyes flashed. "Good," she replied, a dark smile touching the corners of her mouth briefly. Adrian didn't even try to hide the savage grin that settled on his face. After nearly two hundred years, they would finally have their retribution.

CHAPTER

60

Enid made her way toward her room, Dimitri following after. More at his own insistence than for her safety. Word spread fast in the dark city. A human had completed the Elemental Trials and been granted fae status. A human with fae blood. A witch, a seer, who had destroyed the Revenant fire witch, cracking her mind with unknown powers. For the first time since she stepped foot in Dokkalfar, the other creatures let her be. Many avoided her eyes, giving her a wide berth as she walked through the central market.

Her attention flicked to Dimitri. She felt bad for him. He seemed lost. Distracted even. Like a small, solitary boat adrift in an endless sea. The ties to his Queen were severed. His aura boiled and raged around him, frayed edges reaching out for something as if seeking sustenance. He seemed dimmer, as if he was starting to weaken. She wasn't sure how long he would survive on his own without the Queen. Would the other Revenant fade and wither without her as well?

Lost in her thoughts, she turned down the hall to her room. There was still so much to do. The Sirens would want to meet with her. She would need to check in with Jane to see how she was handling everything. She must feel so lost. Enid also needed to stop by the medical ward to check on Hector. Then, there was the matter of her aunt's remains. And she had no idea how she was supposed to get to the realm where Vidar remained captive.

It felt strange to walk the halls, knowing that Vidar was out there somewhere. Imprisoned. Tortured. The door to his room called to her. She was tempted to pass by hers completely. Almost allowed her feet to carry her to his threshold. Would they be her rooms as well now that they were bound? A joint sanctuary. Her fingers fluttered across the mark on her hand distractedly.

She didn't notice the figure leaning against the wall, clothed in shadow. It was only as Enid came closer that she could see the moon-like glow of white hair gleaming in the darkness. What could she want? She stopped before she got too close. Instinct warned that danger lurked within the small fae. An inner turmoil that boiled right below the surface.

The banshee kicked away from the wall and came toward Enid with a steady, purposeful stride. Enid shifted her weight on her feet. Thankfully, either from politeness or indifference, Dagny stopped a comfortable distance away.

"I thought you went with Hector?" Enid inquired.

Exhaustion ate at her. Already it was getting more difficult to keep her eyes open. She just wanted to go to sleep. Dimitri stood at her back—a reassuring presence. The banshee waved the question away, not bothering to answer.

"I hear you met Amaris."

Enid tilted her head to the side. Amaris, the trapped shadow nymph.

"Yes, I met her," Enid replied. "She was...in a sensitive state."

Dagny nodded, a glimmer of emotion—there and then gone.

"And? Did seeing her convince you to help us?" Her voice was low, strained, as though fearful of what Enid's answer would be.

Enid only gave her a confused stare. "Of course, I'm going to help," she said. "That's what I've been doing. I-I don't know what I'm meant to do, other than find Vidar."

Dagny gaped, unblinking. Her mouth opened and then closed. Enid fidgeted in that stunned silence.

"Danu, what have you done to us?" Dagny hissed. She pushed past Enid and Dimitri.

"Wait!" Enid called, spinning on her heel to go after the banshee.

"I would not do that, my flower," Dimitri said quickly. Adrian was coming down the hall, a pleased look on his face that quickly vanished when he caught sight of the banshee storming toward him.

Enid didn't listen to Dimitri's warning, catching up to Dagny, and grabbing hold of her arm. Before she could blink, before she could even think to regret the consequences of her actions, Dagny whirled. A feral look upon her youthful face. Pointed canines flashed as she bared her teeth. Enid gasped and was jerked back, Dimitri standing between her and the wrathful fae. Adrian jogged up, hands held out in supplication as Dagny hissed her anger.

"I want to understand," Enid said soothingly.

The red rings of the banshee's eyes shot to her, pools of red tears forming in their corners. A haze of pink over the whites of them. The banshee glared at Enid as a single tear began to form.

"Understand?" Dagny snapped her teeth in frustration. "We are dying. Danu knew this would happen, and she promised. *She promised*. Danu was meant to send us a savior, a guardian. A guide to lead us home. Instead, we get a clueless, untrained, human girl, who—" Dagny raised her hands in front of her face as she looked toward the ceiling, shouting her irritation to the universe, "DOESN'T KNOW WHAT TO DO!!"

Tears of blood streamed down her face. Her breaths were ragged, heavy pants.

"Shit, shit, shit," Adrian chanted, bouncing anxiously foot to foot.

The banshee staggered back, holding her hands up as if to block Enid. A troubled red gaze shot to Adrian, who nodded in confirmation, his hands shooting out. As her breaths came faster and faster, those red tears fell in a rain of crimson at her feet. A stream of water began to twist its way around her trembling body. With noticeable effort Dagny remained in place, her narrowed eyes glaring at Enid. Then she stilled, slowly drawing in a lungful of air as the water formed a dome around her.

"Dimitri, get Enid out of here!" Adrian cried out.

496

Enid yelped as she was jerked from her feet and thrown over the Revenant's shoulder. He ran as fast as he could. The wall of water thickened and flexed before suddenly starting to vibrate as though beating with a pulse. Soon the image of the white-haired banshee disappeared around a corner. Dimitri ran faster, the hall a blur.

There was a sudden pulse of sound, the deepest vibration passing over Enid in warning, before the blast of a wail struck them. Dimitri and Enid were thrown through the air, landing in a heap on the hard floor. Enid clamped her hands over her ears as the sound drilled into her head, relentless and furious. It made her skull feel as though it were being hammered from the inside. A shriek of such intensity, such fury. Any moment her skull would split open and spill its contents onto the dusty floor. She almost wished for it. For the relief of the pressure. For the end of the sound and the pain it brought with it. She never wanted to hear again.

Dimitri tried to reach her, a hand grasping toward her only to slam back in place. Blood leaked down the sides of his head, dripping from his ears. Enid knew if she were to pull her hands away, they would be the same, coated in her blood. But she couldn't. It was all too much.

She screamed.

And screamed.

And screamed.

EPILOGUE

There was only darkness and silence. Absolute darkness, so complete it left her feeling as though she were weightless in its embrace. The silence though. That sweet, sweet silence. The silence was bliss. She rolled in it, reveled in it, languished in the absence of sound. In nothing.

Nothing but the blackness and her own fuzzy, incomplete, drifting thoughts to keep her company. Distantly, she wondered if she even existed at all. Was she part of this nothing, or did her fragmented cognizance separate her?

A rumble surrounded her. A soft noise echoing through the abyss, filling the silence. Skittering across her skin. Eliciting feeling, a knowing of self. The opposite of nothing. A pale, grey light flickered in the distance, shapeless and blurry. Were these eyes she was seeing with? Were these hands she held before her? It was as though she was only now taking form, or had she been complete this entire time?

The rumble became a low chuckle. It enveloped her, vibrating through the very fibers of her being. Tingling and warm. As the chuckle died down, the light began to glow brighter. She shielded her sensitive eyes with a whimper.

"Welcome, Enid Washbourne, to the Realm of Dreams and Nightmares. I have so many plans for you."

ACKNOWLEDGEMENTS

This has been a long time coming. For more years than I can recall the characters in this story have been in my head, trying to find a way out. Finally, they have made their debut.

There are so many people I need to thank for their support during the process of writing this book. My husband, Stephen, for encouraging me to sit down and write. Despite our hectic lives and many responsibilities, he helped me make the time and find a way. Thank you for being my rock and adventure buddy.

To my parents for their support and encouragement.

Mom, I think you read this about six times just helping me sift through the details. Your patience is endless. Thank you, a million times for a million things.

Mimi, thank you for reading the initial draft and encouraging me to go for it. Even the smutty parts that no one needs to read!

Dad, thank you for not reading this. If you do, please avoid Chapter 43 specifically. I hope you're as proud of me as I am of you. (Again, avoid Chapter 43. And 14. And 2.)

To my sisters, Jenni and Tara, who also sifted through every draft of this story and listened to my endless rants and brainstorming. I couldn't have done this without your input. Without you, I wouldn't have the clear understanding of the details that, while not included in the story itself, were crucial elements of helping me discover the depths of where it needed to go. Sorry for the daily phone calls just to hear me vent. And thank you for the praise that kept me moving forward.

To my oldest daughter, my sweet, brave soul child. Thanks for reading through the clean scenes for me. The look on your face when a twist came to light was the best feedback I could have gotten.

To my smallest daughter, my little warrior. Your fierce enthusiasm for life is endlessly entertaining, but also incredibly inspiring. I hope you keep that fire and determination that burns so brightly.

To my friends who listened, read, and encouraged me to get this thing out there. Erin, for all the support and encouragement. For the hours of venting and days away for some much-needed girl time. A special thanks to the talented Marina for the beautiful cover, and the many other illustrations and designs that brought my work to life. You are amazing. Your enthusiasm for this project from its very inception has meant more than you know. I couldn't have done it without you.

And to you, reader. The brave soul who chose to crack the cover of this tale and travel along its winding road. May your days be filled with adventures, your nights sleepless, and your imaginations satiated.

This is only the first of the series. There are many more stories, adventures, and characters clamoring for my attention. I look forward to the journey with you all.

www.ingramcontent.com/pod-product-compliance
Lightning Source LLC
Chambersburg PA
CBHW010518100726
47903CB00011B/2798